Enjoy

David Magee (signature)

CLOSURE

David Magee

SPINETINGLERS
PUBLISHING

Closure
By David Magee

ISBN - 978-1-906657-36-9

Spinetinglers Publishing
22 Vestry Road
Co. Down
BT23 6HJ
UK
www.spinetinglerspublishing.com

This book has been formatted by
Spinetinglers Publishing
UK

Future releases by the same author

Jokerman

To Square the Circle

For Jacqueline

1

Roisin Byrne stared at the mirror on the lift wall without any awareness of the image it reflected. She was too preoccupied to bother about her own appearance, and her tense, nervy disposition exposed that reality to anyone interested enough to take note. Although in the eyes of her fellow passengers, and there were only two, she went dispassionately ignored as they cocooned themselves in the narcissistic solitude of their own importance. But that could hardly be a criticism since they knew nothing about Roisin Byrne, or her problems. To them she was just a passing irritation, a minor inconvenience that stood in the way of a get-away when they reached their destination. But if you set aside her lack of physical stature, and she really was quite small, Roisin Byrne was anything but insignificant; in fact she could probably be best described as a woman on a mission. A woman with the single minded determination to protect her husband's reputation from the barrage of unfounded rumours that kept crawling out of the woodwork and go off in search of the truth, regardless of how unpalatable or incriminating that truth might prove to be.

Okay, so right now she was having a few last minute jitters, but it was nothing more than that, and they were soon forgotten when the lift slewed to a halt and a soulless monotone voice told her it was time to make her exit. Stepping away from the cold, metal floor of the lift onto the plush carpet of the third floor corridor she hurried off in search of Brennan Associates; a private detective agency that she knew absolutely nothing about, apart from the fact that they advertised in the Yellow Pages and their Irish sounding name had taken her fancy.

Born and raised in the republican heartland of North Belfast, Roisin

Byrne was accustomed, like those around her, to having her everyday life policed by the ruthlessly efficient bully boys of the IRA; a brutal and autocratic regime that demanded complete and unshakeable loyalty from its people, while at the same time suppressing any desire to seek outside help in times of crisis. Indeed any attempt to breach this ruthlessly enforced code of silence was dealt with in summary fashion, and generally provoked a late night visit from a couple of balaclava hooded thugs. A threat that made it prudent to keep such troublesome matters close to one's chest and well away from the prying eyes of officialdom. But whatever Roisin Byrne may have lacked in stature she more than made up for with character and determination.

She wasn't interested in the IRA, or their traditions, she needed professional help and had made her mind up to go and get it, regardless of the consequences. But the enormity of that decision cannot be overstated as it would almost certainly bring her into conflict with the local paramilitaries, and more likely than not with her own neighbours as well. An unpalatable thought that was lingering in the back of her mind as she went about her business.

Just along the corridor, languishing behind a well-polished desk, Jack Brennan luxuriated in the comfort of his newly acquired office suite; his recent up-market move financed to a large degree by an over-generous payment for his last assignment.

However, business wasn't quite so brisk at the moment, and his current list of assignments, which could be counted on the fingers of one hand, were nowhere near the same high calibre. So when his partner Judy advised him of Roisin Byrne's arrival he offered up a silent prayer that he wasn't about to meet and greet another scorned housewife. He'd had enough divorce cases to last him a life time, even though such run of the mill cases were often a buffer between survival and going under in his chosen line of business; a business that by its very nature suffered more than most from peaks and troughs.

Right now it was in a trough, albeit a shallow one, but with his current overheads and meagre outlook he could ill afford the luxury of turning anything away, no matter how mundane. Although any great expectations he might have had regarding his visitor's liquidity were quickly reassessed when she was ushered through the door and immediately slotted into that formidable bracket of upper working class; a category that laid claim to Jack's own lowly start in life, and one that generally caused him little concern. What concerned him more was the fact that he did not see the potential for next month's rent standing the other side of his desk.

What stood there was a quite ordinary looking woman in her mid to late thirties, shrouded in a rather shapeless and unflattering black trouser suit with matching court shoes; a dull and decidedly unfashionable combination, which to the discerning eye did nothing to compliment an otherwise trim figure. In support of this uncaring fashion mode, if it could be called that, her small, oval shaped face was completely devoid of makeup, leaving her ashen features and worry lines openly exposed to public scrutiny, and as Jack was quick to note, there were a lot of worry lines; more than one might expect for a woman of her age. Having said that, she was not entirely without appeal, because in startling contrast to her generally dressed down appearance nature had gifted her a magnificent crop of fiery red hair. An asset clearly deserving of the lavish attention it obviously received, although apart from that one glorious attribute there was nothing else very striking or memorable about her. In fact she could quite easily be passed in the street without attracting a second glance since she made little or no effort to do otherwise.

To her credit though much of that tiresome dowdiness went unnoticed when she opened her mouth to speak; the sound she emitted was soft and lyrical, rolling off her tongue with a gentle, almost musical grace. It was reminiscent of a cool mountain stream meandering gently over well-weathered pebbles.

Sadly for Jack it was every bit as incessant, and rather than let her ramble on indefinitely he felt obliged to cut her off in mid flow.

"Can you just hold it there for a moment or two and let me check that I haven't missed anything?" His timely interruption had her squirming uneasily in her seat, a vacant and almost lifeless expression flashing a warning at him across the desk.

"I'm sorry," she mumbled, her voice noticeably timid and just a touch defensive, "everything has been bottled up for so long -- it's hard to explain what these past three years have been like."

Emotional outbursts like this were a frequent occurrence with Jack's female clients, indeed there are few women in real life who enjoy baring their soul to a stranger, and even more so when that stranger happens to be a man. As a general rule, by the time they got round to seeking help from a professional like him most of his female clients had already reached the end of their tether, and were often suffering some from form of emotional trauma.

But if he allowed himself to ignore her initial outpouring of emotion, then it was clear that his visitor harboured a very single minded determination to pressgang him into taking the job, although right then such a prospect didn't rest easily with him. Although that decision wasn't by any means set in stone as there was still some way to go before he would make his mind up on it.

"Let me see if I've got this right?" he said, checking his hastily scribbled notes. "You say your husband left home three years ago to go to work and has not been seen or heard from since."

She nodded her agreement.

"And you say you have had absolutely no communication from him in all that time and even his bank account has remained untouched -- is that a fair summary?" He waited for her to acknowledge before giving way to a natural instinct to speed things up. His visitor was much more vigorous in her affirmation this time, sending her mass of fiery red hair cascading about her face, its coppery highlights glinting in the cold, white light from the neon tube above her head. He pressed on with little more urgency now.

"You say your husband has no enemies that you are aware of

and you believe it's unlikely there could be another woman involved." His eyes never left her face as he watched for any giveaway reaction, but all he got was another incessant nod of the head, albeit a little slower this time to underline her single-minded opposition to the likelihood of either occurrence.

He allowed her to reflect for a few moments before asking the most obvious question of all.

"What do you think happened to your husband?"

Her hands crept up to her mouth and she stared past him at the wall behind his head, quite vacant in expression, as if he no longer existed, her head moving slowly from side to side; very slowly, and very deliberately as she thought things over.

"I really don't know," she confessed. "I have absolutely no idea. No matter how much I think about it I can't come up with anything that makes any kind of sense. Nothing makes sense to me anymore. I feel as if I'm taking part in someone else's nightmare." Her hands came away from her face and dropped into her lap where they began toying with her wedding ring, twisting the narrow gold band round and round on her finger, a far away, almost dreamy look on her face as she ignored what her fingers were doing. When she re-engaged with him there was an odd hesitancy about her, as if she was about to reveal something distasteful, or perhaps something she was reluctant to admit. "Except ------" her voice tailed off weakly, leaving an uneasy silence as she lingered over what she was about to reveal, an indication to Jack that she was undecided about sharing it with him.

"Except what?" he prompted, with little or no effect as she continued to hold back, as if fearing to voice the unwelcome thoughts that were going through her head.

When she eventually broke her silence her voice was little more than a whisper. "Some people have suggested he was murdered by the IRA." She struggled to make herself heard as she buried her face in her hands and burst into tears, her tiny frame shuddering uncontrollably as she surrendered to her pent up emotions.

It was obvious, even to Jack, that she was a woman close to breaking point, a woman physically wilting under the strain of having to re-live her sorry tale. Her meaningless existence since the loss of her husband had exacted a heavy toll, leaving her struggling to cope with the normality's of life, and although she was finding some release in seeking professional help, her emotions were still very raw and close to the surface.

For his part Jack made a hurried and well-practiced dive for the intercom button that would connect him with Judy in the outside office. "Would you fetch Mrs Byrne a glass of water please, Judy, she's a little distressed at the moment." He remained seated until Judy took over before beating a hasty retreat to the reception area, leaving Judy to cope with the distraught woman on her own.

Little episodes like this occurred frequently enough for him to be well practiced in the art of delegation. He simply off-loaded the problem onto the more than capable shoulders of his hard done by partner, while he waited quietly in the wings for her to resolve the situation.

As it happened Roisin Byrne proved to be much grittier than she had at first looked and regained a reasonable semblance of composure with surprising speed, allowing Judy to get back to her work and Jack to ease gently back to the business at hand.

"Do you feel comfortable enough to go on?" he asked.

She gave him a coy look. "Yes of course, I'm sorry about that. It all gets a bit difficult at times," she confessed, wiping her eyes with a seriously over-used paper tissue, and although he was keen to press on Jack was nevertheless reluctant to push her too hard, and allowed her ample time to gather herself before continuing.

"Why would anyone believe your husband to have been murdered by the IRA?" he asked.

"It's just where we live," she countered, as if such a solitary admission needed no further explanation.

"It's a hard line nationalist area, and lots of people go missing for no apparent reason. It's all part of The Troubles, so I suppose it's the only rational explanation our neighbours can put on Tony's disappearance."

Jack was studying her more closely now, trying to see beyond the outer façade, but even then he believed instinctively that what he perceived her to be was exactly what she was. There were no hidden depths, no artificial fronts, she was just an ordinary working class housewife. A woman in total despair, if nonetheless determined to unravel the mystery as to why her husband had vanished and left her to cope with life on her own.

"Do you have any reason to believe the IRA was responsible for his disappearance?" he asked.

She faced his enquiring gaze without flinching. "No I do not." She sounded seriously resolute on the matter.

"Tony is a wonderful husband and a very law abiding citizen. He's an open book really and we don't keep secrets from one another." Her eyes narrowed noticeably as she looked at him. "I would know if he was involved in something that might cause that to happen -- believe me -- I would know."

It was impossible to ignore the way she insisted on referring to her husband in the present tense. A trait that alerted Jack to the likelihood that she still expected to find her husband alive -- even after three long years, and in circumstances such as those she had described. He perceived that attitude to be an extraordinary act of faith, especially for someone living in a war torn city like Belfast.

"What did your husband do for a living? Where did he work?" he asked.

"He's a heavy goods driver for a local transport company," she explained, deliberately correcting his use of the past tense before giving

15

him the details of her husband's employer.

Reaching across the desk Jack placed a blank sheet of paper and a pencil in front of her.

"I'd like you to jot down the names and addresses of any close friends and relatives you can think of. Telephone numbers as well if you have them. It would be really helpful if you include anyone your husband might have been closely involved with, socially or otherwise, prior to his disappearance."

Getting up from his chair he headed towards the outer office, placing a hand lightly on her shoulder as he passed her by.

"I'm just popping next door for a few moments, so there's no need for you to rush things, take as long as you have to. I would rather you took your time over it and got it right at this early stage, because what you give me now will determine where any investigation is likely to begin." Turning on his heel he went through the door, easing it closed behind him.

Judy glanced up as he approached. She was wearing a well-tailored two piece suit, beige in colour, her naturally blonde hair acting as a shoulder length frame for her delicately tanned and pretty features. As a general rule she didn't wear a lot of jewellery and her choice today was limited to a five stone ruby ring on her left hand, and a large silver locket that hung round her neck and was occupying both hands as she ran it backwards and forwards along the length of its heavy silver chain. When she saw Jack approaching she quickly averted her attention to the computer monitor and carried on working the keyboard.

"Something a little bit intriguing about this one -- if we decide to take it on," he told her, a cautionary note in his voice. The main cause of his doubt being the needling uncertainty over his client's ability to finance what could be a long and drawn out investigation.

"Having said that," he went on, "I'm quite interested -- but only if our dear little lady in there can come up with the necessary readies."

There was a tentative note to his voice that caused Judy to look up from what she was doing. A response he had been hoping for as he was keen to judge her reaction to what he was about to say next.

"There's a slight chance it might involve our old friends the Provo's again."

He took care not to make his explanation sound too threatening, but failed with his effort because Judy's eyes darted back to the computer keyboard in an all fired hurry, too much of a hurry as it happened, and although she didn't actually express any direct opposition, the look on her face told the whole story.

"A decision like that wouldn't be down to you alone," she reminded him, "even if you are the senior partner." She made little effort to disguise her anxiety. "I think in the circumstances it might be more diplomatic to discuss it with Mairead as well before you commit us to anything we might not have the resources to handle."

"Where is Mairead by the way?" he asked, fearing it might need a three way debate to resolve the matter, especially if Judy decided to dig her heels in, she was quite capable of doing just that if the mood took her.

He reached out and picked up the desk diary to check Mairead's schedule.

"She's still hunting down that ghost finance company," she told him, "the one that did a runner on its investor's. She's not due back from London until our next board meeting. I've been trying to get her on the phone about another matter but she must be in a meeting or something as she's not answering."

"Of course," he mused, "I remember now -- well in that case I guess it's up to me to decide, we certainly can't keep that little lady next door hanging around while we try to track her down."

If Judy heard what he said she didn't show it, she remained in her seat with her back turned towards him, stony faced, typing furiously at the keyboard while displaying a total lack of interest in the problem. Jack found her sullen behaviour a trifle irritating and demonstrated his feelings by slamming the desk diary down noisily on the worktop beside her, then turned on his heel and headed back to his visitor, his mind occupied with the unhappy thought that dinner that evening would likely be a silent and tetchy ordeal.

Roisin Byrne appeared not to have moved a muscle during his absence, she was holding the sheet of paper he'd left her with at arm's length, her expression vacant enough to indicate that her mind was somewhere else. Sliding back into his seat Jack reached out and eased it from her grasp.

"Right then," he said with a slight smile, "let's see what we've got." The smile didn't linger, because when he checked the list she had put together he was disappointed to see there were only three names on it; one under the heading relatives and even more alarmingly only two under the heading of friends!

He struggled to suppress the thoughts going through his head and not express them aloud, indeed he had to think very carefully before saying anything at all.

"Who was the last person to see your husband before he disappeared?" He was silently praying it was someone other than the woman sat in front of him, since it was painfully obvious from their earlier conversation that she had nothing more to offer.

"That would be Tony's brother, Alfie, he always gives him a lift to work."

The list he was holding told him that Alfie lived at the top of the Grosvenor Road. A borderline area as far as national allegiances go in Belfast.

"And did he drop your husband off as usual on the day he went missing?"

She nodded briskly.

"Yes, he did, he dropped him off as usual and remembers seeing him waiting to cross the road to go into the depot as he drove off." She paused momentarily before adding. "The strange thing is that none of the other workers in the depot saw him arrive for work that morning, nor have any of them seen him since."

Jack wanted more from her, much more, he needed her to open up and be a bit more intimate; more candid, more emotional even, but she had a stubborn reserve about her that he found less than helpful.

"What sort of relationship do you have with your brother in-law? Are you on good terms with each other?"

It was a question that took them into a very delicate area, but it was a question that simply begged to be asked. Especially where a missing person was involved, and even more so where the outcome of any investigation would probably produce nothing more than a body for burial, perhaps not even that after such a long time.

Statistics leaned heavily in the direction of family members or close friends as the culprits in most murder cases, so it was important ground that needed to be covered no matter how delicate. As it turned out, his immediate concerns appeared to be unfounded as his visitor's reaction was instantaneous and very reassuring.

"Oh yes, we get on like a house on fire -- Alfie's a lovely man - we're very close friends as well as being related through marriage."

She gave the matter some added thought, and being perceptive to Jack's needs, added, with a certain amount of conviction. "Nobody who knows Tony would deliberately cause him any harm."

Her thoughts went straight back to the list she had just compiled and she sensibly concluded that it had some obvious shortcomings.

"To be perfectly honest, I could list every last one of our neighbours as a friend to Tony. He's immensely popular with everyone who knows him and never has a cross word to say about anyone or anything."

Her insistence to speak of her husband in the present tense alarmed Jack a little, and he was unsure whether to mark it down to innocent naivety or lack of judgment? In either event it had all the hallmarks of being a problem further down the line and would need dealing with sooner rather than later, an issue he found rather disconcerting.

"Tell me about this guy, Dessie Graham," he prompted, raising his eyes from the list.

"As I've just told you, Mr. Brennan, Tony is extremely friendly with everyone, but Dessie is a very dear friend, the two of them go back a long way. They grew up together -- even played football in the same team when they were youngsters.

She smiled tamely at the happy recollection before continuing.

"And unlike others I could mention they never allowed the difference in their religious backgrounds to interfere with their friendship, no matter what was going on around them, and at times there was a lot going on as I'm sure you know."

The significance of what she'd said didn't appear to have registered with her, nor was she aware of the impact it had on Jack, who almost fell out of his chair at the frightening possibilities it opened up. Their religious differences might be totally unconnected to the problem in hand, but in Northern Ireland being the wrong religion could quite easily get you killed, especially if you happen to be in the wrong place at the wrong time. A thought that caused a few extra worry lines to visit his brow.

Roisin Byrne's fidgety movement distracted him from the problem as she fumbled with the flap of her handbag; reaching inside she came out with a postcard sized photograph that she slid somewhat hesitantly across the polished surface towards him, looking just a little bit reluctant to part with it.

"That's Tony on the left with Dessie beside him; it was taken the summer before he went missing."

Jack picked it up and ran his eyes over it.

There was nothing unusual about the missing man that could be identified from the photograph, he was just an average looking guy in his mid to late thirties, with neatly combed, dark wavy hair and clean shaven features. He was casually but tidily dressed in a pair of faded blue jeans and a grey crew-neck sweater with loafer style shoes. He certainly had a fresh, easy going look about him that supported his wife's description, although as Jack knew from previous experience, looks can often be deceiving.

The other guy in the photograph had much the same fresh faced appearance, and although he was wearing jeans as well, his were matched with a blue sweatshirt with a large sporting logo across the front in big white letters. Both men had their arms around each other's shoulders and were grinning quite happily and looked to be enjoying themselves, making it the sort of holiday snap one would expect to see of a couple of good friends on a day out together.

Setting it aside Jack concentrated on his visitor's reaction to his next question.

"What have the police said about your husband's disappearance?"

Roisin Byrne looked away, fumbling much more incessantly with the shredded tissue, seemingly mesmerized by the antics of her own busy little fingers as they distributed more litter on Jack's desk.

In reality she was attempting to shield herself from his intense scrutiny, which in the circumstances was probably normal enough. Although it was beginning to look as though she was experiencing some difficulty as she buried her face in her hands and gave a loud sigh. It was some time before she got round to answering Jack's question, and even then her voice lacked enthusiasm.

"From what I can gather their investigation has come up against a brick wall. In fact I haven't heard anything from them for some time."

She made no effort to hide her disappointment and came across as weary and vulnerable at that particular moment.

"I'm sure you know what it can be like when the police try to investigate something like this. No one wants to be seen to be co-operating with them in a nationalist area like ours." The despair in her voice was becoming much more evident. "I honestly believe they did everything they could in the circumstances, and I'm not blaming them for any lack of progress; it's so very difficult for them these days as I'm sure you are aware."

Her charitable tolerance and understanding of the difficulties faced by the Royal Ulster Constabulary took Jack a little by surprise and had him nursing a sense of admiration for the woman, albeit that she was in the process of covering his desk in shreds of torn tissue. Unable to restrain himself he reached out and plucked the shredded remnants from her grasp.

His visitor responded by folding her arms and tucking her hands up under her armpits, as if to keep her mischievous little fingers out of harm's way, while at the same time offering a guilty, almost child-like smile by way of apology.

"If the police were going to make any headway in finding out what happened to Tony I'm pretty certain they would have done so by now-- don't you?" she asked, her expression openly inviting contradiction. An invitation Jack declined, since there was nothing in what she had told him so far to warrant contradiction.

"I think you're probably right," he confessed, using the opportunity to benchmark what was clearly a sad but almost certain reality. There was nothing to be gained from raising her expectations unnecessarily, especially as the case would have long since been filed under the unsolved category by the RUC, maybe not quite a dead file – but after three years, most certainly one in need of life support.

Jack spent the remainder of the session using an open question technique, a well proven routine that ensured a full response to every question he asked rather than a straight forward yes or no. By design it helped to expose as much information as was available in the shortest possible time, but as he was soon to discover, the longer their session went on the more repetitive it became, and it was soon apparent that the woman had nothing more to offer that would be helpful.

In the end there was only one other topic of importance left to be discussed before Jack could make his decision on whether or not to take the case, and it wouldn't wait forever.

"I think we have probably gone as far as we can for now," he admitted, "which takes us to the more mundane matter of my fee I'm afraid."

There were still a niggling little doubt in the back of his mind about her ability to pay the going rate, especially if the investigation proved to be as drawn out as he believed it might be. But even with that concern in mind, there was something about the woman's grit and determination that captured his admiration, and made him hopeful they could work out something agreeable between them.

"There isn't any charge for this initial interview," he explained "but I need a five hundred pound retainer to get me started, which although non-returnable is deducted from any final payment -- after that it's eighty pounds an hour, plus expenses. "

He watched her do some mental arithmetic and was a little surprised that she didn't seem unduly concerned. Indeed her only physical reaction was to clutch her handbag closer to her chest, as if determined to hold on to whatever valuable asset was stored inside. He continued to wonder what her reply would be.

"Tony and I have joint savings of a little over ten thousand pounds, and I will happily spend every last penny of it if that's what it takes to find out what happened to him."

The only indication that Jack had heard her was a slight nod of his head as he reached for the intercom button one more time.

"Can you come in for a moment, Judy?" he said, then quickly switched his attention back to his client. "We will need a few personal details from you before you go, and in the meantime I'll get things under way by seeing what I can find out from the police. I have a few contacts there that might prove useful."

Judy bustled in before he could say any more, an enquiring look on her face.

"Mrs. Byrne and I have agreed terms, Judy, so perhaps you would take her with you and draw up the necessary paperwork."

Judy gave him somewhat withering look, although in fairness it only lasted a second or two before it was replaced by a forced but friendly smile as she turned to their visitor. "This shouldn't take more than a few minutes and then you can be on your way."

Their client left her seat and followed Judy's lead to the door, but stopped unexpectedly before she got there and turned back to face Jack again.

"My husband is a decent, God fearing man, Mr. Brennan -- I'd like you to remember that please. Whatever has happened to him was not of his doing, I'm certain of that, and whatever the outcome of all this, I want him back -- even his bones -- if that's all there is." She turned on her heel and squeezed past Judy to disappear from view.

2

Sometime later, a few hours in fact, Jack was sprawled lazily in his chair, fingers entwined behind his plentiful head of greying, blonde hair, the heels of his well-polished brogues nestling carefully on the corner of his just as well-polished desk. His light grey, double-breasted suit, with matching grey shirt and multi-coloured tie was a tasteful combination, one that might well have earmarked him as just another up and coming business executive. But such a mundane description would not have done him justice. His lean, five foot eleven inch frame carried the definitive stamp of a military man -- okay, so the hair was a bit longer and the glow of physical fitness had dulled somewhat on the taut skin of his handsome face, but the soldier inside still identified itself to anyone with an eye to recognize it.

Twenty two years in the army, fifteen of them with British and American Special Forces had toughened him to the rigours of life and had etched its indelible stamp on his character.

He was the complete article, tough, resourceful, and self-disciplined, a quick thinker with a shrewd analytical mind; a man who had sought out, and mastered, a suitable niche for himself when the army had abandoned him as too old for further service. Having left that life behind he had deliberately shied away from a career in personal security; he'd had his fill of pompous jackasses telling him what to do, and had sensibly declined to even consider the thought of acting as a paid babysitter to some puffed up diplomat or rich Arab Prince. Although such lucrative careers had gained in popularity with many of his contemporaries. In reality he was rediscovering himself, no more mopping up after power crazed politicians who were all too eager to join the American crusade, those days were well and truly behind him and he had no intention of reinventing them.

Lowering his feet to the floor he stabbed the intercom button with the blunt end of his pen.

"See if you can raise Bill Anderson for me, sweetheart," he said, then feeling a need to stretch his limbs got up and wandered over to the double-glazed window that protected him from the noise of the city traffic outside, and stared down at the frantic activity three stories below; wishing like hell it was time for coffee. He would probably have stayed there had Judy's voice not brought him scurrying back to his desk.

"I've got the Chief Inspector on line one for you, Jack."

Clearing his throat Jack hit the speaker button and perched his backside on the corner of the desk.

"Hi, Bill, it's good to speak with you after all this time. I hope everyone at your end is keeping well?"

Chief Inspector Bill Anderson would never class Jack as a friend, although he was undoubtedly a close acquaintance, but being by nature a man of few words, none of them ever wasted, there would be no exceptions on this occasion, not even for a close acquaintance.

"What are you after, Jack?" he asked, inserting an '*I'm too busy*' abruptness into his voice that told his caller he was in danger of being stone-walled. Brevity was clearly the order of the day if Jack was to get any return for his efforts.

"I'm handling a missing person case that your people are involved with, Bill, and I wondered if I might get a look at the case file."

Bill Anderson's reply was blunt, precise, and straight to the point.

"Forget it, you know I can't do that -- now if there's nothing else – I've work to be doing."

Jack gritted his teeth at the bluntness of the refusal, although if he was truthful it was no less than he might have expected. He knew Bill Anderson to be the ultimate professional; a man completely at ease with modern day policing and dedicated, with every inch of his being, to the eradication of crime. He was too professional to waste time on fruitless conversation, even his office décor reflected his no nonsense attitude with its almost sterile furnishings.

The only pictures adorning its magnolia painted walls were obligatory and of office issue. One of them, an exceptionally large portrait of Her Majesty The Queen, showed the gracious lady posed rather stiffly in formal regalia, while staring somewhat condescendingly across the room at a brooding, and rather dour looking Prime Minister on the opposite wall. A Prime Minister, who coincidentally, but quite properly, had his eyes lowered in dutiful deference.

"Come on now, Bill," Jack insisted, "this isn't some crazy crackpot pointing the finger at the police or anything like that, so don't go getting your knickers in a twist. My client is a perfectly respectable little housewife, who quite understandably as I see it, wants to find out what happened to her husband." He let his words sink in for a few moments in the hope that they might awaken the other man's more charitable nature. All he got for his effort was a lengthy and somewhat pregnant pause, forcing him to continue his efforts.

"Surely on this one occasion you can be a little more charitable, Bill." he argued.

Bill Anderson's reply sounded a bit jaded and out of sorts, like he was ready for bed. "You're a damned menace, Jack. I really don't have the time for this right now," he groaned, "who is this bloody woman anyway? Should I know her?"

There was just enough softening of his voice to indicate that the barricades were weakening. It was certainly enough to give a lift to Jack's deflated spirits.

"She's a very distraught little lady by the name of Roisin Byrne – the missing guy is her husband Tony Byrne - he disappeared about three years ago as I understand it. She tells me your guys thought it was a paramilitary killing, although in all honesty, at least from what I can gather, you haven't made a lot of headway." He could almost hear Bill Anderson thinking his way back in time, and it was some little while before he re-joined the conversation.

"Strangely enough I do actually remember that case." The cutting edge had left his voice and was replaced by a more thoughtful, almost inquisitive tone. There was nothing Bill Anderson loathed more than an unsolved crime, basically because it stank of failure and he detested the smell of failure.

"If my memory serves me right there was very little to go on with that case -- it was all a bit peculiar in that respect." The conversation tailed off as he fought to recall the detail of the three year old mystery.

"Correct me if I'm wrong, Jack, but my recollection of it is that the guy just up and vanished one day after leaving home for work. We didn't find a damned lead of any sort to follow up on, and there was no evidence of any paramilitary involvement either, contrary to local gossip. We couldn't find a bloody thing to explain his disappearance. It was all a bit weird in that respect as an investigation usually turns something up, even if it's only a suspect."

Having started the ball rolling the Chief Inspector would stick with it until he had given a full explanation.

"You might want to bear in mind the fact that there was, and still is I might add, the possibility that the guy simply didn't want to be found. Or perhaps as some of the locals chose to believe, just got himself in the wrong place at the wrong time and paid the price for someone else's misdeeds. One thing I do remember very clearly though is that he was as clean as a whistle with us -- and with the army boys too, he had absolutely no form and no dubious connections that we were aware of." He let his offering rest with Jack for a moment, and then added with a touch of cynicism. "Just one of those sad, unexplained events that occur all too frequently in this demented asylum we live in."

A temporary lull fell over the conversation, then quite unexpectedly he came back with an offer that took Jack completely by surprise.

"I tell you what I will do, Jack. I'll give you permission to speak to the case officer involved if that helps, as far as I know Detective Sergeant Dave Jackson is the guy handling it, but that's as far as I'm prepared to go."

Jack's face lit up, it was an offer he hadn't expected; at least now he would have somewhere to make a start and get the ball rolling, and that was a big step in the right direction.

"That's very generous of you, Bill, and I'm really very grateful. It goes without saying that if I do turn up any new evidence I'll pass it straight on to Sergeant Jackson."

"Oh I know you will, Jack." There was the same cynical undertone to his voice that he'd used before, it suggested there would be a bigger price to pay than simply sharing a few snippets of information.

"I'm sure you will want to make a reasonable contribution to the Police Benevolent Fund as well."

The line died before Jack could respond, and as he lowered the phone on to its cradle he pondered over what he had actually gained from the call. If nothing else he would at least have access to any evidence the police had turned up, and could now safely say that his investigation was under way.

Feeling much happier and much more content with life he threw himself back in his chair and considered what his next course of action should be.

3

The most obvious place to begin searching for a missing person is the place where they were last seen alive. With that in mind Jack drove into the transport depot unannounced and looked for a parking space close to the main office block. When he failed to find one he reversed into a spot immediately outside the entrance that was clearly marked 'reserved' and made his way into the pre-fabricated building.

The admin office itself turned out to be a stuffy, dingy little affair, furnished with a variety of cheap wooden desks, three in all, the largest of which doubled up as a reception point, or so the sign on the front modesty panel declared.

Further back, against the far wall, presumably in an effort to keep them out of sight, stood a couple of battered looking filing cabinets, thoughtlessly smothered in a mishmash of meaningless stick-on labels. There was little else by way of furniture on view, except a pair of decrepit old coach seats, so badly worn that the stuffing had burst through their tattered upholstery.

After an unnecessary test of his patience, the chosen one, or more precisely, the young lady earmarked as the receptionist, dragged her attention away from the magnetic attraction of an enormous custard tart and acknowledged his presence. Not as he might have expected by joining him in some form of greeting, or by enquiring into the purpose of his visit, but by senselessly engaging him with a blank, almost idiotic stare, while waiting in silent expectation for an answer to some as yet unspoken question.

Convinced of her ability to speak he waited patiently, and waited some more, but it was to no avail, she simply twitched her nose, snorted noisily through what sounded like a blocked up sinus and bluntly refused to enquire into the purpose of his visit. In fact her limited attention span succumbed once again to the tempting lure of the remnants of her custard tart, allowing Jack to vanish into total anonymity once again.

Even more annoyingly, her two companions, both of a similar age and seated directly behind her, declined to be any more helpful. One remained blissfully engrossed in the contents of a glossy magazine, while the other diligently prepared her over-grown and over-pampered fingernails for whatever important social event lay ahead that evening.

Jack's attention was grabbed by a sign at the far side of the office warning anyone who took notice that the manager resided behind its mock wooden door, and he quickly decided that was where he needed to be.

"Here -- where do you think you're going?" demanded the chosen one as he rounded her desk and made a beeline for the manager's office.

"You can't go barging in there unannounced."

She would have been better advised to have remained in her former state of disinterest as Jack's limited quota of patience was already at a low ebb. Stopping in mid stride he rounded on her and jabbed an index finger directly at the end of her up-turned nose.

"You had your chance, lady," he snarled, the icy glint in his eyes sufficiently threatening to prevent her from compounding her mistake. She jerked back in her seat, at least as far as the backrest would allow, a rush of blood spreading over her startled features that quite coincidentally matched to perfection the blushed pink of her rumpled linen blouse. A few quick strides took Jack to the manager's door where he stopped and knocked quietly on the mock-mahogany panel. After a few seconds without reply he opened it and waltzed inside like it was his God given right to do so.

Crouched workmanlike behind a seriously cluttered desk, the rotund, balding, and bespectacled figure of the area manager looked up in astonishment.

It was obvious from the look on his face that he wasn't expecting visitors, and certainly not an unannounced interruption by a complete stranger. His immediate reaction was to reach up and remove his reading glasses, giving Jack just enough time to grab the initiative.

"Sorry to barge in unannounced like this, but that lot out front appear to be dead from the neck up." He thrust a hand across the desk at the bewildered manager, who responded by sliding uncomfortably to edge of his seat and grasping it in his own soft grip.

"Brennan," he announced in a business like tone, as if his name should mean something to the startled manager, who could only stare back in total confusion.

"Brennan Associates!" he offered again, expectantly this time, inviting recognition, and showing an overstated disappointment when it didn't materialize.

"Do that lot outside tell you nothing?" he asked, jerking his head towards the other office. "We were supposed to have an appointment," he lied, praying not to be challenged, and hoping the guy would be too embarrassed to hold an immediate enquiry.

His uncertainty prompted Jack to push his luck a little further.

"Never mind," he said, with an indifferent shrug, "no harm done I suppose, I haven't been waiting very long really, but we do need to press on as I have another appointment scheduled quite soon."

The hapless manager hadn't a clue what was expected of him and did the only thing he could in the circumstances. He maintained his hold on

Jack's outstretched hand and pumped it up and down enthusiastically.

"Andy Nelson," he advised, apologetically. "Sorry if there has been some confusion but it's been a bit hectic round here this morning. We seem to be under a bit of extra pressure at the moment." He still looked every bit as puzzled as when Jack had first walked in. "Am I supposed to know you?" he enquired, amicably enough.

"I shouldn't think so -- I arranged this meeting with one of your young ladies over the phone. It's to do with an ex-employee of yours who did a disappearing trick about three years ago – a guy called Tony Byrne."

"Oh! I see – right then." Nelson stammered, somewhat awkwardly. Ex-employee's weren't exactly at the forefront of his mind, and especially not Tony Byrne, but now that he'd been reminded of him it only served to bring a tiresome grimace to his face. "That's going back a bit, I'm not sure I can be of much help, what exactly is it you want to know?"

"Why don't you start by telling me what you remember about the guy? You know, what sort of an employee he was – how he got on with the other workers -- that kind of thing." He lowered himself into the only other available chair without waiting for an invitation.

A vacant expression visited Nelson's chubby features as he drifted off on some mental route march, shuffling his thoughts into some semblance of order before opening his mouth.

As a manager he may have had some failings, but impetuosity would hardly list among them. In fact he gave the distinct impression of being a very deliberate sort of person and not someone who could be rushed or press-ganged into anything against his will.

"Well," he said, after careful consideration, "what is there to say about someone as ordinary as Tony Byrne?" His shoulders lifted and dropped nonchalantly. "He was certainly popular with everyone around here, that's for sure. A good, reliable worker, and an excellent driver who never gave me or the company a single problem the whole time he was with us."

He got out of his seat and scurried across the room to a battered looking filing cabinet, returning just as quickly with a large clip file bearing the ex-employee's name. Placing it on the desk in front of him he settled back in his chair and began rummaging through its contents.

"Yeah – just as I thought," he muttered, "he was with us the best part of seven years, and as far as I know he was perfectly happy with the job. I thought it bloody peculiar the way he just upped and disappeared like that, in fact we all did. It was really hard on his wife too, I know for a fact that she took it very badly. Especially as there were a lot of crazy rumours doing the rounds at the time that weren't very helpful to her." He flicked the file cover closed and clasped his hands protectively on top of it.

"What do you think happened to him?" asked Jack.

Nelson's bulky figure eased out of the chair and headed across to the window where he gazed thoughtfully at the busy trailer yard outside, his attention claimed momentarily by the bizarre antics of a forty-footer reversing into a narrow parking space. He continued to give thought to Jack's question, dwelling on it for some time without offering an immediate judgment.

"Let me put that another way," prompted Jack, "what were the other driver's saying about his disappearance at the time?"

Nelson spun round to face him.

"Christ --- there were all sorts of weird stories going about, everything from winning the bloody lottery and running off with the proverbial big blonde, to being shot by the Red Hand Commando's."

Andy Nelson came across, to those who knew him, as a decent enough guy, if perhaps a bit soft, but he was very much a man of the world in many ways, street wise, and with a good understanding of human nature and all of its frailties.

"Most of our drivers do long haul work that keeps them away from their home and separated from their families for long periods – weeks on end sometimes. Who knows what they get up to when they're out on the road like that?"

He shook his head despairingly. "I'm not sure I want to know either," he added quickly.

Jack had convinced himself that Nelson wanted to be helpful, in fact he seemed quite eager to do so, but it wasn't in his nature to deliberately cast aspersions on any of his staff. That clearly wasn't his way of doing things. He flopped back into his seat with his eyes firmly fixed on his visitor.

"Now don't get me wrong," he warned, "all I'm saying is that I'm not responsible for what they decide to do in their own time."

Jack nodded in agreement.

"Yeah -- okay, I take your point, Andy, but Tony Byrne was hardly the sort of guy to get mixed up in anything unsavoury -- was he?"

Nelson raised his eyebrows. "He disappeared didn't he?" he replied meaningfully, seeing no need to elaborate.

Jack's face screwed up in frustration. It was obvious he wasn't going to get anything more meaningful from Andy Nelson and a change of direction was needed.

"Is there anyone left on the staff worth speaking to -- anyone who knew him or worked closely with him?" he asked.

"Yeah – there are still a few guys here who knew Tony, but to be truthful he never socialized much with the other lads, so I'm not sure there's a lot to be gained from speaking to them, but you're welcome to try if you think it will help -- be my guest."

He spread his arms invitingly.

"There is one other thing I need to ask you, Andy," Jack said, a preparatory hint of warning in his voice. "How many Catholic workers do you have on your books?"

The question took Nelson by surprise; essentially because it wasn't something he expected, or imagined he would be asked. And if the tortured expression on his face was anything to go by he was none too happy that the subject had even been raised. His immediate reaction was to leave Jack staring at the back of his heavily creased jacket as he got out of his chair again and retraced his steps to the window, leaving an uncomfortable lull hanging over the conversation.

There was a moment when he seemed uncertain what to do, but having made his mind up he spun round and faced Jack again. "That, my friend, is privileged information that I don't have to share with you or anyone else, apart from the Fair Employment Agency." He looked decidedly uncomfortable as he closed his eyes and raised both hands to his pursed lips in prayer like fashion.

"However, since I believe you are genuinely trying to solve this mystery I will tell you that Tony was the only Catholic we ever had on our books -- but you must understand that that was not by choice" He locked eyes with Jack in a meaningful way. "They simply choose not to seek employment here because of the contractual work we do for the government. The word soon gets about if you handle government contracts; it's a very close knit community round here, as you probably know already."

His chair invited him back and he dropped into it resignedly, giving Jack a very pointed look.

"Whatever thoughts are going through you head right now, Mr. Brennan -- Tony Byrne had no problems of that sort while he worked for us. I would have known if he had -- and I would not have tolerated or condoned any sort of victimization. You have to believe that."

There was enough conviction in Nelson's voice to convince Jack he was hearing the truth.

"Point taken, Andy -- is it okay if I wander round the yard and chat with some of your guys?"

Nelson nodded affirmatively. "Of course it is -- but I'm afraid you will have to do it on your own because I've afforded you about as much time as I can right now."

Jack offered his thanks and turned away just as the phone on Nelson's desk beckoned, doubtlessly bringing more problems his way.

All three of the young females lifted their heads in unison as he re-entered the stuffy atmosphere of the outer office.

Having discussed his presence at length during his absence they had come to the unanimous conclusion that their unscheduled visitor was some sort of inspector from head office, sent to give them the once over. As a consequence they were much more guarded towards him when he reappeared, and even smiled pleasantly as he approached.

They were not to know that he was about to have one last pop at them before leaving.

"I hope I'm not disturbing you ladies, I can see how busy you all are. Anyway, haven't you got nails to polish or something?" he sniped, as he weaved between the desks and out through the door.

The only activity Jack could see when he got outside was in a large hanger-like building at the far end of the yard, and as he made his way toward it he spotted a group of workers milling about just inside the entrance.

They seemed receptive enough when he got to them, and once he'd explained the purpose of his visit they were soon huddled round him in a tight little cluster. Although any response to his enquiry came in generalizations rather than specifics, and it was soon obvious that those who still remembered Tony Byrne shared their manager's high opinion of his as a workmate. Which wasn't a lot of use to Jack; he was looking for information that might offer him some sort of a lead, and not a diatribe of tediously fond memories and character references.

He pressed on with more urgency.

"That morning when Tony disappeared -- did anyone at all see him come in to work?"

"I don't think he came anywhere near the yard that morning. Whatever it was happened to him – it didn't happen in here."

The guy doing the talking was standing right next to Jack, wiping his oily hands on a piece of waste rag.

"Why don't you try asking the guy over in that shop across the way, he has a perfect view of the yard, maybe he saw something." He pointed in the direction of the front gates.

Jack passed his business cards round the group and made ready to leave.

"Thanks anyway guys, I guess the shop has to be my next port of call, but should any of you remember anything at all that you think might be useful I would really appreciate it if you gave me a bell."

4

The shop in question proved to be nothing more than a grubby little general store that had little more by way of information than it had produce on its barren shelves.

The only thing the owner was fit to recall about the day in question was that he had seen a truck park up opposite the shop while the driver nipped in to collect the morning paper, after which it had carried on into the depot.

This apparently took place around the time Tony Byrne's brother would have dropped him off. And the shop owner, a dour individual in his mid-fifties, whose breath stank of last night's whiskey, was unable recall anything else that was any use to Jack. Who by now was wondering if he still had enough active brain cells left to remember what he'd had for breakfast, never mind an event that was three years old!

In the end he left the shop feeling pretty despondent, having genuinely hoped to unearth some little snippet of information that would help get the case moving, when in fact the only thing he had gained from his morning's work was confirmation that Byrne had never set foot in the transport yard on the day he disappeared. As he reflected on the outcome of his morning's work he cheered himself up with the knowledge that he still had one more visit to make before calling it a day, and there was little else he could do but hope it proved to be a bit more productive.

The Graham family home was an end of terrace, two-up-two-down council house at the busy end of a narrow little street in a working class estate.

Jack had to force the badly fitted gate open before taking the three strides necessary to reach the front door. He knocked a few times on the re-enforced glass panel and peered anxiously through the net curtain that obscured from view anyone lurking on the other side. Jean Graham's hazy outline appeared so quickly behind the glass that she might have been lying in wait for him, which of course she wasn't.

After an energy sapping tussle with the ill-fitting door she eventually wrestled it open and Jack found himself looking at a quite blousy thirty-year-old woman who was wearing a pleasant smile, an unnecessary amount of bright red lipstick, and a particularly bad red hair rinse. A combination that might have been slightly more successful had her facial colour not been quite so ghostly. As it was, the overall effect made her look a little bit like a circus clown, but only a little bit, and only because of the hair rinse, nevertheless the ghastly combination undoubtedly killed any potential for glamour.

"How can I help you?" she asked, crossing her arms over a more than ample bosom, and in so doing placing further strain on the already overworked material of her silk blouse.

Jack raised his eyes from the bulging material.

"It's really Dessie I came to see, if he's at home?" he explained, smiling politely.

She sniffed noisily and somewhat indignantly as she made ready to close the door in his face.

"He works during the day – won't be home before seven o'clock this evening – that's if he's lucky?" She might have succeeded in closing the door had Jack not shoved his foot out to stop it. "Perhaps you can help?" he suggested, offering his best Sunday smile as an advance payment for her co-operation. "I'd like to talk to him about the disappearance of his friend Tony Byrne -- his wife has hired me to try and find him."

Jean Graham's over-plucked eyebrows came together in a suspicious frown; she looked Jack up and down like he had stood in something nasty.

"Do you have some sort of identification?" she asked.

With his permit already in his hand in anticipation Jack flipped it open just under her nose.

She gave it a quick once over before taking a half step back into the hall and shoving the door back just far enough to let him through.

"You'd better come in then, the bloody neighbours round here don't miss a trick. They seem to know everybody's bloody business but their own." She took another backward step allowing him to squeeze past the soft cushion of her bosom before slamming the door behind him.

Jack followed her into a tiny front room, where the intrusive wailing of some demented infant was blasting through the walls from the house next door.

"Sorry about the racket," she said, "that poor little bugger never stops yelling. It's nothing short of bloody neglect if you ask me; somebody should report them to the welfare."

Jack ignored the apology, and the noise, he was more interested in having a good look around, and he could hardly fail to take note of the gaudy array of cheap artificial flowers that almost smothered the tiny coal-effect electric fire hidden behind them.

His eyes drifted upwards to an over-sized photograph of the happy couple on their wedding day that was mounted on the chimney breast above, its original colour now fading to a washed-out sepia, thanks to the ultra violet rays seeping through the net curtains on the window opposite.

The rest of the room was liberally festooned with a variety of cheap holiday souvenirs, some bearing the names of the exotic places they had visited to flutter away their hard earned cash. He even had time to notice that she had serious cause to purchase a feather duster, but the thought slid away as he launched a rather provocative opening gambit.

"Tell me about your relationship with Tony Byrne," he invited, deliberately leaving the wording of his invitation open to interpretation.

"What the hell do you mean – relationship?" she snarled, a look of resentful disbelief on her face, her spontaneous and indignant reaction told Jack everything he needed to know, but his ambiguous remark had provoked an angry reaction that was slow to dissipate, and there was a clear warning in Jean Graham's voice when she challenged him about it.

"I hope you're not suggesting what I think you're suggesting," she snapped in angry denial, and while her rebuke had little effect on Jack it did mean he would have to grovel his way back into her good books before he alienated her altogether. "Sorry -- no -- of course not," he stammered awkwardly, "I was only enquiring as to how you got on as friends -- you know, the kind of things you enjoyed doing together -- where you went on your nights out, that sort of thing."

He paused for a moment, endeavouring to look suitably repentant. "I never for one moment meant to suggest anything improper."

Jean Graham was not amused, nor did she look it, her face had coloured up to match her hair.

"Well you should choose your bloody words more carefully," she warned, sinking slowly into the chair behind her and inviting Jack to do the same by pointing a finger at the empty chair opposite.

She'd hardly settled herself before reaching up and lifting a small photograph from the top of the fire surround, her eyes lingering on it momentarily before passing it over to him. It was a small, framed holiday snap of both couples dressed up in grass skirts, clearly a reminder of one of their jaunts to some distant and tropical beach bar.

"We were such close friends until Tony disappeared," she muttered, her voice reflecting a sullen sadness, a sort of regret, a longing perhaps for happier days gone by.

"Does that mean you're not friends anymore?" asked Jack, eager to keep her talking.

"Well," she said, drawing the word out. "Roisin still gets in touch occasionally but she seldom comes to visit anymore." Her voice was laden with sadness now, noticeably more so than before, and that, plus the look on her face, highlighted a genuine disappointment that their friendship was waning. Her eyes appeared a little moist too as she stared into the distance and secreted herself in some distant memory, then quite unexpectedly she switched her attention back to their conversation.

"I can't say I blame her for that mind you, some of the stories circulating round here about Tony were very hurtful." She shook her head in despair. "Why do people have to behave like that?" she asked, more of herself than anyone else.

Jack knew how she must be feeling, mysteries like Tony Byrne's sudden disappearance fuelled the imagination of simple minds; quite often allowing fantasy to take over where reality becomes too outrageous, or lacks conviction.

"There were all sorts of hurtful and shameful accusations about wife swapping and drugs being put about," she went on. "Some bloody idiot even suggested he was gathering information for an IRA hit team." She shook her head in disgust. "I ask you -- really -- where the hell did that come from?" She was clearly upset at having to revisit such painful memories, but beneath it all Jack sensed in her a deep rooted sense of loyalty to her friends that kept her heading in the right direction.

"It was all bloody nonsense of course -- we were just good friends who enjoyed the same things in life, and each other's company." She got up and headed for the door. "I fancy a cuppa tea -- would you like one?" she asked.

"I'd prefer coffee if you have it?" he admitted, getting out of his seat to follow her through the door into a small, but quite well equipped kitchen, which immediately became over-crowded when he squeezed in beside her.

"Did many of your neighbours know Tony was a Catholic?" he asked, ever conscious of the delicacy surrounding the subject. She turned to face him and raised her chin, almost proudly, if not determinedly.

"Tony never hid his religious beliefs from anyone, and neither did we -- why on earth should we? Anyway he was popular with all of our neighbours -- or so we thought, that's why it was so bloody hurtful when all those stupid stories began circulating. People can be terribly insensitive at times," she declared finally.

"Do you know of anyone who would want to harm him?"

Jean Graham peered at him through the steamy mist from the kettle. "That's a bloody daft question if ever I heard one. It's pretty obvious you didn't know Tony or you wouldn't ask a daft bloody question like that. Tony made friends with people, Mr. Brennan, not enemies, he was a very popular guy -- a really nice man to be around."

"Did he seem worried about anything? Did you notice any change in his behaviour prior to his disappearance?"

Jean Graham pursed her lips thoughtfully then shook her head. "No, I can't say I noticed anything unusual, but we went through all of this with the police at the time and they didn't find anything that helped. I don't see how you will either after all this time?"

She passed him his coffee and led the way back to the relative splendour of the front room where she stood with her back to him staring out through the net curtains.

"What do you think happened to him?" He rather sprung the question on her.

She spun round with a puzzled expression on her face. "I have absolutely no idea -- but whatever it was I'm certain it was a case of mistaken identity. I guess I have to keep believing that – don't I?" The same faraway look she'd had earlier returned to cloud her vision again as she wandered off down memory lane. A seemingly pleasant comfort zone, where she would likely as not have stayed had Jack had not dragged her back to reality.

"Where exactly does your husband work?" he asked, "is it nearby?" He felt the need to press on with things since he was learning nothing here that he didn't already know. It was beginning to look like his only chance of turning up something new lay with Jean Graham's husband, who was reputed to have been Tony Byrne's best buddy. Perhaps he could put a different slant on things, especially if they were as close as everyone made out and shared their innermost thoughts like real buddies do.

Although in his heart of hearts Jack felt that even he might not have much to offer. As things stood he would settle for a quick answer to the question he had just put to Jean Graham, especially as she seemed to be in no great hurry to tear herself away from whatever precious memory she was visiting. She remained firmly ensconced in the privacy of her own thoughts and oblivious to everything else, at least until Jack gave a polite but meaningful cough.

"Sorry," she said distantly, "he's a bricklayer." She whispered the words into her chest, looking as vague as ever, wanting to remain connected to that snapshot of the past that offered her a few moments pleasure. "Damned job takes him all over the place -- he's like a bloody wandering minstrel these days, I never know where he's going to be from one day to the next." Her attitude suddenly changed and she became much more animated as her domestic problems focused her mind on more mundane issues that were clearly bugging her.

"It costs him a bloody fortune just getting to some of these building sites. Money we can ill afford I can tell you. He's working in Banbridge at the moment, but one of his workmates who lives close by gives him a lift -- thank God."

She sipped from the hot liquid in her mug.

Jack pulled out his wallet and offered her a business card.

"Perhaps you would ask him to give me a call sometime during the next few days; I really would like to speak with him."

She took the card automatically without thinking about it or even looking at it, almost unconsciously, and duly propped it up beside the photograph on top of the fire surround as Jack made ready to leave.

"I really do appreciate your help, Mrs. Graham, and the coffee too of course. I'm sorry to have taken up so much of your time."

Jean Graham stood up with her hands clasped firmly together, a sad, almost pleading expression on her face.

"Just promise me that you will find out what happened to Tony and give his poor wife some peace of mind." She made no attempt to hide the tears that suddenly welled up in her eyes.

"I'll do my best, you have my word on that. Will it be okay if I call again if I have a need to?" He was already edging closer to the door, keen to be on his away.

"Of course - call any time you want to if you think it will help." She laid her cup down as if to follow him out, but he raised a hand to stop her.

"I can see myself out; you stay right where you are and finish your tea."

With that he was on his way, hurrying back to his car, where he sat contemplating what he had achieved from his morning's work. The sad thing was he hadn't achieved very much, apart from the fact that Jean Graham had rubber stamped what others had already told him.

5

"I find it inexplicable that a guy like Tony Byrne can just vanish into thin air for no apparent reason?" Jack was standing behind Judy with both hands resting lightly on her shoulders.

"All I've got so far is a collection of character references, but nothing to explain what happened or indicate a motive for his disappearance. Maybe the answers lie closer to home, but someone with my background can't go tip-toeing through a bloody nationalist area like north Belfast without drawing attention. The IRA would be on to me like a rat up a drainpipe -- especially if they are involved in this thing, which is becoming a real possibility to my way of thinking."

His hands dropped to his sides and he lowered himself into the chair next to Judy.

"Still, there's one person I can speak to up there without getting a hole in my head."

He got to his feet again and patted Judy on the back.

"See if you can get in touch with Byrne's local priest and arrange a meeting for me." A flicker of doubt crossed his face momentarily. "And I suppose you'd better explain what it's about while you're at it." With that he turned and walked away.

Back at his desk he dialled the central police number and asked to be put through to the Grosvenor Road Incident Room, where he ended up talking to the duty sergeant.

"I've been trying to get in touch with Detective Sergeant Dave Jackson, but every time I phone him he's either out of the office or he's tied up in some meeting or other. Is there any chance you can put me through to him as it's really rather important." All of his previous efforts at tracking down the case officer had proved fruitless, so he wasn't feeling all that optimistic.

"I'm afraid you're out of luck again, Sir, he's got a case up in front of the judge today. Is there anyone else who can help you?"

Jack shook his head in despair, his patience waning; a court case could easily last a week or even longer.

"Not really," he mumbled dejectedly. "Chief Inspector Bill Anderson suggested I talk to him about a case he handled. So I don't see how anyone else can be of much help."

"I see -- well I'm afraid all I can do is leave a priority message for him to contact you as soon as he's free." The duty sergeant was very polite and helpful, but clearly the mention of Bill Anderson's name had oiled the wheels a bit.

"If that's the best you can do I'll just have to go with it, but thanks for your help anyway." After leaving his details he hung up, but he had no sooner set the phone down before Judy's voice piped through the intercom. "I've arranged a meeting with Father Joseph straight after late Mass this evening, Jack. Sorry it's so late but he's away on some sort of retreat tomorrow."

"That's okay, Judy, just so long as I get a chance to grill the guy," he replied.

Judy's eyebrows curled into a frown.

"You might try to remember that it's a man of the cloth you're going to see -- a little diplomacy might not go amiss."

Her rebuke hardly registered with Jack who had much more important things on his mind, like trying to find a way to get the case moving.

Lifting his pen he flicked over to a clean page on his scribble pad and began jotting down some of the key words that came to mind; words that would prompt a more diverse approach to his problem.

Words like -- MURDER -- SUICIDE -- MISTAKEN IDENTITY -- IRA -- RED HAND COMMANDO -- LOVE AFFAIR -- RUNAWAY -- DRUGS -- and many more of a similar vein.

He left a space under each heading to fill in the relevant prompts, like who, why, how, where, when etc. With so little to go on by way of evidence he would need to either eliminate or accept each scenario as the case progressed. Although now that he had time to dwell on the problem, the more plausible became the possibility that Byrne's disappearance was perhaps the result of a sectarian killing. Possibly a random killing by some blood crazed paramilitary who simply wanted to increase his bragging-rites and 'do his bit' for the cause. But no matter how hard he tried to convince himself that such was the case, the less appeal it held for him. He had already accepted that there was more to it than that. The RUC would generally have a good feel for things and would have enough unofficial feedback from their paid touts to be pretty certain one way or the other, even if they lacked the physical proof to act on such information.

No doubt he would learn more from the case officer, if and when he ever managed to track the guy down. For now his main task was to get some momentum going, although if he was honest with himself at this precise moment in time he was already having doubts about taking on such a difficult case.

It was only a fleeting moment of uncertainty, and one that was quickly brushed aside as he contemplated his forthcoming meeting with the parish priest. Someone in his position would get to hear about most things that went on in his parish, one way or another, so he would know more about the local gossip and local suspicions than the police would ever get to hear about. Although any assistance he might actually get from that quarter was for now a matter of conjecture, and one that time alone would provide the answer to.

6

The hordes of late night shoppers were a fading image in his rear view mirror as Jack left the bright lights of the city centre behind and headed for the shadowy and more intimidating atmosphere of north Belfast. He was looking forward to his meeting with Father Joseph, if slightly apprehensive about the kind of reception he might expect. The clergy were hardly renowned for their openness and were more inclined to shy away from things controversial.

As he entered the outer fringes of the nationalist area there was an air of tension about the place that was almost palpable. Most of the street lights had been vandalized to extinction, and the majority of buildings were either covered in IRA, or anti-British slogans, creating a dark, foreboding and intimidating atmosphere. It was no sort of place for an evening stroll that was for sure.

Thankfully he was only a few more minutes behind the wheel before he arrived at the holy residence and was greeted quite promptly at the door by Father Joseph himself and quickly ushered into a well-furnished study, allowing him to enjoy his first close-up of his host.

It was immediately obvious that the dark suit and dog collar were an unnecessary aid to identifying him as a man of the cloth, that fact was as plain as the nose on his face and an integral part of his very nature. He could hardly have concealed his clerical status even if he had wanted to; the only thing missing to confirm it was a halo above his head.

Nevertheless he was genuinely warm and polite in his greeting, although Jack sensed an unexpected guardedness about him from the moment he had opened the door.

"Please make yourself comfortable, Mr. Brennan. I'm about to partake of a drink, perhaps you would care to join me?" He floated off in the direction of an old fashioned but well-polished sideboard, ensuring all the while that he kept his guest firmly fixed in his line of sight as he went about his business.

"I could murder a whiskey if you have one," admitted Jack, as he surveyed the unexpected grandeur of what was a quite spacious and expensively furnished room.

With his visual tour completed he took the opportunity to study his host more closely.

The guy had a strangely calm, almost saintly aura about him; his pale, soft looking skin belied his fifty years and gifted him with a deceivingly youthful appearance, which in turn was matched by a slim, well-proportioned figure.

For the most part he carried himself quite well, with a reasonably upright stance, however, as Jack would later discover, a noticeable stoop developed whenever he became thoughtful or stressed.

Jack studied the priest's expressionless features at some length, the translucent texture of the skin, with its bland, almost lifeless features, somehow reminded him of a death mask; its only saving grace being a pair of startlingly pale grey eyes that were almost hypnotic in their attraction. They taunted and mocked the observer constantly, as if concealing some humorous secret. A trait that persisted even when he indulged in serious debate, as was the case now when he opened the conversation.

"So, Mr. Brennan, you have been employed by Roisin Byrne to find her missing husband!" There was a challenging tone to his voice as he carried on preparing the drinks, tossing several ice cubes into each glass. "Forgive my boldness for asking, but could that not be described as taking money under false pretences?"

There was little humour in his words, nor was there meant to be; in fact it came perilously close to sounding like an accusation; and one that Jack found all the more irritating because it was accompanied by a strong north Dublin accent that took some getting used to, especially for an Englishman who had never been across the border.

Reacting to the challenge Jack's eyes glinted mischievously, he had no intention of being intimidated by his host; he was looking for information from the priest not accusations, so he wasn't about to waste his time on petty point scoring.

"Surely the church recognises the importance of a Christian burial for Tony Byrne -- if indeed he was murdered, as most people around here seem to believe?" he countered.

"Touché, Mr. Brennan," Father Joseph conceded, a wry smile playing on his lips, "but can you honestly say that is the only reason you have for taking on this investigation, to offer a lost soul a Christian burial?" His response was never intended as a question, it was just another way of restating his original accusation.

"I think you know that's not the case, Father, but that's neither here nor there, is it? Roisin Byrne is a very distraught but determined woman who desperately wants to know what happened to her husband, I see nothing wrong in that -- nor should you."

There was a slight unease in the air as Jack suffered a creeping intolerance of the priest's accusative attitude.

"Someone out there knows what happened to Tony Byrne, and I'm making it my duty to discover who that someone is and hopefully unravel this sad mystery. I would appreciate any help or advice you might feel willing to offer, particularly as you know the couple much more intimately than I do."

Father Joseph glided across the room with Jack's drink held at arm's length.

"The Catholic Church in Ireland has a very difficult task these days.

What with this ongoing conflict between state and dissidents." He paused momentarily to choose his words. "So many disenfranchised individuals, and so many groups of people involved in trying to find a formula for peace, each with their own agenda. We priests must be seen to offer spiritual guidance and solace to all of God's children, and that can often lead to conflict in these difficult and trying times."

He sipped from his glass before continuing.

"The church by its very nature is a political animal, but having said that, nothing must be allowed to upset the delicate balance between God and Politics that has survived throughout the centuries." There was something in the way he dropped into his seat that declared he had said enough.

Jack on the other hand was only getting started, and the unfortunate cleric had something of a shock ahead of him.

"You can stuff your delicate balance, Father. I'm employed to find some bones that belong to one of your parishioners -- now you either want to help me do that or you don't. As they say in modern day parlance -- it's make your mind up time."

Father Joseph decided to take to the floor again, less gracefully than before, more stooped and less purposeful in the way he shuffled about the room; his right hand grooming an imaginary beard as it caressed his chin.

"You appear to be assuming that I can be of help." he said guardedly.

Jack looked at him in disbelief.

"There can't be anything of importance happening in this parish that doesn't get back to your ears, Father. You may not be able to verify all the rumours that reach you but you certainly get to hear them." He smiled knowingly before continuing to hammer home his point. "It would help if you stopped dancing around the issue and got on with it. After all, you did sort of indicate a willingness to help when you agreed to see me."

He was convinced the priest was deliberately toying with him, but he believed deep down that it was good practice to keep him on board and make full use of his local knowledge.

Father Joseph eyed him with a bland expression.

"We clerics occupy a very privileged place in the community, Mr. Brennan. We are sometimes granted access to people's inner thoughts, their worries and their doubts -- their fears even."

He was moving away from Jack as he spoke but suddenly swung round to face him again, as if to reinforce the point he was about to make.

"In the privacy of the confessional we uncover their sins and wrong doings, and at such times have a duty to demand penance for God's forgiveness. You must try to understand the burden that places upon us. The responsibility of confidentiality cannot and must not be broken or breached in any way."

He returned thoughtfully to his seat as he continued.

"Our acceptance by the community as God's messengers is very much reliant upon that confidentiality." His grey eyes scanned Jack's face for any inkling of understanding, and when he found none his brow gathered in frustration.

"I'm doing my utmost to explain my position to you."

The first signs of irritation were creeping into his voice.

"As one concerned human being to another I can quite freely offer an opinion on most things, would actually wish to do so under these particular circumstances -- in fact I'm quite entitled to do that."

He squared his shoulders defiantly.

"What I cannot do however is divulge a confidence - I'm afraid you will just have to accept that."

Setting aside the brusque finality in his voice, there was sufficient tetchiness in his body language to show a degree of personal irritation at the position he found himself in. Jack wondered if it was an indication that he knew something that he felt might be important. On the other hand he could just be fencing with him, setting out his stall by limiting the boundaries of Jack's expectations.

There was no denying the difficulties facing the cleric, even if he did feel obliged to help. He was after all wholly governed by the restrictions placed upon him by his faith, and while Jack thought he detected an element of frustration in the priest regarding those restrictions, it hardly meant he was going to be any more forthcoming because of it. It was difficult to be absolutely certain but he chose to allow the priest the benefit of the doubt for the time being. The future would quickly tell if he had got it right.

"Okay, Father, I take your point."

He had seen enough in the priest's demeanour to believe it was still worth trying to win him over, even if it meant reining in on his own aggressive approach to do so. A thought that reminded him of Judy's warning about exercising an element of diplomacy.

"I can see that what I'm asking might not sit too comfortably with you, Father, but I find it hard to understand how you can offer an opinion on something like this without that opinion being influenced by knowledge that has been confided in you -- from whatever source?"

Father Joseph gave him a wry smile.

"Then I suggest we pursue the matter a little further and see where it takes us." He rolled out of his chair in a seemingly well practiced movement that lined him up on a direct compass march with the drinks cabinet. "There are certain opinions that I have regarding Tony Byrne that have absolutely nothing to do with his disappearance, or the confessional; opinions that have been forged over many years of knowing the man and his family personally and intimately. Those opinions haven't changed because of his disappearance, and while they may not tell you why he disappeared, they may allow you to discount certain theories that have already had an overgenerous airing around these parts."

He pursed his lips, pinching them between thumb and forefinger in a thoughtful pose.

"What you might call a process of elimination, Mr. Brennan, since they stand outside the influence of any stories or theories that may have come to my ears since his disappearance."

He carried on talking as he refilled his glass, while absentmindedly failing to do the same for his guest. "It may not be much, but under the circumstances it's the best I can offer."

Jack put on his happy face.

"You have my undivided attention, Father," he assured him, smiling agreeably, before purposefully draining his glass and holding it out at arms-length.

"Well now," said Father Joseph, "having said all that, where do I begin?" He ground his hands together in preparation, then on spotting Jack's empty glass remedied his earlier oversight by pointing towards the cabinet. "Please -- help yourself while I gather my thoughts."

To Jack's surprise he got quickly into his stride.

"Let me begin by saying that Tony Byrne was a good and practising Catholic. His whole life revolved around those close to him; his wife, his friends, his work, and the church, and probably in that order as well."

Jack struggled to remain patient, a difficult task in the circumstances as he was fed up listening to glowing character references about the guy. If he had been such an uncomplicated and saintly individual why the hell had he gone walkabouts?

He was tempted to voice his thoughts but the priest took the opportunity away from him.

"Tony Byrne was a genuinely honest and sincere person and very charitable with it. He was also a valued friend to all who knew him." He eyed his visitor from across the room, and seeing the frustrated look on Jack's face, smiled mockingly.

"If you know what a man is, Mr. Brennan, then you may also determine what he is not. You should listen carefully, because what I have to say might give you some direction."

His words of caution registered a warning with Jack making him much more attentive.

"Tony Byrne was a non-political individual, a man of integrity, who strongly disliked seeing other people suffer."

He sipped from his glass while arranging his thoughts.

"His charitable work within the parish required a great deal of commitment, but he was involved in other charities outside of the church as well, which, from what I can gather, required even more commitment. He was a truly valuable asset to this community -- one that will be sadly missed by all who knew him."

Jack edged to the front of his seat, a questioning look on his face. What he had just heard triggered an alarm in his over suspicious mind. No one had mentioned anything about any charity work to him, and while it might be completely irrelevant it was still something that set him apart from his friends, and therefore something that needed following up.

"Tell me more about this charity work, Father," he said casually, concealing his excitement.

The priest angled his head to one side in a manner that posed a question; a question that he soon put in front of Jack.

"There's nothing much to tell really, but why would you attach any importance to his charity work?" He curled a well-manicured fore-finger round his upper lip as he tried to figure out what Jack was angling at. "It was nothing more than a local fund raising project based here at the church -- nothing of any great importance, other than its charitable purpose in life of course."

He had been quick to sense Jack's sudden interest, and it continued to puzzle him.

"You mentioned other charities, Father, ones that were outside the influence of your own church. What was his involvement with them?" Most likely the whole thing was perfectly innocent, but he would want to look very closely at everything and anything that took Tony Byrne away from his family circle. The only thing he felt certain about at this stage was that Roisin Byrne had played no part in her husband's disappearance. Everything else was up for grabs.

"There was only one that I am aware of really, and as I understand it Tony's only involvement was to offer his services as a driver. But I'm not the one you should be asking about it as our church had no connection with it at all."

"Do you know what charity it was, Father, or where it was based?" Jack asked, his interest deepening.

"It was one of those off the cuff Romanian or Bosnian appeal things, I'm not sure which. I do know Tony volunteered as a driver on a couple of emergency convoys that went out from here. But you would do better to ask his wife, she can tell you much more about it than I can."

It looked as if he was politely indicating to Jack that his time was up. As it was Jack believed he had exhausted his conversation with the cleric, but before he headed for the door he posed him one last question.

"Are you sure there's nothing else you can tell me that might help my investigation, Father?"

The priest shook his head firmly and got to his feet.

"I fear not, Mr. Brennan, but if you are genuinely trying to solve the mystery of Tony's disappearance then I wish you all the luck in the world." He offered his hand in a parting gesture.

"I think I'm going to need some luck, that's for sure" Jack admitted, pulling a fifty pound note from his wallet.

"A small contribution towards the church fund, Father." He smiled as he laid it on the table, enjoying a quiet inner chuckle at the thought of bribing his way into heaven!

Father Joseph followed him to the door and laid a hand on his shoulder when they got to the top step, much like an old friend might.

"I'm sorry to say we live in troubled times, Mr. Brennan, which makes it very difficult for some of us to accept things at face value. I sincerely hope that you understand my position of neutrality regarding certain circumstances that prevail within my parish." Jack smiled half-heartedly as he turned his back on the priest.

There was nothing more to be said.

As he made his way home he weighed up the evenings events with the cold objectivity that only hindsight can provide. He had been less than convinced about the priest's willingness to co-operate when they had first met, but on reflection he realized that the guy had probably been more helpful than he'd given him credit for, or for that matter had acknowledged.

His disclosure regarding the second charity that the missing man had been involved with opened up a new approach to the investigation as he had known absolutely nothing about prior to their meeting; that was something to think on. He was just about ready to accept that Byrne seemed an unlikely type to have been involved in anything unlawful, not intentionally anyway. Everyone he had spoken to had been very convincing about his good natured approach to life. The information about his charity work was new and needed following up, but thanks to Father Joseph he could eliminate some of his original suspicions about the guy's disappearance, and that would help focus his future approach to the case.

Top of his agenda was to discuss his findings with his client and ascertain the full extent of her husband's involvement with both charities, especially the overseas one. There was something quite tantalizingly about that scenario from an investigative viewpoint, and the sooner he knew more about it the better.

7

"See if you can raise Roisin Byrne for me, Judy. I'd like her to pop in for a chat later on if she's available. Something came up last night that I need to run past her." Jack was perched on the corner of Judy's desk rummaging through the morning's mail. Having arrived home late the previous evening with Judy already in bed he'd had no chance to brief her on his meeting with Father Joseph. For now though he watched in silent witness as she topped up her caffeine levels, accepting that until she had righted that little shortcoming it was a waste of time trying to explain anything.

Her zombie-like expression dictated that it would take at least one more caffeine fix before she would be capable of rational thought. Until that happened there was no sense in trying to engage with her in sensible conversation. In fact his somewhat guarded silence was a well-rehearsed part of their daily ritual, a ritual that kicked off each morning with their muted journey to the office, and his lover's need to boost her depleted caffeine intake. Rather than say anything untoward he would let her suffer in isolation as he crept off into his own office without his partner even noticing his absence.

His first call of the day was another futile attempt at contacting Dave Jackson, and having failed to do so it left him wondering if the guy was deliberately stone-walling him. That said, he did at least discover that he was scheduled to give evidence at a case being heard in Downpatrick Court House that very morning, which left him thinking that if Mohammed wouldn't come to the mountain, then the mountain would just have to go to Mohammed. He jabbed a finger at the intercom button in hopeful anticipation that Judy was back in the land of the living.

"If you haven't contacted Mrs. Byrne yet, Judy," he explained, "try scheduling the meeting for later this afternoon. I'm heading off to Downpatrick shortly and I don't know how long I'm going to be. You can give me a bell on the mobile when you have it sorted." He drummed his fingers impatiently on the desk top as he waited for her to acknowledge.

When she finally graced him with an answer it was every bit as caustic as he had assumed it would be.

"It might be a good idea to let the lady get out of bed before we start pestering her -- the whole bloody world isn't suffering from the same sleep disorder as you -- some of us actually enjoy a few hours in bed."

Jack threw his head back and chuckled quietly to himself, convinced the caffeine had worked its magic and his lover was once again firing on all cylinders, but his humour was short lived as he needed to rush and make ready for his trip to Downpatrick.

8

The first thing Jack did when he arrived at the courthouse was to head straight for the public notice board, where a quick scrutiny told him that Downpatrick was no longer the crime free zone its patron saint had hoped to establish. Not if the long list of cases published for hearing that day was anything to go by, and since he hadn't a clue what Dave Jackson looked like he had to go back to the entrance and the uniformed cop who stood there ready to help.

"I wonder if you could point me in the direction of a Detective Sergeant Dave Jackson -- I believe he's involved in a case that's being heard here today."

The young constable scanned the crowded lobby but failed to pick the detective out amidst the milling horde of learned members and their nervy looking clients, all of whom were locked in tight little huddles of whispered urgency as a prelude to whatever fate awaited them.

"It looks like he might be inside already, or perhaps he's not even here yet." Having made his pronouncement the young cop gave Jack a quick once over. "Who are you anyway, and what do you want with him?" he asked.

Jack produced his permit and offered it up for inspection.

"I need to talk to him about a case he worked on that has now ended up on my plate, but he's a bloody difficult guy to track down, and as I'm a bit strapped for time and I was hoping I might catch up with him here."

The young cop gave it a few seconds thought and eventually decided he would help out. "You stay right where you are," he insisted, "I'll go and see if he's inside for you."

With that he wheeled away and disappeared through the first set of doors he came to, re-emerging within a couple of minutes accompanied by a neatly dressed young man wearing a dark, pin stripe suit.

The newcomer was perhaps an inch or so taller than Jack, with dark, wavy hair and a neatly trimmed moustache. His finely chiselled features were set in an agitated grimace that made him, temporarily at least, less handsome than he might otherwise have been. As he headed in Jack's direction his facial expression became ever more aggressive. In fact if looks could kill then Jack considered himself to be at least mortally wounded!

"What the hell is this all about?" he snapped, his curt remark portraying the same degree of venom that simmered behind his dark eyes.

Ignoring his abrasive approach Jack introduced himself with a friendly, almost amicable smile. But as he got down to explaining the purpose of his visit, the other man took him quickly by the arm and guided him away from the busy concourse in the direction of an empty bench close to the main entrance.

"Well -- I guess if Bill Anderson gave it the okay - who am I to argue?" he muttered, his mind on other things as he frisked himself in a frantic search for a cigarette. In desperate need he dug a pack of Marlboro out of his shirt pocket and scrambled one between his lips. Then, with a well-practised movement that came close to being an art form, he flicked the top of his Zippo lighter open, fanned the wheel with the heel of his hand and lit up, drawing his much needed toxic entitlement deep into his lungs before releasing it through flared nostrils in a steady grey stream.

"So it's the Byrne case you're interested in," he muttered, sucking greedily at his cigarette, as if his very life depended on it. "What can I say, there's not a lot to tell really. The guy went missing a few years ago and has not been seen or heard of since - mystery done - over and out. There's nothing more can I tell you?" He stretched his neck into his collar and jammed the cigarette back between his lips, drawing deeply on its toxic fumes. Jack looked on in frustrated silence, puzzled by the young man's stroppy attitude and noticeable lack of interest. After all, as it was a case the young detective was personally involved with one might expect him to be just a tiny bit nosey about Jack's involvement, if nothing else.

"Supposing you start by telling me why you think Tony Byrne went missing? There must have been some sort of official line on what happened to him." Jack hadn't driven all the way to Downpatrick to be stonewalled by a cocky young cop with a nicotine dependency.

"There never was an official line," Jackson replied, flicking the ash from his cigarette in cavalier fashion, while ignoring the sign directly above his right ear that declared he was in a no smoking zone.

Jack began to wonder if their lack of rapport had anything to do with the fact that he was a private investigator. It was unlikely the guy was being awkward just for the hell of it, but whether he was, or whether he wasn't, it was time to present him with a proverbial kick up the ass.

"I don't believe your case report could have been quite so obtuse, but if you know so little about an important case you're meant to be handling then perhaps I should be looking to Bill Anderson for my answers." The veiled threat was perfectly in order in Jack's book; he knew the introduction of the senior officer's name in such a familiar way would almost certainly invite a more helpful attitude -- which was exactly what he got.

"I hardly think you need trouble the Chief Inspector again. I'm being perfectly serious when I say there is nowhere to go with this case." He drew in another lungful of nicotine, more greedily this time, almost as if the cigarette owed him something!

"Nobody saw anything -- nobody heard anything -- nobody knows anything." He shrugged his broad shoulders. "The guy just vanished off the face of the earth for no apparent reason."

He began pacing about in a tight little circle in an effort to curb his impatience, while Jack kept pressing for him to get involved. "What was the word on the street back then?" he asked, trying to draw a conversation from the other man.

Jackson studied his shoes for a moment or two then gave him an unwelcome bland look.

"There was no word on the street -- at least not in the nationalist area where he lived. Byrne was a Catholic who chose to have Protestant friends, and that obviously generated a few wild stories, particularly amongst the loyalists. But there was no information of any consequence coming back from any of our usual sources." He dropped his cigarette butt on the marble floor and ground it underfoot.

"They -- the loyalists I mean -- had him marked down as an IRA spy who was fingering potential hits, but there was no evidence whatsoever to support such an accusation. The guy was just your average Joe Bloggs, who on the face of it, disappeared for reasons known only to himself." One side of Jackson's face attempted a smile, but it looked more like a grimace from where Jack was standing. "Maybe he's shacked up somewhere enjoying the comforts of a good woman. Or maybe his disappearance was the unfortunate result of mistaken identity?" He pulled another cigarette from the packet and dangled it between his lips, determined to get his full quota of toxic intake before heading back to the court room.

"It's always possible that he did fall victim to some blood crazed loyalist looking for an easy kill – there are plenty of them about. They would certainly have seen him as an easy target as he was on their patch often enough to have been noticed."

Jack wasn't overly impressed with what he was hearing; in fact he found it all rather depressing.

"So if we cut to the chase – you're actually telling me that you think the guy is dead."

Jackson eyed him invitingly.

"Don't you?" he asked, with an air of incredulity. "Is that not what this is all about -- finding a few bones to bury?" He turned away and stamped on his half smoked cigarette. "I have to get back inside now, if it's any help come over and have a look at the case file sometime."

He was about to leave when Jack nodded towards his discarded cigarette butt.

"You should give those things up before they kill you." he said, half-jokingly.

Jackson raised his hand in a two fingered salute and wandered off.

Jack was no more than twenty minutes away from Belfast when he got a call on his mobile phone and pulled over to the side of the road to take it.

It turned out to be Judy.

"Hi, Jack, I'm afraid the Byrne woman can't make it today, she has some tradesman or other coming to service an appliance and she's not sure what time to expect him. It looks like you will have to get your ass up to her place if you still want this meeting to take place."

Jack thumped the steering wheel in frustration; the last thing he wanted to do was visit his client at home; that was a seriously bad practice, because it had the potential to bring the spotlight down on her and produce a security issue if the IRA were involved.

"I really don't want to go near her place -- being seen anywhere near her house is bad practice -- it declares our involvement sooner than I would like, but it appears I don't have much choice. I should be back with you in about twenty minutes or so anyway so we can discuss it then." He tossed the phone aside and switched his thoughts back to his earlier meeting with Dave Jackson. If nothing else, it had gone some way towards clearing up a couple of points that had been at the forefront of his mind. For starters he could almost take it as read now that Tony Byrne had no paramilitary connections, and none of his friends, nor indeed the police investigating team, held out any hope that he might ever be found alive. Which rather shortened the odds on the guy having been murdered. The big question of course was why?

The laws of probability were heavily stacked against his death being accidental, and that in turn undermined the popular theory of mistaken identity, but the likelihood that it might have been a sectarian issue was still very much alive and kicking.

The unpalatable truth was that it mattered little to Jack one way or the other because either scenario meant he was hunting for a dead man, and bodies were notoriously easy to hide, especially for those who were practiced in that particular art form.

The more he dwelt on the problem the more disappointed he became at the lack of evidence uncovered by the RUC's investigation, he had hoped for something more positive from them. The name of a suspect would have helped, even if any evidence gathered fell short of being case proven -- but it wasn't to be. In fact they had given him nothing that he could rely on

It suddenly became clear just how difficult it was going to be to achieve a positive outcome with the case, if he even decided to see it through. It wasn't in his nature to waste a client's hard earned savings on a futile search if her husband had been killed by one of the terrorist groups. That was a road to nowhere, and he did have some scruples.

In any case, if that was what had happened then the body was probably buried under some fly-over, or under the foundations of some multi-story car park, which was generally where such victims ended their days. One thing was absolutely certain, there would be no digging them up from there -- not in this lifetime -- not with the monumental costs such an exercise would incur. It was a disturbing thought that made him take stock of his situation. His final decision, prompted mostly by the lack of police evidence, was that if his investigation into Byrne's charitable work revealed nothing of any significance he would call it a day and not waste any more of his client's money.

It was a few minutes short of four o'clock when he turned up the Grosvenor Road, an area he knew all too well from his undercover days with military intelligence. And it took him hardly any time at all to pick out her neat little semi, although it gave him a decidedly uncomfortable feeling that he was in the area at all as it resurrected some unhappy and best forgotten memories. Stepping away from the protection of his car gave him the eerie feeling that a dozen pairs of eyes were secretly watching his every move. This part of Belfast was a law onto itself, bandit country in the true sense of the word, an area were strangers were instantly taken note of and monitored every inch of the way until they went back the way they had come. If they were allowed to!

Fortunately for Jack his client's front door opened with hasty consideration and he was spirited into the living room without undue ceremony.

The first thing to grab his attention, and it would be hard to have missed it, was a long, knee high mahogany table that stretched a third of the length of one wall. Its polished surface festooned with framed photographs of the woman's missing husband. However it wasn't the photographs alone that impacted on him, but the fact that they shared their resting place with an array of multi-coloured candles, lots of candles in fact. Their garish looking arrangement had the potential to qualify as a shrine, and probably would have done had the candles had been lit, which thankfully they were not.

There was little else of particular note in the room, except that it was dust free, comfortably furnished and well maintained, much as he had expected it would be. But he wasn't here to inspect the furnishings and needed to be getting on with things.

"I think it will be better for both of us if I am completely honest and up front with you, Mrs. Byrne, and I'm afraid that means admitting that

I'm making absolutely no headway whatsoever." He laid it out exactly as it was, without any frills, knowing that to do otherwise would be a waste of everyone's time. "I'm sorry to say that it's very much like you said, Tony seems to have vanished off the radar without trace and without reason."

His client appeared unmoved, and faced him with a deadpan expression. "We both knew that when you took the job, so nothing has changed; nothing is any worse than it was before." The soft lilt of her voice deserved to sound happier.

"To be perfectly honest," Jack explained, with a hint of warning, "the general consensus seems to support the theory that your husband was the victim of a sectarian killing. Even the police unofficially support that theory, and at this precise moment in time I'm almost convinced of it myself." He resisted the temptation to say more.

His client angled her head to one side and peered up at him, her top lip pinched firmly between forefinger and thumb. She had no wish to over-react and hesitated momentarily before saying anything, but when she chose to do so there was no lack of resolve in her voice, she sounded as determined as ever, possibly even more so! "If bones are all there are to find --- " She left the remainder of the sentence hanging in the air unfinished; not that it needed finishing, it was simply a reminder of her determination to keep going, and an indication that she was not about to let Jack wriggle out of their contract.

For his part Jack found himself admiring her all the more for it.

She was forcing him into a corner and leaving him no alternative but to get on with what she was paying him to do. Having accepted that fact there was still the matter of her husband's charity work to deal with, which was the original purpose for his visit.

"Okay, Mrs. Byrne, if you want me to continue looking for your husband then that is exactly what I propose to do."

She endeavoured to grace his response with smile, but it got lost somewhere among the worry lines.

"I hope that wasn't the only reason for your visit," she said pointedly.

"No -- of course not" he replied hastily, "I need you to tell me about this charity work your husband was involve with, especially this Bosnian, or Romanian thing?"

Her brow gathered in an enquiring way.

"Do you believe that has some relevance to what happened to Tony?" She sounded much too optimistic and hopeful, which clearly needed reining in before she got carried away.

"Now don't get over excited about this -- I don't want you getting your hopes up unnecessarily, it was just something that Father Joseph mentioned in passing and might have no relevance whatsoever," he warned, tactfully weaning her off her current course.

She drew back, looking a little perplexed.

"You've been to see Father Joseph?"

She was genuinely surprised.

"Was he able to offer any help? I wouldn't ever have thought so."

Having answered her own question Jack let it pass without comment. "I still need you to tell me about this charity," he insisted, bring the conversation back to where it needed to be.

He could almost hear her brain moving up a gear, but he didn't want her going off on some detailed explanation, all he wanted was a quick overview, nothing more.

"Please, Mrs. Byrne," he stressed, "can we stay focussed."

She shook her head, as if coming out of a trance.

"It was just a local idea, one of those spur of the moment things -- you know -- collecting blankets and clothes for those poor souls who were trying to survive out there. Especially the children."

She gave him a wry smile.

"Tony was mostly concerned about the welfare of the children and offered his services as a driver to try and do his bit; it's what he's best at after all." The endless fidgeting of her fingers was systematically dismembering the paper tissue that substituted for a security blanket, leaving shreds of paper scattered all over the carpet at her feet. "He even sacrificed his holidays so he could fit it in -- but he's like that, is Tony." A tiny pearl of moisture hovered on her lower eyelid, ready to trace a line down her face the next time she blinked.

Jack dreaded what he thought was about to happen, but he needn't have bothered because she spotted his discomfort and dealt with it instantly.

"Don't fret yourself, Mr. Brennan" she assured him, "I'm not about to have another emotional outburst." Her eyes twinkled, and her face lit up in a cheeky half smile. It was the only smile he had seen on her face since she had first entered his office, and while it rather surprised him, it also confirmed his belief that she could be very resolute when the mood took her.

"How long would he have been away on these trips?" he asked, leading her back to the memory of her husband's last movements.

"The last time -- which was just before he went missing -- lasted about three weeks." She was trying hard to remember all the detail she could and it showed on her face.

"There was some sort of last minute re-routing or something on the return journey that added a few extra days to the trip, which turned it into an extremely long overland drive. Tony and another man planned the route. The other man knows his way round Europe quite well and was by far the most experienced driver on the convoy, but Tony was always in on the planning stage."

She abandoned the shredded tissue altogether and switched her attention to the trailing ends of her hair, twisting them round and round her index finger.

"Did he seem alright to you when he got back? Was there any indication that something out of the ordinary might have taken place during the trip?" It was vain hope that she might recall something useful. There was always the possibility that it was simply a case of -- boy meets girl on long trip away from home -- boy runs off with girl after long trip. It was a totally inappropriate time to be having such thoughts because he was conscious of his client's inquisitive eyes watching him intently. A look that suggested she was reading his mind, and from the expression on her face she was anything but pleased.

"No, Mr. Brennan, let me stop you right there, you are quite wrong if you think Tony has run off with someone he met on that trip. Do you think I haven't already considered such a possibility?" She threw her head back defiantly. "I'm going to say this once more so that it's perfectly clear and you understand exactly what it is I'm telling you -- Tony is not that sort of man --anyway, apart from being worn out and distressed at what he saw out there he was his normal self when he got home."

Jack sighed like a defeated athlete, then gave her something else to think about.

"Who actually organized these trips?"

She shrugged her shoulders offhandedly.

"Just a local neighbourhood group; the whole thing was nothing more than a spontaneous reaction to the situation we saw played out on television. One of the guys in the next street was the mastermind behind it -- Joe Devlin is his name -- he floated the idea at the leisure centre one night and things just took off from there. The idea sort of captured everyone's imagination, and I suppose it gave us all something useful to do during the summer. It also helped to take our minds off the riots and everything else that was going on around here at the time."

Jack was growing ever more intrigued by this whole charity thing.

There was ample potential for something to go wrong on a long trip abroad like that. It certainly warranted some sort of follow up, in fact it was crying out for it if the truth be known.

"Would this guy Devlin be willing to talk to me about it if I paid him a visit?"

"I don't see why not, although from what I hear he's a bit of a law unto himself. A hard line nationalist by all accounts, if you know what I mean, so I dare say he might not be too receptive to discussing something with a stranger like you." She thought over what she had just said, then added. "Perhaps you shouldn't read too much into that as it's very much the nature of things round here, what with the troubles and all. Everyone's a bit guarded about who they speak to."

Jack was once again impressed with her generosity of spirit: especially with her husband going missing in the way that he had.

Such an event would test anyone's faith in humanity, yet here she was showing a level of tolerance that was nothing short of inspirational. Although even he had to agree that it was all too easy to make a rash judgment, or jump to a wrong conclusion with all the side issues that tainted people's rationale.

Desperate and often horrific events were played out in the back streets of Northern Ireland that would never be tolerated in any other part of the United Kingdom. So much of everyday life was shrouded in sectarian and political overtones; not to mention the feuds and internal squabbles within the paramilitary organizations themselves, and the drug dealers and local gangsters who hung onto their coat tails.

The whole place was a bloody mess, one big churning cesspit of hatred and criminality, stoked, in part at least, by a government that had broken its promise to the people and were intent upon releasing mass murderers, thugs, drug pushers and perverts back onto the streets, and more importantly back into their former strongholds to continue their persecution of the population.

It was all part of an extremely fragile peace process that was being force fed to a war weary population struggling to survive.

Jack sighed at the naivety of some politicians, but he had let his mind wander and needed to get it back on the case. Clearly the only way to move things forward was to contact this Devlin character and see what developed, a task that would be difficult for him personally because of his military background.

"Would you class Devlin as a close friend of Tony's?" he asked, seeing the relationship between the two men as an important issue. Especially as Devlin's name had not surfaced anywhere before, nor was it on the list of friends she had provided him with, and that in itself was enough to make him curious.

She grimaced slightly and wrinkled her nose at the suggestion.

"No -- they have never been as close as that." she admitted. "They only came together because of their charity work. I suppose you could really only describe him as a – a," she searched for the right word, "an acquaintance -- yes that's it -- an acquaintance."

Her explanation only served to strengthen Jack's interest, and while he didn't like the vibes he was getting about Devlin, he felt he was in danger of condemning the man before they had even met. Clearly an early meeting was essential, although from what he had just learned he did not feel confident that Devlin would be up for it. One thing was fairly obvious though, he would need to find a suitable go-between to set the thing up, and it would have to be well away from the prying eyes of the local paramilitaries. The less attention he got from those guys the safer it would be for all concerned. It was a fact of life that nothing of any consequence happened on their patch that didn't feed back to the godfathers of the republican movement, and with his own history of involvement in the troubles during the latter years he would need to take particular care not to over-expose himself.

"It would be very helpful if you broke the ice for me with Devlin," he suggested, "maybe ask him to get in touch so we can arrange to meet.

Do you think you could manage that?"

Roisin Byrne knew nothing of Jack's military background, but she recognized an English accent when she heard one, and being perceptive, knew very well the danger Jack would face if he went storming in off his own bat. He was a complete stranger to Devlin, and as she already knew from her earlier experience with the police investigation that even her closest of neighbours had been reluctant to offer their help, never mind a hard-nosed republican like Joe Devlin.

"I can see you might have problems there," she admitted, "from what I have learned about him Devlin was less than helpful to the police during their investigation, but then again -- who wasn't?"

She brushed an irritating lock of hair aside, but it fell back and continued its irritation.

"I'm honestly not sure that I can make that much difference as I hardly know the man myself, we're only on nodding terms really." She looked a little uncertain as she tucked the offending lock of hair behind her ear out of harm's way. "But when you think about it, what possible reason could there be for anyone not wanting to help me find my husband?"

Jack nodded his agreement.

"You can only do your best, Mrs. Byrne, and if visiting my office proves a problem for Devlin I'm quite happy to meet him somewhere else, but at the end of the day I need to meet the guy face to face, a telephone conversation won't give me what I want." He pulled a notebook from his pocket and held it out to her. "I need his address and phone number if you can dig it out for me." His client only had to go as far as the telephone table in the hall to get what he wanted, and with his notebook tucked safely back in his pocket he was ready to take his leave.

There was just one other thing he had promised himself he would do before leaving.

"You might not realise it, what with everything else you've had to put up with, but you have a really good friend in Jean Graham, and it's obvious to me that she misses your company since you stopped calling with her." He grinned good-humouredly in anticipation of what he was to say next. "Believe it or not she has even dyed her hair the same colour as yours -- well -- almost, although to be perfectly honest it doesn't really work on her, and she could do with someone telling her to do something about it."

She returned him the gentlest of smiles.

"Thank you, Mr. Brennan, I appreciate your thoughtfulness." She smoothed the skin on the back of one hand with the palm of the other, then clasped both hands tightly together in her lap. She remained that way for a few moments, deep in thought.

"You are right of course, I do owe Jean a visit, and I promise to go and see her again very soon." The guilty look on her face suggested it was a promise she intended to fulfil.

Jack got up and moved in the direction of the door.

"I'll keep you updated with anything that develops," he promised, "but my main priority at the moment is to get to work on this guy Devlin."

He took another step towards leaving.

"Don't you disturb yourself," he told her, "I'm a big boy now -- I can see myself out." Smiling good-humouredly he turned away, leaving his client staring longingly across the room at her husband's photographs.

He had no sooner turned his back on her before the smile left his face, he had other more pressing matters that needed his attention, like an explanation for Devlin's reluctance to assist the police. Unless the guy had a valid excuse for doing so it seemed very odd indeed, and even if there had been some kind of old boy cover up in operation at the time, it had been made redundant with the likelihood that it had now become a murder enquiry. Devlin certainly needed closer inspection to determine that there was nothing sinister in his unhelpful attitude. A quick check with his colleagues in the RUC might shed more light on the matter.

9

"See if you can get me any background on this guy from our friends in blue." Jack said, pinching his nose like there was a bad smell about the place as he set his notebook down in front of Judy. "And while you're at it," he added, "You might as well have them do a quick check on Father Joseph at the same time -- I'm sure he's okay, but you never know; better safe than sorry -- eh!"

Judy gave him a look that would have fatally wounded a lesser man. It seemed incomprehensible to her that he would even consider adding a parish priest on his list of suspects.

She was still looking churlish as he wheeled away and headed back to his office to attend to the list he had compiled the previous day. Without a moment's hesitation he picked up his pen and drew a thick line through the word suicide, then pushed the list aside and headed across the room to the window; his hands buried deep into his trouser pockets.

As he watched the bustling activity below a niggling little twitch crept into the back of his mind over something he should have done, or should be doing, but the memory of what it was eluded him. His attention focusing on a queue of vehicles that were backed up on the road below, and seeing a couple of trucks nose to tail like that was enough to jog his memory.

He rushed back to his desk and buzzed Judy.

"Be an angel, sweetheart, and see if you can raise Sergeant Jackson for me, he's up at the Grosvenor Road barracks."

He hardly had time to plant his backside before his phone rang. "I've got Sergeant Jackson for you on line one," Judy told him, hanging up immediately afterwards.

Following a few initial pleasantries Jack got straight down to business. "How are you fixed if I nip over to take a look at Byrne's case file? There's something I need to check out if you can spare me the time?"

There was a slight gap in the conversation that didn't inspire confidence.

"Much as I'd like to accommodate you, Jack, I'm about to hit the road and as I won't be back until late evening I don't really see how I can fit you in."

Jack screwed his face up and cursed his luck under his breath. "Just give me a time that suits you, Dave, and I'll be there, any time you're free will do."

When he got no immediate response he provided his own answer to the problem.

"Forget that idea, why don't you just come over to my place for dinner this evening when you're finished? That would solve the problem and give me a chance to run a few other things past you at the same time."

"That's very decent of you, Jack, but I'm afraid I'm not permitted to remove case files from the office. Even you should know that."

The rebuke brought a weary sigh from Jack, but he wasn't inclined to give up that easily. "Come on, Dave. You must have checked out my credentials by now. I'm hardly likely to mug you and take the bloody files now am I?" He hung on for an answer but didn't get one, just a series of frustrated moans and groans that warned him Jackson might be about to hang up. .

"Jeez – why can't I have a nice cosy little nine-to-five job like every other bastard out there?" He wasn't really envious of others, just momentarily pissed off with his own unhappy situation.

"I can tell you're not going to let me off the hook, are you, Jack? So why don't you give me your address and tell me how I get there --- and you better give me your phone number as well just in case something crops up and I can't make it."

Jack quoted him the number and a time then found himself cut off with embarrassing haste, but he was feeling too pleased with himself to even give it a second thought.

He placed a lot of importance on building a good rapport with the young detective, and was convinced in his own mind that having him round to dinner would help cement a more fruitful relationship. He had always held the belief that people were much more forthcoming when they were in a relaxed social environment than they might otherwise be, and he definitely needed the young detective on his side.

He was still toying with that thought as he wandered through to Judy's office to warn her about their dinner guest.

10

Dave Jackson timed his visit like a military exercise, arriving at Jack's house at precisely eight thirty as arranged. He had both hands fully occupied as he climbed out of the taxi, his left arm hugging a bulky box file and an unwrapped box of chocolates close to his chest, while his right hand steered a bunch of flowers out of harm's way as he elbowed the cab door shut behind him. The gifts were a last minute idea, and were warmly received by Judy, but her show of appreciation, genuine though it was, didn't do a lot to relax their visitor, and the conversation remained rather stunted in its early stages. Which probably had more to do with the fact that Jackson's last encounter with his host had been a somewhat abrasive affair, and one that remained firmly planted at the forefront of his mind.

Jack on the other hand looked completely relaxed and at ease with himself, secure in the belief that the twelve year old malt he had just served up would justify its exorbitant price tag and help the conversation flow more readily. In fact he was proved right sooner than even he had hoped when Jackson moved to the edge of his seat with an inquisitive look on his face. He mused over the rapidly melting ice cubes in the bottom of his glass before raising his eyes and making it known that he had done his homework since their last meeting.

"I believe you spent some time here with our friends from Hereford." There was nothing in his enquiry to make it an issue of any importance, just an acknowledgement that it was something he was aware of.

"With that in mind, I presume you must have acquired some understanding of the way we do things on this side of the pond."

Jack grimaced ever so slightly, the last thing he wanted was to portray himself as a mister-know-all. In fact he was keen to play down any reference to his past, seeing it as a possible barrier to a good working relationship with his visitor. He believed it necessary to avoid that at all costs.

"You might well think that to be the case, Dave, but I'm pretty well out of touch with mainstream security matters these days. I try to hold on to the odd useful contact to keep me in the picture but they're drying up fast -- everyone moves on in time and you just lose contact in the end."

A momentary silence ensued, but Jack believed he'd done enough to put the matter to rest.

"I imagine life must be quite challenging for you over here. It's hard to imagine there's enough demand for your line of business to actually make a serious living from it?"

The quick change of subject was enough to ease Jack's fears and he was more than happy to keep the conversation going along the same vein if it helped break the ice.

"You'd be surprised how many people don't like paying their bills, Dave, and how many wealthy women there are out there who want to know what their husbands get up to." He stretched his legs out in front of him and relaxed into his chair. "We get our fair share of divorce cases too of course – far too bloody many for my liking if I'm honest." He shrugged his shoulders resignedly. "This case we're on at the moment is an unusual one for us -- but it certainly makes life a lot more interesting."

He was about to elaborate further when Judy intervened.

"We have a small, start-up agency in London as well that is currently being run by a third partner, but it's only just getting off the ground so the jury is still out on that."

Jackson's eyebrows shot up.

"I didn't know you worked the mainland as well, does that not make control a bit of a problem?"

Jack shook his head and grinned. "Don't get the wrong impression, Dave, it's not a big operation by any means, in fact between here and London we only have four full time staff and a couple of part-timers to call on if things get busy."

He gave a little smirk.

"But if you're ever interested in a change of career we're always on the lookout for people with your background." The offer was nothing more than a light-hearted conversation maker and not meant to be taken seriously. But Jackson had a thoughtful look about him when he replied. "I might just take you up on that one day," he said, not altogether frivolously.

Such a reply was symptomatic of an attitude that was rife among many serving members of the security forces in Northern Ireland. They were always looking to keep their options open, in what was, quite ironically, because of The Troubles, a very insecure employment.

The conversation drifted along in a similar vein until they went through to the dining room some three drinks later; it was at this point that Jack broached the matter in hand and the real purpose behind the detective's visit.

"This Byrne case has me stumped and I don't mind admitting it. I'm getting nowhere fast and I could do with some serious help from you guys."

Jackson stopped toying with his food and looked up, although he didn't actually say anything, just looked a mite cautious really.

"You're the guy handling this case at your end, Dave, and I'd say if we were to pool our resources and get a result it would be a win-win situation all round."

Jackson's left eyebrow raised enquiringly.

"Don't stop there on me, Jack, keep going and tell me how you think we can help."

Jack scratched his head, and massaged the back of his neck as he decided where to begin. "Well for starters, you must have taken statements from everyone in and around the vicinity of that transport depot on the morning in question."

Jackson nodded. "Of course we did." He reached down for the file lying at his feet and hoisted it onto his lap.

"So apart from his brother's car that gave him a lift that morning, were there any other vehicles parked in the street, or near the depot entrance when Byrne was dropped off?"

Jackson opened the box file and began rummaging through its contents.

"We have a statement from Byrne's brother of course, confirming that he dropped him off outside his workplace at their usual time, and there is one from the owner of a little shop directly opposite the depot entrance – oh yes -- and another from a seemingly unconnected individual who just happened to be walking his dog past the depot around the time in question."

He carried on rummaging through the file until he found the statements he was looking for and passed them to Jack.

"I'm not sure they will be any more use to you than they were to us," he said, closing the lid on the box file and dropping it down by his feet again.

With Jack fully occupied rummaging the case file Judy made a valiant attempt to resurrect the conversation, but the young detective had no interest in idle chat, his only interest was in Jack's reaction to what he was reading. And having failed to hold his attention Judy decided to cut her losses and headed for the kitchen to prepare the coffee.

Jack on the other hand was so engrossed in what he was reading that he didn't even look up when he popped a question. "How do you think Tony Byrne disappeared?"

The young detective was caught unawares and had to think for a moment or two before answering. Jack looked up from what he was doing and cocked an eyebrow at him in the hope of prompting an answer.

"I subscribe to the theory that he was the victim of a loyalist hit gang." Jackson replied.

"That's hardly an answer my question," muttered Jack, under his breath.

Jackson looked slightly alarmed, he hadn't expected a rebuke, and his failure to say anything in his own defence forced Jack to look up again from what he was reading, and seeing the look of alarm on his visitor's face realized he had been misunderstood.

"Sorry, Dave, we seem to be at cross purposes here. I was really asking what the practical mechanics of his disappearance were. How was it made to happen? That's what I'm really trying to find out," he explained, giving Jackson just enough time to consider his answer before giving him another prompt.

"Was he bundled into a car and spirited away after he was dropped off -- was he dumped in the back of a truck and driven off, or was he imprisoned inside the depot and moved on later? What were the actual mechanics of his disappearance -- if, as you say, he was bumped off by some loyalist nutter?"

The peevish look eased from Jackson's face as he unfolded his arms and eased back into his seat. "If we knew the answer to that little riddle we would be a lot closer to solving this case," he admitted lamely, too lamely in fact, because his voice was sufficiently lacking in confidence to have Jack shifting in his seat ready to have another go at him.

"Let's be honest with each other, Dave, if you don't have answers to these questions then you really have no idea what happened, or who was responsible -- you're simply guessing." Having said his piece he switched his attention back to the statement he'd been reading, ever hopeful that some little snippet missed by everyone else might come to light.

Jackson didn't rise to the bait, he just looked on in stony silence.

"This statement here," said Jack, waving the offending sheet of paper in the air, "is from a witness who says he saw the brother's car turning into the street on the morning in question, but there's nothing to indicate that he saw Tony inside the car, or getting out of it either for that matter."

Again Jackson didn't comment and Jack took it a signal to carry on.

"Conversely, the owner of the shop does actually say that he saw Tony Byrne getting out of the car and crossing the road in the direction of the depot, but from where he was stood in the shop your own investigator reckons he had no clear view of the depot entrance. So he doesn't really know if Tony continued on into the depot or not." Setting the papers aside he rubbed his face with both hands. "If Byrne disappeared between getting out of his brother's car and crossing the road to the depot then somebody had to be lying in wait for him, and to my reckoning they must have moved pretty bloody sharpish. I would calculate they had no more than twenty or thirty seconds at most to spirit him away. Wouldn't you agree?"

The lack of input from the young detective was becoming a slight irritation to Jack, who had a gut feeling the guy was deliberately shying away from becoming too involved. A thought that was reinforced by the fact that when he did respond it was preceded by a somewhat perplexed expression, and was accompanied by an over dramatized sigh of weariness.

"We've been down that route more times than I like to recall." He shook his head in weary resignation as he had a shrewd idea where Jack's line of thought was leading, and from where he was sitting it was difficult to argue a case against it.

"The guy who saw Alfie Byrne's car that day was quite adamant that no other vehicle followed it into the street. So if Byrne was lifted by someone after he got out of his brother's car and before he reached the depot that someone had to be parked close by and lying in wait -- and I mean really close by for it to go unnoticed. So I imagine that's at least one thing we can both agree on."

Jack nodded his agreement; he wanted Jackson to keep talking now that he had him involved. It had taken long enough to get him started and he didn't want him to stop now.

Jackson slumped back in his chair and stretched his legs under the table.

"There were only three vehicles in the street that morning that were within striking distance of the depot entrance. Two of them were articulated trucks -- one parked either side of the depot entrance, plus a privately owned hatchback that had been parked up overnight and was unoccupied -- at least according to the shop owner, but all three vehicles checked out okay with us."

His comment about the other vehicles brought Jack the edge of his seat, soaking up everything on offer. He thought this might be the only opportunity he would get to challenge the outcome of the police investigation, and he did not want to miss some little piece of information that could prove useful or revealing.

"You know, Jack, if you apply simple logic to all of this you would be inclined to suspect that whatever happened to Tony Byrne must have occurred inside the depot itself." Having nothing else to say on the matter Jackson leaned back in his chair and raised his half empty wine glass to his lips.

Jack was just about to make another suggestion when Judy came charging back into the room and interrupted him.

"Well -- what's the verdict you two?" she chirped merrily, "has the universal brain come up with an answer, or does the mystery linger on?" She eased into the chair she had vacated earlier and slid the coffee tray along the table in front of them. But she might just as well have stayed in the kitchen for all the impact her reappearance had, because Jack simply ignored her remarks and carried on his debate with Jackson as if she wasn't there.

"Are you now telling me that the RUC believe Tony Byrne's vanishing act was orchestrated from inside his place of work?" He angled his head to one side and cocked a questioning eyebrow at Jackson.

"If that is the case then you're pointing the finger of suspicion at his fellow workers -- unless I'm missing something here?" His eyebrows went up in disbelief, although he continued with the conversation. "Is that because Tony Byrne was the only Catholic employed by the company?" He gave Jackson a look that said he was unconvinced. "That's a little bit convenient isn't it?" he said, challenging the idea. "In fact it's almost a ready-made excuse to lay everything at the feet of some loyalist hit squad." There was a hint of cynicism in his voice. "In all honesty, that sounds a tiny bit too convenient for me."

Jackson shrugged his shoulders, he had nothing more convincing to add. He had already decided to accept the criticism and ride out the moment, but that didn't mean he wouldn't defend his own ethics against criticism, and he leaned across the table to get closer to Jack add emphasis to what he was about to say.

"We can only run with what we've got, Jack. We don't fabricate evidence; we just gather it up and interpret it. Anyway, there wasn't a lot to go on by way of evidence, none of his bloody neighbours wanted to talk to us or share any information with us -- not willingly anyway -- so don't go criticizing our investigation out of hand."

He took a breather to reflect on how difficult things had been during the early days of their investigation. But he didn't remain quiet for long.

"This whole thing happened during a very busy time for us. There was a hell of a lot going on just then -- a lot of terrorist activity; bombings and shootings, and we were seriously short of manpower on top of everything else." He paused again to gather his thoughts.

"I'm not suggesting that if we'd had more resources we would have solved the case or handled it differently, but we did the best we could with what was available." Breaking away from the conversation, he allowed himself a few moments thought, A few moments that lingered too long to be comfortable, and only survived interruption because of the hesitant expression that clung to his face. An expression that suggested he was having difficulty keeping his thoughts to himself.

"I find it a wee bit offensive that I should be required to defend my professional integrity, or that of my colleagues, so what I'm about to say I never want to have to repeat -- and I do mean never."

He turned his eyes in Judy's direction, inviting her into the conversation as well.

"Some misinformed individuals, incensed by their own anti British agenda, have accused the RUC of not investigating this case thoroughly enough because the victim was a Catholic who came from a predominantly nationalist area. I find that a reprehensible accusation -- a total and absolute fabrication."

His eyes never flinched as he held Jack's enquiring look.

"We want this case solved and put to bed, and if someone out there is responsible for Byrne's disappearance -- and I have to say that remains as yet unproven - then we want them brought to book and off the streets like every other right minded person - more so if the truth be known."

He kept up his steely vigil on Jack's face until he saw what he was after — an expression of acceptance.

"I'm not the one who needs convincing, Dave, I'm on your side, remember." Jack assured him. "But setting that particular issue aside, where do I go from here? I'm the one being paid to solve this bloody mystery and right now I'm no further on than I was at the beginning."

The defensive expression fell away from Jackson's face and he shuffled the papers he was holding back into their folder.

"I'm relieved to hear that, Jack -- because I could not continue this liaison if you were harbouring any doubts."

He raised his arms above his head and stretched the tension from his shoulders with a noticeable grunt.

"You had better tell me what you're investigation has come up with and we can take it from there," he suggested.

Jack suddenly felt the need for a change of scenery, he was hoping they might leave the tetchy atmosphere at the dining table if they got up and changed venues.

"Let's go through to the lounge and Judy can bring you up to date with things while I sort out the drinks."

Judy smiled condescendingly at their guest, she was frequently side-lined during working dinners and it no longer bothered her the way it used to, unless of course she chose to let it.

"That's the best idea I've heard all night," she chirped in. "there's a nice cosy fire going in there and I'm ready for a good stiff drink." Pushing aside the unheeded coffee tray she stood up and led them from the room.

Jack took longer than he might have over pouring the drinks and by the time he had finished Judy's briefing was running out of steam. She was quite adept at summarizing events, and as Jackson was a good listener who chose not to interrupt, it didn't take her long to update him. As a consequence, when Jack re-joined them the young detective was eagerly awaiting his return.

"From what Judy tells me you haven't interviewed Byrne's brother yet -- is that right?" he asked.

Jack nodded, but as he was raising his glass to his mouth at the time he left it to his visitor to carry on talking.

"He appears to be a straight forward sort of guy, who gave us every indication of being completely overwhelmed by the whole sorry episode when we interviewed him -- but I guess that's only to be expected." He seemed to be reasonably sympathetic towards the guy from the way he was speaking.

"From what I know of him it appears unlikely that he had anything to do with what happened. More importantly than that, he could think of no valid reason as to why his brother should disappear."

Jack was obliged to note that his list of suspects had just been reduced by one. If the RUC gave Alfie Byrne a clean bill of health who was he to argue? But he wondered if the same all clear applied to all the other possible suspects?

"Did you give Devlin a clean bill of health as well?" he asked, expecting the response to be just as forthcoming.

Jackson jerked upright in his chair looking a little puzzled.

"Who the hell is Devlin?" he asked, his relaxed demeanour departing somewhat hurriedly with the realization that after three years there was suddenly a new name in the frame; a name that neither he nor his colleagues knew anything about. He looked decidedly uneasy as he waited for Jack to tell him more.

Sadly for him Jack was in no hurry to oblige, at least not right away. After all, it was answers he was looking for not questions, and he was genuinely taken aback by Jackson's ignorance about Devlin, and asked himself what else the police investigation might have missed if they knew nothing about a potential main player.

"I take it you're aware of this charity group that Byrne was involved with?" he asked, tempering a growing excitement at the prospect of uncovering something else that hadn't been checked out by the police.

Jackson looked even more dismayed, in fact he appeared to be totally confused and made no effort to keep it under wraps.

"No, Jack – I can honestly say that I have never heard any mention of it." If the ground beneath him had opened up and swallowed him Jackson would have been a happy man. But it did no such thing, and nothing changed, he was left with the embarrassing fact that his lack of knowledge reflected poorly on him as a professional investigator, and that of his investigating team as well.

With his moment of glory safely in the bank Jack saw no advantage in prolonging the young detective's misery, so he pressed on with a full and detailed explanation of everything he knew about the charity. By the time he'd finished Jackson looked even more astonished than before he'd started.

"Nobody mentioned any of this to our team at any time during our investigation," he confessed, "I'm absolutely gob-smacked that Byrne's wife chose to keep it from us. Surely to God she must have known how important something like this could be to an investigation?"

"She never mentioned it to me either," Jack admitted, "I only got wind of it from the local priest."

He was a little disappointed at the police investigation's lack of diligence, but hindsight told him that if he hadn't taken the trouble to visit Father Joseph he wouldn't have known anything about it either.

"Well -- what can I say?" Jackson declared. "You've turned up something that we all missed." He still looked ill at ease, but at least some of the anxiety had left his face.

"Clearly something like this needs following up." His eyes narrowed inquisitively. "But what's your take on it, Jack? Do you think it has any bearing on the case?" There was an air of expectancy in his voice.

Jack dithered for a moment or two, not quite sure what kind of spin to put on it.

"No – I wouldn't go quite that far," he said, "I wouldn't put it as strongly as that, *but* ------", he stressed the word and let it hang in the air to help emphasize what he would say next. "I don't necessarily think we should waste any time on the charity itself, although I have a gut feeling that this guy Devlin is worth a second look. Maybe you could run a check on him and let me know what you come up with." He wondered if Jackson would show willing, or give in to temptation and allow self-interest take over.

"You can bet your bottom dollar I will," Jackson told him, very convincingly. "But I can't do anything about it until tomorrow morning I'm afraid."

Jack glanced up at the expensive looking carriage clock holding pride of place on his mantelpiece.

"It's getting late now anyway, Dave, but can we keep in close touch on this?" he asked.

Jackson nodded affirmatively.

"I wouldn't want it any other way. You've given us a new angle on the case. Okay -- it might not lead anywhere, but let's work it through and see where it leads us – I'm feeling quite optimistic about it to be honest."

Without further ado he was on his feet with his hand held out in Judy's direction.

"That was a lovely meal, Judy, and I do apologise for hogging Jack's attention all evening but I'm afraid that's just the nature of this particular beast." She brushed his apology aside. "Don't even go there, Dave, anyway, as you probably guessed, I'm quite used to it by now."

All that remained was to swap telephone numbers and Jackson was on his way, gagging for the cigarette that he had been denying himself all evening.

Having seen their guest to his taxi Jack rushed back inside, eager to get Judy's take on the evening's events and her reaction to their visitor. They had agreed earlier in the day that she would exercise a watching brief on the young man and try to assess his reliability and possible usefulness. It was indicative of how highly Jack valued her judgment on such matters that he chose to do so, and his faith was well founded as she was recognized by all who knew her as an extremely good judge of character.

"Well -- what do you reckon -- do we have him on board?" he asked, as he seated himself facing her.

"Oh -- I think so, don't you?" she confirmed, "I believe he's quite happy to have us on his side as well. I'm certain he wants this bloody mystery cleared up just as much as we do; I think he's a genuine sort of guy." Getting up from her seat she made her way over to the door, aware from the attitude Jack had displayed during the course of the evening that she was simply confirming his own feelings on the matter. "Having said that," she added over her shoulder as she went through the door. "I don't think the RUC have earned any brownie points from the way they handled this case. Although it's probably fair to admit that they don't appear to have been deliberately neglectful."

She carried on into the kitchen with the task of clearing up the after dinner mess still ahead of her, while Jack sat where he was, quietly nursing the glass in his hand, pondering over what his next move would be.

11

The drive to Banbridge didn't take as long as Jack had anticipated, and he was even fortunate enough to find the building site he was looking for without too much trouble, and having done so he was in quite a good mood when he got there.

The development itself appeared well on its way to completion and proved to be one of those modern, up-market estates that was becoming increasingly popular with young, upwardly mobile first time buyers. The kind of buyer who would probably only occupy a property for a few years before moving ever onwards and upwards towards their ultimate dream home.

Having parked his car out of harm's way he trudged through a mass of builder's rubble in the direction of some unfinished houses at the far end of a makeshift road that split the estate right down the middle.

After a few strides his shoes were covered in wet, sticky mud making him regret having agreed to meet Dessie Graham at his place of work.

Looking just a little bit lost some guy who was handballing a huge pile of topsoil into shape took pity on him and pointed him in the right direction, and he eventually found his quarry humping a barrow load of cement in the direction of a garden wall he was working on.

Dessie Graham had changed very little from the photograph Jack had seen of him, making the task of picking him out relatively easy.

"Good morning, Dessie," he greeted, sticking his hand out to cement the greeting. "I'm Jack Brennan."

Graham wiped a hand on his mud splattered jeans before accepting the handshake.

"Good to meet you, Jack. My wife has told me what you're trying to do." He looked around for a piece of dry ground to stand on, but it was not to be, the whole site was covered in a thick layer of sticky, clinging mud.

"Is there somewhere we can go for a cup of coffee and a sit down?" Jack asked.

Graham screwed his face up. "I don't think my boss would be too happy if I just bale out and down tools. We're a bit behind schedule here as it is, what with all this bloody rain we've been having, and as he so frequently reminds us -- there's a penalty clause for late completion." He smiled impishly at some private thought that tickled his fancy.

"Yeah, I guess life must be a real bitch for all these poverty stricken property developers." Jack's cynical remark was greeted with a robust burst of laughter, sadly it was so over the top it was almost embarrassing, but the look of expectation on his face soon brought the bricklayer back to the matter in hand.

"We could try the site canteen," he offered, "there shouldn't be anybody in there this early in the day." Turning on his heel he headed off through the clinging mud in the direction of the site entrance and a ramshackle cabin that had clearly seen better days.

To afford it the grand title of canteen was an elaborate extortion of the truth as its only furnishings consisted of two wooden tables, a collection of seriously disabled chairs, and a hot air blower. Well, that plus an unhealthy collection of litter. It also contained something of a shock for the bedraggled bricklayer in the shape of the site foreman.

"What the hell are you doing in here at this time of the day – don't I pay you to lay bricks or something?" His verbal attack might have come across as aggressive to Jack but his body language didn't back it up, and the mischievous twinkle in his eye softened the whole thing, in any case Jack was quick to dive in and take the blame.

"I'm sorry, I just need a few minutes with Dessie about a private matter. If you'd like me to explain ----"

The site foreman cut him off with a wave of his hand. "If it's got nothing do with laying bricks, then it has nothing to do with me." He turned to face his prized bricklayer.

"Whatever it is, Dessie -- make it short -- I need you back on the job as soon as -- okay?"

Having said his piece he grabbed a bundle of drawings from the table, shoved them under his right arm and shuffled out through the door, snorting like an old bull.

Graham didn't look any the worse after the little episode.

"His bark is worse than his bite," he confessed, "he's actually an alright sort of guy most of the time."

That said they settled down either side of the rickety old table and waited for each other to say something.

It fell to the bricklayer to make a go of things.

"Jean has explained what you're trying to do, and you can take it as read that I'm on your side -- I'll do anything I can to help, although I don't see how you can achieve any more than the police did, and they didn't get very far. You must bear in mind that it's been more than three years since Tony disappeared, and nobody will ever convince me that my good friend is out there somewhere still alive."

His eyes wandered over to at an old canvas rucksack dangling from a hook on the back of the door.

"I'm afraid I can only offer you black coffee, that's all I've got."

Jack shook his head and looked on with envy as Dessie filled his mug. "I think I'll give it a miss, if you don't mind," he said allowing Graham enough time to enjoy a few mouthfuls before getting down to business.

"Why don't you tell me what you think happened to your friend that made him vanish the way he did?"

Dessie raised his eyes over the rim of his mug, although didn't say anything until he'd taken another mouthful.

"It's like I said earlier – Tony has got to be dead, but don't ask me how I know because I can't answer that -- but I'll tell you one thing that I do know -- Tony Byrne would never put his wife through all this suffering if he was still alive." He poured some more liquid into the heavily stained mug.

"And you can forget all that crap about him being murdered by some hot head loyalist because he wouldn't have disappeared the way he did if they'd murdered him, it's not their style."

He set the mug down and leaned his elbows on the table.

"They would have just shot him one dark night when he left my place to go home. What reason would they have for hiding his body? What were they gonna gain by doing that – where's the street cred in it?" He pursed his lips and shook his head in denial. "That theory doesn't stand up for me -- it's a load of old cobblers."

His voice had gained noticeably in pitch as his emotions took over, but he took a deep breath and expelled it somewhat noisily through puffed up cheeks to help settle himself. "I honestly believe this whole thing is the result of some bloody awful mistake."

"You could be right," Jack conceded, having no good reason to think otherwise. "In the absence of any other evidence that would seem to be the most likely scenario, but you know something, Dessie --------," there was a prolonged, inviting pause before he continued, "these things are generally not that simple. There's always a possibility that he was killed because of something he saw or something he heard; something he wasn't meant to see or hear -- something that made him a threat to others. I don't for the life of me know what that could be, but it's always a possibility in cases like this."

Dessie was rummaging in his pockets for his cigarettes, but he stopped abruptly in reaction to Jack's suggestion. "Bollocks," he snapped, "that's absolute bollocks -- what the hell would Tony Byrne know that would make someone want to kill him?"

There was a look of utter dismay on his weather beaten face.

"Christ -- he never went anywhere without his wife by his side, or me and Jean, he literally didn't go anywhere without us."

"He went to Romania." Jack argued, somewhat emphatically.

Graham sprung to his feet like he'd been jabbed in the ass with a sharp object.

"Are you telling me something happened to him out there that brought all this about?" He looked seriously perplexed as he toyed with the idea for the first time.

Jack left him to it and waited for a reaction.

"But he was only out there on charity work for Christ's sake -- you don't get knocked off because you help out with a lousy charity." The idea was too preposterous to contemplate; he just couldn't believe it.

Jack prompted him a little more.

"I know it was a long time ago, Dessie but can you remember if there was any difference in Tony's behaviour after that last trip he made to Romania? You know -- did he seem depressed or nervous in any way? Was he drinking any more than usual? Was there any noticeable difference in his attitude towards his wife?"

The vacant look on Dessie Graham's face, and the weary, almost methodical way his head went from side to side told Jack that he had been down this route too many times in the past. It was only out of loyalty to his friend and his desire to help unravel the mystery that forced him to revisit those particularly unsavoury memories. "It may have happened some time ago, Mr. Brennan, but I've been over it with a fine tooth comb so many times that it remains as fresh as ever in my mind's eye. Tony was my best friend after all -- don't ever forget that. But I've not been able to zero in on anything that seemed out of place or unusual in his behaviour before he left us." He threw his head back and sighed dejectedly. "Christ almighty -- the cops went through all this with me time after time, in every tiny detail."

He shook his head in bewilderment.

"They questioned me so much that I was beginning to think they had me down as a fuckin' suspect," he said accusingly, pinching his top lip as his thoughts drifted to some far off memory.

Jack held his tongue and allowed Dessie to drift back to the past uninterrupted. He wanted him to remember everything and anything that might help.

"If there was any noticeable difference in his behaviour then I guess he might have been just a little bit stressed out after that last trip. Tony never told his wife much about the awful sights he witnessed out there -- it would only have worried her, but he would occasionally open up to me about it." He stopped to consider where next to take the conversation, then added. "What depressed him most was the ages of the young children he saw running around with guns and things. He told me of one occasion when he gave a fourteen year old boy a ration pack and some second hand clothing and the lad offered him an automatic rifle in exchange -- without Tony even asking him for it."

Jack jumped in immediately.

"What did he do with the weapon?" he asked.

Dessie shrugged. "He told me he smashed it to pieces. The availability of weapons out there was one of the things he found most depressing -- but then who wouldn't?"

Having screwed the lid back on his flask he got out of his chair, indicating that it was time to get back to work.

Jack followed him to the door.

"Thanks for your help, Dessie, I know it's not much, but every little helps in a case like this. Although between you and me I don't hold out much hope of ever getting to the bottom of it."

He laid a casual hand on the bricklayer's well-padded shoulder. "Take some advice from a well-meaning outsider, my friend, Roisin Byrne still considers you and your wife to be her best friends, you should make more of an effort to keep in touch with her. She really could do with your support these days."

Graham nodded in a way that said he didn't need reminding, just prompting.

Jack walked away thinking it unlikely that the two of them would ever meet again -- except perhaps by accident -- or at Tony Byrne's funeral, because there was no doubt in his mind now that Byrne had not gone walkabouts just for the fun of it. He had very definitely been removed against his will.

12

When he got back to Belfast he found an unexpected visitor waiting for him, and although he had never met the guy before he needed no telling that it was Tony Byrne's brother, the family resemblance was undeniable, and really quite striking. He even had the same laid back look about him that his brother carried off so well, albeit that he had carried it a few years longer. And he possessed an endearing habit, when he wasn't engaged in conversation or serious thought, of allowing his facial expression to relax into a friendly, welcoming smile that immediately inspired affection to the onlooker.

If there was an undesirable trait in his make-up it had to be his fixation with his nose. He was forever picking at it, blowing it, or constantly fidgeting with it in a way that was very off-putting. He also had an obsessive fixation with protecting the creases in his trousers, constantly ensuring that they weren't under undue strain, although on this occasion anyway, it didn't deter him from opening the conversation.

"Can I say right away, Mr. Brennan, that I fully support my sister-in-law's decision to employ someone like your good-self. If your efforts help to bring this awful mess to some sort of conclusion then we will both be very grateful." He attended to his trousers again before re-engaging Jack with a rather enquiring look.

"Have you uncovered anything new? Are there any developments? Is there anything I should know about?"

His barrage of questions slipped by unanswered. Not because there wasn't anything new, although that was probably true enough, but because Jack had no intention of putting a damper on the guy's apparent enthusiasm. He was also mindful of the fact that although his visitor was a close relative of his client, he was not the person footing the bill, nor was he the person to whom Jack was answerable.

"It's good of you to come and see me like this. It's quite helpful really because I had planned to get in touch with you tomorrow anyway, so you've actually saved me a journey."

He ran his fingers through his hair.

"There are a few things I'm following up on, but whether or not they lead us anywhere only time will tell."

The half-smile fleetingly deserted his visitor's face and he leaned back and crossed his legs, then quickly uncrossed them again, ever protective of his trousers.

"Are you getting any help from the police with this new investigation?"

It was an innocent enough question on the face of it but Jack knew what was really being asked of him.

"Well -- I've been in close touch with the case officer, as you might expect, and it seems to me that he is as keen as we are to solve the case. The police have given me access to everything they have on your brother's case, and I'm completely satisfied that they are doing all they can and are co-operating fully. I'm sure you must be pleased to hear that."

His admission brought a very subtle change of expression to the other man's face, mostly around his eyes, it was hardly noticeable to be fair, but it didn't go unnoticed by Jack, who asked himself was it a look of relief that he saw there? He wasn't exactly sure, and in any event before he had time to think about it properly his visitor re-engaged with him.

"It's been a while since my sister-in-law heard anything at all from the police, so I guess there can't be much happening or I'm sure they would have been in touch."

From what Jack had read in the police file Alfie Byrne had had very little to offer during their investigation, apart from explaining how he had dropped his brother off at work on that fateful day, he had offered little else of any consequence.

"How well do you know this guy Joe Devlin?" Jack asked, springing the question on him without warning.

Alfie Byrne was clearly caught unawares, and it showed, the smile that had been threatening to hold permanent residence on his face quickly went walkabouts and he developed a more serious expression.

"I don't know him at all," he stammered quickly. "The first time I heard his name mentioned was last night when Roisin told me of your interest in him."

He leaned forward and put his elbows on the desk.

"In a way that's actually what prompted my visit. It seems to me that this charity thing is a new line of enquiry and I wanted to discuss it with you. Particularly as it was never something the police mentioned."

He leaned back into his chair again.

"I'm curious to know what brought it to your notice."

Jack gave him a dismissive shrug.

"I really don't want you to leave here thinking that this guy Devlin might be in any way connected to your brother's disappearance." He shook his head slowly and deliberately, hoping to knock the message home. "Right now I see his involvement as nothing more than a loose end that has never been followed up."

He leaned back into in his chair.

"Having said that, and as you so rightly pointed out, it is a line of enquiry that was never explored by the police." He smiled at his visitor. "But that can hardly be seen as their fault since no one told them of your brother's involvement with the charity." Alfie Byrne leaned back as well and thought things over for a moment.

"I appreciate everything you've told me, Mr. Brennan, I really do, but if it turns out that this charity is implicated in Tony's disappearance then I would like to know about it. Roisin tells me this guy Devlin who set it up has a bit of a local reputation, but I wouldn't think he was involved in what happened to Tony, and neither does my sister-in-law for that matter."

Hearing about Devlin's background from a different source was useful, and Jack was certainly keen to find out everything he could about the guy, but he had no wish to leave his visitor with the impression that he had made some sort of breakthrough, that was something he was very wary about.

"Involved is probably too strong a word don't you think? From what Roisin tells me he and Tony only knew each other through these charity events, and on the face of it there is nothing to suggest that it wasn't all quite innocent." He raised a questioning eyebrow. "Unless of course you can tell me something different."

Alfie fidgeted uncomfortably in his chair.

"I do know he hasn't been in jail or anything like that, even if he does sail pretty close to the wind. But I imagine you will be taking a closer look at him and I would be keen to know if he becomes part of your investigation."

Jack had already asked for a police report on Devlin, but that report wasn't through yet, and until he got his hands on it everything he was hearing now was just so much hearsay.

"All I can tell you is that they guy is part of an ongoing investigation, no more and no less than that at this moment in time."

Alfie Byrne had looked a bit tense for a moment or two but he seemed more relaxed now that Jack had explained himself.

"Well, I just wanted to touch base with you and see how you were getting on. If I can help in any way at all you only have to ask."

He got out of his chair.

"I really have to go now, but I would appreciate it if you kept me in touch with any developments."

He offered his hand in a parting gesture, and Jack could not help noticing that it was a bit clammy.

"I'm sorry, but I'm afraid that's not something I am authorized to do," he told him bluntly. "I have a responsibility to your sister-in-law and to no one else. She's the one paying the bills and the only person I report to."

Alfie Byrne looked fit to challenge what he'd been told but checked himself at the last moment. Choosing instead to simply nod a reluctant acceptance and walk away, although there was a look about him that said he wasn't entirely happy with the way his visit had panned out.

Jack gave him enough time to clear the outer office before wandering through to join Judy.

"See if you can raise Dave Jackson on the blower for me," he said, heading past her work station in the direction of the coffee machine, his mind firmly focussed on Alfie Byrne and his unscheduled visit. A thought that preoccupied him so much that he ended up overfilling his mug!

The incoming call from Dave Jackson coincided with Jack draining the last dregs of his coffee. "Hi, Dave," he chirped brightly. "I know you haven't anything new for me otherwise you would have been in touch, but I'd like to pick your brain about something that's on my mind?"

"Anything to help, Jack, and thanks for your hospitality last night, I thoroughly enjoyed the evening."

There was a more relaxed familiarity in the young man's voice this time around.

Jack smiled to himself, a little smugly.

"No problem, Dave, we very much enjoyed having you – but look -- I need to know who owned the two trucks that were parked outside the transport depot when Byrne disappeared?"

Jackson came straight back at him. "That's an easy one, mate, they were both from Zipline Transport -- the company he worked for."

Jack had suspected as much, but there was another consideration that interested him.

"That's a fairly long street outside that depot, Dave, can you explain to me more accurately where they were parked?"

He heard a cackle of light-hearted laughter at the other end. "Christ -- two easy questions in a row, Jack – you are being kind to me this morning." He was clearly relieved that the answers came readily to mind and didn't require any rooting through case files.

"They were both parked on the same side of the road as the depot, one either side of the entrance. I mean literally right outside the gates."

Jack formed the picture in his mind's eye and considered the implications of what it meant before asking. "Which way were they pointing, Dave?"

There was a bit of pause while Jackson rummaged through his memory banks.

"They were both pointing in the same direction actually, towards the main road. Why do you ask?"

"Oh! Nothing really -- just a thought, although my interpretation of that scenario suggests that one was probably going into the depot and the other had probably just come out."

"Is there a point to all this, Jack -- or am I being bloody stupid and missing the obvious?"

The guy did sound a bit puzzled.

Jack's immediate reaction was to keep his thoughts to himself, but on hasty reflection he decided the safer option was to stand by his promise to share everything that came to light. He was after all looking for the same consideration from the guy at the other end of the phone.

"It really is just a thought, Dave, nothing more than that for the

moment, but when I questioned the guy who owns that crappy little shop facing the depot, he distinctly told me that one driver had parked up and called in for a morning paper before driving on into the depot. That would have to be the truck that was parked to the left of the entrance as you look at it. The other vehicle must have just come out of the depot and parked up if it was pointing in the same direction. Now you really have to ask yourself why he parked up right after leaving the depot if he never went into the shop to make a purchase. What other reason could he have for stopping there?"

Jackson fell quiet as he tried to recall the detail of his interviews with the driver concerned.

"I'm sorry, mate, I'll have to consult the case notes before I can answer that. I can't remember off the top of my head what the driver had to say for himself, but whatever it was it must have made sense at the time or we would have given it more attention."

Jack chose not to air his disappointment.

"I'd be grateful if you'd let me have the names of the two drivers and anyone else who was accompanying them, I think it might be useful to have a quiet word with them."

"I don't have a problem with that, I'll give you a bell later this evening when I'm back at the station, if that's okay?"

Their conversation ended with both men staring at their phones, each wondering what the other was thinking.

For his part Jack was nursing a grudging suspicion about the mysterious second truck. It bugged him to know why it had been there. The most obvious reason would have been for the driver to visit the shop, which they knew had not been the case, so until he got round to interviewing the people concerned this annoying little issue was going to plague the very life out of him. In order to circumvent any delay he decided not to wait for Dave Jackson to get back to him, opting instead for a more readily available source of information by lifting the phone and dialling the Zipline number.

"Hi, Andy, Jack Brennan here. We met up the other day when I called with you," he prattled his greeting off quickly to help jolt the other guy's memory. "I wonder if you would be good enough to help me out with a little matter."

"Oh yeah, what is it this time?" asked Nelson, a tetchy weariness in his voice, which in itself was warning enough to make Jack dispense with the small talk and get straight to the point.

"On the day Tony Byrne disappeared two of your trucks were parked on the road outside the depot gates -- I'd like the names and addresses of both drivers, if it's not too much trouble." Something else suddenly came to mind.

"I'd also like to know their journey plan for that day. I'm presuming, as it was part of a police enquiry at the time that you've kept a record of them."

Andy Nelson sighed loudly down the phone, issuing another warning that Jack was on borrowed time.

"I really don't have time for this right now. It means delving into records that are three years old. You'd better leave me your number and I'll have one of the girls dig out the information and ring you back with it." His words were rushed and clipped, indicating there was something more important on his agenda. Jack quickly recited his phone number and rang off.

When the information finally came through, much later in the day as it turned out, Jack was surprised to discover that one of the drivers had an address in Scotland. Which in turn made him wonder if Zipline had a depot there as well? It was something he would need to check out, but that was for later, right now he shoved his notes into the case folder and made another quick phone call before leaving the office.

13

Dave Jackson looked for all the world like he was ready for the knackers yard as he peered round the door that was wedged open by his left foot. Nodding positively to the duty sergeant perched behind the bullet-proof barrier at the reception desk, he invited his visitor into the inner workings of the building.

"Come on through, Jack, it's been one of those days I'm afraid, I've been up to my ass in alligators all morning and boy do I need a break."

He caught the eye of the duty sergeant again as the automatic locking device secured the door behind them.

"I'll be in the canteen for the next twenty minutes or so, Bert," he explained, as he led Jack down a narrow corridor that was flanked on either side by a continuous duplication of glass fronted boxes. There wasn't a window anywhere in sight, leaving the air heavy with the smell of cigarette smoke and stale body odours, plus the persistent noise of incoming radio traffic. Added to this was the continuous racket of telephone ring tones that accompanied them all the way to a flight of stairs at the far end. The whole building was a maze of narrow, brightly lit corridors, causing unbelievable congestion to the overloaded human traffic that scurried purposefully in all directions. A scene that was probably no different to that of any other fortified police station in Northern Ireland at that particular moment in time.

"A guy could get trampled to death in here," jibed Jack light-heartedly, "is it always like this-- or do they know something I don't?"

The level of activity was really quite daunting, and Jack was more than a little relieved to shut it off behind them as they went through a set of double swing doors into the more spacious and calmer environment of the station canteen.

"There's a bit of a flap on at the moment, that's all." Jackson muttered from the corner of his mouth, as if letting Jack in on something he shouldn't be privy to.

They each grabbed a mug of steaming coffee from a serving hatch and parked themselves at the first available table they came to.

"Sorry I didn't have time to chat with you when you phoned earlier, but I'm sure you know how it is." He pulled a fag from a brand new pack and Zippo'd it into life, sucking in a couple of deep drags before relaxing in his chair. "Christ -- I needed that." he gasped. "I don't know if I'm punched, drilled, or bloody centre bored at the minute. I feel like I'm living my life inside a bloody pressure cooker."

He drew deeply on his nicotine stick one more time, becoming noticeably more relaxed as his toxin levels adjusted.

"About this guy, Devlin," he said, between puffs. "No sweet charity there I'm afraid. We don't actually have anything official on record so to speak but he's a known face to some of our people, which I suppose has to be a concern."

He ran a hand over his unshaven face to wipe away the tiredness, an indication perhaps that if he had not had time to shave then he probably hadn't had much sleep either.

"I'm grateful for you seeing me like this, especially when I can see how busy you are. Can you tell me why your people have an interest in Devlin?"

Jackson continued sipping at the hot liquid before getting off the mark. "To be perfectly honest I can't be very specific, it's not as clear cut as that," he began, "but it would appear that he's been seen too frequently in the company of some known faces at some dodgy venues, which I guess is enough to give our intelligence people more than a passing interest in him." There was an odd look on Jackson's face that suggested he had more to tell if he had a mind to.

Jack felt it important to make it comfortable for him to do so.

"You do know that anything you tell me is in strictest confidence and will never be repeated. You have my solemn word on that."

Jackson swirled the remains of his coffee round the bottom of his mug and kept his eyes diverted. There was no doubting that he looked a little hesitant, although Jack hadn't a clue why that should be.

He eventually set his mug aside with what was a very deliberate and thoughtful movement before clasping his hands together on top of the table.

"If I didn't believe it might have some bearing on this case I would not be telling you what I'm about to disclose."

He paused for effect.

"Our boys have suspected for some time that Devlin is a quartermaster for the IRA's North Belfast Brigade."

Jack's eyes opened wide in astonishment, but just as he opened his mouth to speak Jackson stuck a hand up and warned him off. "Before you get carried away you should understand that at this precise moment in time there is no proof to support what I have just told you, it is purely circumstantial -- so make bloody sure that I don't hear any of it coming back at me."

Jack was familiar enough with security matters to know that where and when a terrorist suspect is observed can very often identify their role within the organization. So if the anti-terrorist branch suspected Devlin of IRA involvement then they must have a jolly good reason for doing so, even if they didn't have positive proof to support their suspicions.

Jack's eyebrows gathered in a frown as he considered how this latest bombshell might affect his investigation.

"Well now -- that certainly puts a different slant on things. Although in an odd sort of a way it helps to reinforce my belief that there could be a link between Devlin and Byrne's untimely disappearance."

"I can see where you're taking this, Jack. It's so bloody ironic that nobody mentioned Byrne's connection with this charity back in the early days of our investigation. It would almost certainly have given us a reason to pull Devlin in for questioning, and might even have given us a more positive outcome to the case."

There was an uneasy edginess in the way Jackson squirmed in his seat that suggested he was still holding something back. Jack had a notion what it might be, but thinking was never the same as knowing -- and he needed to know. "There's something you're not telling me, Dave," he said accusingly.

Jackson stretched his neck into his collar to ease the tension, then almost as if he was relieved at doing so he let his resistance drop.

"When I began asking about our friend Devlin in connection with this Byrne case, I was very quickly, and none too politely I might add, hauled to one side and told not to pursue my enquiries any further." His shoulders lifted and dropped just as quickly. "It turns out that Criminal Intelligence have a particular interest in him that is part of a much bigger picture. The nuts and bolts of it are that they don't want me muddying the waters and chasing one of their targets underground, not while they're running a watching brief on him."

He shrugged his shoulders resignedly with the action of a man who was overdue a night's sleep.

Jack on the other hand looked decidedly animated.

"Well now – you've been very candid with me, Dave, and I certainly appreciate your situation -- but hey -- if that's the way the land lies then there's not a lot we can do about it, is there?" He watched Jackson closely through narrowed eyes. What he was about to say next would tell him a great deal about the young detective's willingness to help solve the case.

"You need to understand that I have no such concerns about tramping on anyone's toes, and I intend to make it my business to see if Devlin is involved in what I am investigating."

Jackson smiled wryly. "That has to be your decision, Jack - you go for it - as far as I'm concerned this conversation never took place."

Had he taken just a moment longer to consider his reply it would have caused Jack some concern, but it was so spontaneous that he felt it must be genuine, and he quickly switched the conversation to a more mundane topic?

"What are the chances of me getting a look at the statements you took from the two drivers we discussed?"

Jackson gave him a crafty little wink. "I think we can accommodate that. If you've finished your coffee we can nip back to my office and you can read through the whole damn file if you've a mind to."

He gave a little smirk.

"Bill Anderson has already authorized it after all – hasn't he?" He got to his feet and led the way back through the maze of corridors to his own little sweat box, which was precisely what it turned out to be.

The statements Jack had been so keen to get his hands on proved to be a bit sketchy to say the least. They contained nothing of sufficient interest to make them stick in Jackson's mind, or anyone else's for that matter. The only thing of any significance concerned the truck that had driven out of the depot and parked up immediately outside the gates. That statement was taken from the guy called Barratt, the driver with the address in Scotland. It explained how he had forgotten to collect a vital delivery docket before leaving the depot and had to go back inside to get it. It wasn't something that could be easily verified at this late stage, as the likelihood of anyone remembering something so trivial was pretty remote, but Jack thought it needed pursuing.

"This guy Barratt," he said, "the one who says he went back to the office for a delivery docket -- did his story check out okay or were there any inconsistencies?"

Jackson reached out and pulled the file towards him.

"I'll need to check my notes, Jack. I can't be expected to remember every bloody dot and comma, but I imagine it must have done if we didn't do a follow up on it."

He rummaged through the file until he found what he was looking for then eased back into a more relaxed position.

"Yeah, I remember now," he muttered, thinking aloud rather than talking to his visitor. "The guy isn't actually employed by Zipline, or wasn't at the time we took our statements, he operated as a sub-contractor back then. He had ferried a container across from Scotland that very morning and was intending to return by the same route until his rig broke down. In the end he had to borrow a rig from Zipline to fulfil an urgent delivery. I don't think there was anything unusual in that, just common business practice I should think." He looked to Jack for agreement, but he had his eyes closed at the time formulating the events described in his mind's eye.

Allowing for everything he now knew he viewed Barratt with some suspicion. The guy had been in exactly the right place, at the right time, even if he didn't appear to have any connection with the missing man. The only way to remove him from the equation was to have a conversation with him and find out what he had to say for himself. Although judging by his address in Scotland that wasn't going to be easy, but it was a problem Jack would have to overcome, one way or another.

He was still considering how he might do that when the phone on Dave Jackson's cluttered desk sounded and broke his concentration. The young detective snatched it up angrily, annoyed at the unwelcome intrusion.

"Jackson," he snarled impatiently, instantly regretting his bluntness as he took note of the incoming message.

Jack watched his expression turn to one of weary acceptance as he clamped his brow between finger and thumb to relive a sudden rush of pain.

"I have to go, Jack -- I'm sorry -- but this is something I can't wriggle out of." Clearly there was some sort of panic or emergency in the offing that couldn't wait.

"There's no rest for the wicked, eh!" Jack quipped light-heartedly, although his humour was lost on his host, who was already on his feet and guiding him out through the door.

"I'll see you out then I really do have to go," he said, and being good for his word he didn't even take time to say goodbye as he bundled Jack through reception and out onto the street.

14

To his surprise, not to mention amazement, Jack was greeted with a suspiciously welcoming smile by Judy when she saw him coming through the door.

"Well, how did you get on?" she enquired, catching him completely off guard with her show of interest. An interest that seemed rather out of place following her open resentment when he had accepted the Byrne case against her wishes.

It wasn't that her feelings on the matter had gone into reverse, but rather that she had been so impressed by their new client during their initial meeting that she had taken a genuine liking for the woman.

Ignoring her niceties Jack pulled out his notebook and flicked through it.

"Nothing very startling really, just a couple of things that need following up on."

He leaned over her with his note book in hand.

"The most urgent right now is for you to try and make contact with this guy Barratt for me. There are some questions he needs to answer to put my mind at rest." He studied his own notes on the guy, reflecting on how little he knew about him. Jack's facial expression was more than familiar to Judy, she had seen it many times in the past and knew exactly what it meant.

"I can read you like an open book, Brennan. This is your gut instinct at work again -- am I not right?"

He gave her one of his 'more innocent than thou' looks before denying it.

"No sweetheart -- you're quite wrong this time. In fact as things stand I'm not particularly interested in Barratt, but I'm quite interested in the truck he was driving." Turning on his heel he headed for his office, casting more instructions over his shoulder along the way.

"Get on to that manager guy at Zipline again. I know he thinks he's busy but find out what the scheduled run was for Barratt's truck on the day Byrne disappeared. We need to know what it was carrying, where the delivery point was, and what he was taking back to Scotland on his return trip."

He came to a halt with one hand on the door knob.

"I know he was headed for Dublin to make some sort of urgent delivery, but it would be worth knowing if there were any complications along the way."

No sooner had he finished than another thought popped into his head. "And check out if the vehicle mileage was recorded for the journey, and if the delivery was made on time." That said, he slipped behind the door out of sight, only to quickly pop his head back round the door frame. "And I could absolutely murder a cup of coffee while you're at it." Judy folded her arms and gave him a look that would have cut through ice. "Which would you like me to do first -- or don't you have a preference?" she snapped.

"Why the coffee of course, what else?" he said indignantly. "I'd like to think I take precedence over a dead man."

Judy's jaw dropped and she stared at him open mouthed; his tactless and cruel revelation exposed a complete lack of expectation that Tony Byrne might still be found. She found it particularly hurtful as she had it in mind that they would still find him alive, sadly Jack had thrown a dark shadow over that ambition and she wasn't best pleased about it.

"What makes you think you have all the answers?" she snapped. "You could be wrong you know."

She snatched up the phone to begin making the calls, but she had one last piece of advice for him before doing so.

"And you can get your own bloody coffee or go without, I'm not here to work as a kitchen maid."

Jack ducked out of sight without delay, leaving her to get over her tantrum in her own good time, which experience told him wouldn't be any time soon.

15

As the last remnants of daylight disappeared below the skyline and the weather grew steadily darker, it suddenly became one of those nights when it was safer to be indoors than out. Which was exactly what Judy had in mind as she lounged beside the fire nursing a well-earned pre-dinner drink.

Jack had bailed out of the office in an all fired hurry long before she had, and hadn't even taken the time to mention where he was going or when he would be back. As a consequence she found herself struggling to keep a rein on her feelings, mostly because she was still nursing a grudging hostility over the tactless comment he had made earlier in the day, and with nothing else to occupy her mind she began to wonder what he was up to that was taking so long.

Before she could think up an answer the familiar crunch of car tires on the gravel driveway outside sent her scurrying across to the bay window. Her spirits lifted when she saw his lengthy frame unwind itself from the driver's seat, but they quickly went flat again when she spotted Mairead flashing her long limbs as she climbed out from the passenger's seat on the opposite side and totter round to join him.

She felt a shiver run up her spine as an uneasy chill swept over her; in truth it was more like an icy draft, a feeling she experienced almost every time she saw the two of them together. It wasn't something she couldn't readily explain, because she knew in her heart of hearts that it wasn't jealousy, well not quite, it had more to do with knowing that they shared a similarly disciplined background, he being an ex-serviceman and she a former agent with the MI5.

They enjoyed a synergy of thought processing that had her believing them capable of communicating without the use of words, a trait that freaked her out and left her feeling isolated, almost like an outsider.

There was no doubting they shared a special kind of intimacy that she was no part of, and although she made every effort to keep her feeling under control it was beyond her to keep them fully suppressed, and they always found an opportunity to re-surface and come back to haunt her. Even though she was much more content with life now that Mairead was heading up their London office as it meant they only met up at board meetings, which had recently been reduced to once every quarter, except in unusual circumstances, but it was a frequency that Judy was happy to tolerate.

For now though she wore a troubled look as the door behind her opened and the two people occupying her thoughts came in to join her. Mairead cutting a strikingly handsome figure in her fitted pink suit; its pastel shade highlighting her ebony hair and tanned complexion to great effect.

The last time Judy had seen her she had been artificially blonde, an inconvenient but necessary disguise at the time, although even she would concede that she looked much more attractive in her natural colour. The contrast between the two women could hardly be more striking. Judy's honey blonde hair, fine features and pale complexion contrasting vividly with Mairead's alluringly dark sultry looks. But while she might not be aware of it, no matter how alluring Mairead might be, she was no threat to Judy's claim on Jack's affections. In fact she had long since lost any ambition in that direction, having already discovered, much to her embarrassment, that Jack was a one woman man who made absolutely no bones about telling her so.

Judy had enough self-pride to ensure the troubled look had left her face before she turned to greet them.

"It's good to see you again, Mairead, how are things working out across the pond?"

"Hi, Judy, about as well as can be expected I guess, although if I'm honest it's all a bit too quiet right now." She draped an arm over Jack's shoulder with an unnecessary and deliberate familiarity that got right under Judy's skin.

"Your loving partner here has been bringing me up to speed with this missing person case you guys have landed-- it sounds like all the interesting stuff is happening on this side of the pond." The wishful look on her face declared how badly she wanted to be back in Belfast, and back in the thick of things. But the London job had been a blessing in disguise, because at that particular time operating in Northern Ireland had become much too hazardous for her.

Her final and most dangerous under cover mission with MI5 had taken her to the very the heart of the IRA leadership in Londonderry, where she had taken some seriously scary risks that had put her life in genuine danger. A threat that became much more imminent when she discovered there was another agent working undercover on the same patch, one that she had not been briefed about.

As it turned out the other agent wasn't just working the same patch but was also acting as a double agent for the IRA. In the end the powers that be had no option but pull her out, and as quickly as that, her usefulness as an MI5 agent in Northern Ireland came to an end.

Fortunately for her, a mutual contact, who was aware of Jack's ambition to expand his business, had put the two of them in touch, after which it was a simple case of like-minded people looking after their own.

"You might want to run some names past me later on and see if any of them strike a chord." Mairead suggested, being keen to get involved in any way she could.

"Although I suppose I'm mostly out of touch with what's going on over here these days." It was a simple enough truth as her sudden but necessary departure from the scene meant there were few of her old contacts left who felt they owed her any allegiance.

Jack shrugged her arm from his shoulder and dropped into a nearby chair. He was keen to cut out the small talk and get the board meeting out of the way post haste. It had only been convened to discuss profitability and future growth, there had been no plans to discuss specific cases, apart from any pending legalities. In essence the whole thing was obligatory and tedious, and quite simply bored the pants of him.

"I suggest we get this bloody meeting over with so we can go out and make a night of it."

He turned his attention to Mairead.

"Judy has booked us a table at that Japanese restaurant we used last time you were over."

Mairead smiled contentedly. "That's fantastic, I seem to remember we had a very enjoyable meal there." She was on her feet and reaching for her briefcase.

"Since we don't have a lot to discuss we might as well get on with it. I haven't had a bite to eat all day and I could certainly do with something any time soon."

With everyone in accord and eager to get to the restaurant they were soon embracing the job at hand with business-like intensity.

16

The information Jack had requested on Barratt's trip to Dublin was already on his desk when he got to the office the next morning. In fact it had been there since mid-afternoon the previous day, thanks to Judy's diligent sense of urgency. Although its priority status seemed to have slipped a few rungs down the ladder as he gave precedence to his early morning coffee. Still, it was only eight o'clock and being alone in the office he was in no great hurry to deal with something as mundane as paperwork.

Their intended quiet night out of the previous evening had turned into something of a marathon that had drifted into the wee small hours, leaving him sensibly disinclined to bother the girls before leaving the house for work.

He had most of his coffee finished before it took effect and he was suitably inclined to look at what Judy had left him.

Crouching over the single sheet of paper he browsed through it rather off-handedly at first, then went back to the beginning and read the whole thing again, more thoroughly this time. Although, if he thought reading it twice would unearth something new he was to be disappointed. In fact it contained nothing of any great importance, and little that he didn't already know. According to Andy Nelson, Barratt was a run of the mill, freelance contractor who ran a one man show from his own home in Scotland, not too far outside Sterling. The trip to Dublin had been a first for him and appeared to have fallen his way more by default rather than design.

As far as his business relationship with Zipline was concerned there was no binding agreement or contract of any kind, just a loose arrangement that suited both parties. He simply acted for them on a casual basis as and when they found themselves short-handed.

The logistics were fairly straight forward, Zipline would load a trailer onto the ferry at Larne and Barratt would collect it at Stranraer for onward delivery. The same procedure worked in reverse when an urgent load from UK Mainland or Continental Europe was destined for Northern Ireland.

There was a short note at the bottom of the page to say that Andy Nelson found him to be more than capable of handling what was asked of him and he appeared to be very reliable, but as there was nothing else in the short brief to make him sit up and take notice Jack read all this in disappointed silence. He had been hoping for something that might cast doubts on the guy's character, and he felt a bit let down when he didn't find it.

Tossing the report to one side he drained the remnants of his coffee and mulled things over for a while. His interest in the Scotsman had been nothing more than a vague suspicion to begin with, and it now looked like he had been barking up the wrong tree. It was a thought that lingered in his mind as he wandered across to the window and gazed down at the early morning traffic jostling its way through the city centre. But try as he might he still couldn't make his mind up about the Scotsman, and the more thought he gave to it, the more he realized that regardless of what he had just read it was too soon to drop him from his list of suspects. The fact remained that he was the only known person who had been in the right location to have been involved in whatever happened to Byrne, there had been no one else at the scene who could be afforded the same opportunity.

"Sorry pal," he muttered to himself, giving voice to his thoughts, "I'm afraid you're not off the hook just yet -- not by a long shot." He was about to leave his viewing station at the window when he spotted the girls getting out of Judy's car.

Neither of them looked ready for a day's work and he wondered if they were even fully awake. A thought that took him through to the outer office full of mischievous intent to await their arrival, and no sooner were they through the door before he descended on them. "Good evening, ladies," he goaded, with a very deliberate and meaningful check of his watch.

"Piss off, Brennan," Mairead retaliated loudly, "it's not our fault that you're a chronic insomniac -- if you can't sleep you should go see your bloody doctor." She was clearly in no mood for his banter, and judging by Judy's sullen expression she was hardly alert enough to try parrying with him either, her brain numbed by the previous night's indulgence. Jack though was revelling in his moment of triumph and quickly set about perpetuating his earlier offence.

"I'll be next door when you two are ready for work, if the caffeine ever manages to kick start that old grey matter." He bounded through the door leaving both girls quietly cursing him under their breath.

It was a full thirty minutes before they graced him with their presence, ambling in without a word and making a beeline for the comfort of the settee, each nursing a steaming mug of coffee and showing precious little interest in anything else.

Jack's earlier ribbing was evidently at the forefront of their mind, because in almost perfect unison, like some pre-choreographed ritual, they set about wilfully over-dramatizing the feminine art of making themselves comfortable. They continued in this vein until they had achieved their goal of stretching his patience to the limit, by which time he was only too pleased to let them know they had succeeded.

"If you're both quite comfortable perhaps we might get down to business?"

Mairead took up the challenge and opened the conversation. "This guy Barratt that you and Judy were on about last night, is there anything I can do to help out with him?"

"Don't you dare go anywhere near him." Jack snapped irritably. "I'll tackle him myself just as soon as I can arrange something with Andy Nelson. Right now I want us to concentrate on local connections. I don't like what I'm hearing about some of them, and it's a damn sight easier to get that out of the way first." He idled over and dropped into a seat on the other side of the coffee table, directly opposite the girls, aware that Judy was busily shuffling through her case notes in search of something. He was keen to know what it was before moving on.

"Didn't you say we were looking for anything out of the norm that happened on that last trip Byrne made?" She didn't wait for an answer. "Well, according to what you have in your notes, his wife made an issue of the fact that it took a lot longer than anyone expected. Apparently there was some sort of re-routing at the last minute that added a few extra days to the return journey."

She glanced round at Mairead sitting next to her, then at Jack.

"Is that not the sort of thing we're looking for?"

Mairead jumped straight in.

"It bloody ought to be. In fact that's exactly the sort of thing that needs looking into." She looked for some show of interest from Jack, but he hadn't stirred a muscle.

"Come on, Jack" she urged, "we're supposed to be looking for anything different that went on out there, and I'd say changing the route home at the last minute is highly significant. In fact it's bloody strange to say the least."

Jack leaned over the coffee table. "How do you work that out?" Mairead looked at him in disbelief, expecting him to show a bit more awareness. "Check it out if you don't believe me, but it's a known fact that any aid convoy needs official clearance to travel in or out of a conflict zone and are issued with a specific route before being permitted to leave their home shore. You can't just roll up to a bunch of border guards and tip your hat like some weekend camper, not in a bloody war zone. These things need careful planning."

She seemed so sure of herself that her argument galvanized Jack into immediate action. Jumping to his feet he pulled his address book from his inside pocket as he reached for the phone. When he'd found what he was looking for he punched in Andy Nelson's number.

"Now why did I not think of that?" he muttered, making it sound like an admission of failure.

Andy Nelson's abrasive young receptionist had done nothing to improve her people skills since their last encounter, and was every bit as abrupt and unwelcoming as she had been then. She offered no proper greeting, no enquiring introduction; a simple "Hello," was the best she could manage.

Jack responded in kind. "Put me through to your manager," he snarled, "and don't even think of putting me on hold -- you'll only live to regret it."

His no nonsense approach appeared to do the job and the delay was only minimal before Andy Nelson's Belfast twang came down the line at him.

"Good Morning, Nelson here -- how can I help?" He made it sound like he was expecting to greet an irate customer.

"Hi, Andy, it's Jack Brennan again. I hope you don't mind me calling like this but I need a bit of professional advice and I think you're the best man to provide it."

"What is it, Jack?" Nelson asked glumly. "You seem to be living inside my bloody telephone lately, but you had better get on with it since you're here now. In any case advice is free -- for the moment at least."

Jack chuckled into the mouthpiece. "Thanks, Andy, you'll be pleased to hear that it's nothing too difficult, I just want to know if these charity aid convoys that go to places like Bosnia and Romania are required to clear their routes with the overseas authorities before they leave home shores. Or would they just take a chance on getting clearance once they got there?"

Nelson gave a cynical snigger.

"No way that's going to happen, you don't take a multi vehicle convoy to places like that without securing the necessary clearances well in advance, and more importantly, Jack, you stick to the agreed route if you know what's good for you. Some of the roads in these conflict zones are mined to hell and back."

Jack massaged his forehead with his fingertips and grimaced uneasily, whether he liked it or not he was going to have to concede that Mairead's advice had been spot on.

"So I take it anyone running one of these convoys would be unlikely to alter a route once a convoy was actually under way or already out there?"

"That's not something to be recommended, Jack, especially if the convoy is heading into a live conflict zone. The authorities issue a very detailed route plan that they believe can be secured. A food convoy is no use to anybody if it's shot to pieces."

Jack nodded thoughtfully.

"Thanks for that, Andy, you're an absolute scholar --that's all I needed to know. You've been a big help -- I owe you a beer next time round." He was about to hang up when Nelson came straight back at him. "If it's that important to you, that guy Barratt you were asking about earlier could probably throw more light on the subject. He does a lot of those charity runs. Don't quite know how he manages it, being self-employed and all that, but I can remember him being unavailable for maybe a month or more at a time because of it."

Jack had been resting his elbows on the desk in a fairly lazy stance, but he suddenly jerked upright and charged round to his chair and collapsed into it. The ensuing silence had Andy Nelson wondering if he had been disconnected.

"Are you still there Jack?" he asked.

"Yes -- I'm still here, but can I take up a tiny bit more of your time? He sounded thoughtful, tentative even. "Would you know if Barratt and Tony Byrne ever went on the same convoy?"

His question was greeted with some surprise. "Bloody hell, Jack -- of course they did, I thought you would have known that. Barratt is the main organizer for these things; he plans the routes and gets all the clearances necessary for any convoys leaving from Scotland or Northern Ireland. He's been doing it for years. He's the guy with all the contacts and the expertise. He spent years driving round mainland Europe and knows the place like the back of his hand."

He suddenly broke away from the topic. "I'm sorry, mate, but much as I'm enjoying our little tête-à-tête I have some important things that need doing here so you really must excuse me. If you need to ring me again try and make it between five and six o'clock in the evening -- I might have more time then."

He was about ready to hang up, but hadn't quite finished. "Don't forget that beer you owe me."

The connection died after that, leaving Jack with the phone stuck to his ear and a worried frown on his face. What he'd just had confirmed shot Barratt up the pecking order on his list of priorities and was now topping his list of things to be urgently attended to, which left him pondering about how to go about making contact with the Scotsman. A serious thought that drew a prolonged and pensive silence from him and alerted Judy's curiosity.

"Don't bother telling us what that was all about, Jack, we can sit here all day and grow old together while we wait to hear what the hell

is going on?"

Jack squirmed to the edge of his seat. "Sorry, girls -- but you would not believe the conversation I've just had with that guy Nelson from Zipline." He ruffled his hair and screwed his face up with a 'where do I go next' sort of expression. "I don't want to go over it all in detail right now, but I'm more convinced than ever that our man's disappearance is in some way linked to that bloody aid convoy."

He switched his attention to Mairead. "I know this is not your case, and

I know I said we did not want you getting involved, but I need you to get someone at your end to run a check on this guy Barratt for me. Judy will give you everything we have on him. I want to know anything you can find out about him -- and bloody quickly too." He cocked a questioning eyebrow at her. "Can you manage that okay?"

She nodded enthusiastically. "I'll get on it right away."

Rising from the settee she turned and invited Judy to come with her, but Jack stuck his hand up in protest. "Just hold it there, Mairead, there's no need for you to go anywhere, I'm on my way out so you can stay right where you are and work from here."

He tapped Judy on the shoulder as he breezed past.

"I may be late back, so I'll see you at home later this evening. You can organize a taxi to get Mairead to the airport when she's ready to go, but I need you to stay in the office all day in case I need to get in touch."

He swung round and pointed an accusing finger at Mairead. "Don't you even think of getting too involved in all this, just run a check on Barratt like I asked, that's all I want. It's not your case, so bear that in mind.

He was through the door before she could argue, but his sudden change of plan left them both wondering what had caused him to up sticks and bail out in such a hurry. Whatever it was, it helped to inject a sense of urgency into their attitude as well, and they became much more purposeful without even realizing it.

17

The city centre traffic was crawling along at a snail's pace taxing Jack's patience to the limit. Not that he ever had much to start with, but right now he was sat in the shadow of a huge articulated lorry that was completely blocking his view. He wasn't aware of it at the time, but he was actually stuck at the wrong end of a mobile security check-point, and by way of rubbing salt into his wounds, he could only sit and watch with irritation as an elderly man on a push bike passed him by.

It took ages to clear the bottleneck and when he did he drove like a bat out of hell through the city centre and across town to where Roisin Byrne lived. When she opened the door it looked like she was dressed for going out, and although she invited him in, she pointed out, quite forcefully in fact, that she was on her way to work and had no wish to be late. She went on to explain that she had only recently acquired the job as a dinner lady at the local school and needed to be punctual.

"I won't detain you very long, Roisin," Jack promised. "I just need to know if you've had any luck getting in touch with Joe Devlin yet. I really need to be talking with him sooner rather than later."

The apologetic grimace on her face warned him that it wasn't going to happen.

"I did speak with him as it happens, but he was adamant that he doesn't know anything at all about Tony's disappearance. In his own words, he sees no reason why he should talk to you or anyone else about something that has nothing to do with him." Her expression didn't change much as she went on to explain what had happened. "I did my best to talk him round but he's not an easy man to deal with I'm afraid." She fiddled nervously with the strap of her handbag.

"I really don't want to be late for work, Mr. Brennan. You know how it is when you've just started a new job." Her anxiety was understandable and Jack wasn't minded to add to it, he knew she had enough problems in her life to be getting on with without adding to them.

"Don't worry yourself about that," he said soothingly, "I'll drop you off and you can show me where this guy Devlin lives as we go -- how's that?"

"That's most considerate of you. It won't take very long as Joe only lives in the next street." She substituted her anguished look with a timid little smile.

"Let's be on our way then," Jack prompted, opening the door to let her through.

If the Byrne family home had been two doors further down the street it would have run back to back with Joe Devlin's house in the next street, although it would still have been separated by the length of two long, narrow back gardens.

In fact Devlin's house was an exact replica of the one they had just left, even down to the colour of the exterior decoration.

The most noticeable difference however was that the front door was wide open and a tall, heavily built figure, dressed in jeans and a stained grey sweatshirt, filled the space where it should have been.

"That's Joe over there, standing by his door." Roisin said, winding her window down to get a better view.

Jack could only afford a quick glance as he weaved his way between some parked cars, but he slowed right down to walking pace to give himself a better look at Devlin and gauge his reaction to seeing the two of them in the car together. What struck him right away about the other man was his large, dome shaped head, completely bald on top, and what little hair there was on the sides was the whitest shade of grey possible, although it was cropped so close to the skull that it was really incidental.

Jack guessed his age at around forty to forty five; it was hard to be precise as he looked to be a pretty fit and robust sort of a guy. He was certainly a big man, in every sense of the word, with a huge breadth of shoulder and chest, which together with a square, well-muscled jaw and heavy brooding brow combined to give him an ugly, brutish appearance. If he had to choose a suitable occupation for him Jack would probably have marked him down as a prize fighter, or bare knuckle pugilist.

One thing was very certain; he was no choir boy. In fact he had a face that resembled a bull mastiff with a nose job.

As they drew level with Devlin's house his passenger greeted her neighbour with a cheery wave of her hand through the open window.

"Good morning, Joe," she gushed hurriedly, having little time to say anything else as Jack kept the car moving. However it was obvious from his startled expression that the last thing Devlin expected was to see his neighbour cruising down the street in a posh car, his jaw dropped and his mouth gaped open. It was every bit as noticeable that he didn't appreciate what he was seeing, and declared his contempt by blatantly ignoring her greeting. He clearly had something more important on his mind because as Jack's car edged slowly forward so did he, straining his neck to peer through the windscreen in an attempt to see who was driving the car.

Both men locked eyes for the briefest of moments, but it was long enough for Jack to note the dispassionate and unwarranted iciness the guy showed towards him. Indeed it took nothing more dramatic than a lowering of his eyebrows, and a tightening of his lips to convert his icy glare into something altogether more overtly threatening.

Being no stranger to such aggressive behaviour; having been on the wrong end of it frequently enough in the past, Jack had to concede that this was the first time he'd seen it on the face of a charity worker! Having seen all he was going to see he leaned on the accelerator and drove away feeling much the wiser for his short encounter. But he remained deep in thought for the rest of their short journey, although he kept his thoughts very much to himself as his passenger directed him to her place of work, where he was relieved to drop her off and get under way again.

There was plenty to keep him occupied along the way, as his brief sighting of Devlin had left him in a thoughtful and retrospective mood.

A mood that stayed with him all the way back to the office, where he was no sooner through the door before Judy picked up on it. "I can tell from the look on your face that your trip didn't go exactly as planned, but before you get too involved in anything else I need a few minutes of your time." There was an anxious, slightly disconcerting frown on her face that bade him to take the invitation seriously.

"How about now?" he invited, "come on through -- I was hoping to meet up with Dave Jackson this afternoon but it didn't pan out as I couldn't get in touch with him. Anyway, what's on your mind?" He spun away and slipped through the door with Judy hard on his heels. "What's the problem then?" he asked, settling his backside on the edge of the desk, immediately aware from her expression that he wasn't going to like it. Whatever it was?

"It might be nothing at all, Jack, and maybe I'm making a mountain out of a molehill, but after you bailed out this morning Mairead planted herself in your chair to make a few calls, which in itself was nothing unusual, but the minute she saw that photograph of Tony Byrne and his friend that you left on your desk her expression changed completely, and I'm convinced she recognized at least one of the guys in that picture." She cocked an enquiring eyebrow at him. "I know it sounds daft but I'm certain she was trying to hide it from me, but she was too slow and I spotted it." She stopped and waited for him to respond, only to be disappointed with his reaction.

"Well?" he asked.

"Well what?" she snapped, looking slightly confused.

"Well -- did she or didn't she know someone in the photograph. I presume you did ask?" He looked at her expectantly, anxious to hear the whole story without having to drag it from her one syllable at a time.

"Of course I did, that's what was so strange about it, she just brushed my enquiry aside and mumbled something about phoning you later when she was back in London. Whether that's to do with the photograph or not I can't say. You know what she's like sometimes, less than willing to recognize me as an equal partner." She screwed her face in horror at the realization of what she'd just said, since it brought to mind an unwanted memory of an occasion when Jack had accused her of being jealous of Mairead, and she had no desire for either of them to revisit that old argument.

"Anyway," she went on, hoping for a clean get out. "I've told you what I think. It's up to you to decide whether or not you should follow up on it." She turned away to leave, wrongly believing that her presence was proving something of an irritation to him.

"You have every right to be inquisitive, sweetheart," he assured her, "and if she does know either of those guys then you were very perceptive to spot it. I've no doubt we'll discover the answer to that in due course, and you're right, she can be a bit of an awkward bugger at times, even I know that." He looked a little doleful as he watched her go through the door, if only because he was still nurturing the hope, forlorn though it might be, that one day there would be less rivalry between the two women. But he also knew how much impish pleasure Mairead got from playing her mischievous little games. It was an inherent part of her nature to be secretive, which frequently complicated matters unnecessarily, and he firmly believed that was what really got Judy's dander up. Not that he believed for one minute it was intentional; it was more complicated than that -- it had more to do with the schooling she had received in her previous career with MI5, and he had often ignored it in the past believing she would grow out of it in time. However he was now beginning to wonder how much time it would take for her to 'blend in' properly.

They had only just seated themselves at the dining table with Judy ready to serve up dinner when Mairead's call came through and dragged Jack away from the table to answer it.

She was in a bright, cheery mood, mostly due to the fact that her flight back to London had arrived exactly on time; which in itself was something of a success story as she had an unlucky history with air travel.

"I hope I haven't caught you at a bad time, but I'm about to head out and wanted a quick word with you before I left." Jack wondered if she was being deliberately flippant just to annoy him.

"No doubt Judy has mentioned our little episode with the photograph?" The mischievous undertone in her voice was too obvious to be missed, which was undoubtedly how it was meant to be.

"I know all about it, Mairead, so you can cut the shenanigans and get to the point -- if there is one -- we're about to have dinner."

A smile visited Judy's face when she heard Jack's blunt rebuttal.

"Okay - okay, I get the message, but I need you to brief me on one of the guys in that photograph you left on your desk, the one with the black hair."

Jack was slightly mystified by her request, but it made him sit up and pay attention. "That's Tony Byrne, the guy we're looking for -- the guy we're being paid to find – the one who vanished three years ago." He shook his head in wonderment before asking. "Why the hell are you interested in him? Do you think you know him, is that what this is all about?" he asked, recalling that she had a virtual photographic memory for faces. More worryingly, she had operated undercover within the upper echelons of the IRA, so if she had come across Tony Byrne in that connection then the guy was not as lily white as everybody tried to make out. He got a sudden rush of adrenalin as he waited to hear what would come next.

"I just want to tell you that he looks familiar to me. I can't say any more than that at the moment, but I have a gut feeling he was involved in something I was handling, I've come across him somewhere before, I'm absolutely certain of that."

Jack clamped a hand to his forehead despairingly, asking himself why he had even bothered to take the call.

"It will come back to me, Jack, don't worry about that -- it always does -- and when it does I'll let you know straight away. I just thought it best to warn you of a possible situation. Sorry I can't be more helpful right now, and I'm sorry for disturbing your dinner. Give my love to Judy and I'll see you both in about four weeks." She disconnected without waiting for a reply, leaving Jack feeling anxious and perplexed as he replaced the phone and re-joined Judy at the table.

"Well, what did she have to say for herself?" she asked. "It must have been mighty important if she couldn't share it with me." There was a spiteful edge to her voice.

"Not a lot, sweetheart, to be perfectly honest, in fact it was an awful lot about nothing as it happens," he told her, looking more than a little bemused. "She has some crazy idea in her head that our man Byrne looks familiar, but I think we should leave that possibility out of our thinking for now unless she comes up with something more positive." His calm, outer appearance masked the anxiety he was feeling inside. When he had taken the call from Mairead he had actually hoped it might be Dave Jackson at the other end, and he was slightly disappointed that he hadn't bothered to get back to him yet. It meant he would have to chase him up again first thing in the morning.

18

There were a number of genuine reasons why public bars didn't figure highly on Jack's list of places to visit. Apart from the obvious security issues, he saw them as little more than social shelters, smoky little hideouts where less fortunate mortals sought refuge from the harsh realities of life. Nevertheless that was exactly where he found himself to be, if only because Dave Jackson had arranged to meet him there.

As he sat amidst a bunch of total strangers, whose backgrounds were secreted from him, waiting for the young detective to put in an appearance he felt decidedly ill at ease. The building itself was located smack in the middle of a staunchly republican area close to the docks, an area Jack would normally have steered well clear off had he been given a choice, but the young sergeant had been very persistent and convincing.

Having already seen off one whiskey he was attending to his second before Jackson put in an appearance.

"I take it this isn't your normal watering hole," Jack sniped at him, expressing his displeasure at the poor choice of venue. Jackson ignored the obvious rebuttal, indeed if anything he looked to be rather pleased with himself. "No, I can't say it is, Jack, but it does have an interesting clientele, as I hope you will discover before long."

Catching the barman's eye Jack ordered a round of drinks, which allowed him time to figure out what the young man was on about.

Jackson leaned closer to him and whispered in his ear. "You wanted to know more about this guy Devlin -- well this is where you get to find out about him."

His eyes narrowed slightly as he scanned the room for anyone who looked familiar, or anyone showing too much interest in their presence.

Devlin had been the last thing on Jack's mind when he'd accepted the invitation, he'd had other more important things to think about at the time, like the reason why he had asked to meet up with Jackson in the first place, and clearing all thoughts of Devlin from his mind he pressed on with his own agenda.

"I think we need to give this guy Barratt some close attention, I'm not entirely comfortable with him. I don't like the idea of his vehicle being parked up so convenient to the depot entrance when Byrne is reputed to have disappeared – that whole scenario bugs me a bit." He peered over the rim of his glass at his companion. "Did you know Barratt accompanied Byrne on his charity trips abroad?"

Jackson's jaw dropped and he looked surprised, maybe even shocked, it was hard to tell as he had a face of a poker player.

"We didn't know anything about the bloody convoys until you told us about them, Jack, so how the hell were we supposed to know anything about Barratt's involvement with it? Mind you, if what you're telling me now is true, then I would see that as a huge coincidence."

Jack accepted that the police didn't have privy to all of the information he had unearthed, so he wasn't about to make an issue of it, but the topic of the parked truck was forever popping up in his thoughts, and as Barratt was the driver of that truck, so was he. He eased his chair a little closer to Jackson's

"In my book it's much more than coincidence, Dave, because it provided opportunity, and when you have opportunity you can sure as hell start looking for motive because the two are seldom far apart." He took a quick drink before going on. "I can't shake off my suspicions that this whole damned mystery revolves around that aid convoy." He looked at Jackson, half expecting an argument, but with none forthcoming he pressed on regardless.

"I guess I'm really looking for something out of the ordinary that happened during that last trip. Something that was important enough for Tony Byrne to want to disappear afterwards, or for someone to arrange his disappearance."

He searched his mind for something to help convince the young detective he was right, but Jackson had his own ideas and he wasn't slow in voicing them. "There's nothing in what you say that convinces me their last trip was in any way different to any other trip. You need to produce some evidence to back that up if you want to convince me of it. Personally I can't see where you're going with this theory because we are still looking closer to home for our answers. You'll need to come up with something more conclusive to change our approach. Guess work and conjecture won't do it I'm afraid."

"Well I'm telling you now that there was something radically different about that last trip, at least on the return journey anyway." He waved his companion closer, not wanting the whole world listening in on their conversation. "For starters, it took a good deal longer than originally planned as the route for the return journey was changed at the last minute for no obvious reason." His announcement had no effect on Jackson who still looked nonplussed.

"Christ, Jack -- that's hardly an earth shattering revelation. Nor is it a valid reason for someone to disappear." He cocked his head cheekily to one side. "What is it you're trying to say – that because they arrived home a little bit later than planned Byrne had reason to disappear? Come on, mate, you will have to do better than that."

Clearly Jackson had failed to grasp the significance of the point Jack was making, although his contemptuous expression eased a fraction and he did at least become a little less dismissive looking.

"Listen, Dave, I've checked this thing out with people who know, and I can assure you that any deviation from an authorized route into or out of a conflict zone is absolutely taboo. In fact each and every route has to be clearly defined and certified by the authorities before a convoy can even leave these shores."

Jackson fished his cigarettes out and lit up, making an issue of blowing the smoke away from his companion. Jack watched him top up his nicotine fix without saying anything, at least until Jackson gave him a quirky 'what are you waiting for' raised eyebrow expression.

"Get on with it, Jack, don't just come to a grinding halt on me -- follow through with this theory of yours and let's see where it takes us."

Jack leaned his elbows on the table, taking him closer to his companion.

"I think there was a more sinister reason for that change of route. If you remember it was Devlin who floated the idea of this charity trip in the first place, and from what you've told me of his probable IRA connections, and from what I've seen of the man myself, I don't see him getting involved with any sort of charity just for the fun of it."

An alarming change came over Dave Jackson; he suddenly became extremely agitated and tense looking, almost panic stricken. He shifted nervously in his seat, his eyes flitting anxiously round the room in each and every direction. When he failed to find what he feared he might, some of the panic left him, but his whole demeanour had changed and he looked more like a trapped animal than a confident copper. Jack couldn't understand the reason for it, nor did he like it.

"For fuck sake, Jack!" he spluttered, "are you telling me that you actually met Devlin?" His voice was loaded with anxiety.

Jack lifted his elbows from the table and backed away, bemused by his sudden change in attitude and wondering what all the panic was about.

"Nooooo," he replied, drawing the word out, "I haven't actually met him, but I did catch a glimpse of him standing outside his front door." He shrugged his shoulders offhandedly. "Why are you getting so worked up over something as trivial as that? What's so bloody important about it?"

Jackson massaged the back of his neck, but the fearful look in his eyes remained in place. "For Christ's sake, Jack, this pub just happens to be Devlin's watering hole. I arranged to meet you here so that we could get a look at him together, from a distance. My information is that he comes here every afternoon around about this time." His words were rushed and panicky, as if there was insufficient time for detailed explanation.

"For fuck sake, Jack, tell me he didn't get to see you," The anxious look on his face said that something really serious was bugging him, something Jack wasn't yet party to.

"I don't know why you're getting so worked up, but as it happens he did see me --- but what difference does that make to anything we're doing?" He was bewildered by the young detective's strange behaviour and at a loss to make sense of it.

"I'll tell you exactly what difference it makes, I have instructions from our Criminal Intelligence Branch to steer well clear of Devlin – or have you forgotten. I'm only here because I'm doing you a favour, but I'd better make tracks before he gets here because if he recognizes you, then it will become his business to find out about me as well. You're in danger of compromising me, Jack. I can't stay here – I've got to leave right now."

He was half way out of his seat when the pub door opened and Joe Devlin walked in, bold as brass, looking for all the world like he owned the place. Jack grabbed the young detective by the coat tail and pulled him back into his seat.

"You're a bit late, old son," he muttered from the corner of his mouth, "Doctor Barnardo has just joined the party." He hadn't meant to sound flippant; his choice of words just came out in the heat of the moment.

They both lapsed into silence as they watched the brutish figure of

Devlin shuffle his way over to the bar, the arrogant nature of his body language indicating that this was his domain, his regular haunt. A few customers smiled sheepishly as he passed them by, while others raised a glass in timid salutation as he acknowledged their presence with a hardly noticeable nod of his bullet like head. Others simply shifted uncomfortably in their seats and pretended not to have noticed him coming in, which on the face of it was pretty unlikely as his huge, lumbering frame took up so much space it wasn't easily ignored.

Having ensured his presence was suitably acknowledged Devlin planted himself on a seat at the bar, where a tankard of beer was immediately placed in front of him, a sure and certain indication of his high status within the establishment. Jack was convinced that he had spotted them when he came in, even though he appeared to pay them scant attention. He also knew Devlin was watching everything that was going behind him in the full length mirror behind the bar. What he had no knowledge of however was what Devlin was thinking.

By now Jackson had accepted the inevitable, and although he made some effort to protect his identity by turning side-on in his seat, he had no doubt Devlin would recognize him again if they ever met; a thought that put a big question mark over his promotion prospects. Especially if those who had warned him to stay away from the guy ever found out he had been so close to their suspect. And if Devlin ever found out he was a cop it could well cause even bigger problems as it might alert him to the possibility that he was under surveillance. An issue the young detective dreaded to give thought to.

Jack edged his seat closer to his companion to get a better view of what Devlin was up to. He watched him raise the tankard to his lips and empty its contents down his throat in one long, continuous swallow. Having finished his drink he sat quietly contemplating the empty tankard for a few moments before placing it on the bar in a very precise and deliberate manner, almost reverently, as if his actions were a prelude to some greater event. Then with a shrug of his bull-like shoulders he turned and headed straight across the room in the direction of Jack's table, his aggressive body language declaring to all present that he wasn't planning a social call.

Jack watched him approach with some trepidation, although in truth he was well prepared for anything that might happen, both mentally and physically. Devlin looked cock sure of himself as he bore down on their table, his big fists balled into fleshy hammers in an openly aggressive manner.

When he reached their table he locked eyes with Jack for only the second time, and although he maintained eye contact with him, his outstretched arm was undoubtedly pointing in the direction of the young policeman sat beside him. "I don't know who you are and I don't much care, but do yourself a favour and keep out of this."

His eyes didn't flicker for a moment, boring into Jack's in a blatantly threatening manner as he folded his heavily muscled arms, stuck out his chest, and spread his feet in an aggressive stance.

"You, on the other hand," he said, continuing to glare at Jack, "are something of a pain in the ass, because a little bird tells me you're trying to involve me in this fucking Byrne thing." He paused for a moment before leaning across the table in an even more aggressive and threatening stance.

"You can take it from me that's not a healthy pastime to be indulging, but you look like a nice enough young man, so why don't you take my advice and go back where you came from and leave well alone -- okay?"

There was no doubting Devlin's determination to pick a fight, but for the life of him Jack couldn't understand what he had done to provoke it. At first he thought it must be some sort of misunderstanding that he hoped could be sorted out amicably, after all, he still had a case to pursue and he had no wish to alienate one of his potential witnesses along the way. At least that was the immediate thought going through his head, but that was before Devlin's surly attitude raised the red mist and triggered his own survival instincts.

Jack remained in his seat, immobile, elbows resting lightly on the table in front of him, hands clasped with his fingers lightly entwined and hovering over his glass.

Every eye in the room was focused on their table and you could have heard a pin drop throughout the bar, the only sound to disturb the silence was a slight scraping noise as Jack straightened his long legs under the table and eased his chair back a little; a purely tactical move on his part. Bullies like Devlin and his ilk needed to get up close and personal to make their threats work. A trait Jack expected from him, and one he hoped he could entice him into following.

"And what if I don't take your advice?" he taunted, hoping to provoke an even angrier reaction. Devlin had too much of an advantage towering over him as he was; Jack knew he needed a leveller, something to even the odds, and to his relief Devlin took the bait. He did exactly what Jack expected him to do and leaned across the table to get closer to his quarry, placing the palms of his hands on top of the table, with his upper body weight weighing directly down on them he leaned over, close to Jack's face.

"Oh I think you will -- don't you?" he threatened, shoving his face into Jack's to add muscle to the threat.

Jack glared up at him.

"I think not pal," he said, unclasping his hands and sweeping them downwards and outwards with lightning speed.

He caught Devlin completely off guard as his hands were flung aside and his face headed on a collision course with the table top. Jack's hands carried on full circle until they ended up behind Devlin's neck, allowing him to drive his face into the hard wooden surface. The unnatural silence that had befallen everyone in the bar was suddenly disrupted by the sickening sound of cartilage and bone impacting with the table top, quickly obscured by a screaming bellow of pain as Devlin collapsed across the table in agony, both hands clutching frantically at his injured face. But if Devlin thought his troubles were over then he was about to be disappointed because Jack hadn't quite finished.

He shot round behind a bewildered looking Jackson, shoving him to the floor out of harm's way as he rounded the table to get behind Devlin. Grabbing hold of his right wrist he twisted his arm up his back, locking it off, while his other hand grabbed hold of his neck and smashed his face twice more into the hard surface of table, causing further damage to his face and removing five of his front teeth in the process, three from the top and two from the bottom. Devlin was completely restrained and at Jack's mercy as he bent down and whispered in his ear. "Just so you know -- I'm not the nice young man you thought I was -- not really -- but I imagine you've probably guessed that by now." He ground Devlin's broken face into the polished surface one last time before turning on his heel and heading off at a steady, unhurried pace towards the bar exit.

Everything had happened so quickly that no one else had time to react, apart from offering a few startled gasps, although Jack was pretty certain he detected a smug look of satisfaction on a few of the faces he passed them on his way to the exit.

Jackson scrambled to his feet and charged towards the door behind him.

By this time Jack was only a few strides from the heavy glass fronted entrance that led out to the street, but he never got that far. He suddenly changed direction without warning and veered off towards the bar, causing the panic stricken young detective following in his wake to collide, rather unceremoniously, into his back. Jack brushed him aside like he wasn't there and headed straight for the barman, who was standing with his mouth open wondering what the hell he'd just witnessed.

"Would you be good enough to tell your friend back there that I'll chat with him again sometime when he's in a more receptive mood?" Turning his back on the bewildered barman he headed for the exit just in time to see Dave Jackson's well clad figure disappearing through it. He looked strangely relaxed as he went after him in what can only be described as casual pursuit, leaving a stunned and silent audience behind him.

"What the fuckin' hell was that all about?" Jackson snarled through gritted teeth. His every thought centred on the frightening vision of his once promising career sliding down the tubes at a rapid rate of knots.

"Sorry for bundling you aside like that but it seemed the only way to keep you out of it, I really didn't want you getting involved."

"Fuckin' wonderful, Jack! I'm doing my utmost to keep a low profile and you decide to start world war three while we're sat in full public view in a well-known republican drinking den – fuckin' marvellous -- you sure make it easy for people to fall out with you." There was nothing Jack could do to placate the guy, except listen to him gripe and let him get it off his chest.

"That's it for me I'm afraid, I can't be associated with someone who goes around creating that sort of mayhem in a public place."

They were still retreating poste-haste in the direction of Jack's car with the young detective continuing to let off steam. Oblivious to everything else around him he was working himself up into a real old fashioned frenzy, ignoring passers-by who might overhear, including a pair of grey haired old ladies who shuffled past with an over-laden shopping trolley and a startled expression.

When they reached the car Jack flung the door open and leaned on the roof to address his companion.

"Why don't you stop fuckin' panicking for a minute and get in the car."

Jackson responded with a look that would have curdled milk, but the situation that Jack had created dictated that he didn't have a lot of choice. He had arrived at their meeting by taxi and with everything that had gone on since his arrival he could hardly hang around waiting for another one to pick him up. He didn't want to get into Jack's car, or even be seen anywhere near him, but in the circumstances he had little choice.

"For Christ's sake," he repeated, "what the hell was that all about? You almost gave me a fuckin' heart attack back there. What the hell were you thinking?" His face was the colour of unbaked dough. "I need a fuckin' drink, because unless I'm mistaken you have just sent my bloody career into freefall."

Jack shifted the car into gear and booted the accelerator.

"Calm yourself down," he advised, "we can have a drink back at my place when we get there." He glanced round at his companion. "What are you getting so worked up about anyway, you know as well as I do that Devlin isn't going to report what happened. Why in God's name would he? If he's as mucky as you say he is then he's not going to invite an inspection from any of your boys." It was a valid enough argument and one that Jackson, even in his heightened state of agitation, had to accept, albeit with a great deal of reluctance. And while Jack disguised his fears behind a calm and confident outer façade he was actually furious with himself at the way he had reacted to Devlin's threats. He had completely lost control and reverted to his base instincts, reacting in the way he'd been trained to react, instinctively, without too much conscious thought, except survival. He certainly hadn't planned a run in with Devlin, he wasn't even aware that he would be in the pub, but it had happened and he needed to put it behind him and move on. It was no good worrying over spilt milk, he needed to weigh up the likely consequences and work out a strategy to deal with them, and it looked like he would have plenty of time to do so as his stony-faced passenger was in no mood for conversation.

By the time they got to the motorway and were nearing home he had already sorted out his immediate priorities. Pulling out his mobile phone he dialled the office number and waited for Judy to pick up, when she did he got straight to the point.

"Hi, Judy. I want you to pay close attention to what I'm about to say," he warned. "I need you to get in touch with Roisin Byrne and make her drop whatever she is doing and get a taxi to our place. In fact it would probably be easier and quicker all round if you took a taxi and went to fetch her. Don't accept any argument from her, just get her back to our place as quickly as you can. I'm relying on you, sweetheart, so don't let me down"

He tried to mask the feeling of impending doom that was crowding in on him, but it was a wasted effort because his partner quickly recognised the veiled hint of panic in his voice.

"I'll do my best, Jack, but she might not be at home," she warned, sensing his need for urgency. "Is there something I should to be aware of?" Jack cringed and closed his eyes momentarily. "I'm not sure," he admitted, "not yet anyway -- but you must keep phoning her until you make contact, and don't hang about, phone her as you go and get her to pack enough clothes and things for a weekend stay. The minute you lay eyes on her take her straight to our place, that's absolutely essential." He was back at her again before she could ask any questions. "Don't let me down on this, Judy. I'm relying on you -- it's really important. I'll probably be home before you as I'm headed that way now, so I'll see you when you get there."

Listening in on the conversation had a strangely calming effect on the young man sat beside him, who hadn't uttered a word since getting into the car. But after witnessing Jack's brutal attack on Devlin it came as something of a contradiction that his first thought should be in consideration of his client's welfare. It was enough of a surprise to draw him out of his enforced silence.

"I'd say that's a smart move, my friend," he conceded, not ungraciously in the circumstances. "That little lady could be in real trouble if she stays where she is."

Still in a state of shock over what had happened, and concerned about how far Jack was willing to go in pursuit of a goal, he was anxious to know what his next move would be. "So where do you go from here – what's your next plan of action?" he asked.

"I was about to explain exactly that before everything kicked off with that bastard Devlin. Our people across the water are checking out this guy Barratt for me as we speak. I'm not convinced it's going to lead us anywhere, but I feel it's important to have a face-to-face meeting with him if it can be arranged. I'm working on an idea that might help set it up."

He didn't elaborate further, just smiled and glossed over it like it wasn't important. The break in conversation suited Jackson, who needed time to evaluate how much damage Jack's little episode might had been done to his career, a distinctly worrying prospect that remained at the forefront of his mind, mostly because it threw up the possibility of a similar episode taking place if and when Jack met up with Barratt?

Later that evening, much later in fact, when the initial feeling of panic had subsided and they were sitting side by side in Jack's living room sharing their company with a bottle of Black Bush whiskey, Judy walked in with their rather dishevelled and confused client in tow. She had suffered a really trying time persuading her to drop what she was doing and leave her home at such short notice. A task that was made even more difficult by her inability to explain the rationale behind it, although she had sensibly determined, from the panicky edge in Jack's voice, that something quite serious had happened.

As soon as she entered the room Roisin Byrne spotted Dave Jackson and a look of recognition lit up her eyes, although it did little to erase the dour expression beneath them.

"Good of you to come at such short notice, Roisin," Jack acknowledged, with an apologetic smile. "There have been a few developments that we need to discuss sooner rather than later, hence the need for such urgency."

He was being vague and indecisive, unsure how best to explain the situation without causing his client undue alarm. His only objective, for the moment at least, was to get her out of danger and into a safe refuge. They couldn't afford to leave her exposed to the possibility of a run-in with a brute like Devlin after what had happened.

Roisin Byrne was bewildered and confused by what was going on and it showed on her strained expression. She had no understanding of why she had been spirited from her home with such unexplained haste, and it was now up to Jack to conjure up an explanation that she would understand, and an action plan that she would buy into.

"We believe, or should I say, we suspect, there is a connection between your husband's disappearance and the charity aid convoys he was a part of, and we're convinced that Joe Devlin is in some way connected to whatever went on out there." He watched her confused expression change to one of disbelief. He'd deliberately made no mention of his assault on Devlin, nor did he intend to, he was only concerned with telling her what she needed to know to fall in with his plan, nothing more.

"If we are right, then we think it would be safer for you not to be living quite so close to that man for a while, at least until we see how things pan out over the next few days."

Judy was nothing more than a background listener to the proceedings; she had no knowledge of Jack's run-in with Devlin, but she recognized a sense of urgency when she saw it, and what she saw in her partner as he tried to console their client wasn't just a sense of urgency but something close to panic. Nevertheless she trusted him to put their client first, and was convinced that there had to be a very good reason for what he was doing; what happened next only served to reinforce that faith as Dave Jackson spoke out in support of Jack.

"I suggest you take that advice very seriously, Mrs. Byrne, this guy Devlin knows he's under scrutiny right now and he may take it upon himself to do something about it. He's a pretty nasty piece of work and we don't really know what he's capable of doing, but it makes sense for you to take precautions."

The distraught expression on Rosin Byrne's face gave warning that he'd said too much, prompting Jack to give him a withering look as the little woman buried her face in her hands, burdened with worry. She lacked the emotional capacity to cope with what was being asked of her. Jack rushed to her side to comfort her, as did Judy.

"But what am I to do?" she asked, "Where am I supposed to go that would be any safer than my own home?" The tremor in her voice bore witness to the anxiety she was suffering, making Judy embrace her more tightly.

"Why don't I get us both a nice warm cup of tea, Roisin, we can come back to this discussion afterwards when you're more composed." She gave Jack a wide eyed look that told him to keep his mouth shut and say nothing else. "Come through to the kitchen with me and don't go getting yourself all worked up over this. There's absolutely nothing to get worked up about, you can stay here with us until we get things sorted out, and you have my promise that you will be perfectly safe." Having consoled her as best she could, she guided her through the door and out of sight.

Having bided his time until they were on their own Jackson was quick to demonstrate that he was far from being a happy bunny. It was Jack's insane reaction to Devlin's challenge that was directly responsible for the crisis they now faced, not to mention his own frustration at having been unwittingly roped into something that had absolutely nothing to do with him, and he didn't hold back from saying what he was thinking.

"If you'd had enough sense to keep your fuckin' hands in your pockets none of this would be necessary," he whispered, endeavouring to keep the conversation between the two of them. Jack shrugged the accusation aside; he didn't wholly agree with that particular analysis, being minded to believe that his client's safety had been compromised from the moment Devlin had seen the two of them in the car together, so he wasn't overly concerned with Jackson's interpretation of events.

"What do you intend to do now?" Jackson asked.

"Get that little lady off-side as quickly as possible. I'll send her across the pond to stay with our people in London for a while -- at least until it's safe for her to come back home." The truth was he was flying by the seat of his pants, but he picked up his mobile phone and dialled a pre-set number. Mairead answered almost immediately, and after a quick update she agreed to help out without giving it a second thought.

"I don't see why we can't handle that for you, Jack, just give me the flight details and leave the rest to me."

"Thank you, Mairead, I knew I could depend on you." An undisguised sigh of relief accompanied his response. "I'll get back to you as soon as we've sorted things out at this end. Speak to you then." He hit the disconnect button and tossed the phone behind him on the chair.

Having nursed his empty glass for some time Jackson reached out and placed it on the table in a way that said he was preparing to leave. "There's no reason for me to get involved in any of your private arrangements, nor do I want to be, so I guess it's time I was making tracks."

Having made his point he said his farewells and rang for a taxi, and within seven or eight minutes he was climbing into a black cab and on his way, relieved to be untangling himself from the obvious problems facing Brennan Associates.

It was impossible for Judy not to have heard Dave Jackson leave, yet she lingered on in the kitchen in the company of their client long after he had gone, providing Jack with some space for quiet reflection and an opportunity to sort out an action plan.

In fact it was quite some time before he was ready to face them, and when he did he found Roisin Byrne in the same agitated mood, although in fairness she had at least accepted the fact that it was in her best interests to be kept under wraps for a while.

"It would appear I don't have any other choice but to do as you ask, although I must say I find it hard to accept that someone living in the very next street to me could be responsible for what has happened to Tony."

She shrugged her shoulders resignedly.

"I gave you the job of finding out what happened to my husband, so I suppose I must accept your decision and go along with whatever

156

you decide to do." She gazed thoughtfully at the remnants in her tea cup for a moments, then looked up to face him with a much more determined expression on her unadorned face.

"I may appear slightly naive to someone like you, Mr. Brennan, and no doubt you see me as a fragile and emotional little woman, but please have no illusions about my intentions. I'm absolutely determined to find out where my husband is, and exactly what has taken place to keep him from me. It's important to me that you understand that."

For a second time since meeting her Jack found himself admiring his client's dogged spirit, and he wondered where such a diminutive little lady like her found the stamina to keep going in such trying circumstances, he also found it very refreshing and just what he needed to raise his own bruised spirits.

"I don't doubt your commitment for one moment, Roisin -- but we do need to put some arrangements in place to secure your safety. That's the most important issue right now."

He guided her to a chair.

"The immediate plan is for you to stay here tonight and then get you off to London first thing in the morning. I'm not sure yet which airport you will be flying in to, but one of our people will meet you at the other end and look after you until it's safe for you to return. Please bear in mind that this is only a precaution, although I do feel it's a necessary one in the circumstances."

He sidled over to the worktop and poured himself a coffee, then carried it back to the table where both women were now seated.

"I have to go and sort out your flight tickets and a few other things, but you make yourself comfortable until I get back. Judy will be here to keep you company."

Knocking back what was left of his coffee he got up and left the two women in quiet reflection.

***

It proved to be an early start for everyone as they escorted Roisin Byrne to the airport. She was booked on the early morning commuter flight, which was the first one out of the city, and she looked a forlorn, and lonely little figure as she fought the gale force wind that tore across the wet tarmac on route to the aircraft.

Judy had insisted on accompanying them and was stood beside Jack as they watched their client board the plane from the comfortable surroundings of the airport viewing platform. They stayed that way until the plane had taken off before searching out a much needed cup of coffee at the airport cafeteria.

"I have a wee job for you this morning," Jack told her, as they took their place at a table. "I need you to get in touch with Father Joseph and see if you can arrange another meeting, preferably early next week."

His hand made a dive for his inside pocket and retrieved his mobile, he pressed the keys and waited for a response, tapping his fingertips impatiently on the table top while waiting to be connected.

"Hi, Mairead, our friend is on her way, make sure you take good care of her for me because she's a little bit fragile and confused right now and definitely in need of some good old fashioned TLC. Oh – and while I think of it -- that consignment we discussed -- you need to arrange for it to be delivered on Friday, and for God's sake don't forget to confirm that they can deliver on time."

Judy gave him a curious look from across the table. She knew nothing of any consignment and was quite intrigued to hear about it.

"What consignment is that?" she asked.

Jack brushed her enquiry aside like it was unimportant.

"Nothing to bother yourself about, sweetheart."

He was already on his feet preparing to leave.

"I've got things to do that won't wait. You take a taxi back to the office and when you have a moment ring Andy Nelson for me and tell him I'll be in to see him this afternoon."

Having made his hurried excuses he turned on his heel and walked away, sensing Judy's eyes burning a hole in his back to help him on his way.

19

The loading yard at Zipline Transport was a hive of activity when Jack drove in, with most of the vehicles on site in various stages of loading and unloading, some even cross loading, attended to during this mad rush by a seemingly endless fleet of fork-lift trucks.

Driving straight past the loading bays he parked up outside the office block and went inside, finding the atmosphere thick with stale tobacco smoke and sweaty body odours, courtesy of a somewhat boisterous collection of drivers eagerly waiting to get their paperwork and hit the road.

He gave them a curt nod as he wandered past on route to Nelson's office, where he rapped on the door a couple of times before walking in to find him feeding his computer its daily ration of statistics.

"Hi Andy," he greeted cheerfully. "I see you're busy so I promise this won't take very long."

Nelson looked up briefly while continuing to feed the computer. "Your young lady told me you would be calling. What can I do for you this time?" He appeared receptive enough, and Jack guessed that was probably down to Judy's powers of persuasion rather than any natural curiosity on his behalf.

"I'm hoping you might agree to do me a little favour," Jack confessed. Nelson was dressed in a heavy donkey jacket that seemed seriously out of place in the hot and stuffy atmosphere of his office. He was undoubtedly feeling overdressed as well because he quickly undid his tie and popped the top button on his shirt.

After saving whatever statistics he'd been feeding into the number crunching gismo he swung his chair round to face Jack.

"You had better get whatever it is off your chest then," he invited.

Jack smiled as he debated where to start.

"I consider you to be an up-front sort of guy, Andy, so I'm going to be really candid with you and lay my cards on the table." Apart from a bemused little smile, which was so incidental it was hardly noticeable, Andy Nelson's only other reaction was to lean back in his seat and wait for whatever was to follow.

"For a variety of reasons it has become imperative that I get to grips with this guy Barratt. I'm convinced he was in a position to know something about Tony Byrne's disappearance, so I need to hear what he has to say for himself. But I need to meet him face to face to make a judgment on that, it's not something that can be done any other way. To cut a long story short I'm arranging for him to deliver a package to me at my office here in Belfast."

He paused to let Nelson digest what he'd been told.

"As I understand it, at least from what you told me, Barratt would normally drop off any deliveries with a Northern Ireland address here at the depot for onward delivery by your Belfast crew. Is that right?"

Nelson wasn't at all sure where the conversation was going or what Jack was leading up to, but he decided to play it by ear for a while and see what happened.

"That about sums it up, but it would help if you were a little less circumspect, I don't like mysteries. I'd much rather you got to the point and told me what it is you want." He was definitely a bit guarded, but then he wasn't the type to take a gamble anyway.

"It's nothing terribly difficult really. When Barratt arrives here with my consignment I want you to convince him that the customer has been hounding you on the phone for an urgent delivery. You have to make out that all your drivers are too busy to make the drop and convince him to do it for you."

Seeing a less than convincing expression on Nelson's face Jack pressed him a bit harder.

"It's not a lot to ask, Andy, but it's extremely important to me that Barratt makes the delivery so that I can have a word with him face to face."

They eyed each other up for a few seconds, until eventually the transport manager broke the contact and allowed a distinctive hesitancy to take over as he shuffled through a pile of papers in front of him.

"I really have no wish to get involved in any of this bloody cloak and dagger stuff." Having said his piece he got up and crossed the room to the window, and shrugging off his heavily creased jacket along the way he draped it over the top of a filing cabinet that was near at hand. He stayed like that for quite some time, just gazing out into the yard with his back to his visitor, contemplating nature.

"I'm trying to run a business here," he explained, "and it's difficult enough to keep on top of things these days without volunteering for any of this crap,"

He undid his tie another notch and shuffled back to his seat, beads of sweat running from his sideburns down his cheeks.

"Christ, Andy, it's not much to ask," Jack insisted. "Tony Byrne was one of your most reliable drivers, you told me so yourself, so surely to God you would want to find out what happened to him as much as I do?" It was Jack's turn to take the short hike over to the window.

"The way I see it, if this guy Barratt has nothing to hide then he'll hardly hold it against you if he ever finds out. Surely you can see that?" He turned round to face Nelson. "On the other hand, if he is in some way involved in Byrne's disappearance then you really don't owe him anything – do you?"

He wasn't leaving Nelson much room for manoeuvre.

"You're a right determined bastard, Brennan, I'll give you that, but I think you're being a bit unfair dragging me into this." He smoothed his hair back with both hands. "Although you're right of course, I do want to know what happened to Tony, and of course I want to help -- don't we all? I'm just not any sort of hero when it comes down to it. You may not know it but Barratt is a big man and I'm not in the best of shape, as you can see." He spread his arms to let Jack appreciate his ample girth.

Jack grinned and made light of his excuse.

"There's no reason at all for you to feel threatened by Barratt, so come on, Andy, just anti up -- are you willing to help, or not?" Time was pressing on and Jack needed an answer one way or the other, otherwise his plan would need a complete rethink.

Nelson stared blankly at his desk as he debated the problem, and much to Jack's surprise he made his decision quite quickly in the end.

"Okay -- I give in, but you had better keep my name out of it. As far as Barratt is concerned I'm merely responding to a customer's request for an urgent delivery."

He dug into his trouser pocket for a handkerchief and wiped the sweat from his glasses before wiping his brow.

Jack gave him time put his glasses back on. "That's more like it, Andy, I knew just you wouldn't let me down -- but don't forget that I'm relying on you to get it right." He cocked an eyebrow at him, it's very important that you do." He let his warning sink in for a few moments before explaining his plan.

"I've arranged for Barratt to have my parcel here on Friday, but I need to know just as soon as he is on his way to my place, you'll have to warn me. I could do with his mobile number as well, that might prove useful down the line."

Nelson scribbled the number on a piece of paper and handed it over, and after a brief but grateful handshake Jack was on his way, happy to escape from the stuffy atmosphere.

Following his visit to Zipline he was in a much more jovial mood when he got back to Judy, whistling light-heartedly and causing her to look up in surprise as he walked in on her.

"What has you in such a good mood?" she asked, relieved to see him looking more like his old self. "Do I take it things went well?"

"Couldn't be better, sweetheart, and you're quite right, they did go well." He failed to elaborate and in so doing produced a tardy response from his inquisitive partner.

"Well thanks a bunch for the update, Jack. That really brings me up to speed." Her snappy rebuke brought a mischievous smile to his face. Of course she would need to know what he was planning if only to update the case file, that was her job after all, but until he was ready to tell her, he would enjoy teasing her for a little while longer.

20

Jack dragged his little secret out until Friday morning before telling Judy the detail of what was going on, and only then because he wanted her off the premises before Barratt arrived.

She put up a token resistance at first, but the truth of it was she was pleased to know he was concerned enough about her welfare to give her the afternoon off in case his meeting with Barratt got a bit heated.

They had already been in touch with Mairead earlier in the day to check on how their client was settling in, and were delighted with the report they got. It appeared she had adapted well to her new surroundings, taking it upon herself to act as chief cook and bottle washer while her host was at work.

"She's an absolutely perfect house guest, Jack, I think I'm going to miss her when you take her from me."

Mairead's enthusiasm came as a welcome relief as he had been nursing the thought that she might not entirely fit in at her upmarket residence. It was a welcome bonus to know that there was one less problem for him to worry about.

The news from Mairead also put Judy in a good mood, and she took herself off just before lunch, leaving Jack alone in the office to await Barratt's arrival.

Sitting around with so much time on his hands he soon became restless and ill at ease, finding it almost impossible to concentrate on anything but what lay ahead. His mind was totally preoccupied with planning his next move, but he was unable to advance any sort of rigid plan as so much depended on the outcome of his meeting with Barratt. If indeed that yielded anything useful.

It was close to four o'clock before his much awaited call from Andy Nelson came through. "Barratt's on his way over to you, Jack, and I have to say it took a lot of persuading to get him to do so." He was whispering into the mouthpiece and Jack was unsure if that was due to a guilty conscience or because he didn't want to be overheard by any of his staff. In any case when he replaced the handset he was in a thoughtful mood trying to figure out how long it would take Barratt to get across town.

"Twenty minutes at most I reckon," he murmured to himself, finding comfort from the sound of his own voice in the nervy silence, and not being of a mind to take any chances he unlocked the desk drawer and reached inside for the Colt forty-five he had placed there earlier. He had no intention of using it, but he might need it to help persuade Barratt to talk, time would tell.

After checking the chamber he tucked it into the back waistband of his trousers, where it remained out of sight under his jacket. Satisfied that everything was in order he wandered through to the outer office and the intercom that would link him to the duty doorman at the desk downstairs. He hit the button and waited for what seemed an eternity before a broad Belfast accent boomed out at him through the speaker.

"Front desk."

The loud and abrupt greeting provided no other information, but it was a voice that Jack knew well. "It's Jack Brennan here, Tom. I'm expecting a small parcel by urgent delivery that I have to sign for it myself, would you buzz me when the driver gets here and send him straight up." He thought for a moment about what might go wrong, then added. "Whatever you do, Tom, do not accept the delivery on my behalf, I really must see the driver myself."

It had just occurred to him that Barratt might try to dump the delivery on the doorman.

"Sure thing, Mr. Brennan, you can safely leave that to me." The security man, come doorman, come part time receptionist, was an ex-serviceman like Jack. A guy in his early fifties who could be relied on to do exactly what he was asked to do. Jack thanked him and settled down to await Barratt's arrival.

It was a bit longer than the twenty minutes he had allowed for before the intercom buzzed into life, and although he had been sitting for the whole of that time waiting for it to happen, it still caught him off-guard and made him jump.

"Your delivery has arrived, Mr. Brennan. I'm sending the driver up as soon as I book him in." Jack thanked him and leaned back in Judy's rather flimsy typist's chair with his eyes glued to the door, not really knowing what to expect.

Barratt kneed the door aside and breezed in with both arms wrapped around a smallish cardboard container. He was dressed in jeans, a black tee shirt and a pair of Doc Martin boots.

The first thing to enter Jack's mind was that Andy Nelson's description had been quite accurate, Barratt was a big man. In fact he stood about five eleven with long, greasy, jet black hair that hung well below his collar. His angular face sported a couple of day's growth, which along with his dark hair gave him a rather Middle Eastern appearance. Whatever his birth right he looked anything but Scottish.

As the door swung shut behind him he nodded a greeting to Jack and hoisted the parcel up on the desk in front of him, then flicked through his delivery pad looking for the required docket.

"Just sign on the bottom line and print your name and the time of delivery beside it for me please." He might not look Scottish but Barratt sure as hell sounded it with his really heavy Glaswegian accent. Jack gave him a quick once over, and noticed right away that his left cheek sported a faint but unmistakable scar some four or five inches long that was partly hidden beneath the dark stubble. On top of that he had a face that portrayed a somewhat arrogant attitude, in fact it was a face that could easily get its owner into trouble, and Jack believed the scar he was sporting bore witness to that.

"You're Barratt I believe?" he said, accusingly.

The Scotsman jerked back in surprise, his eyes sweeping the room nervously, as if he was expecting to find someone he should know, someone who could have identified him to the stranger in front of him. To his amazement there was no one else in the room.

"Do I know you?" he asked, looking genuinely surprised, his heavy shoulders flexing under the cotton tee shirt.

Barratt clearly didn't like surprises and he most certainly didn't relish this one as he had a decidedly uneasy look about him.

"No you don't know me, so don't go worrying about it, but we have a mutual friend you and me. Someone who gives us both a wee bit of well-paid charity work now and again."

He paused for a moment to let the information sink in.

"I'm talking about Joe Devlin of course."

Barratt was clearly unprepared for what was happening and it showed in the way he reacted, but the guy was no fool and quickly regained his composure, even if he was unable to stop the frown from deepening on his swarthy features. He took a couple of backward steps, putting a little distance between himself and the reception desk.

"I haven't a clue what you're going on about, pal. You've obviously got me mixed up with someone else." He made as if to leave but Jack came out from behind the reception and blocked his path.

"You're going nowhere, my friend, not yet anyway," he warned, reaching for the door and snapping the security lock in place. When he turned back to face him Barratt had adapted a much more defensive posture, and it was noticeable from his stance that he wasn't lacking in street experience because his heavy frame hung loose and ready for action. There was an unmistakable air of confidence about him that Jack found dauntingly disturbing. The guy definitely looked primed and ready for action.

"Fuck you," he mouthed.

"I had hoped we could do this the easy way," Jack told him, "but it's immaterial to me, I'll go along with whatever cuts your grass." He pulled out the Colt and waved it at a chair close to the wall directly behind the Scotsman. "Plant your ass in that chair and don't try any heroics, this thing makes an awful bloody mess, and my cleaning lady has the day off."

Judging by the alarmed expression on his face his earlier show of bravado appeared to have called time as he shuffled backwards without even looking where the chair was; too frightened to take his eyes off the weapon for a single second. He was clearly bewildered by the sudden change in his circumstance.

"There are two ways we can play this." Jack explained. "One -- you tell me what I want to know and be on your way -- or two -- you don't tell me what I want to know and I hand you over to the cops and tell them all about your cosy little relationship with Devlin."

A sudden change came over Barratt's expression, it was as if someone had turned a light on inside his head.

"I bet you're the silly bastard who gave Devlin the face job – aren't you?" His more respectful tone expressed a definite change of attitude, but he still looked threatening enough to keep Jack on his toes. Although this time around it was Jack's turn to look surprised, he hadn't expected Barratt to know anything about his run-in with Devlin. He found that rather puzzling.

"How the hell did you find out about that?" he demanded. Barratt smirked knowingly. "Devlin met me at the docks this morning. He always meets me when I come over, and I'd say you made a serious mistake there pal -- big Joe's not a man to be crossed and he'll have his pound of flesh, you can bank on that." He calmly crossed one leg over the other as if he had all the time in the world, still looking far too cocky for Jack to put the gun away.

"Tell me about Tony Byrne," said Jack.

Barratt looked at him like he'd lost his senses, his brow gathering in a way that indicated he had no understanding of what was being asked of him.

"What do you mean -- tell you about Tony Byrne? What the hell can I tell you about Tony Byrne?" There was no doubting the guy's confusion, and Jack was convinced that he wasn't play acting or feigning his bewilderment. He quite clearly had no idea what was being asked of him.

"Let's just take stock for a moment," suggested Jack, feeling a little less sure of himself now. "You do know about Tony Byrne's disappearance -- right?"

Barratt looked even more confused, and had to think about what to say before answering. "Yeah -- of course I do -- I heard he went walkabout -- so what, am I supposed to be his fucking nurse maid or something?"

"Maybe not, but you had better explain what your truck was doing parked up outside the depot at the exact time he disappeared?" He had been suspicious about Barratt's truck and its close to hand convenience ever since he had heard about it. It had been in a perfect position to assist in spiriting Tony Byrne away, if indeed that was what happened. Unfortunately at this stage he had no way of knowing if the Scotsman was the actual perpetrator. Indeed there was always the possibility that others were involved who hadn't been identified yet.

Barratt looked at him in disbelief.

"Look pal, I may be up for the odd shady deal here and there -- I admit that, but I don't go around making people disappear, believe me, that's way out of my league."

He sounded convincing, and more to the point he looked convincing, so much so that Jack began to question his original suspicions about the guy. It was beginning to look as if Barratt had no involvement in whatever had taken place, at least not intentionally anyway.

"I really don't need this now -- do I?" he said, tucking the Colt back into his waistband out of sight.

Barratt looked visibly relieved.

"Is there anything in that pot?" he asked, pointing at the coffee machine. "My mouth is dry as a bone."

Jack weighed him up for a few moments, then headed over to the percolator and filled a couple of mugs with the steaming black liquid. Barratt got up from his chair and joined him, albeit a little sheepishly at first, although he was quick to switch on to the fact that he was no longer under threat, and as a result became a little more talkative.

"Look pal," he explained, "I hardly knew Tony Byrne, although from what I did see of him he seemed a pretty inoffensive sort of guy, but I can assure you I know absolutely nothing about his disappearance."

"Okay, I get the picture, but you can sure as hell tell me why that last convoy the two of you went on was re-routed on its return journey?"

Barratt turned his face away unexpectedly, shielding himself from Jack's scrutiny. A blind man could see he was hiding something and Jack needed to force it out of him while he still had the upper hand.

"If you tell me what I want to know then as far as I'm concerned the matter ends here and now, but if you try holding back on me, then I make you a promise that you will be finishing this conversation downtown with the boys in blue."

Barratt tightened up and looked decidedly edgy, but it was hard to determine whether it was fear that Jack detected in his eyes or just nervousness; either way he needed to get everything he could out of the guy while he had the opportunity.

"My only interest in all this is finding out what happened to Tony Byrne. I couldn't care a toss what sort of scam you and Devlin are running."

Barratt jerked away, startled. "What fucking scam?" he protested, "All

I did was pick up some goods for Devlin's people on the way back." The words gushed from him in a defensive outburst, he hadn't even thought to refute the accusation that he was scamming the charity he was supposed to be helping. Nevertheless his determined denial and the mention of a pick-up triggered a ray of hope in Jack.

"You said Devlin's people. Who exactly are Devlin's people?" he asked, his interest in the re-routing of the convoy growing by the minute. Barratt eyed him up and down as if weighing up the opposition, although he was looking decidedly uneasy as he did so.

"Look pal, you don't know who you are dealing with here. Do I have to spell it out for you?" He folded his arms over his barrel chest and shook his head in disbelief. "Surely to God you know who Devlin is mixed up with?"

It wasn't in the Scotsman's nature to divulge a confidence in front of a total stranger, but reading between the lines Jack believed he knew who the Scotsman was talking about and it gave him plenty to dwell on. If he was right then what he had suspected from the very beginning, and in many ways dreaded, had suddenly become a reality. "You mean the IRA," he said, not wishing to question it, just seeking confirmation.

Barratt was showing all the signs of being uncomfortable with what was going on. He was being forced to discuss something he didn't even want to think about, never mind talk about, but the pressure was slowly building and getting to him.

"For God's sake -- can you not see the position you're putting me in? I'm not part of any organization, I'm just a private contractor earning a few extra quid by picking something up on the side, and making the odd delivery that doesn't show on the books. I don't need any of this shit."

Jack was busy trying to figure out why the IRA would choose someone of Barratt's lowly status to smuggle contraband for them. To his way of thinking none of it added up, and was completely alien to their normal method of operation.

"Tell me about this consignment you collected when you were rerouted -- what exactly was it?"

Barratt had his face buried in his hands, but he dropped them away and looked up.

"How the hell would I know? I never laid a bloody finger on it -- it was loaded on my truck during a routine halt and taken off again at the other end outside Dublin."

The more he engaged with Barratt the more convinced Jack became that the guy was telling the truth, at least the truth as he knew it. He sounded far too convincing to be lying, although he had it in mind that the Scot must have at least set eyes on the mysterious package.

"You did see this consignment at some time or other though didn't you? So just describe it to me" The one question that kept going round and round in Jack's head was why the IRA would use a complete outsider to do their smuggling for them? It was so totally out of character; even Jack knew that, and Barratt certainly had him convinced that he was an outsider.

"It was just a big package, probably weighing about a hundred kilos or so. It was wrapped in thick hessian with clear polythene on top to keep out the damp." His brow knit as he thought about it. "What's the difference anyway?" he asked, then added as an afterthought. "I don't question what the boys tell me to do, I just get on with it, like any sensible person would."

His facial expression suggested he had already said more than he wanted to, but Jack was having serious doubts about what he was hearing as none of it made sense. In fact he was quite perplexed by it all, and decided to air his thoughts to the Scotsman. "I have a feeling you're being conned," he suggested, chewing on his bottom lip as he thought about what to say next. "I would bet my last dollar it was drugs you were transporting, and I'm pretty certain the IRA would never use someone like you to do that for them."

He scratched his head in puzzlement.

"What on earth gave you the idea that you were working for the IRA?" His suspicions were leading him down a specific route and he felt he was just beginning to make sense of things. It was purely guesswork of course, but an educated guess nevertheless, and if he was right then Devlin had been taking a mighty big risk by operating as an independent -- independent of his lords and masters in the IRA that is.

"Well," Barratt drew the word out slowly, "Joe never actually said it was the IRA -- not in so many words, but he was always talking about the boys and what the consequences would be if I ever let them down. What the hell would you take that to mean with his background?" He had uncertainty written all over his face as he endeavoured to explain himself, and against his better judgment Jack found himself having some sympathy for the guy, especially if his theory stood up. Because if he was right then it meant that Devlin had worked a rather crafty sting on the Scotsman, and with all he had found out recently, that particular theory made much more sense than any other.

"Where did this package eventually end up?" he asked Barratt.

"How the hell would I know? I just parked up in a pub car park like I was told and went for something to eat. I presumed the package would be gone when I got back. I didn't even look at the bloody thing after it was loaded, I simply follow instructions." Barratt continued to find the conversation unnerving, and it was starting to show in the guise of a fidgety edginess as without warning that he leapt to his feet, causing unnecessary alarm for Jack in the process.

"Have you nothing stronger than this crap?" he asked, waving his coffee cup at arm's length. "I really could use a stiff drink right now."

Jack seized on the opportunity, hoping that a drink or two might loosen his tongue even more.

"Follow me," he said, leading the way to his own office, where a quick rummage in his desk drawer uncovered a bottle of whiskey. Grabbing a couple of glasses from a wall cabinet behind his desk he set about pouring a couple of good measures.

"Here," he said, "this should help settle your nerves."

Shoving the glass into Barratt's eager hand he watched him down the half of it in one gulp before he was ready to take up the conversation again.

"You don't believe the IRA is behind Devlin, do you?" He made no attempt to disguise the relief in his voice.

"I just can't see it," Jack agreed. "They would never let someone like you know what they were up to, and from where I'm sitting you should think yourself damned lucky that they don't."

"I'll drink to that," Barratt whimpered, downing the remnants from his glass. "I could use the other half if that's alright?" Without waiting for a reply he lifted the bottle and recharged his glass.

"I think you've told me just about everything I need to know." Jack told him. "But you really ought to take my advice and get the hell away from here and not come back for a while. I'll find out soon enough if the

IRA is involved in this mess."

He looked directly at Barratt in a meaningful way.

"I actually believe you when you say you had no part in Byrne's disappearance, and quite honestly that's all I am interested in. But setting that aside, you will have to take your own chances with the RUC if they come looking for you -- if it helps I will try and put a word in on your behalf."

He had no particular liking for Barratt, or any of his type, but he could see how easily he might be exploited by someone like Devlin, someone with enough insider knowledge and connections to make a story stick. But that was Barratt's problem, not his, although what he had learned as a result of their conversation had put an altogether different perspective on things.

"I suggest you finish that drink and get the hell out of here," he told the Scotsman, who readily tipped the remnants of his glass down his throat and made a beeline for the door.

As soon as he'd gone through the door Jack reached for the phone, with Barratt no longer topping his list of priorities other more meaningful things had to be done.

Father Joseph's response to Jack's call was almost instantaneous.

"It's Jack Brennan here, Father," he warned him. "I could do another chat if you can fit me in sometime soon."

The uneasy lull that ensued seemed to drag on forever as the cleric awarded more time than was necessary or deserving of such a simple request.

"If you really consider it to be important, Mr. Brennan I suppose I shall have to fit you in." The stony silence came back into play, although marginally less prolonged this time.

"But I really do hope this is not going to become a habit." There was an unmistakable lack of interest in his voice, which in the circumstances was probably natural enough. It was obvious that he was only agreeing to another meeting out of sufferance, or curiosity perhaps

"That's very generous of you, Father. I'll see you straight after morning Mass tomorrow if that's okay?"

"Agreed, Mr. Brennan, it so happens I have some free time round about then. Goodbye for now."

Jack dropped the phone on its cradle and headed for the door, setting the office alarm as he left the building.

He was feeling quite upbeat as he walked out to his car, his mind entertaining the happy thought that he had achieved an unexpectedly successful afternoon. For the first time since he had taken on the case he could feel some momentum building. There was a down side as well however, because the plan he was currently formulating in his mind, whilst a courageous one, involved a great deal of personal risk.

21

Nothing in the room appeared to have been changed since Jack's last visit; not noticeably anyway. Even the garish and oversized cushions appeared to be in exactly the same regimented formation as before, indicating the attendance of a housekeeper who was undoubtedly something of a perfectionist.

"Good of you to see me again at such short notice, Father." Jack began, with over stated gratitude as he sought to gauge from the priest's expression what sort of reception he might expect. It proved to be a forlorn effort because he was none the wiser in the end as the priest's pale grey eyes gave nothing away, prompting Jack to wonder if he was a regular poker player.

"To be perfectly honest, Mr. Brennan, I'm only seeing you to quell my own rampant curiosity." He was informally dressed in a pair of grey, light-weight slacks with a crew necked sweater and canvas loafers. Having been pottering about the garden when Jack arrived he had downed tools instantly to greet him.

"The good Lord has given me a day off for good behaviour," he joked, giggling a trifle girlishly at his own sense of humour. "But what is it you think I can do to help you this time?" he asked. His voice more serious now, reinforcing Jack's belief that he chose his words very carefully and deliberately.

"I've been provided with some new information since we last met that had given our investigation a more focused line of enquiry.

The cleric's features remained determinedly impassive. He didn't appear over interested in anything Jack had to say, contrary to his admission about his 'rampant curiosity', or at least if he was he was keeping it well under wraps. His reaction, or lack of it, caused Jack a little concern, leaving him unsure how best explain himself without raising too much alarm.

"It's not so much what you can do for me, Father -- more a case of what you can get others to do."

Jack's uninspiring explanation drew a cool reception from his host, who cocked a quizzical eyebrow at him, followed almost immediately by a look of outright suspicion.

"I think you had better explain yourself in more detail," he suggested, easing into the first available chair, while indicating with a casual flick of the hand that Jack do the same.

"You have a certain well known individual within your parish that I need to meet up with rather urgently, and quite honestly if I don't have someone of your good standing to act as go-between then it is unlikely that it's ever going to happen." He kept a steady eye on the priest as he lowered himself into the chair. "And as I'm sure you might have already guessed, I'm here to persuade you to arrange that meeting for me."

Father Joseph studied his visitor much more intently.

"And who exactly is this mysterious person who has no wish to meet with you?" he asked solemnly. "Does this reticent individual have a name?"

"He undoubtedly does, Father, but I'm afraid I have no knowledge of it," Jack admitted, creating even more confusion in the process.

The mocking expression that greeted his response had him wishing that he'd put his request more succinctly.

"You must lead a very complicated existence, Mr. Brennan -- most certainly a very confusing one. How on earth do you propose that I arrange a meeting for you with someone you are unable to identify?" The mocking expression vanished just as quickly as it had arrived, replaced by one of mischievous amusement as he looked to his visitor for clarification.

"It's someone you will know by reputation, Father. Someone you can get a message to on my behalf."

Father Joseph stared at him like he had lost all sense of reason.

"I want you to arrange a meeting for me with the commander of the local IRA unit." The cleric almost fell out of his chair. He hadn't expected anything of this nature when he had asked the question. Standing up he strode rather purposefully towards the door. "I think you had better leave, Mr. Brennan. I wish to have no further part in this conversation." His brusque tone underlined a decisive finality in his words.

It was obvious to Jack that he had broached the subject much too quickly, too abruptly, but he remained in his seat refusing to give up, almost daring the priest to leave the room without him. "Please hear me out, Father," he pleaded, a little anxiously. "This is not what you think, and if you give me a couple of minutes to explain perhaps you might want to reconsider." It was a last ditch attempt to explain his proposition. His host stopped in mid stride and swung round to face him, his blank expression giving no clue to his inner thoughts.

"How on earth are you going to convince me that I should consider such an outrageous request?"

Jack clasped his hands under his chin, prayer like, pleading for the priest to hear him out. "Just give me a moment to try and convince you. I explained to you earlier that we're following a more definite line of enquiry now."

He looked up at the priest towering over him. "We have enough evidence to convince us that one of your parishioners, a guy by the name of Joe Devlin, was involved in Byrne's disappearance. We also know he has a loose connection with the local IRA unit, although I believe his involvement in the Byrne case has absolutely nothing to do with the IRA. If I am right about this, then you can bet your bottom dollar that the IRA won't take kindly to any attention Devlin inadvertently brings their way. They might just consider it to be in their interest to help me prove my theory, after all doesn't everyone want this fragile attempt to secure a peace agreement to get under way and succeed?"

The priest's facial expression softened a little, and it could well have been reflecting nothing more than a moment of perverse curiosity, had it not been for the challenging glint lurking behind his pale grey eyes.

"I am indeed familiar with this man Devlin that you speak of, in fact he lives no more than a stone's throw from here," he said, looking seriously thoughtful. "But having told me on the one hand that he is a member of the IRA, and that he is involved in Byrne's disappearance, you then go on to say that you don't believe the IRA are involved. I think perhaps you should explain the rationale behind this insane and contradictory observation, because right now you have me totally confused."

Jack felt more at ease now that he had triggered a show of interest in the priest, but his interest appeared short lived when he suddenly turned away and glided off in the direction of the drinks cabinet. "May I get you something, Mr. Brennan?" he asked, with boring politeness.

"A large whiskey wouldn't go amiss." Jack admitted, thankful for a little respite and the chance to rearm himself for his next bout of verbal jousting.

He was finding Father Joseph much too pedantic for his liking, the man seemed intent on analysing every single word that was put to him, and even Jack's limited knowledge of the guy had established that given half a chance he would choose to put his own interpretation on everything he was told.

Having armed Jack with his drink the priest planted himself back in his chair, wriggling with undue necessity against the floral cushions to make himself comfortable. "The floor is all yours, Mr. Brennan," he invited, with an elaborate flourish of his arm.

Sensing that this was probably his last chance to get the priest on board Jack was in no hurry to rush things and get it wrong. To allow himself a little breathing space he took a lingering sip from his drink while viewing the priest over the rim of his glass

"Rightly or wrongly, I'm assuming that you want the mystery of Byrne's disappearance cleared up as much as I do, Father?"

His intentionally meaningful snipe brought no reaction from the priest, who remained annoyingly impassive. He took another sip from his glass to let the message sink in. "We have uncovered a link between this guy Devlin and the driver of a truck that was parked at the exact spot where Tony Byrne was last seen. We also have Devlin and this other driver linked to an aid convoy that took Tony Byrne to Romania. To my reckoning this gives us a scenario that defies simple coincidence, in fact this aid convoy is the one common denominator linking all three men." He was looking for some feedback from his host, something to indicate a willingness to get involved, but he just fiddled with his glass and remained obstinately immune. His attention disturbingly focused on the wall directly behind Jack's head, as if that was of more interest to him. One thing he wasn't doing was showing any inclination to get involved, and even went as far as to say so.

"What you appear to have uncovered, if indeed that is the correct terminology, would seem to me to be nothing more than a simple coincidence, and one you appear particularly eager to deny. The fact that three innocent people offer their services in a simple act of charity provides little motive for one of them to disappear." Jack was tempted to go across and shake the guy by the throat, he had known from the outset that it wouldn't be easy to bring him on board, but even allowing for that his patience was wearing a bit thin.

Nevertheless, he was still left with the problem of finding a way to prove, one way or the other, that there was real substance to his theory.

There was nobody else he could trust to act as a go-between with the IRA. Whether or not they would agree to such a meeting was another matter altogether, and not the issue at hand. Right now he needed to gain the priest's confidence without divulging too much information along the way. It would be ill advised to disclose more than was absolutely necessary before securing some form of binding agreement from him.

"Without labouring the point, Father, I have enough evidence to convince me that Devlin was up to something sinister when he got involved with this charity. I'm just as certain that Tony Byrne somehow got wind of it and paid the heavy price for doing so. There was another individual involved in this who believed he was under threat from the IRA if he didn't carry out Devlin's instructions. In fact he was actually convinced that he was working directly for the IRA and not Joe Devlin, a belief that I consider to be extremely unlikely."

Father Joseph stroked his non-existent beard continuously as Jack worked to convince him. His eyes were tightly shut now and looked, on the face of it anyway, to be deep in thought, but his body language, and the way he shifted about in his seat when Jack stopped talking indicated that he remained unconvinced by anything he was being told.

"You seem pretty well convinced that the IRA are not involved in any of this, but for the life of me I don't see how you can make such an assumption. Perhaps you would take a little more time to enlighten me."

He seemed blatantly intent on missing the whole point of Jack's argument, although in fairness to him he was at least still open to argument.

"Whatever went on under the guise of that aid convoy was important enough to get Tony Byrne - - -" Jack stopped short of uttering the one word that came all too readily to mind. "Let us just say removed for now, shall we."

His thoughtful sensitivity was rewarded with a wry smile, which wasn't a lot of recompense for what he believed had been a very patient approach, although he perceived it as a possible indication of a breakthrough in winning the cleric over.

"One thing I'm sure of," he explained, "if what was going on out in Romania was so sinister that it brought about Tony's disappearance, and if the IRA were involved, they would never entrust such an important overseas operation to a complete outsider, which is what we are being asked to believe."

His attempt to lock eyes with Father Joseph in a show of determination failed as the priest was miles away, staring off into space, an inexcusable habit that Jack found more than a little irritating. Although when he returned from his mental meanderings Jack detected a slight change in his attitude.

"I have to say that I'm beginning to understand your rationale, Mr. Brennan. I can even see where you're coming from with this, and I suppose if I'm honest I must acknowledge that if the substance of your story is accurate, then I might be inclined to make exactly the same assumption as your good self. Regarding the IRA's involvement that is," he added quickly.

Rising from his chair he brushed aimlessly at the front of his sweater, as if to dislodge something that was not at all evident to the naked eye. Then turning to Jack he took the empty glass from his hand and made another visit to the sideboard, looking hunched and intense as he poured the drinks. A clear sign that he was toiling with some inner moral restraint, certainly not a sign that he was about to volunteer his services.

"I'm actually offering the IRA a chance to clear their name on this one," Jack told him, "because when this whole shebang comes out into the open, which it eventually will, it could well be seen as a breach of the cease fire by some observers and jeopardize the whole peace agreement, especially if the IRA are assumed to be the culprits. All I'm asking is that you get that message across to them and ask them to agree to meet with me. They can name the time and place, I'm sure they wouldn't have it any other way anyway, and I know I have to accept that."

Father Joseph cocked an eyebrow at him, suspicious of his motives.

"Why are you so interested in the IRA's reputation?" he asked.

Jack grinned innocently. "I'm not, but if they do confirm that Devlin has been working as a freelance on this scam he's running, then I'm hoping they won't stand in the way of my investigation." He screwed his face up at what he was about to say next.

"I don't relish the thought of looking over my shoulder at every twist and turn because of some loose connection both parties might have. You know as well as I do what the implications would be if a situation like that were allowed to develop."

He waited for some sort of response from his host, but was taken a little by surprise when Father Joseph, instead of doing so, simply motioned for him to carry on.

"All I'm trying to do is track down what remains of Tony Byrne and let his wife put her grief behind her. She deserves to have her life back on track, but her loyalty and devotion to her husband won't allow her to do that until she knows for certain what has happened to him. The only thing she's married to at the moment is a piece of paper and a few happy memories. That's no way to live out the rest of her life."

Father Joseph passed him his recharged glass and reclaimed his seat opposite him, balancing his glass on the arm of his chair without drinking from it.

"You hand me quite a dilemma, young man. For all I know this whole thing could blow up in my face if I was to accommodate your request. It's certainly not beyond the bounds of imagination to consider that your theory could be completely misjudged."

Raising his glass he fidgeted uneasily with it. "It goes without saying

Roisin Byrne is the most important factor in all this, and I sincerely want her to enjoy peace of mind. Probably more than you will ever understand -- and incidentally -- I do actually believe your sincerity -- much to my surprise. I even respect your very courageous tactics. Nevertheless, what you ask of me could have consequences far beyond what you or I may perceive at this moment in time. Officially, I should take advice from above on matters of this importance before reaching any decision."

He spotted the quizzical look on Jack's face and smiled cheekily. "No -- I don't mean from up there." He cast his eyes skywards in appreciation of Jack's confusion. "I mean from my Bishop." He grinned at the humour in the situation. "Although I will need all the help I can get from Him as well."

Jack felt a little twinge of excitement. Was this was to be the defining moment he asked himself? If it was he wanted to have it confirmed. "I'll take it that's a yes then."

Father Joseph stretched his legs in front of him and took a deep breath.

"It's a yes that I'll try, but you must understand that I'm moving into unknown territory here, so don't go fooling yourself into thinking that what you ask will be easy to accomplish, or will be accomplished at all." Downing what was left of his drink he stood up to place his empty glass on the fireplace.

Jack did the same; he knew the priest was finished with him. Pulling a card from his wallet he handed it to him. "Someone will need that number if they are to make contact." He paused for a second or two. "If we are successful in this, then for obvious reasons I would appreciate it if you would be in attendance during the meeting."

"If it happens at all, you may be absolutely certain that I will not be the one dictating the terms. You can almost certainly rely upon that."

Having said all he needed to say he headed for the door, letting Jack know, that for the time being at least, there was nothing more to be said.

They exchanged handshakes at the door and Jack made one last plea before taking his leave.

"You might have a word with Him up there, Father." He looked to the heavens, "maybe He can give us both a little help."

"Have a word yourself, Mr Brennan -- why don't you?" There was a caring sincerity in his voice. "It might surprise you just how much help that can be."

Jack gave him a weak grin and turned away.

As he caught sight of the holy residence fading in his rear view mirror the full implication of what he was entering into descended over him like a dark cloud. For the first time since he had conceived the idea of talking to the IRA he realized that his theory was founded on very little substantial evidence, and there could be serious consequences if it turned out to be a misjudgement.

"You'll be one sorry bastard if you are wrong Brennan," he told himself, although he brushed the thought aside quickly enough, knowing his decision was made and he would have to live with it. In any case, the information Barratt had provided him with had convinced him that Devlin was dealing in drugs, and was in all probability freelancing. Whatever he was up to, it was unlikely he was running munitions, because the package described by Barratt wasn't big enough for that. But he would clearly need to be more circumspect in his dealings with Devlin's mob in the future. Their connections within the IRA, and the criminal underworld they were connected with, meant he needed to be careful not to end up as the meat in a very appetizing sandwich.

22

Years of military training had honed Jack's powers of observation to a level where it was more than just a skill; it was a valuable asset; it provided the ability, even when intensely focused, to maintain an objective overview, a broader perspective than most people were capable of. Right now his attention was focused on the road ahead as he made his way home. The traffic was light and he was enjoying the accompanying music coming from the car radio.

The brown Mazda 626 following in his wake didn't go unnoticed as it was maintaining a steady thirty yards distance behind him, and as a matter of practiced routine he memorized the registration number. However the tinted privacy glass windscreen made it impossible to see anything of its occupants, nevertheless the fact remained that the same vehicle was stuck in his rear view mirror for longer than it might have been and raised his suspicions, forcing him to veer off his normal route and make a quick diversion before re-joining his route again. It was unlikely that anyone else would have cause to make such a diversion, unless they were forced to, and he was alarmed to see that the Mazda was still there when he got back to the main road.

Having repeated the routine a second time in order to dispel any lingering doubts, he experienced a genuine sense of relief that the Mazda was nowhere to be seen, nevertheless the seeds of suspicion had been sewn and remained at the forefront of his mind.

As it turned out he saw nothing of the other car for the remainder of his journey, although there was no denying the experience had given him a touch of the jitters and had compelled him to get a move on. He floored the accelerator heavily and was thrust back into the seat as the Jaguar lurched forward in response.

Two questions occupied his mind as a result of what had happened, firstly, who was it that had been following him, and secondly, what was the purpose behind it? Neither question would resolve itself easily for him, and the more he dwelt on it the more convinced he was that it was probably Devlin or one of his cronies, and although he had no reason to completely write off the IRA's involvement, on the balance of probability he came down on the side of Devlin.

If the experience did nothing else it awakened him to the fact that he needed to tighten up on their personnel security and ensure that his personal protection weapon was close at hand at all times. His own security was less of a problem than Judy's, as years of experience with the SAS had taught him to adjust readily to such situations. Indeed his former military service was the reason why he'd been granted a personal protection weapon in the first place -- but Judy was a different proposition altogether. For while she had strong family connections with the RUC through her father, and consequently a sprinkling of knowledge of the basic requirements, she would still need advice on how to vary her routines and her journey plans and other minor but essential precautions that Jack deemed essential.

Convincing her to accept such changes was a separate issue altogether as it was unlikely she would take kindly to having her personal liberty curtailed. A worrying thought that became a reality all too quickly when he got home and explained the events of the afternoon. Although it turned out that his played-down explanation was an open invitation for her to throw an almighty tantrum. And after an initial verbal outburst that could only be described as an indoor hurricane, she wheeled away and bolted from the room.

When she eventually returned, having considered all of the implications, she squared up to him with her arms folded across her chest looking like she meant business.

"This is all down to your thoughtless bloody attack on Devlin -- you do know that don't you?"

Jack didn't even bother defending himself, he knew better than most that with the mood she was in it would only prolong whatever misery she had in store for him.

"Okay," he conceded, "I hold my hands up to that, but we can't alter what has already taken place." Edging closer to her he clasped his arms round her waist and drew her to him.

"We have to deal with the situation as it is right now, at this moment in time, not dwell on the past, so you see, sweetheart, one way or the other you are going to heed my advice. You might as well make it as painless as possible, because it does neither of us any good to go tossing accusations about."

He inched back slightly to look at her. "I just want to ensure that we don't take any unnecessary risks, that's all."

He gave her his best Sunday smile in an effort to smooth the waters.

"Anyway, it's only precautionary really as nobody has actually threatened to do anything. But I think it's better to be cautious now, rather than sorry later -- don't you agree?"

He drew her to him again and planted a lingering kiss in the hollow of her neck, holding her like that until she eventually caved in and relaxed her body into his. When she eventually opened her mouth to speak her voice was weak and had a noticeable tremor, but at least there were no more accusations.

"Look how difficult this case has been already, Jack. Roisin Byrne has had to vacate her home, and now you and I might be under threat as well, what next -- what else is going to crawl out of the woodwork?"

What next indeed, Jack wondered, although he dared not voice his fears aloud.

"Come on, Judy," he urged, "lighten up a bit -- we're being paid to find out what happened to Tony Byrne, and maybe I'm the only one thinks so, but I actually believe we're getting a bit closer to achieving that, and that has to be our main focus – it's what we do after all – is it not?"

He looked her straight in the eye.

"If you're feeling so uneasy about the way things are going why not go and stay with your folks for a while. I can handle things here without too much difficulty, and it would put my mind at rest if you were under your father's wing, in the short term at least, he knows exactly what's needed to keep you out of mischief.

Judy's father was a retired police inspector; one of the old school who had the right credentials to know how to keep her out of harm's way, although deep down Jack doubted that she would agree to his suggestion, and as it turned out he was right on the money as her immediate reaction was to pull away from his embrace and put on her stubborn face.

"Some partner I would be if I ducked out every time the going got a bit tough." She threw her head back defiantly. "I came in to this partnership and this relationship with my eyes wide open. I knew back then we would have to take the occasional risk, and I'm not going to chicken out on you now -- no way Jose -- we'll see this through together."

She backed further away from him.

"I'm about to start dinner, we can discuss whatever it is you have in mind after we have eaten. You can make yourself useful by getting me a drink." Leaving him floundering in the middle of the room she took herself off to the kitchen.

Having anticipated much more opposition from her Jack felt he had got off rather lightly, although it was pretty clear, even to him, that his partner needed her own space for a while. She just needed time on her own to think things through and reflect on the issue at hand. That was mostly how she coped with personal issues when they came at her unexpectedly, it was an essential part of her make-up, part of her core-self, stubborn and single minded to the bitter end.

Okay, so she would probably give him the cold shoulder for a few days, but he saw that as a small price to pay if she consented to take his advice.

Without even thinking about what he was doing he turned to the sideboard and poured a couple of drinks, one he set on the corner of the coffee table to await Judy's return, and the other he took with him as he dropped into his chair by the window. There was a lot of sorting out to do, and he needed to get his thoughts in order if he was going to achieve a favourable result.

Dinner that evening was a muted, slightly tetchy affair, at least it was until the phone rang and breached the uneasy silence. Jack reacted the quicker of the two and scurried across the room to answer it, and being in no mood for social niceties his greeting was somewhat less than cordial.

"Brennan," he snapped, uninvitingly.

"Well now, don't you sound pissed off." Dave Jackson had cottoned on to his mood right away, leaving Jack to blurt out a hurried apology.

"Sorry Dave," he said, "you can mark this one down to domestic harassment." He had been totally wrapped up in his own thoughts prior to the call coming in and was intrigued to know why the young detective was phoning him. "I'm more interested in what has brought you to the phone."

"Nothing special, Jack. I just wanted an update on how the Byrne woman is coping with life over in the big smoke?"

"That's very thoughtful of you, but from what I'm told she's doing fine. I haven't actually spoken to her personally mind you but I'm reliably informed that she's coping really well. To be perfectly honest I've got more pressing matters on my mind right now." He had already taken the decision to come clean and tell Jackson all about the afternoon's events.

"Someone has taken an unhealthy interest in my rear bumper." He stretched the phone cable as far as it would go and reached out for Judy's untouched whiskey that was still sitting where he'd left it. Raising it to his lips he took a good mouthful as he waited for Jackson to come back to him.

It took the younger man some time to decipher what Jack was on about, although once it struck a chord he wasted no time in chasing the matter up.

"Did you get the registration, Jack?" The whole evening had been such a misery that Jack hadn't even thought to seek Jackson's help in tracing the Mazda.

"Sorry, Dave, I'm not even thinking straight at the minute, I should have been on to you straight away." Drawing out his little pocket notebook he recited the details down the line.

"How long before you think you might have something?" he asked.

"Shouldn't be more than a few minutes, I'll ring you straight back."

Jack took himself back to the dinner table not knowing exactly what to expect, and was surprised to learn that Judy's silent treatment had finally run its course.

"I take it from what I just heard that our friendly policeman is checking that car out for you."

Her tone had lightened noticeably and was a lot more upbeat than it had been, confirming Jack's theory that she could cope with most problems if she gave herself enough time out to think them through.

"In a word -- yes -- he reckons it should only take a few minutes. They only have to press a button these days and they get straight through to the Central Vehicle Register."

Judy leaned across the table to get closer to him.

"If it does turn out to be the IRA who followed you I want this case dropped immediately, no quibbling, no disputes, just bloody dropped." She shoved her plate of partially eaten food to one side and stood up, determined to make him listen to what she wanted to say.

"We don't need this kind of hassle, Jack. We simply haven't the resources to deal with it. It would mean watching our backs every minute of every day and I don't think I could put up with that." Her voice carried a certain finality that left no room for misunderstanding, and the problem was that Jack knew her fears were justified, and if he was totally honest about it, a true reflection of their situation.

He was thankful now that he hadn't divulged the whole truth about his meeting with Barratt. God knows, she was edgy enough without knowing everything about it. He dreaded to think what her reaction would be if she ever found out he was planning a meeting with the IRA, especially if she got wind of it before the meeting actually took place. One thing was very certain; he wasn't going to be the one to enlighten her -- not in this lifetime.

Slipping from his seat he rounded the table and draped an arm over her shoulder. "Look, sweetheart, whatever it is Devlin is up to I'm convinced he's just freelancing and none of this has anything whatever to do with the IRA. It would help if we just chewed things over for a while before jumping to conclusions. We need something more evidential to go on, and I'm sure if we bide our time we'll get it before too long."

It was a last ditch attempt to allay her fears, although he was less than hopeful that anything he said would succeed in doing that, but he had to keep trying.

"Barratt has me convinced that the IRA aren't involved and you are just going to have to trust my judgment on that."

He led her away from the table and through to the settee by the fire.

"You don't honestly believe I would deliberately put you in danger – now do you?" Gathering her in his arms he felt her body melt into his, and that was how they stayed, clinging and nuzzling each other like a couple of newlyweds. He was just about to kiss her on the neck when the phone rang and spoiled their precious moment. He made a hasty grab for it, hoping to hold on to the moment they were sharing. "Stop worrying -- okay." He mimed the words silently to her as he put the handset to his ear, not at all surprised to hear Dave Jackson's voice at the other end as he'd expected him to call back quite quickly.

"Thanks for being so prompt, Dave. What have you got for me?" The sound of a chair scraping on the floor came down the line as his caller seated himself before answering.

"Well, there's certainly enough to set you thinking, Jack. That Mazda you spoke of belongs to an out of town relative of Devlin's by the name of Towey -- Padraig Towey."

He sniggered loudly.

"He's nasty piece of work, Jack, with some serious form. I have a printout here of his recent CV and believe me it makes interesting reading."

Aware that Judy was inching her way closer to listen in Jack put the phone to his chest and gave her the thumbs up in the hope of reassuring her. When he got back to the conversation he had missed part of what had been said. "I'm sorry, Dave -- I missed that, can you give it to me again?"

Jackson groaned noisily.

"For God's sake, Jack, listen up. Now as I was saying, this guy Towey has been done on a number of occasions for armed robbery. He also has a string of convictions for assault and bodily harm – that sort of thing, although as far as I can see he doesn't have any paramilitary connections. Which I must say surprises me a little judging by the company he keeps." There was a rustling of papers being shuffled about at the other end and Jack wondered what was coming next.

"He's a bad pill, Jack -- a really bad pill. We know for a fact that he's involved in some serious racketeering, but the bastard always manages to avoid conviction by threatening the witnesses, he's just the sort of guy Devlin might call on for a little help after what you did to him."

The strained look on Jack's face eased a little. "Believe it or not, I'm actually relieved to hear that -- it supports my theory that it is just Devlin we're dealing with and not the IRA."

He glanced round to see if Judy was still listening, hoping his words were of some comfort to her, sadly, although she gave him a timid smile, they didn't have any noticeable effect and she continued to look underwhelmed.

"Well now." Jackson's voice carried a hint of warning. "I wouldn't necessarily side with you on that issue, Jack, for all we know they could well be involved."

Jack didn't comment; he wasn't about to argue the point in front of Judy, not when he had just got the makings of a smile out of her. "Anything else of interest that I should know about?" he asked.

"Well, I could go on all day about Towey, but what's the point, you know enough to be warned."

There were other conversations going on in the background that Jack couldn't quite make out, although it sounded as if some sort of panic was going on behind the scene. Jackson took it upon himself to enlighten him.

"Sorry to cut you short but I have to go now -- duty calls and all that, but let's keep in touch, and take my advice, mate, watch your back."

Jack replaced the handset like it was a precious object, slowly and carefully, ensuring Judy saw nothing of the apprehension he was feeling.

Jackson had given him plenty to think about, much of which Judy would never get to know about -- not for a while anyway. She had made every effort to eavesdrop the conversation but had heard nothing that gave her cause for concern. Now back on her feet she was about to go and clear away the dinner dishes when Jack intervened.

"Why don't you leave those for now, they're not going anywhere.

Come and sit down and have a drink while I explain what our friendly policeman was on about." His easy going, relaxed manner made it difficult for her to refuse, and in the end she relented and went over and to join him.

When they were both settled with a drink in hand Jack went into an elaborate, almost word for word explanation of what he had discussed with the young detective. Omitting the most important fact that the IRA might still be involved, even though that single thought was buzzing around inside his head like a bee in a bean can.

23

It's nearly always the case that when you're waiting for something important to happen, every day that it fails to materialize feels like a life sentence, and that was exactly how it was for Jack. Tied to his desk, playing catch up with the paper work he had been neglecting of late, helped take his mind off Father Joseph, for a short while at least, but all too quickly the tedium set in and he was driven to push his work to one side. He'd been at it nonstop for two solid hours and was in need of a break, more than that he needed to stretch his legs, and both issues brought him to his feet and away in search of a caffeine fix.

The endless waiting for something over the last couple of days had him feeling decidedly jittery and unsettled. It was impossible to concentrate on every-day matters with his mind constantly awash with thoughts of Father Joseph and what he was endeavouring to do. It would have helped no end to have been free to share his worries with Judy, but he couldn't do that, they were his and his alone, since none of his furtive arrangements with the priest had been discussed with anyone else, not least her.

The very notion that she might find out about his plan before the event took place filled him with a constant dread. But at least there had been no further episodes of the car following routine, which although welcome, puzzled him enough to give rise to other concerns. Like what Devlin might be up to? A thought that was worrying enough to make him reach under his jacket and touch the butt of his weapon for reassurance.

Having poured his coffee he began pacing aimlessly about the office with his mug in his hand, untouched, as he wrestled with what was next on his agenda. He was sorely tempted to ring Father Joseph and find out if he had made any headway but somehow held his eagerness in check, fearful that if he hassled the old boy too much it might make him change his mind altogether. And although his case was at a standstill, he rightly decided to stick with his original plan and do nothing until the priest got in touch with him.

Judy eyed his antics with suspicion as he wandered up and down in front of her work station, she was seriously concerned by his uneasy attitude.

"Why don't you get on with some bloody work?" she snapped irritably. "You're pacing about there like a demented bloody leprechaun?"

She shook her head in despair.

"Why are you hanging around in here anyway?" she asked. "Isn't there anything you can be getting on with to move this case forward? It seems to have come to a grinding halt, and quite honestly it's not like you to spend so much time in the office getting under my bloody feet. I find it rather disturbing to be perfectly honest."

She knew her man well enough to know that something was amiss, she just couldn't put a finger on it. Before his unwelcome intrusion she had been busy typing, a necessary but unnatural skill as far as she was concerned, hence the need to stop occasionally and work the tension from her neck and shoulders.

"I'm perfectly fine, sweetheart - honestly - I've just been putting the finishing touches to our statement of evidence on that divorce case that's up for a hearing next week, and you know how I hate that sort of thing, it's so bloody boring."

He did his best to sound genuine, but Judy swivelled her seat round to face him.

"You can cut the crap, Brennan, I know you too well to buy a sob story like that. You're definitely up to something, I can smell it, and it would make life an awful lot more bearable if you told me what it is instead of prancing about like an expectant father." Her eyes never left his face in her determination to find out what was on his mind. "Are you still worried about..." She was interrupted by the phone on her desk, but she still maintained her vigil on Jack's face as she reached out blindly and picked it up.

"Brennan Associates -- Judy speaking -- how may I help?"

The cheery look of recognition on her face said it was a familiar caller. "Certainly, Father, he's right here beside me. I'll put him on directly."

She hit the privacy button on the handset.

"It's Father Joseph. Do you want to take it here, or in your own office?" The very mention of the priest's name sent Jack scurrying through the adjoining door without answering, the apparatus on his desk flashing continuously when he got there. Snatching up the handset he listened until he heard Judy hang up before saying anything.

"Good morning, Father, I hope you're still in good health." There was little else he wanted to say to the priest, he was only interested in what the priest had to say to him.

"Thank you for asking, Mr. Brennan, I'm very well as it happens." There was a short pause after the greeting.

"I would consider it less than prudent to discuss confidential matters over the phone, so I'm afraid I must burden you with yet another visit to my place of abode. I believe that would be the most suitable venue in the circumstances."

The formal ring to the invitation caused Jack to question if it had been rehearsed.

"That's fine by me, Father."

He needed a bit more information, if he could get it.

"But tell me does this little get-together involve just the two of us or might there be a third party present?" It was inconceivable to him that a meeting with the IRA could have been arranged quite so easily, but he had no intention of walking into any situation that he was less than properly prepared for.

"Please don't be silly, Mr. Brennan. That's just romantic foolery. This afternoon would be most suitable for me, if that fits in with your itinerary."

Jack struggled to keep his laughter in check at the pretentious tone of the priest's voice. He sounded like a school master chastising a wayward child.

"It's just about lunch time now anyway, so how does two o'clock suit?" Jack was eager to have the meeting dispensed with as quickly as possible.

"That would suit me admirably. I shall expect you at about two o'clock then." The line went dead.

Had she bothered to indulge herself Judy could easily have listened in on their conversation, but even though she had been seriously tempted, if only to quell her rampant curiosity, it was not in her nature to do so. She was too up-front to do anything quite so underhand, but with her curiosity aroused she left her desk and made a beeline for Jack's office with a purposeful look about her. When she got there she was immediately struck by her partner's noticeable change of mood. He was poised on the edge of his desk looking pretty tense and wound up, but he was also displaying a familiar smugness that she had seen all too often in the past, usually in association with a major breakthrough in a case, or some sort of business coup. Right now it was enough to convince her that whatever Father Joseph had imparted to him, it was obviously something he had been eager to hear.

"Come on now, Jack, out with it, what's going on between you and that priest? And why are you looking so bloody smug, like the proverbial cat that got the cream?"

His wide eyed, innocent look denied her accusation.

"I haven't a clue what you're on about -- Father Joseph has a vested interest in this case and wishes to be kept up to date with our progress, Roisin Byrne is one of his parishioners after all. In any case he was only telling me a few things he had found out about our friend Devlin, but they merely confirm what we already know." He cringed at the thought of spinning her another lie; but he simply had to keep his plan covered up, even though he was having serious misgivings about it. But past errors were fresh enough in his memory to remind him of what life would be like if she found out. In the circumstances one little white lie was much the safer option.

Unfortunately he only had to look at Judy's face to see she hadn't fallen for his cover story. "Bloody nonsense, Brennan," she snapped. "Do you really expect me to believe that load of hogwash? I know you're up to something; I can see it written all over your face -- but if you insist on playing your little games then so be it."

Jack threw his head back in an outburst of forced laughter, it was the only thing he could think of doing to hide his guilty look.

"You really are a suspicious young madam," he teased. "You ought to have been a copper like your dad." He wasn't thinking properly or he would have known better than to raise that particular hare as his diversionary tactic backfired on him big time. Instead of pacifying her, all he did was open up an old wound and she wasted no time in reminding him of it.

"That was precisely what I had planned to do with my life. Or have you forgotten? It was you who colluded with my father to talk me out of it." She headed back to reception, accepting that there was nothing to be gained from further argument, although she wasn't about to go graciously.

"Are you buying me lunch or am I expected to eat bloody sandwiches at my work station today again?" she asked, determined to make him pay in some small way for keeping things from her. In the circumstances he was getting off lightly, and he knew it.

"Just tell me where you wish to eat, Madam, and I'm at your disposal," he quipped, with an exaggerated Sir Walter Raleigh sweep of his arm. Then spoiled any chance he had of gaining any reprieve by adding. "You had better be quick though – I have an appointment at two o'clock."

Judy threw her arms up in despair.

"How very thoughtful of you. So that's how it's to be -- we can have lunch together as long as I agree to eat at a pace dictated by you. Nice one, Brennan – well you can stuff it. I'll see to my own lunch thank you very much."

Spinning on her heel she bolted for the door.

"And you can see to your own dinner tonight as well."

Jack sat in stunned silence watching her leave, although his silence was probably good practice for what lay ahead that evening if she remained in her current mood.

24

The holy residence was beginning to take on a certain familiarity for Jack, and as he drew up alongside its imposing outer façade the gentle purr of his two and a half litre engine was masked by the noisy crunch of his car tires on the gravel driveway. A sound that alerted Father Joseph to his arrival and had him scurrying into view from round the side of the house and make his way to the front door, where he waited for Jack to join him. There was something about his posture that warned Jack he was in a sombre mood, although he smiled readily enough as he checked the time on his watch with an elaborate gesture.

"You're very punctual, Mr. Brennan, would that have anything to do with your military training?"

There was nothing accusative or cynical in the question, but it had a worrying effect on Jack, because it took him completely by surprise. Whether that was the intention or not he couldn't say.

Father Joseph made things easy for him with his follow up.

"We all have a past, Mr. Brennan, and I'm certainly not challenging yours, so please don't go into defensive mode on me. I'm simply alerting you to the fact that I am aware of yours -- although you might perhaps call it a career rather than a past I imagine. Either way, I am sure you were a perfectly good soldier, and since our dealings at the moment only concern you in your current capacity as a professional investigator it is of little consequence to me. I only choose to make you aware of it out of a simple act of courtesy because of what you have asked me to do on your behalf."

They were inside the house now and Jack was being led into the same room he had visited on both previous occasions.

"I'm not ashamed of my past, Father, why would I be? But I must admit to being a little surprised that you took it upon yourself to research my background."

When his admission failed to invite an answer he carried on.

"To be perfectly honest I'm even more surprised that you have the resources at hand to trace my background in such a short space of time." He was feeling a little unsure of his ground, even though there was nothing untoward in the priest's attitude. In fact he was politeness personified, but Jack was still a bit wary. After all he was in Northern Ireland, and although the main terrorist groups were on their way to signing up to the peace agreement they hadn't actually delivered on it yet, and there were many nationalists who were still very much at war with everything British. He had no way of knowing where the priest stood on that.

"You give way to self-flattery, Mr. Brennan, I can assure I took no such trouble." A wry smile played on his lips as he treaded the familiar route to the whiskey decanter. "Quite the contrary in fact, it was the very people you wish to meet with who provided me with the information on your background."

An icy shiver ran down Jack's spine that made his skin tingle like an adrenalin rush. The priest's unwelcome revelation unnerved him enough to make him feel very exposed and vulnerable, even here, within the sanctuary of the cleric's living quarters!

Father Joseph sensed the change in his guest right away. The uneasy silence, and the way Jack's eyes flitted about the room in search of any uninvited guests told him what he was thinking, but he carried on to the sideboard unhindered, pouring the drinks before turning round to face to his visitor again.

When he did so there was an odd, almost apologetic expression on his pale features. "I took the liberty of pouring you a large one as you look as if you could do with it." As he passed Jack en-route to his favourite chair he handed him his drink.

"Do take the weight off your feet," he invited, as he made himself comfortable.

A whole host of questions were stacking up in Jack's mind. Important questions, questions that needed answering in a hurry, but something warned him not to rush things. It might be more beneficial to bide his time and listen to what the priest had to say, especially as he appeared to be in a talkative mood.

"There appears to be bit of a problem here for both of us – a small matter of personal security, wouldn't you agree?" He combed his hair back with his hand. "Perhaps you can tell me how I can contemplate placing an ex-soldier in front of his sworn enemy?" He eyed Jack with a questioning look, his pale grey eyes unwavering. "You must surely see my dilemma?"

He held back for a little while before continuing to air his views.

"I have no doubt that your courage will see you through such an ordeal, but I have no such courage to call upon, only a Christian conscience. And while courage is a requirement of the momentary act, conscience remains imbedded in the soul forever."

He stretched his neck into the cushions behind him and stared up at the ornate ceiling above his head. When he resumed the conversation his head was still nestling against the back of the chair and his eyes were shut tight.

"What am I to do about my conscience?" he mused, the words slipping from his mouth in a hushed, self-questioning whisper.

A question that wasn't directed at Jack, and he knew it, he also knew that the priest's conscience was very much his own concern. That said, there was no denying that his concerns were born out of a genuine and understandable Christian attitude, however from where Jack was standing they were simply getting in the way of progress. A thought that convinced him they had arrived at a crucial moment and needed a renewed meeting of minds to get things moving again. As they were he wasn't entirely convinced that they would ever achieve it, but he had an inkling that neither of them would give up trying, and that was enough to spur him on.

"Your concern for my well-being almost has me convinced that the IRA has already agreed to a meeting."

A tired looking Father Joseph bolted upright in his seat. Having been immersed in his own private little world studying the intricately carved plaster ceiling above his head it suddenly ceased to hold the same magnetic attraction.

"My apologies, Mr. Brennan -- I assure you I wasn't asleep. I was actually contemplating our mutual dilemma." He got to his feet a little unsteadily and drifted over to the window, his ungainly gait providing a suspicion that perhaps he had already been visiting the drinks cabinet prior to Jack's arrival.

Whatever the cause, he looked decidedly jaded and off colour, although he was still quick witted enough to pick up on Jack's unvoiced criticism, and made a point of telling him so.

"No," he assured him, "contrary to that suspicious glint in your eye, I have not been over indulging of the amber liquid. My lack lustre appearance simply reflects the fact that I had precious little sleep last night toiling over what I should do about your request." He shrugged a solitary tired shoulder. "As you can see, I might just as well have slept soundly since I have in no way resolved the issue."

"Why don't you let me resolve it for you?" suggested Jack, ignoring the rather pointed rebuke. "Just tell me what the arrangements are for this meeting and let's get on with it."

"That would certainly be a simplified answer to your problem, but how do I overcome my concerns about your safety?" Searching Jack's face for an answer, he found nothing to make him feel any better. His own tired facial expression held on to an anguished look that aged him another few years.

For his part Jack gave him the only answer he could think of.

"I haven't a clue what arrangements you have made for this meeting, Father, but it would be really helpful if it were to take place here at your residence, if at all possible. I can't believe the IRA would be stupid enough to try anything while you are in attendance." His voice was gaining in pitch, underlining his growing frustration at the pace things were moving.

Father Joseph gave him a very curious look.

"Why is this so important that it drives you to take such a monumental risk," he asked. "Explain to me why it's so important?" Slumping back in his chair he looked every bit as frustrated as his guest.

"Because it's what I do, Father," Jack told him, "and because Roisin Byrne came to me for help and I agreed a contract with her. That contract makes me morally bound to do everything in my power to honour our agreement. Not only for the money, but because it's my duty to do so."

The priest gave a cynical smile.

"Ah yes – your duty -- I see it all now -- the soldier and his duty." Again there wasn't anything mocking in what he said, he was simply airing his thoughts aloud.

"Don't knock it, Father," Jack argued. "A soldier is merely a product of the society he comes from. His duty is what he performs to protect that society under the laws that it lays down. A nation votes in its decision makers, and it is they who determine the laws that govern his duties." He was building up a real head of steam and in danger of going overboard, but he caught himself on and decided to say nothing more in case he caused too much friction.

Father Joseph toyed with his glass.

"I can't argue with that, Mr. Brennan, and believe me, I more than most understand the constraints of duty." A short lapse in the conversation took over that allowed him to study Jack for a few moments, and when he chose to re-engage with him he had clearly made his decision.

"I'll not stand in the way of your duty, and I promise to do my utmost to arrange things so that both of us have some degree of protection, but it is only a wish, and one that I can't promise will be successful." He was back on his feet before Jack realized what he had just said. "I'll see you to the door, then I'm off to bed to catch up on some lost sleep." The merest ghost of a smile touched his lips, but it looked laboured and out of place, an indication that the burden of acting as a go between for such a perilous venture was putting a severe strain on his nerves, more of a strain than Jack had allowed for. He was just about to make mention of it when the priest raised his hands and warned him off. Realizing there was nothing more to be said he walked away without so much as a backward glance.

The idea of meeting with the IRA was fraught with danger. Not least in terms of Jack's personal safety, and that danger might well extend to those close to him as well, especially if his judgment on the matter wasn't as sound as he thought it was.

The risk factor was so glaringly obvious that it plagued him all the way down the Falls Road as he headed back into town. Yet no matter how much he toiled with it, the fact remained that he had convinced himself the IRA would stand by any commitment they made. He judged it inconceivable that they would do him any real harm with a man of the cloth involved, and surely not while they were on a negotiated cease fire as a prelude to a final peace agreement with the British Government. Experience had taught Jack that such meetings between sworn adversaries were anything but unique, especially when there was a common objective involved. Indeed they had even taken place with regular monotony between the IRA and the British Government throughout most of the IRA's current campaign.

The only fly in the ointment was the dreaded possibility that Devlin might not be freelancing. A niggling little doubt that was really quite scary when he thought about it, and one he was keen to put out of his mind, for now anyway. But pushing that thought to one side simply produced another much more serious issue to consider; that knowingly making contact with a subscribed terrorist organization was against the law. On the face of it that particular issue was a much more of a threat and couldn't be ignored quite as easily as the Devlin issue. But being stuck behind the wheel of his car allowed Jack plenty of time to dwell on it and brought the full implications of what he was attempting to do into perspective. Prompting him to realize that he had chosen a very uncertain and eventful career since leaving the army.

25

Instead of switching off and putting his feet up after their evening meal Jack found himself labouring over the realization that three whole days had drifted by without any word from Father Joseph. His irritating tetchiness was there for all to see as he snatched at his cell phone every time it rang in case he missed an important call. However, for one reason or another the call he was so eagerly waiting for never came, and as a consequence his over-active imagination was rummaging through everything and anything that could have gone wrong.

So deeply engrossed was he with the problem that he had only a vague awareness of Judy's voice in the background. Her attempted conversation being far enough removed from his conscious awareness to pass him by and disappear into the ether without earning a reaction.

"I might just as well talk to myself," she snapped, fully intent on dragging him away from his closeted isolation; even then it took him a while to switch on and get back to the real world.

"Sorry, sweetheart, I was miles away -- what did you just say?" he asked glibly.

"I'm wondering what I have to do to get some attention round here. You've hardly said a word to me all day." She was having great difficulty keeping her feelings in check, mainly because she suspected something was going on that her partner was keeping from her, and she was unwilling to tolerate his sulky behaviour any longer.

"If I've done something to upset you then for God's sake get it off your chest, because this sullen silence you have suddenly become addicted to is driving me round the bend."

Her words struck home with a vengeance and made Jack sit up and take notice.

"I'm sorry, sweetheart," he said with genuine regret, "It has nothing to do with you, believe me, it's just that I'm not making any headway with this Byrne case and it's really beginning to bug me." He rushed over and wrapped his arms round her, wondering to himself why he hadn't thought to do so more often.

"I tell you what," he said invitingly, shaking off his own miserable mood. "Why don't you go and get your coat and I'll take us out for a drink. I could certainly do with something to cheer me up." His big smile, and as he thought, unnecessarily gracious invitation got a decidedly frosty reception.

"For God's sake, Jack I'm not asking you to take me out -- I just want you to let me in." Having given way to her pent-up emotions Judy found herself close to tears, and determined as she was not to let it show, she buried her face in his shoulder out of sight. "Just because you were in the army doesn't mean you have to be mister macho man all the time and bottle everything up. You need to stop shutting yourself off from me like this. I'm your partner in life as well as your business partner -- or have you forgotten that?"

With her face buried in his lapel her words were muffled and weak, but Jack was sensitive to her mood and knew he had no one to blame but himself for the state she was in. All he could think to do to redeem himself was to gather her closer to him.

"I'm sorry, sweetheart, I know I can be a bit of an independent bugger at times, but it's not something I do intentionally. And I promise to cheer up and not let this case get under my skin anymore -- how's that?" He bent over and kissed the top of her head.

"Oh what's the use -- you'll never change, so why bother making promises you can't live up to?" Resigned to her lot she knew deep down that his momentary lapses were unintentional, but that didn't make them any less annoying. And when she thought about it more seriously she grudgingly accepted that her own emotional sensitivities might be part of the problem, although she would never openly admit to it.

She drew closer to him for the moment, then released him and stood back, having made her mind up to accept his invitation.

"Okay, Mr. Brennan," she said, half -jokingly, donning a comically aloof manner. "I accept your invitation to join you for drinks." The cheery note in her voice gave Jack's spirits a lift, but his expectations were somewhat in vain as her tone quickly took on a sterner note. "But only on the grounds that you leave your problems behind you and concentrate on me for a change."

She broke away and headed upstairs to get her coat, throwing one last challenge over her shoulder as she went. "And you can leave that bloody mobile phone behind as well."

Shaking his head in vain Jack pulled the phone from his pocket and placed it on the arm of the settee as Judy's voice came at him again from out in the hall.

"I'm ready when you are, Brennan, so shift yourself."

They got as far as the front door unhindered before the high pitched, attention seeking ring-tone of Jack's mobile phone screamed at them from the front room. They both stopped in mid stride like a couple of statues, rooted to the ground, staring at one another, Judy's angry expression forbidding any attempt to go and answer it. "Don't you bloody dare," she warned, unaware that he had no option but to get to it before the caller rang off. He'd been waiting for three days to hear from Father Joseph and he simply couldn't afford to miss a single call in case it was the one he been waiting for. He had to make himself available; there would be no second chance with the IRA, if they shouted he had to jump, that was the only way his plan would work. He knew they would give him no warning, no time to arrange any underhand trickery or ambush. More likely than not they would run him round a bit on a dummy run or two, so he would never be quite sure which call was the genuine one when it came along.

Right now his problems were more immediate; Judy was marking time out on the front step, openly cursing the ring tone that seemed to grow louder and more impatient in its demand for attention. The angry look on her face a further warning of her defiant mood, if one was needed.

"I'm sorry, sweetheart, I really am sorry," he grovelled, "but I simply can't ignore that." His voice was laden with regret, that sadly meant nothing to Judy as he turned from her and rushed indoors, praying his caller would let him get to the phone before ringing off.

"Brennan," he spluttered, conscious of Judy storming into the room behind him and throwing her bunched up coat over the back of the settee, livid with anger.

"Stuff you, Brennan," she snapped "I've had just about enough of this crap for one night. I'm off to bed." Her furious outburst completely drowning out what Jack's caller had said.

"I'm sorry, could you repeat that -- I was a bit distracted." His apology invited a very sympathetic clearing of the throat from the other end before his caller re-engaged with him.

"So it would seem, Mr. Brennan, so it would seem." Father Joseph's north Dublin accent was never more warmly received.

"Ah -- Father Joseph, it's great to hear from you," Jack enthused, with an enforced calmness, for although he tried to mask it there was a noticeable undertone of expectancy in his voice. "I hope you're the bearer of good news.

The cleric appeared reluctant to enlighten him, posing a question of his own instead. "Where exactly are you at this precise moment in time, Mr. Brennan?"

"I'm at home -- in Lisburn." Jack said hesitantly, the question taking him by surprise.

Another pause ensued, another irritating break that deprived him of what he wanted to hear, although it didn't stem from a lapse in conversation this time, but more obviously from a hand being placed over the mouthpiece. He suspected the priest had company, there was certainly an unnatural rhythm to his voice, indicating perhaps that he was being prompted in what to say?

"Are you alone at the moment, or are you in company?" Father Joseph's voice was flat and controlled, leading Jack to believe that his suspicions were right, the priest was almost certainly being dictated to.

"I'm entirely on my own, Father," he admitted, "so we are unlikely to be disturbed."

The priest made no reply, and Jack was left listening to a muffled conversation going on in the background. Then out of the blue came a rather rude awakening.

"Listen very carefully to what I have to say, Brennan, and don't open your mouth again until you're told to." The harsh Belfast accent sent a shiver up Jack's spine. He had no idea who this new voice belonged to, but the pronunciation had an authoritative air to it, and the heavy accent did nothing to hide the autocratic style of delivery. Clearly this was someone who expected his instructions to be carried out without challenge. Someone used to giving orders and having them obeyed, a cold and calculating terrorist no less.

"It's suffice to say that I would not be speaking with you now if we had not given due consideration to the request you put to us. You have laid certain-----" he hesitated for a moment, "unfounded accusations against a member of our organization that cannot be ignored, but you would do well to understand one thing, Brennan -- we take our responsibility to police the nationalist people of North Belfast very seriously. Which in turn requires us to protect them against all forms of anti-social behaviour, including injustices by officials of the state, or indeed crimes of self- interest."

He coughed lightly to clear his throat.

"You have made a very serious accusation against one of our volunteers that requires an investigation to determine its validity."

Jack detected the faintest rustling of paper in the background, alerting him to the fact that he was listening to a recital from a prepared script. It was enough to tell him that whoever it was on the other end of the line, he was unlikely to be the decision maker, which undoubtedly explained why he had been warned not to ask any questions.

"Our organisation has no desire, nor indeed any responsibility to help solve the riddle of this missing individual you appear to be concerned about. However, we do see some merit in this meeting you propose. Although any such meeting will only take place if you obey, absolutely and without question, all instructions as they are dictated to you by us."

There was more rustling of paper that again sounded like the turning of a loose page.

"You will make your way by taxi to the Carlisle Circus roundabout, and remain there at the junction of the Crumlin Road and the Antrim Road with your mobile phone switched on. You will be unaccompanied and unarmed, and you will get there at precisely eleven o'clock tonight and stay at that exact rendezvous point until someone contacts you."

The line died on him without warning.

Jack sat still for a few moments trying to assimilate what he had just heard. Then he tossed his phone aside and strode briskly across the room to the whiskey decanter. The hairs on the back of his neck were standing on end and his mind had gone completely blank out of sheer panic, his ability for rational thought having completely deserted him. When he eventually gathered his wits and tried to recall the instructions he had been given his mind remained a complete blank.

Pouring himself a large measure of whiskey he knocked it back as if it was his last, then with the decanter still in hand he poured a much needed refill and knocked that back as well; the alcohol hit home this time and the feeling of panic began to subside.

As the alcohol got to work and he became more relaxed the detail of his conversation came flooding back, almost word for word, like a stop and pause tape recording.

A worried glance at his watch told him he still had a couple of hours in hand before he needed to be on his way, if indeed he still minded to do so, because at that particular moment in time he was concerned that the whole charade might be nothing more than an elaborate set up. It was a given fact that he would be a prime kill for the IRA, if that was what they were intent upon. Taking out an ex-member of the British Special Forces without putting themselves in any danger would be a real feather in their cap, so there were obvious and frighteningly genuine reasons for his concern. Apart from Father Joseph no one else even knew what he was up to, so if he suddenly vanished into the ether, like Tony Byrne had done, no one would have a clue where to begin a search. He had always assumed, wrongly as it turned out, that any meeting would take place at Father Joseph's residence, but that idea had clearly been given a by-ball, which in turn upped the ante to a seriously critical level.

With so much to think about he looked anything but calm as he collapsed into a chair and drew temporary comfort from the amber liquid, trying as best he could to settle himself and take a more positive outlook. It was time to show his true mettle and not give in to the fearful thoughts that were beleaguering his current state of mind, otherwise he might as well abandon his plan altogether.

He needed to remain calm, think rationally, and do nothing in a panic.

There were things that needed doing out of necessity in case the whole thing went belly up, urgent and important things. Fortunately it was at times like this that his training stood him in good stead, and he headed for the sideboard in search of some writing materials.

Settling at the coffee table he began composing a letter to Judy, explaining in words of one syllable what he planned to do, and any information he believed might be of use to the police in the event that he didn't survive the night's activities. He had been warned not to carry a weapon, which tempted him to put together an escape kit that he could conceal within his clothing in case he was taken prisoner. But then on reflection he accepted that if the evening's activities were a trap, it would almost certainly be a death trap, and the IRA would likely follow their normal procedure and strip him naked before having their fun, in which case an escape kit would be worse than useless. It was a sobering thought that convinced him to run with his instincts as they rarely let him down. However it flashed through his mind that he was taking a monumental risk for a lousy two hundred quid a day Peace agreement or no peace agreement!

When he'd finished his letter to Judy he placed it inside the cover of his passport and returned it to its resting place in the bureau drawer, feeling safe in the knowledge that it would only be found if she needed to go through his personal effects, and that would only occur if things went belly up. After another sip from his glass he wrote her another note to cover up his immediate absence. All it said was that he had gone to see Father Joseph -- nothing more. This one however he left in a prominent position on the mantelpiece where he knew it wouldn't be missed, he then relaxed back in his chair and finished what was left of his drink.

26

As luck would have it the taxi he had ordered was late in arriving, and although the driver assured him they would be at Carlisle Circus before eleven o'clock it was an uneasy journey. But true to his word, and just ahead of schedule, he had Jack pacing up and down the footpath at the pre-arranged meeting place with time to spare. It was a depressingly wet night, and Jack scrutinized every approaching vehicle with nervous expectancy, but as his nervy vigil passed the hour mark he began to doubt that the meeting was going to take place. Then as midnight drew near and the pubs tossed their well-oiled customers out onto the street the pedestrian traffic increased noticeably. Coinciding with this sudden burst of people traffic Jack found himself the target of some challenging looks; his reason for loitering at the street corner in the pouring rain being viewed with suspicion, but that was only to be expected and he simply ignored it.

By half past twelve the area resembled a ghost town and was completely deserted. The sudden onslaught of people that had emptied from the pubs had dried up as if by magic, and after a further hour and a half of fruitless waiting Jack was convinced that the proposed meeting had been abandoned and decided it was time to grab a taxi and head home. Unfortunately he would have to make his way into the city centre on foot to get one as there was no sign of any cruising the area. The only thing to brighten his mood was that it had stopped raining.

Cutting across the main road he headed downhill in the direction of the city lights, feeling pissed off and angry at having been taken in so easily by the IRA. He guessed the whole charade had been nothing more than a test to check him out; an opportunity for them to ensure he obeyed instructions and turned up without a surveillance team in tow. Which he accepted would have been a sensible thing for them to do. Indeed there was a distinct possibility that he might have to endure a number of such dummy runs before they finally made live contact. One thing he was very sure of; if the IRA were genuine about having a meeting they would have been watching his every move from the moment he arrived at the proposed rendezvous. It was an unsettling thought that did nothing to ease his frustration, or his disappointment -- at least not until his phone rang and stopped him in his tracks. Diving into a shop doorway he almost dropped the phone in his panic to get at it.

"Brennan," he gasped, unable to conceal his nervousness.

"You were told to wait at Carlisle Circus, Brennan -- are you one of those soldiers who doesn't know how to obey orders?"

The voice was the same one he had listened to earlier in the evening, with the same autocratic and authoritative snappiness. Clearly its owner was enjoying his own little game.

Jack scanned the nearby buildings, fruitlessly trying to spot their observation post, but there were too many unlit, multi-storey blocks with nothing but darkness behind every window. It was almost impossible to see anything on a night like this, so he had no way of telling where they might be.

"I had just about given up -- I thought you must have called it------ ----" he was cut off before he got finished. "Get your sorry ass back up the street and wait there like you were told." The line died again without warning, just like the last time. Pulling his collar up against the driving rain that had come back to haunt him Jack headed back up the hill and across the roundabout to reclaim his little piece of territory.

In the circumstances there was little else he could do.

The next twenty minutes felt like an absolute eternity, but if Jack thought he was over the worst then he had better think again. The driving rain certainly made life uncomfortable, but there was worse to come when the street lights suddenly dimmed and went out altogether, leaving him more vulnerable and exposed than ever before.

By now there was hardly any traffic to be seen, and when the odd car did appear, or approach his position, the tension he was already harbouring increased significantly. Which was a senseless waste of energy because any traffic that came along passed by without giving him a second glance, leaving him anxiously waiting for the next one to appear.

It took a while before he spotted what he believed was the vehicle he'd been waiting for, and he could hardly have missed it in the circumstances. It was cruising down the road with its headlights on full beam at a speed little above walking pace. When it got within fifty yards or so of his position it came to a halt on the opposite side of the road and flashed its headlights twice in quick succession.

Jack waited for something else to happen, fully expecting it to move closer, or for someone to get out and approach him, but when neither happened he became confused and unsure what to do. As there was no movement from the car or its occupants that he could see, he decided to take matters into his own hands and crossed the road, making his way towards it with both hands by his sides and in full view.

He had only taken a few steps when the car suddenly lurched forward and raced up the road level with him. A couple of masked men leapt out, one from the front and other from the rear. Working like a couple of professionals they grabbed both of his arms and forced a black bag over his head, then dragged him up to the waiting car and bundled him into the back seat before climbing in after him, one either side. Before they even got the doors closed the car did a screeching U-turn and went tearing back up the road the way it had come.

After a minute or so of furious driving the driver eased his foot off the accelerator and slowed to a more moderate speed, one that he maintained for the remainder of the journey.

No one uttered a single word during the journey, but Jack could tell from the way he was tossed about that the driver was executing a number of unnecessary diversions in an effort to confuse his sense of direction. All he could do was count the seconds in his head and try to estimate how long they had been travelling, he worked it out at approximately eleven minutes before the car came to a halt. But he had absolutely no idea at all about the direction they had taken.

Once they had stopped he was quickly and efficiently bundled out and frog-marched a short distance over some level ground with an escort on each arm forcing the pace. After about twenty paces he was forced up a series of short flights of stairs, and from the echoing sound of their footsteps on the surface underfoot he surmised they must be in a tower block of some sort.

At the top of the fifth flight he was suddenly dragged to his right and allowed to stumble a few paces before being brought to an abrupt halt. Before he even had time to gather himself he was aware of the unmistakable sound of a door being opened; accompanied by a violent shove from behind that sent him sprawling inside, struggling to stay on his feet.

He had no idea where his captors had taken him, but wherever it was the heat inside the room was almost unbearable, and that, plus the discomfort of his dusty cloth hood, made him feel completely unbalanced and a little queasy, not unlike the sensation one might experience from vertigo.

Someone shoved him forward a few more steps before dragging a chair across the floor and forcing him into it. There was a flurry of movement behind him, which he presumed was his escort taking up a position by the door to prevent any attempted escape.

It was difficult to be precise, but from the noises he was picking up around him he surmised that there were at least three other people in the room -- then someone directly in front of him spoke -- and that made it four.

"Now then, ***Mister*** Brennan, I think it's about time you explained yourself." The word Mister, was stressed quite heavily, as though it was an unworthy title, but more importantly Jack knew straight away that he was listening to the same voice he had heard on the phone. It carried a middle class Belfast accent that strangely enough was easy on the ear, unthreatening, yet demanding a reply. Jack faltered for a moment then decided it was best to get straight to the point -- after all that was why he was here.

"You have a guy called Joe Devlin in your ranks who I believe is using his connection with your organisation to feather his own nest." With his vision blocked Jack waited in isolated silence for middle class Belfast to respond. When it failed to happen he decided he was probably meant to carry on.

"As Father Joseph no doubt explained, I've been hired to investigate the disappearance of one of his parishioners, a guy called Tony Byrne, and that, and absolutely nothing else, is the sole purpose behind me being here. It's important that you fully understand that, because I need you to believe me when I say there is absolutely no underhand motive in what I'm trying to do."

He paused and waited for a reply -- but once again he was to be disappointed, so once again he took it as an invitation to carry on. "My client is convinced that her husband is still alive, although to my reckoning if he hasn't turned up in three years I don't think he ever will, the problem is she won't accept that, so I have to keep on looking."

With his head stuck inside a dusty cloth bag his breathing was quite laboured and he had to pause occasionally to gather some saliva to stop his tongue sticking to the roof of his mouth. When he had generated enough saliva he continued with his explanation.

"Tony Byrne was heavily involved with your man Devlin in shifting aid out to Romania. On his last trip, just before his disappearance, the convoy was re-routed on its return journey so it could pick up an unscheduled consignment, possibly contraband of some sort, most likely drugs, but I'm not completely certain about that. Whatever it was -- it was something Byrne wasn't meant to be privy to, something he wasn't meant to know about."

The guy to his front cleared his throat and Jack heard a creaking noise as he dropped into a chair.

"I'm as certain as I can be that Byrne uncovered something he wasn't meant to and paid a heavy price for it. I'm just as positive that Devlin, or one of his Armagh sidekicks had him removed, although again I can't be sure what actually happened to him to cause his disappearance." Jack had no way of telling what impact his explanation was having, but he hadn't been interrupted thus far and he took that as a positive sign.

"I have no interest in bringing Devlin to justice, that's not within my remit. I simply want to find Tony Byrne's remains and return them to his wife for burial. But I'm not stupid enough to believe I can achieve a successful result if your organization chooses to make things difficult for me."

He stopped to run his tongue over his paper-dry lips.

"All I'm trying to do is return Tony Byrne's remains to his wife." There was nothing else he could say that would further his cause. He had said his piece, and although he felt some relief that he had managed to see it through, his mouth was bone dry and rivulets of sweat were pouring down his face beneath the dusty cloth hood. Even the musty smell of his own rain sodden clothes managed to creep inside the hood and attack his senses, adding to his discomfort.

With his nerves stretched to the limit the ensuing silence only served to make him realize that whatever his inquisitor said next would probably determine his fate, one way or the other. It was time to pray that his theory was correct, because if the IRA were involved in operating the smuggling racket then he was as good as dead. His judgment on such matters was about to be put to the test.

There was no obvious reason for the long lapse in the conversation, but it made for a seriously worrying few minutes for Jack, and in spite of his most determined effort he became fearful of the reason behind it. Indeed he was so disturbed by it that eventually that his nerve gave way and he was forced to bring it to an end himself.

"An organization that is about to sign up to the peace agreement can do without negative publicity, or having the finger of suspicion pointed at it, especially for what on the face of it appears to be a senseless and unnecessary criminal act."

Under the dusty hood his mouth was now so parched that he could hardly pronounce his words properly, his tongue as dry as blotting paper.

"It's very generous of you to consider our reputation, Mister Brennan." There was a very different reason for stressing the title 'Mister' this time around, it was meant to indicate something more than his civilian status.

"This is a very unusual situation for us both. However you are correct in your assumption that the IRA has nothing to do with drug running, if indeed that's what is involved here, although as yet you have done nothing to convince me that is the case. It is perhaps time you revealed exactly where this ridiculous theory comes from?"

The middle class accent was calm and unhurried, confident of being in control, while on the other hand Jack's nerves were fit to snap, and his resolve to keep calm was under severe pressure. It was only the fact that his captors were still engaging with him that kept his hope of surviving alive. He tried to moisten his lips before answering but his tongue was too dry to fulfil the task.

"I've had a long discussion with the driver who collected the goods for Devlin and he has assured me it was a regular event, not just a one off. More to the point, he was forced into it because Devlin threatened him with a visit from your people if he stepped out of line."

The temperature of the room, and the dusty atmosphere inside the cloth hood combined to make it seriously difficulty to keep talking. His dry, swollen tongue seemed to fill his mouth completely, and his parched lips stuck to his teeth whenever he tried to speak.

"I'm sorry," he stammered, exaggerating his distress, "but I need a drink, my mouth is bone dry and I'm choking inside this bloody hood."

His plea brought a cynical snigger from one of the guards behind him, followed quickly by the sound of shuffling feet from the same direction, and sooner than he might have expected a glass was pressed into his clammy hand.

"Don't even think of taking that hood off." He was warned.

Easing the cloth sack away from his face he slipped the glass under it, and although the water was little tepid his taste buds welcomed it with relish. As he lowered the glass again he heard the guy in front of him slide his chair back and get to his feet.

Jack followed his every footstep in his mind's eye as he circled behind him with menacing speed, then frighteningly, and without warning, the cold, hard metal of a gun barrel pressed into the back of his neck. His first instinct was to lash out, and it placed a severe strain on his nerves to remain statue-like and not retaliate, but the situation demanded steely nerves and he had no intention of being found wanting. With a gun barrel pressed against his neck any sudden movement had the potential to be fatal, indeed if this was to be where he met his end he knew there was nothing he could do to prevent it.

The guy with the middle class accent bent down and whispered in his ear.

"You're an enemy of my people, Brennan -- so before I squeeze this trigger and bring your grubby little life to an end, why don't you tell me what you're really up to?" The muzzle pressed deeper into the flesh of his neck, emphasizing the threat. Jack's flesh tingled as a rush of adrenaline surged through him bringing about a flash back to another time when he had been taken prisoner. He re-lived, all too vividly, the adrenaline rush he had experienced back then, and how when it had subsided he had felt completely washed out and lifeless. The situation he was in now was no different, except that on the last occasion he had been rescued from his Arab captors by his own unit. There was no chance of that happening this time around as no one else knew where he was, or what he was up to. His mouth had dried up completely and he craved another drink, but even though he still had the glass in his hand he didn't dare make a move to drink from it. Any movement on his part might easily be misread, with fatal consequences.

It was beginning to look as if his plan had backfired, and he questioned in his own mind why, if they were going to kill him, they hadn't already done so. He decided to try one last throw of the dice. "I've told you why I'm here – you can't possibly believe I would willingly put myself in a position like this if I was not being totally truthful. I'm not completely fucking mad." His heart was beating so fiercely that he could hear its every beat inside his own eardrums.

He wondered if anyone else could hear it.

"You signed up with the SAS, Brennan, so don't tell me you're not fucking mad -- although I might accept that you're not totally insane." The cold metal eased away from the base of his skull, and his light-footed inquisitor retraced his steps back to his original position.

"Maybe I'm fucking mad as well, but I'm inclined believe your story. I don't see that you have anything to gain from seeking this meeting unless you are telling the truth."

Jack tried to restrain his euphoria, knowing he was not out of the woods just yet. He was very aware of an uneasy shuffling of feet behind him, an obvious sign that someone was not altogether happy with the way things were panning out. Fortunately for him middle class Belfast was in no mood to be challenged by his underlings.

"This is my decision," he insisted forcefully, aiming his remark at the shoe shuffler behind Jack "I want no argument about it -- for now anyway."

Jack knew the remark was directed at whoever was behind him and not him, and although his feeling of relief was beyond description he also felt completely drained, limp as a wet rag, and grateful to be alive.

"You can thank Father Joseph for getting you off the hook," middle class Belfast explained.

"I'll make a point of doing just that, first chance I get." Jack confessed, his voice thick and lisping as he mustered the last remnants of saliva to help get the words out. "Is it okay if I take another drink?" he lisped.

"Same rules apply." The voice behind him warned.

Easing the glass under the hood he gulped down what left of the tepid liquid.

"Okay, Brennan, you've won a reprieve this time, and we will have our little chat with Devlin and see where that takes us."

Jack cringed at the very thought of that happening -- what if Devlin failed to survive their little chat? It wasn't in anybody's interest to have him depart this world just yet. That would do nothing to help his case.

"I've seen evidence of your little chats before and I don't think that sort of behaviour will help my investigation at all. I need a little bit of latitude with Devlin." He held his hands up in mock surrender. "I need just enough leeway to follow my investigation through in my own way. If you put Devlin out of action then my case is done with. I promise not to tread on anyone's toes; you have my solemn word on that."

"I'll have more than your word on it, Brennan, I'll have your life on it -- you can bet on that, and understand one more thing -- this meeting never took place. Be sure to remember that." This final directive was decisive and to the point, with nothing lost in translation, but middle class Belfast had one more thing to add that Jack was mightily relieved to hear, even though it was not all directed at him.

"Take soldier boy back to where you found him, and you bear in mind, Brennan, there is always a next time."

The glass was whipped from his hand and he was dragged from the chair and bustled back out the way he had come in, hopefully to start his journey back to freedom.

It hardly mattered one way or the other to Jack, but the journey back to the pick-up point, if indeed that was where he was being taken, seemed to take hardly any time at all compared to the outward journey. It certainly ended much more abruptly when the car suddenly lurched to a standstill and he was shoved out onto the pavement with his head still encased in its cloth hood.

Before he could scramble to his feet someone charged into his back and drove him into the wall, his face, still hooded, was then ground into the rough brickwork with a vicious twisting motion.

But if he thought that was the end of things he had another think coming, because before he could gather himself the two heavies who were escorting him took it in turns to pummel his lower back with a volley of vicious punches that forced him to his knees. As he stumbled to the ground under the viciousness of the assault he gathered himself into a protective ball, only to be kicked even more viciously in the ribs from both sides.

After both assailants had vented their anger one of them bent down and whispered in his ear. "Take that as a down payment on what to expect if we see your face again, and a little reminder that we haven't all gone soft on you fuckin' Brits."

Curled up in agony on the wet pavement Jack was never more thankful to hear the screech of tires and the smell of burning rubber as his assailants sped off into the night. Even then he waited until the sound faded well into the distance before tearing off the hood and attempting to see if anything was broken.

The ferocity of the beating made him feel nauseous, but try as he might he couldn't make himself throw up, not even when he put his fingers down his throat. Struggling into a more upright position he stayed that way until the nausea passed and the clammy sweat on his brow dried to a salty grit. Then wedging his head between his knees he filled his aching lungs with great gulps of fresh air that helped revive his senses.

When he finally scrambled to his knees he was still weak and unsteady, although thankful the feeling of nausea had all but subsided. He had taken a few serious beatings in his time, mostly in the line of duty, but this was very different, this time his beating was for nothing more than a few miserable quid, and that painful realization made him question why he had put himself through such an ordeal.

With that sobering thought bedevilling him he struggled upright and took refuge against the wall for support until his strength and sense of balance returned, and as soon as he felt strong enough he headed off on the downhill journey to the city centre, praying for the comfort of a warm taxi to take him home. Every part of his body hurt, especially his ribs and kidneys, and his head pounded like the worst possible hangover he had ever known. On the plus side however, if there could possibly be one, much of the pain he felt was dulled by the euphoric feeling of relief that he had survived the encounter mostly intact.

When he finally made it home he found the house in total darkness, but he hardly noticed any of that as he made a beeline for the drinks tray and poured a couple of large measures, knocking them straight back one after the other. After which he literally crawled up the stairs and eased quietly into bed beside Judy and eventually slumped into thankful unconsciousness.

27

Waking up was a painful and unpleasant experience next morning. Any sudden, or strenuous movement was punished by excruciating pain as he slid from the anaesthetizing comfort of his warm bed and hobbled the short distance to the bathroom, going about his business like a pantry mouse so as not to rouse his partner. He wanted to be well clear of the house before she was up and about, and needed some time alone to get his stiff and aching body active again before she arrived on the scene with her eagle eyes. If she ever got wind of his injuries she would only be fussing over him like a mother hen, and that was something he could not handle in his present state. Anyway, he had always been a quick healer and a few non eventful days would soon have him as right as rain.

Having said that, when he checked his ribs in the full length bathroom mirror the stark glare from the neon tube overhead gave them an angry brownish hue, making them look much worse than they really were. He slid the shower door closed on the mirror image and turned the knob to full power, letting the needle like jets of scalding water sting his body back to life.

By the time he was fed, dressed, and ready for the off he was feeling much livelier. The couple of painkillers he had taken along with his coffee had started to kick in, and before he knew it he was immersed in a feeling of quiet satisfaction. Satisfaction that the risk he had taken the night before had proved worthwhile and he was now able to pursue Devlin without any kick-backs from the IRA. There were of course other factors to be considered, not least Devlin's connection with the

Armagh mob. They had the potential to prove troublesome if they put their minds to it, but they were much smaller fish, and he had already convinced himself that with a little caution, and a sprinkling of common sense, he could handle anything they might throw at him.

It was a major achievement to have the IRA off his back, and for all his suffering the night before, what had taken place proved that the IRA were not involved in Devlin's smuggling racket, and knowing that was another big plus.

His next major hurdle was to get to grips with Devlin, and that would need to happen well away from the guys own cosy little patch, somewhere quite isolated would be preferable. It would also require an element of surprise to make the odds more favourable. For now though he hadn't a clue how he was going to go about it, in fact that very thought had just this moment entered his head, but he was certain in his own mind that he would think of some way of achieving it. His main ambition, for the moment anyway, was to get to the office and keep a low profile as far away as possible from Judy's prying eyes.

Before the lift doors had even closed behind him he heard his office phone beckoning in the distance, its insistent shrill pitch generating a false sense of urgency, if only because it was so early in the day and he had no idea who could be looking for him at such an unearthly hour. By the time he had punched in the security code and scrambled through to reception it had lapsed into silence. His first reaction was too scowl angrily at the innate object as he shrugged off his overcoat and tossed it over the back of a chair. Then with one hand inside his jacket tending his aching ribs, he ambled through to his office and sat down rather gingerly, frisking himself for his mobile phone. When he switched it on the digital readout told him he had one unanswered call, and although it was a local number he had no idea whose number it was. Placing it on the desk he reached for the land line and dialled the number on the readout and waited expectantly.

Whoever the caller was they picked up straight away, almost as if he had been waiting for the call.

"Good morning, Father Joseph, how may I help?"

Hearing the priest's voice really took Jack by surprise.

"Good morning, Father. Its Jack Brennan, I'm returning your call -- although I can't imagine what could be so important that it has you phoning me at this -- dare I say it -- ungodly hour?"

There was a gasp of breath at the other end.

"You have no idea what a relief it is to hear your voice again. I have been up half the night worrying about your wellbeing, although it would appear my loss of sleep was an unnecessary sacrifice." He gave another mighty sigh. "Thank God my worries were unfounded -- perhaps I should have had a little more faith."

Jack's eyebrows went up in surprise and a big grin opened up his face. Evidently there was more to this solemn looking cleric than he had given him credit for.

"I know exactly what you mean, Father, and believe me it's a relief to be able to speak at all this morning. Although at one stage last night, round about the midnight hour, I had my doubts about that."

Father Joseph groaned into the mouthpiece. "I do wish you had not told me that, I doubt you realize just how concerned I was. You shouldn't forget that I was instrumental in placing you in that dangerous position, and I don't know how I would have dealt with it had anything regrettable happened to you. But I thank God that everything has turned out all right."

The short silence that followed generated its own form of relief.

"I very much hope your courageous exploits were worth the risk. Not that I wish to know anything of what took place - heaven forbid - that's entirely your business, but I do hope it justified the serious nature of your mission." If he was hoping for an explanation then he was to be disappointed because Jack had no intention of giving anything away, even though the guy's efforts in negotiating the meeting deserved recognition of some kind. "I got what I had hoped to get, Father, and I'm immensely grateful to you for all your help."

"I appreciate your gratitude, Mr. Brennan, but I don't need your thanks, I did not put myself out on a limb solely for your benefit, my efforts were entirely in support of Roisin Byrne. I'm simply phoning you now to satisfy myself regarding your safety, and to erase my own feeling of guilt, and I must say that I now consider this to be an end to my involvement."

"Be that as it may, Father, but I'm grateful none the less, and I doubt very much if there will be any need to call on your services again."

"That's good to know, I just hope it all proves to have been worthwhile, but I dare say only time will provide the answer to that. I'll say goodbye now and wish you every good luck in your endeavours." The call he ended with Jack wondering if there was something else he should have said.

28

When Judy finally turned in for work she found Jack chatting on the phone with Dave Jackson. She mouthed a muted greeting in his direction and dropped into a chair facing him, trying, unsuccessfully as it happened, not to appear terribly interested in what was going on.

"Don't ask me how I know, Dave, just take my word for it when I say the IRA has no involvement in this Byrne case, or for that matter in Devlin's drug running scheme. We're dealing with nothing more than a bunch of hoodlums, not terrorists. It's unfortunate that you can't haul him in for questioning, because we might get to the bottom of this whole saga much quicker if that were to happen."

Judy could only hear one side of the conversation otherwise she might have had a better understanding as to why Jack was wearing such a sullen expression.

"There's nothing I can do to accommodate you with that I'm sorry to say. I have my orders, Jack. I'm afraid you will have to handle Devlin all by yourself -- unless of course you can give me something concrete that proves he was involved in Byrne's murder." Jackson paused for a moment then added. "It really is murder we are talking about -- isn't it?"

Judy was watching her partner closely, looking for any reaction that might give her a clue as to what was going on, and what he said next dispensed with some of the mystery.

"I'm sorry you're not convinced enough to arrest Devlin, believe me

I know he's the guilty party in all this. I guess I'll just have to find a way of proving it to you."

He winked knowingly at Judy.

"How do you feel about popping over to my place tomorrow night, I have an idea that might produce something useful, and I could do with your help, any chance you can manage it?"

It took a while for Jackson to make his mind up.

"As long as you don't involve me in any direct contact with Devlin, and you don't pull any more of your heavy handed stunts. You're not exactly helping my career prospects with the way you go about things, the proverbial bull in the china shop comes to mind."

Jack grinned, but it was hard to tell if he was grinning at Jackson's honesty, or the caustic tone of his remark.

"Okay -- okay -- I get your drift," he conceded, light heartedly. "So I'll see you tomorrow evening then."

Judy had bided her time in bemused ignorance throughout the conversation, but her natural curiosity wouldn't allow her to remain completely in the dark. "What was that all about?" she asked.

Jack plunged straight into a long winded, if somewhat tailored version of events, a version that made no mention of the previous night's exploits, except to say, by way of a red herring, that he had been to another meeting with Father Joseph. And when he considered her to be suitably satisfied he steered her away from the issue altogether by asking. "Are you okay with Dave coming tomorrow night?"

She gave a nonchalant shrug of her shoulders.

"It's important we keep him on side, sweetheart," he insisted. "He's got an inside track on what the boys in blue are up to, and anyway I'm almost certain we'll need his help again before this case is put to bed."

Yet again she neglected to show any real interest, which made her verbal response all the more bizarre when she voiced it.

"If that's what you want, Jack, then so be it, but I'd rather it didn't turn into another late night session like last time if you don't mind."

There was something in her attitude that didn't rest easily with Jack, a niggling suspicion that she was angling for something, but she was on her feet and turning her back on him before he had the chance to challenge why she was looking so smug.

As she left the room the thought slipped from his mind and he settled down to planning his next move on Devlin. He didn't exactly have a lot of options going for him, as it was hardly likely brute force alone would achieve very much, not with Devlin's pedigree. It would need to be something more subtle than that. He needed to manufacture an opportunity to catch the guy with his guard down if he hoped to get any sort of disclosure on the whereabouts of Tony Byrne, or his remains. How that might be achieved was nothing short of a mystery for now, but he was convinced in his own mind that Barratt was the key to the whole thing. With that thought lingering in his head he rummaged through his pockets in search of the scrap of paper Andy Nelson had given him with Barratt's phone number on it, then he picked up the phone and dialled.

It took a while for the Scotsman to pick up the call, and just when Jack was about to hang up his gravelly voice, accompanied by the sound of Neil Diamond prattling on about his Sweet Caroline and the screech of a high revving engine filled his earpiece.

"Barratt," he bellowed down the line, making the background noise sound muted by comparison.

"Brennan here," Jack told him, every bit as loudly in order to make sure he was heard. "You and I need another little chat, but if this is a bad time phone me back whenever you're free, but you had better phone me back and bloody quickly too, otherwise the cops might want to hear what I have to say." If Barratt was on the road he could hardly expect anything more than a quick acknowledgement, which was exactly what he did get.

"I can't talk now - I'm in traffic - I'll have to ring you back."

Jack stretched back in his chair with a look of quiet satisfaction chasing the worry lines from his face, the lack of argument from the Scot gave him a positive feeling and things seemed to be moving in the right direction at last. His gut feeling about Barratt had been right on the money, the guy would probably agree to anything to keep the cops, and the IRA off his back. Not that he was under any real threat from either organization, not yet anyway, but of course he wasn't to know that, and Jack intended to exploit the guy's ignorance for all it was worth.

Stretching his legs out under the desk he allowed himself a momentary feeling of satisfaction that things were beginning to take off at last. All he had to do was wait for Barratt to return his call and get his latest plan under way, or so he thought, but only until Judy's voice reached out to him over the intercom, pushing all thoughts of Barratt aside.

"You have a couple of visitors, Jack."

His immediate reaction was to dive for his desk diary and check his appointments, only to find proof that he hadn't missed anything -- he didn't have any appointments scheduled, and he certainly wasn't expecting visitors.

"Who is it, Judy? I'm not expecting anyone -- I've nothing entered in my diary."

"Apparently they're from Special Branch, Jack -- I'll bring them straight through -- okay."

Bolting upright in his chair, his attention was suddenly focused on the office door.

One of his two visitors was a few inches taller than the other, at around six foot three, although both were tall enough to stand out in a crowd. Smartly dressed in mid-grey suits they looked for all the world like a couple of Mormons out on a recruiting patrol.

Judy ushered them in and took up an observation post just inside the door, shrugging her shoulders at Jack to indicate her ignorance as to the purpose of their visit. She eased the door closed behind her and tucked herself behind the smaller of the two men, leaving it up to them to introduce themselves.

The taller one was about to do just that when Jack stuck his hand up cutting him off in his prime.

Thank you, Judy -- that will be all -- I'll let you know if I need you again." With no idea why he was getting a visit from Special Branch he had no intention of finding out in front of his partner. There was always the possibility it might be something he would rather she didn't get to know about, like what he had been up to the previous night. She gave him a withering look and spun on her heel to retrace her steps, her body language anything but inviting.

Jack waited until the door was closed before returning his attention to his visitor's.

"Now then, gentlemen -- what can I do for you?" he asked calmly, belying the sickening dread that was churning up inside him.

The taller man pulled out a warrant card and waved briefly it under his nose.

"Inspector Campbell," he announced grandly, before making an exaggerated display of returning the warrant card to his inside pocket. "Sergeant Baxter," he went on, flicking a hand in the general direction of his muted companion, who, until now anyway, had done little else but glare suspiciously, or as he probably believed, menacingly across the desk at Jack. Unfortunately his heroics didn't achieve their intended effect but he displayed such an obvious air of confidence with his arrogant manner that it made Jack feel decidedly edgy.

Campbell, the senior of the two, had the distinct appearance of someone who perceived the whole nation to be guilty of something, his own mother included. Everything about him was abrasive and brash, and what could be seen of his coarse features behind the bushy growth on his upper lip, was set in an untrusting sneer.

The other one, the sergeant, had a clean-shaven, much leaner face, almost devoid of character, other than a forced expression that portrayed an ambition to look hard and mean. A fruitless effort that was wasted on an old soldier like Jack, who, not knowing the purpose of their visit, refrained from making any unnecessary conversation. Even though he was certain from their attitude that their visit wasn't likely to end in pleasantries.

In any case he had taken an instant dislike to both men, mostly due to their apparent reluctance to communicate, a ploy that was probably meant to intimidate, rather than generate mystery. Either way it failed in its ambition because Jack was having none of it, as his visitors were about to find out.

"I'm sorry, gentlemen," he said dismissively, "but I'm a very busy man so if you've got nothing to say perhaps you should go away and come back when you have it written down."

He knew right away that he had declared his annoyance too readily and immediately regretted it, especially as both men looked set on being confrontational. But Jack could be every bit as confrontational himself, and generally when he felt under pressure his singular instinct was to get the first blow in, and since he couldn't take back what he'd already said he had no option but to brazen it out.

"If you would like something interesting to read, I can always come back with a warrant," Campbell countered.

'*Touché*,' thought Jack, although the threat was enough to make him pull back and take a rein on his attitude.

"In that case, gentlemen, I suggest you sit down and explain to me what this is all about as I'm not a bloody mind reader." They each found a chair and placed them as close to Jack's desk as they could before sidling into them in perfect unison, like some aerobatic display team.

Campbell pulled the customary notebook from his inner pocket, flipped it open, and searched its contents for something he quite obviously didn't need.

"It has been reported to us that on the tenth of this month you viciously, and without provocation, assaulted an innocent member of the public by the name of Devlin --" He made a quick reference to his notes, "a Mr. Joseph Devlin -- and that on the aforementioned occasion you caused the said Mr. Devlin actual bodily harm that necessitated emergency hospital treatment for a badly damaged nose and the removal of a number of front teeth." He flipped the cover of his notebook shut and slipped it back into it resting place with a cynical smile.

"Do you still wish me to go away and return with it in writing, Mr. Brennan?"

Jack was speechless. He certainly wasn't expecting anything of this nature, it was inconceivable that Devlin had reported him for assault, it simply didn't add up. The whole thing was nonsensical, and as far as any witnesses at the scene were concerned, no one else would dare report it to the cops without first clearing it with Devlin. He couldn't believe what was happening, and unfortunately he didn't have enough time to think it through before Inspector Campbell thought to enlighten him.

"We haven't fully concluded our investigations at this time." He was back on his high horse doing all he might to look mean and threatening, but again he was found wanting, at least in Jack's eyes.

"The purpose of this visit is to advise you of our ongoing investigation and your own rather precarious situation. We treat this sort of offence very seriously, and you should be warned that any future approaches, or threats, against the victim during our investigation will be viewed as intimidation and could result in your immediate arrest. I hope I have made myself clear?"

He cocked a questioning eyebrow at Jack.

"Or perhaps you would prefer that it in writing as well?" he sniped.

'*Pompous bastard*,' thought Jack, suppressing a natural urge to voice the sentiment aloud, at least until he knew exactly why this was happening, especially as he found his two visitors less than convincing. From what he could make out the only reason for their visit was to put the frighteners on him, which made him wonder if he was being quietly warned to stay away from Devlin.

His conversation with Dave Jackson on that very subject suddenly sprang to mind and convinced him that he was more than likely right in his assumption.

One thing he knew for sure, a cheap hoodlum like Devlin would never turn the spotlight on his organization by running to the cops to complain about being done over. Such a suggestion was not of this world

"I have no idea what you're talking about, gentlemen, so I suggest you go away and get your facts straight. It seems to me that someone has given you a bum steer -- and unless you have something of more relevance to discuss, I suggest it's time you got out of my face."

He had no desire to sit chewing the fat with a pair of ego inflated cops, but he needed to be careful not to say too much and expose the fact that he had access to inside information. That would only throw suspicion on Dave Jackson and he dare not let that happen, otherwise the guy would drop him like a hot potato, and rightly so. Campbell glanced at his companion before replying.

"We always check our facts very carefully, Mr. Brennan. It would serve you well to remember that, a private investigator like you could easily have his license revoked if he was found guilty of assault, or causing bodily harm."

With his threat delivered Campbell got to his feet, and followed by his dutiful supporting act, vacated Jack's office without saying another word.

Overcome with a sense of relief Jack slumped back in his chair, relieved that the whole episode was over. Although he was seriously concerned, not to mention a little amazed, that the police were taking an active interest in him. Who, or what, had pointed Special Branch in his direction was something of a mystery. It was certainly a problem he could do without, having already invested a huge effort, not to mention a massive risk, in order to get the IRA off his back and deal with Devlin unhindered. Now it was Special Branch who were warning him off Devlin and not the IRA. Things were definitely becoming much more complicated.

"What next?" he asked himself as he stared at the office door, expecting Judy to come waltzing in any time soon. It was unlikely she could hold her curiosity in check much longer. In fact he had hardly finished the thought when the door opened and she wandered in with her coat slung over her arm.

"What was that all about?" she asked.

He shrugged nonchalantly and gave her a blank look. "Nothing much really," he lied. "It looks like we're treading on someone's toes with this Byrne case -- but it's nothing to get alarmed about, just more routine crap from our wonderful boys in blue."

She eyed him with suspicion.

"Whatever you say, Jack," she muttered, "I'm off now anyway -- see you later tonight." That was all she said as she spun away in the direction of the door.

"Where in the blue blazes are you off to?" he yelled after her. She reappeared almost immediately, popping her head round the door frame. "If I'm expected to work tomorrow night entertaining you and your friend Jackson, then I'm taking time off in lieu." She gave him a no nonsense look, then added with noticeable pleasure. "We're governed by European employment laws now, Jack, or haven't you bothered to read the last directive I put on your desk – it's called flexi hours, in case you're wondering."

Grinning mischievously she disappeared from his line of sight.

He listened as the outer door slam shut and was hit with the realization that he had just been done up like a proverbial kipper, but that was how life was between them, a constant battle of wits, especially when Judy thought she was being treated as anything less than an equal.

Mind you, when he took time to think about it, and he quite often did, he would be the first to admit that all too frequently in the past he had given her ample cause for complaint. And if nothing else, he had learned from experience over the years, often to his cost, that her emotions lay very close to the surface. Especially when there was the slightest hint of danger to anyone close to her. So although it meant living with a guilty conscience from time to time, over the long haul there was usually more to be gained from sticking to his guns and not deviating, rather than trying to placate her over-protective nature.

For that very reason he would take every precaution possible to ensure she discovered nothing of what he planned to do. There would be ample time to salve his conscience about it when things returned to normal.

29

Jack arrived home just in time to catch Judy on the phone with Mairead, and from the little he did hear they seemed to be having a good old chin wag. Although he didn't really get to hear a lot of the conversation because as soon as he entered the room Judy brought the conversation to an abrupt end and plonked the phone down, as if to deprive him from getting a word in. It never ceased to amuse him the way she could be perfectly amicable towards Mairead when he wasn't around, but as soon as he put in an appearance it orchestrated a complete change in her attitude.

"You might have let me say hello before you cut her off like that. You know how much I enjoy a chat with Mairead."

She swung her legs off the settee and gave him a frosty look.

"Of course you do, Jack, and don't I know it."

His mischievous grin declared to the world that he was only teasing, but she hadn't spotted it in time, and it was too late to retract what she'd already said. "Stuff you, Brennan," was all she could think to say as she headed for the drinks tray, furious with herself for falling for his charade.

"Pour me one while you're at it, sweetheart, there's a good girl," he said, hoping to keep up the charade.

"I'm on a half day, Brennan – or have you forgotten? So you can find some other bloody skivvy to dance attendance on you." She was in no mood for his antics, and he knew it, but he wasn't about to let it end there. "I wouldn't have to ask Mairead twice," he teased, with pretentious innocence.

Judy stopped what she was doing and rounded on him like an injured vixen, all primed up to deliver another verbal onslaught.

At least she was until she saw the exaggerated look of innocence on his face and her attack crumbled in a fit of laughter, although in all honesty she might just as easily have burst into tears.

"One of these days you really will go too far," she warned. Jack followed her to the drinks tray with a self-satisfied smile on his face. To him the whole thing was nothing more than a bit of light hearted banter, but he still had to follow her advice and pour his own drink, she hadn't given way on that.

He was just about finished doing so when the phone rang, and making a quick grab for it before Judy could reach it he was greeted by Barratt's dour Scottish accent at the other end.

"What the hell do you want from me, Brennan?" There was a snappy irritability in his voice, but in the circumstances was no less than Jack expected.

"The last time we spoke you told me Devlin meets up with you every time you come over to Belfast. Why does he do that?" he asked.

Barratt took his time about answering.

"Well," he said, "there are times when he needs something shifted in a hurry between your side of the pond and the mainland over here, and the same in reverse of course. But why are you so interested in our meetings -- what have they got to do with anything?" There was a hint of caution in the way he phrased the question, suggesting that he wasn't too keen on what might be coming next.

"It's just a thought." Jack muttered, almost to himself. "I need to know how involved Devlin was in Byrne's disappearance, and finding that out isn't going to be easy." He was really hoping Barratt would volunteer his help, rather than forcing him to resort to threats and blackmail to bring him on side.

"And I suppose you think I can help -- is that the way of it?" he said guardedly.

"I had it in mind that you might relish an opportunity to get one over on him after the way he tricked you into being part of his little scam. It should be some comfort for you to know that the IRA has nothing at all to do with this drug running racket he's into. I have a guaranteed assurance that they are not involved in it in any way, shape, or form. Devlin is operating his scam purely for personal gain and nothing else -- and more to the point -- the IRA doesn't even know you exist -- at least not yet."

The little add-on was a deliberately muted threat, a warning to ensure Barratt took account of the likely consequences if they were to find out.

When there was no immediate response Jack continued to pile on the pressure.

"What I'm telling you now comes straight from the horse's mouth, believe me. So it hardly matters what other worries you might have, you can take it from me that the IRA does not have to be one of them, unless of course you decide to be stubborn."

Barratt snorted down the phone at him. "And I'm supposed to take your word for that am I?" The underlying hint of relief in his voice suggested that he wanted to be convinced, and Jack sensed for the first time that he was winning him over. It only needed a little more pressure to bring him in line

"I would much prefer to lessen the likelihood of the IRA finding out about your involvement, but of course I can't guarantee that if I have to resort to other tactics to bring Devlin to book." He left the rest unspoken, giving free reign to Barratt's imagination.

There were a number of reasons why he needed the Scotsman on board. The fact that Devlin trusted him being the main one, but also because he was the one who had driven the truck to Dublin with the drugs on board, so he knew first-hand what Devlin's instructions had been on that fateful day. All he could do now was wait and see if the Scotsman had the balls to face him down.

"What is it you want me to do?" Barratt asked dejectedly, resigning himself to the fact that Jack was calling the shots.

"For starters I need you to contact Devlin and tell him you've been questioned by the police over Byrne's disappearance. When he hears that it's bound to bring about the kind of reaction I'm looking for, if for no other reason than the fact that he knows you had nothing to do with it. You need to convince him that you're really worried the police are showing so much interest in you. Drop him a gentle hint that they've mentioned his name as well, then tell him you're heading this way with a delivery and set up a meeting to discuss the problem."

Jack toyed aimlessly with his pencil as he waited for the Scotsman to say something. He heard him cursing under his breath and mutter something unintelligible before replying.

"Devlin can be a nasty bastard like you've never seen. What if he decides I'm no use to him anymore? Am I gonna end up like your friend Byrne?"

He had good reason to be concerned, there was no denying that, but Jack believed if he gave him a little more reassurance it might do the trick.

"I won't be far away when the two of you meet, and believe me I can handle Devlin."

Barratt cleared his throat before acknowledging. "Yeah -- I saw the result of your last encounter -- remember. But what happens if Devlin doesn't come by himself? What if he turns up mob handed -- what then?" His Glaswegian accent sounded more pronounced as the first signs of real panic set in.

"Cut crapping about, Barratt." Jack yelled at him. "You're either up for this or you face the fucking consequences. I don't have the time to stand here chewing the fat all bloody night.

"Okay – okay -- don't get your knickers in a twist. This is all a bit scary for me, I haven't a fuckin' clue what I'm letting myself in for." Jack hardly gave him time to finish. "For Christ's sake, Barratt. All I'm asking you to do is arrange a meeting with Devlin and let me know where and when it's going to happen. Surely that's not too difficult a task -- even for you."

"Alright," Barratt conceded, "but you can be certain of one thing -- if Devlin sounds the least bit suspicious when I meet with him then I'm calling the whole thing off. You can go to the cops if you want to, but I'd rather have that than end up with my toes pointing skyward in some goddamned Irish bog."

"Okay, I accept that," Jack agreed. "Just give me as much warning as you can about the arrangements for the meet, and make sure you have some time in hand so that I can make the necessary arrangements at this end."

"I'll let you know the minute I have something, don't worry about that, but you better make sure you have some protection laid on for me in case things go wrong, because there won't be anyone else there to help me."

Jack dropped the handset in its cradle and turned away to find Judy watching him from her perch on the settee.

"Why are you telling Barratt the IRA aren't involved in this case?" she demanded. "We don't have any evidence to support such a claim."

"Of course the IRA aren't involved, even Dave Jackson admits that." He made it sound casual and convincing, as if he was stating the obvious. "There won't be a problem for Barratt if he does as he's told. In any case, he got himself involved when he started running drugs."

Judy looked anything but convinced. She knew just how ruthless her partner could be at times, how he could manipulate people to achieve his own goals, especially if he was convinced that the end justified the means.

"One minute you're telling me Tony Byrne is dead. The next minute you're proposing to put someone else's life at risk just to recover the guy's remains. Where the hell is the logic in that? Where exactly is the cut-off point with you Jack? Where's the point when you decide the risk is too great?" She was allowing herself to get worked up over the issue, and as Jack had no desire to prolong the conversation he delivered a snappy retort and hurried from the room.

"Wherever it is -- we haven't reached it yet."

Judy flopped back in her seat and stayed there long after he had gone, pondering over his cavalier attitude. She knew her man well enough to know that when he killed a conversation like he just had it was usually because he had something to hide. She resolved to find out exactly what that little secret was.

30

Alec Jameson shoved the device he was working on to one side and reached for the phone, allowing his irritation to show at being interrupted. When he heard Jack's familiar voice at the other end a smile settled on his lips and his thoughts travelled back to the last time their paths had crossed. On that occasion his old army chum had wanted an electronic search carried out on a property to check for any hidden listening devices that might have been planted. The search had been a success, and Jack had paid well above the going rate for his services. The two men went back a long way, having served together in the SAS until Alec had finished his time and left to set up his business, Electronic Securities Ltd.

Electronic surveillance was what he excelled at, having spent most of his time in the military specializing in that field at the very highest level,

"What's it to be this time, Jack?" he asked, without so much as a friendly word of greeting, but then neither man bothered much with pleasantries when they got back in touch, simply picking up on their friendship where they had left off, as if they had never been apart, when in fact they had hardly seen anything of each other since leaving the service.

"I'm hoping to borrow a piece of equipment, Alec." Jack explained, safe in the knowledge that his friend was almost guaranteed to have something suitable.

"No you're not Jack -- you're looking to hire a piece of equipment," he corrected, his somewhat caustic remark bringing a smile to Jack's face.

"Still as tight as a fish's ass, Alec -- some things never change. But listen up mate, I need one of your electronic gismos that will let me listen in on a conversation and record it at the same time -- and it needs to be something that's user friendly, I don't have electrodes running through my veins like you do." His admission brought a hearty laugh from his old pal.

"I'm sure we can sort something out for you, Jack. Why don't you pop in so we can discuss it properly? I'll need a few basics for starters, like the operating environment, distance from the target and such like before I can make any sort of recommendation. It is not as simple as you might think if you want a guaranteed result."

"That's great, Alec. I'll nip in later this afternoon if that's okay with you?"

"See you then, Jack," his friend replied, making a mental note to check his whiskey supply to see if it would survive another visit from his old chum. It had taken a serious hit the last time they had met.

Judy caught the tail end of their conversation as she wandered in without warning, but what she heard was enough to rouse her curiosity.

"What on earth are you up to now?" she asked, "and what's all this about electrodes?"

Jack turned to face her. "I'm hoping to use Barratt to put the squeeze on Devlin and make him open up about his shady dealings. That way we might learn something about what happened to Tony Byrne. I need to get him into a conversation with someone he trusts and get it recorded on tape, there's every chance he will let something slip when his guard is down and he thinks he's in friendly company. I know it's a bit of long shot but apart from beating the crap out of the guy to get him talking, I really don't see any other way to get things moving. Something has to be done to move this bloody case forward, it's stuck in a mire and going nowhere fast."

He grabbed for the phone as a diversionary tactic and called Dave Jackson to confirm their dinner date was still on. The call was a quick one because he still had to get across town to see Alec and needed to get a move on. But even though he was in a hurry he still took the time to make one last effort, albeit in vain, at wiping the frown off Judy's face and bringing back a smile.

"Cheer up, sweetheart -- it might never happen," he said glibly. She didn't even reward him by looking up, but as soon as he was out of earshot she muttered to herself. "I've a feeling it already has."

There was neither a sign nor a name plate to advertise the presence of Electronic Securities, which was no inconvenience to Alec Jameson's secretive and highly sensitive patronage. The people who used his services would themselves shun publicity at every opportunity. Although in reality the lack of a name plate was no more than a tactic on Alec's part to remain unobtrusive and well hidden from the prying eyes of the general public. His premises were sited no more than a stone's throw from the police headquarters in what had once been a fairly upmarket Victorian residential area. The exterior of the building had been renovated fairly recently and been returned to something like its former glory, while only the furniture and furnishings betrayed it's new role as a business premise on the inside.

Feeling in a playful mood when he got there, Jack made a comic face at the security camera above his head to announce his arrival to whoever lurked behind the mahogany doors. When he heard the electronic lock undo he pushed the door open and went inside. The receptionist, who had been watching his antics on the monitor with muted pleasure, turned out to be a business like little red head, who greeted him with an amused smile and wasted no time in ushering him up to Alec's office on the next floor.

"Come on in you old bugger." Alec teased, as he charged round the desk and embraced Jack like a long lost brother. An embrace that might more accurately be described as a rugby tackle, Jack unwound himself and stood back to get a proper look at his old pal.

"It's great to see you looking so well. It feels like ages since we last met up, yet it's only been about nine or ten months."

Jack had always felt at ease in Alec's company. Their familiarity stemmed from sharing a hole in the ground for weeks on end during reconnaissance missions back in the days of the Soviet threat. A particularly difficult series of missions when they had to dig into the side of a hill on the East German border in total darkness, camouflage their hide to blend in with the surrounding countryside, and spend seemingly endless weeks watching and reporting on eastern bloc troop movement. Only venturing out once a week to replenish their water supply from the nearest source, whatever that might be.

On one such mission Jack had crept out of the hide just as daylight was breaking to find a German farmer standing right on top of them, searching for mushrooms. The poor guy took off like a scalded cat at the frightening sight of this dirty, un-kept apparition appearing out of the ground from under his feet. They still enjoyed a good old chuckle about it, even though it meant their mission was compromised and they had to up sticks and pull out. It was impossible to share such a confined space and not develop a true understanding of one another's strengths and weaknesses, and that was how it was with the two of them, a familiarity that even family relatives might never enjoy.

"Plant your ass, Jack," invited Alec, grinning at him like a banshee, his strong west-country accent dragging Jack away from his fleeting recollection as he brought into view a bottle of whiskey he'd conveniently stored close at hand.

"Let's get the important things out of the way first," he said jokingly, "we can get down to the other business later."

Producing a couple of glasses from his drawer he gave each a generous helping. Shoving one in front of his friend he raised his own in the air, declaring in a solemn salute. "Absent friends."

"Absent friends." Jack repeated, throwing his head back and emptying his glass in one swallow.

"So how has the world been treating you, Jack? Still living off other people's misfortune?"

"Don't be like that, Alec. I simply offer a service to those who need it, but yes, I am still making a crust thank you very much. Anyway, who are you to talk? We both make a living from other people's failings, so don't you go knocking it."

Alec reached out and refilled their glasses. "What's this gear you're after?" he asked.

Jack screwed his face up with a look of uncertainty, "I need to eavesdrop on a conversation, but the problem is that I don't know when or where it's going to take place. It might be in the cab of an articulated truck, or in a pub, or even in a car park." He stopped talking and sipped from his drink.

Alec viewed him over the rim of his glass. "Are the participant's hostile or do you have a friendly face on board?" he asked.

"There's every possibility it will only involve two people, and one of them is friendly, well -- maybe friendly is over stating it a bit, let's just say he'll do as he's told."

Alec smiled knowingly. "Nothing has changed there then, Brennan. Anyway, it shouldn't be a problem to find something suitable, it's technically very simple in fact, as long as your guy is willing to co-operate and wear a rig -- will he do that?"

"Like I said -- he'll do as he's told." Jack replied with confidence.

"If that's the way of it then I don't see a problem. In which case I only need to run you through the set up procedure and show you how to fine tune the system. They can be a bit lady-like in temperament sometimes and in need of a delicate touch to get the best out of them." He grinned and leaned back in his seat. "A bit like old times you and me together again like this -- eh mate?"

Before Jack could answer his friend was out of his chair and heading for the door.

"We might as well run you through the procedure while you're here now and get it over with." He was talking and walking at the same time, and at pretty much the same speed as he trotted nimbly down the stairs, past the receptionist desk, and on down into the cellar.

Forty minutes later Jack left the old Victorian house and was on his way home, the equipment he had hired nestling beside him on the passenger seat in a cardboard box. He had no way of knowing when the meeting between Devlin and Barratt would take place, but he needed the equipment on hand just in case things moved quicker than he expected. It meant some extra cost for the extended hire, but that was a price he simply had to bear.

31

Dave Jackson was part of a larger group milling around the bar when Jack arrived but he wasted no time detaching himself and rushing over to join him. It was hardly a secret that the rest of his group were policemen as they all had that bold, upright bearing that oozed confidence and stood them apart from lesser mortals.

"What's happening with your case, Jack?" The young detective asked. There was plenty of background noise going on and Jack waited until he was seated before answering.

"Not a lot," he confessed, "Although I could do with some advice on a small matter." Jackson pulled his chair closer. "Anything I can do to help, you know that -- but before you get started, I have someone I would like you to meet while you're here. There's no great panic about it, it can wait until we're finished."

Jack had other things on his mind and didn't show much interest, just a brief nod of the head to accommodate the guy.

"I'm putting a little plan together that I think you should know about. I've persuaded this guy Barratt we spoke about to be a little more helpful, and if things pan out the way I expect them to we may get this case moving again."

The guarded look on Jackson's face forced him to go into more detail.

"Barratt drove the vehicle that was parked up outside Zipline the morning Byrne did his disappearing trick."

Jackson looked a touch sceptical -- or perhaps it was something else, there was no way of knowing. "Are you telling me you've been in touch with the guy?"

"I have indeed," Jack confirmed, "we had a delightful little chat, which is one of the reasons why I'm here. He has me convinced that Devlin was using the aid convoy as a cover for smuggling drugs." Jackson looked ready to argue the point before Jack raised a hand in protest.

"You will have to trust my judgment on this, Dave, because I've no intention of going into much more detail. Let me just say that I've managed to talk Barratt into arranging a meeting with Devlin in the hope of cajoling some sort of admission from him about what happened to Byrne. If he does give anything away, I hope to get it down on tape. But I need to be sure that any evidence gathered in this way will stand up in a court of law? What's your slant on that?"

Jackson was taken by surprise, and it showed. It was also clear from his attitude that he was fearful of being dragged into something shady.

"I admire your persistence, Jack. I really do, but you're asking me to accept this theory about drug smuggling when you have no conclusive evidence of any sort." He thought things over for a moment. "But none of this actually involves me, does it -- so what the hell, if you're only looking for advice I don't imagine it can do any harm." He folded his arms stubbornly, displaying a gritty determination not to get too closely involved. "I would think it safe to conclude that if no physical force is applied, or any other means of physical persuasion or coercion is used, then there is no reason why such evidence should not be accepted in a court of law. But remember – I'm just an ordinary Joe plod -- not a legal expert -- not by any stretch of the imagination." He fell silent for a moment, but he had the look of someone chewing on a problem.

"You have me a bit confused, Jack. I was under the impression you were looking for a body to bury. Has something changed that I don't know about? Surely you're not dreaming of getting this Byrne guy back alive and securing a prosecution -- are you?"

Jack shook his head.

"No -- nothing like that, Dave, a prosecution is for you guys to deliver, if and when we get enough evidence for a conviction. I promised you that little bonus in return for your help remember. I'm only looking to give Byrne's wife some peace of mind, but believe me, when this is all over, jail might be a safer place for Devlin to be than walking the streets." He caught the waiter's eye, waved him over to order a round of drinks.

Jackson gave him a quizzical look but didn't say anything until the waiter had gone away.

"I get the distinct feeling there's something you're not telling me?" Jackson had been a criminal investigator long enough to know when someone was holding back on him.

"Not really, Dave. I just think life might become a little bit ---- he searched for the right word, "hazardous for our friend Devlin if a certain organization ever found out what he has been up to."

Jackson eyed him with even more suspicion.

"And you would hardly be the one to put that little snippet their way -- would you?" There was something in Jack's attitude that didn't rest easily with him. "I advise you not to go down that route either, otherwise you might well become part of the problem rather than part of the answer."

Jack raised his hands in mock submission.

"Now would I ever do that, Dave?" he mocked, unconvincingly.

"As long as we understand each other," Jackson warned.

Jack felt it was time to change the subject.

"Is there nothing new at your end?" he asked.

Jackson shrugged offhandedly. "This isn't a current case with us, as you know, Jack, so I haven't really been on it. In fact I've had a couple of quiet days in court, and glad of it -- I needed the break."

"You mentioned something about a guy you wanted me to meet?" Jack prompted, steering them onto a less contentious topic.

"Oh yes -- I'm glad you reminded me." He nodded towards the group of people he had been associating with when Jack had arrived. "You see the guy at the far end of the bar in the light grey suit -- the one with the pint glass in his hand."

Jack swivelled round in his seat and identified the guy he was talking about. He stood a few inches over six foot, with broad, shoulders and a head of thinning grey hair. His face was mostly hidden because of the angle they were at, but Jack judged him to be in his mid to late fifties and reasonably fit looking, he definitely wasn't carrying any excess baggage.

"What about him?" he asked, as he waited for the guy to turn round and offer him a better view.

"Well," Jackson said stretched the word, "he's just finished his time with us --- in fact this is his very last day -- which is what this shindig is all about. We gave him a bit of a send-off at the office before coming here." He smiled at the recollection then carried on. "He had a successful career with uniform branch before finishing up in Criminal Intelligence. He's an up-front sort of guy, Jack -- very highly thought of by his peers and as reliable as rain in an Irish summer." He leaned closer not to be overheard. "Between you and me the guy is so bloody honest and up front that it got in the way of his last promotion, and there's one thing I can safely say, he's as loyal as an old sheepdog." He gave Jack a knowing wink. "It might be worth your while to have a word with him, I know he's interested in your sort of work now that he's been pensioned off."

Jack had already guessed what was coming, but he was in no position to take on another overhead, not until they had more work on their books.

"I'm sorry, Dave," he told him outright, "I really don't need another body right now, maybe some other time if things pick up a bit." Jackson looked disappointed, but he knew better than to fight a lost cause.

"Oh well," he said ruefully, "I just thought I'd give it a try. Guys like us have a hard time finding something challenging to do when our time is up." He gave a quick grin. "I imagine you had exactly the same problem when you left the army." He hadn't expected Jack to be quite so emphatic about it, but neither was he going to let that deter him.

"It wouldn't do any harm to meet him you know -- after all -- what have you got to lose?" Jack screwed his face up, he wasn't really interested, but there was nothing to be gained by putting the young detective down too brutally.

"Well, you may be right," he said, "but I wouldn't want to build the guy's hopes up unnecessarily." He could easily recall his own difficult experience when he had quit the army, and without looking for it, the tiniest nub of empathy began to take hold.

"Why don't I fetch him over anyway," Jackson suggested, "just to introduce the two of you - what harm can that do?"

Before Jack could get a word in he was on his way, elbowing a route through the crowd to get to his friend. After a quick word in his ear he literally towed him back to their table, allowing Jack his first opportunity to get a real look at the guy.

A boyish quiff of thinning grey hair topped a high, intelligent forehead, and a cheery looking, slightly chubby face that was brought to life by the bluest eyes Jack had ever seen. There was a determined set to his jaw without any hint of arrogance, while the rest of his general demeanour made him look no more than his probable years, although his purposeful bearing indicated a well-being that went unaffected by that.

"Jack Brennan -- Peter Dunseith." Dave's introduction was short and snappy as he rushed to take himself off-side. "Now if you two will excuse me, I need to take a leak." With his excuses made he wandered off in search of the toilets, giving his friend the opportunity to demonstrate that he was a straight talker who got quickly to the point.

"Look Jack," he began, setting the scene. "Dave has given me a quick update on your set up and I see no sense in beating about the bush. I have a keen interest in the sort of work you're involved with, but if you haven't a position available right now, or you don't think I can be of any use, just say so and let's not drag things out."

He was about to leave it there, then decided there was something else needed to be said.

"Dave has told me a little about the case you're working on right now, and I imagine it's my inside knowledge of your guy Devlin and his cronies that made him think I might be of some use to you." He saw the look of surprise on Jack's face and did his best to salvage the situation. "You probably didn't want to hear that, Jack, but I'm telling you so you know from the outset that I don't keep secrets from my employers."

The very fact that Jackson had discussed his case with another cop came as a bit of a shock to Jack, but right then he had more important things on his mind. Like trying to figure out why Jackson had made no mention of Dunseith's previous knowledge of Devlin. That was much too important to have been overlooked, and he wasn't at all sure how he felt about it. It was an early reminder, if he needed one that the Byrne case was still considered an 'unclosed file' with the RUC and was bound to be discussed between colleagues. Casting his doubts aside he pointed to the vacant chair beside him.

"Exactly how were you involved with Devlin?" he asked, his interest gaining momentum as Dunseith slid into a seat and shook his head.

"To be perfectly honest I didn't have any direct involvement with the guy," he confessed, "but I worked for a lot of years in Criminal Intelligence so I know more than most about the criminal fraternity in Northern Ireland, especially in the Greater Belfast area." His explanation wasn't meant to be boastful; he was simply laying out the facts to explain his background.

Jack fingered his forehead thoughtfully. "There's no doubting you have an interesting pedigree, Peter -- no doubt at all -- and I know Dave wouldn't recommend you lightly -- but I don't have enough going on right now to justify taking on extra staff -- I'm sorry to have to admit it but that's just how it is." He genuinely regretted having to turn the guy down when he had so much potential. On the face of it he appeared to have many of the attributes he looked for in his staff, which made him a really attractive proposition. But attractive though it was, taking on more staff simply wasn't a viable proposition, not financially anyway.

"There's no need for you to apologise, it was only an idea that Dave dreamed up while we were chatting at the bar. But if I might make a suggestion -----" he stopped and waited to see if Jack was interested in listening to his idea.

"Go on then," urged Jack, keen to hear what he had to say.

"I have had a lot of experience with the very people you're hunting down, so it might be worth your while to think about using me on a casual basis, at least until you have this particular case put to bed. It wouldn't cost you much, we could agree a rate for any time I put in, and it would give me a chance to bolster my pension and help tide me over for a while until I find something else." He shrugged his shoulders. "That way there would be no obligation on either side and we both be getting something out of it. It would also give me a chance to show you how useful I can be -- what do you say?"

Jack was impressed with the guy's originality. The idea he'd come up with merited serious consideration, especially as it wouldn't commit either of them to a long term contract. And if nothing else, his suggestion illustrated a canny ability to think creatively without being pushy. In fact there was a lot more merit to the suggestion than Dunseith himself probably realised, especially as Jack needed someone to ride shotgun and watch his back for a while. There was also the separate issue of providing protection for Barratt, if and when the meeting with Devlin took place. The problem of making such an arbitrary decision without consulting his partners had to be considered of course, although that was no more than a fleeting thought as he had already made his mind up.

"I quite like your idea, Peter -- I believe it has enough potential to warrant a trial at least. Let's give it a go, although I'm afraid the pay won't be great until we see where we're going."

He stuck his hand out to have it greeted with obvious enthusiasm.

"Thanks, Jack – that's brilliant and I promise you won't regret it." He pumped Jack's hand up and down like he was jacking up a car.

"I'm presuming from the cheesy grin on your faces that you two have come to some sort of agreement." Jackson's cheerful tone brought the handshake to an end with Dunseith grinning from ear to ear.

"We have indeed, Dave -- it's only a bit of casual work to start with, but it's enough to keep me busy until I get myself established." He turned to Jack. "Let's have a drink to celebrate." The waiter was already being hailed before anyone could deny him the opportunity, and by the time they'd finished their drinks Jack had arranged for Peter to call in with him the following morning so they could tie up the loose ends and run him through a short induction.

In reality Jack was looking for any opportunity to pick his brain about Devlin and his associates, which he was loathe to do with Dave Jackson still in attendance, and once they had finalized things Jack took his leave and left the others to re-join their friends at the bar and continue with their celebration.

32

"What makes you think this guy Dunseith can help us with the Byrne case?" asked Judy, sounding as though she actually wanted to be convinced. There were very good reasons for her to welcome an extra man about the place, especially after the car following incident. She was well aware that Jack over-exposed himself at times, leaving him vulnerable to all sorts of dangers. So having a man of Dunseith's calibre about the place could be a blessing in disguise. She wasn't to know it of course, but Jack had already made a conscious decision to clear the air on the matter before Peter even arrived on the premises.

"To start with I want to pick his brain about Devlin; that much goes without saying, but I also need someone to ride shotgun on Barratt the next time he meets up with Devlin. I can't do it because he already knows me, but I have every confidence that Peter can handle it without too much fuss."

Judy dropped the subject just as quickly as she had brought it up. She might not openly admit it, but she was quite content with the new arrangement as it provided a bit of extra support for her partner. However that was as far as they're discussion went because right then Peter Dunseith walked in on them.

Jack whisked him straight through to his own office where he grilled him for the best part of an hour on Devlin and his underworld connections. In return, Peter offered a detailed brief on the whole criminal family, confirming that it operated almost exclusively out of south Armagh. His detailed briefing turned out to be much more enlightening than anything Dave Jackson had provided.

One point of major significance that came to light regarded a police tout, who some two years earlier had put Devlin's name firmly in the frame for a drug related killing. But as no one was willing to come forward and offer any evidence and as he was living outside the RUC's jurisdiction in the Irish Republic at the time, no further action had been taken. But at least it explained how he came to the attention of the RUC in the first place. It also acted as a warning to Jack over his own cavalier attitude towards the man.

After a lengthy session together Jack was keen to know how Peter rated Devlin in the grand scale of things, and in order to get a balanced judgment he told him about the run-in that had taken place between them and waited to see what he would say.

"Christ, Jack -- that was a serious mistake. Devlin won't let go of something like that -- no way. Even if he wanted to you can bet your bottom dollar his family of cheap thugs won't allow him, it would totally undermine his authority within the mob, not to mention the mob's reputation as well. You would do well to keep your head down for a while"

"Thanks for the warning, Peter, but I'm afraid it comes a bit late as I think the damage has already been done." Dunseith gave him a forced smile that failed to hide his concern.

"Anyway," Jack told him, "getting back to matters at hand, I have a specific job in mind for you, although after what you've just told me you may not be quite so keen to take it on."

Dunseith's expression never wavered, although he shifted his weight from one foot to the other as if to spur things on.

Jack gave him a quick run-down on how he planned to use Barratt.

"If he does manage to tempt him into giving something away, and we get it down on tape, then perhaps we can unearth Tony Byrne's remains and put this thing to bed. The only fly in the ointment is my lack of faith in Barratt's ability to see it through. I don't know if he has the balls to keep Devlin talking long enough to divulge something useful, especially if things go pear shaped, or Devlin gets wind of what's going on.

He draped an arm loosely round Dunseith's shoulder.

"And that's where you come in my friend, because your job will be to go over to Scotland, meet up with Barratt, and accompany him back over the pond. To all intents and purposes you'll be acting as his co-driver, but you'll actually be riding shotgun on him."

There was little reaction from Dunseith, in fact if anything he looked genuinely interested.

"It's unlikely Devlin will let his guard down and drop anything incriminating in the presence of a total stranger, but if he believes you to be just another driver you might be able to stay close enough to the action to keep an eye on things for me."

When he'd finished talking Jack suddenly thought of something he had overlooked.

"I hope I'm right in assuming that you and Devlin have never met?"

"No need to panic, Jack, the guy doesn't know me from Adam. I worked quietly behind the scenes on guys like him for years -- but none of them ever got to know me."

"Thank God for that, Peter, because I want you with Barratt as a support mechanism to help bolster his courage and my own peace of mind. I have to know for certain that we have all the bases covered in terms of everyone's safety."

Dunseith didn't look adversely affected. "I know I have to prove myself to you -- well -- we both know that -- but when things start to pick up round here I'll be expecting you to consider me on a more permanent footing. But for now I don't have any problem with what you're asking me to do, especially if Devlin turns up without a bucket full of heavies.

On the other hand if he does decide to turn up mob-handed I don't see that there's anything any of us will be able do about that. The important thing is that Barratt picks a venue that's not too secluded, or cut off from the general public. We don't want this meeting taking place down some dark alleyway."

Jack gave a reassuring nod. "We have to rely on a little bit of luck regarding that I'm afraid, but as long as you're still up for it it's all systems go for me."

There was something about Peter Dunseith that instilled a feeling of confidence in Jack. The ex-cop's instinctive feel for the business suggested he would settle in really quickly and not need too much chaperoning.

Dunseith folded his arms and stuck his chest out a little.

"What sort of impression would it give if I backed off at the first hurdle? Of course I'm still up for it, but I haven't heard your whole plan yet. I need to know what precautions you plan to put in place."

Hi admission earned him a friendly pat on the back from his new boss.

"We can go through all that when Barratt lets us know what the deal is," Jack promised, "in fact there's no better time than right now to check that out."

He picked up the phone and punched in Barratt's number, but the guy failed to pick up. All he could do was leave a message on his voicemail and pray that the Scotsman wasn't giving him a deliberate by-ball. Time alone would provide the answer to that.

33

After what had been a fairly lengthy introductory session that was rounded off with a brisk walk round the block to clear their heads, Jack returned to the office with his new employee still in tow. They seated themselves side by side on the settee and continued discussing the case, at least until they got to a point where Jack noticed an odd expression on Dunseith's face that he found worrying.

"If there's something bothering you, Peter, just spit it out?"

Dunseith stretched his legs out in front of him.

"I don't want you to take this as a criticism, Jack, but are you not in danger of losing sight of your real objective?"

"What do you mean?" asked Jack.

"Well, as I understand it you've been hired to find this guy Byrne, but the way I see this investigation going you seem to be more interested in finding out who was responsible for his disappearance." There was more he wanted to say, and he only reined himself in not to overstep the mark on his first day.

"Go on," urged Jack, "I can see you're biting your tongue over something -- finish what you've started."

Peter grimaced uneasily as Jack shrugged off his jacket and settled back to listen.

"Look at it this way -- we might well dig up some evidence, or get a break of some kind that leads us to Byrne's whereabouts, or what's left of him, but it won't necessarily follow that we'll ever find out who was actually responsible for what happened to him." He pointed an accusing finger in Jack's direction. "It seems to me you're stuck in a rut right now, and there's not a lot of evidence available to move you forward. You need to focus your attention on the real issue, concentrate on what we know to be fact."

Jack edged forward a little on his seat and let his new employee continue uninterrupted.

"I've always followed one very simple rule when an investigation goes cold, or comes to a dead end -- go back to the scene of the crime. Go back to what you know to be fact."

He waited to see if Jack was accepting his criticism, but he was soon talking freely again.

"When was Byrne last seen? Where was he last seen? Who was the last person to see him? You need to focus on the known facts, because that's where the answers lie. If we can't see those answers then we're missing something."

Dunseith's wake-up call was more effective than he immediately grasped because it made Jack sit up and take stock almost straight away. There was no question he had deviated from the main focus of the case, but when he had considered all of the known facts it had failed to get him anywhere. It was only after he had discovered the connection between all the people involved with the charity that he had gained some momentum. But even allowing for that, he wasn't a lot further on. He had been chasing a consignment of drugs in the hope they would lead him to Tony Byrne, but what if there was no such connection -- where would he end up?

"So what are you suggesting?" he asked.

Peter got to his feet. "We run with what we know to be fact," he insisted. "From what you have told me nobody claims to have seen Byrne getting out of his brothers car on that fateful morning." There was a questioning tone to his voice. "Okay -- I agree there is some questionable evidence that suggests he was seen in his brother's car before he disappeared, but you have to ask yourself how reliable that evidence is ----" Jack cut in before he could finish. "Are you suggesting we challenge his brother's evidence?" he asked, a look of disbelief on his face.

It was the first time his investigative skills had been being put under the microscope, and it irked him, just a little.

"Let's try to remain objective about this." Peter's calm assertiveness produced the desired effect and Jack sat back and let him continue.

"Remember what it is we're trying to do here, I'm simply suggesting that it would be best practice to look more closely at what we know for certain. If someone other than his brother had picked Tony Byrne up from his house that morning, then without doubt that person would now be your prime suspect. Do you see where I'm going with this?"

There was no faulting the logic in his argument, and it made Jack look uncomfortable enough to bury his face in his hands.

Peter ignored his obvious discomfort and carried on regardless, giving him something else to think about.

"Let's assume for arguments sake that Byrne did arrive at the depot in his brother's car, and let's take things from there. You have already indicated that you don't believe Barratt played any part in whatever it was happened to him. So how the hell did Byrne vanish so quickly like that?" He stared at Jack for a few moments with a questioning look on his face.

"For my money Byrne was either never in that bloody street at all -- or he ended up in the back of Barratt's truck." He gave a kind of conspiratorial wink. "As it happens, I suspect the former might be the case, but that's because experience has taught me that the majority of murders are carried out by someone close to the victim's social circle, or a family relative."

He dropped into his seat and leaned forward with his elbows on his knees, his huge hands clasped together like a pair of hammers. "What makes you so sure Byrne's brother wasn't involved in what happened?" he asked, posing another question for Jack that he had no answer to, although he dwelt on it for some time before conceding that he might now be having serious doubt on the subject.

"To be perfectly honest I don't think I am anymore, I thought I was, but now I'm not so sure. I've been taking Alfie Byrne's innocence for granted. Not because I took any particular liking to him when we met, but because Roisin Byrne speaks so highly of him." It took him a few moments to sort out what he wanted to say next. "You're right of course, he had the perfect opportunity, there's no denying that, and he could easily have dumped his brother in the back of Barratt's vehicle without Barratt even knowing anything about it. I'm convinced in my own mind that Barratt is innocent, and he has admitted leaving his truck unattended in a Dublin car park on instructions from Devlin. That was apparently so that whatever contraband he was carrying could be removed." He put his hand over his mouth as he pictured the scenario in his mind's eye. "Whoever carried out that little manoeuvre could have been responsible for removing our missing man at the same time. Whether Byrne was dead or alive at the time is an entirely separate issue, but if we can find out who picked up that consignment in Dublin it might lead us somewhere."

Peter leaned back in his seat and gave a loud sigh. "They would never have handed those drugs over to just any old Tom, Dick or Harry. It was either Devlin who met that truck, or one of those jumped up bastards from south Armagh. But if what you say is true then it's pretty clever the way Barratt has been used in all this. It's possible he didn't see anything, didn't know anything, and possibly didn't even touch anything. And to top it all the silly bugger doesn't even know who he's risking his nuts for." He ruffled a hand through his thinning hair before going on. "Meanwhile Devlin sits back with a clean pair of hands and collects a packet of readies as soon as the goods are delivered south of the border." He smiled grimly. "It's quite possible Byrne discovered what they were up to and had to be silenced. Classic movie stuff really when you think of it?"

He stretched his legs again and settled back with a thoughtful look on his face, but it didn't take him long to come to a conclusion.

"Go after the brother, Jack, he was the last person to see Byrne alive. It all starts there or I'm a bloody Dutchman. If you lose something, don't you always go back to the last place you had it to begin your search?"

Jack stretched his long frame and stood up, then reached across the desk for the intercom. He buzzed Judy and asked her bring them some coffee, then made his way over to the window where he stretched his arms behind his neck and turned round to face Peter again. As he opened his mouth to say something Judy rang to tell him she had Mairead on the line and he headed for the phone instead.

"Hi, Mairead -- what's the buzz?" There was no apparent reason for her to be phoning, and Jack was in no mood to put up with her usual frivolous chatter.

"Hi yourself, Jack, how are you?" she asked sweetly, testing his patience.

"For Christ's sake, Mairead -- I'm busy right now. Have you not got something more important to discuss than the state of my health?" He stuck his hand over the mouthpiece and turned to Dunseith. "Sorry about this, Peter, it's our London office."

Peter donned an amused smile and shrugged indifferently, and while Mairead decided to apply the silent treatment Jack had this picture of her in his mind's eye shaking her fist at the telephone and cursing him under her breath. The thought brought an impish smile to his otherwise strained expression.

"Who pulled your chain? You haven't had a tiff with the lovely lady of the house have you?" she asked.

"Mairead," Jack growled impatiently, "are you going to tell me why you're bugging my earhole or do I have to read the fucking Tarot cards to find out?"

"Okay, okay, keep your bloody shirt on."

She cleared her throat with a delicate cough before continuing. "That guy in the photograph we talked about – the one I thought looked familiar -- well I've remembered where I know him from." She was in danger of having Jack hang up on her.

"For God's sake, just get on with it -- I haven't got all day." She cleared her throat yet again before obliging.

"Before you and I met up last year, while I was still working undercover with MI5, I was tasked to identify all of the fund raising activities the paramilitaries were involved in. There was a lot going on back then as they all lined themselves up for the signing of the Peace Agreement, protection money, tax scams on building sites, VAT fraud, bank robberies, smuggling contraband across the border from the south, particularly agricultural diesel, and of course that other old chestnut -- drugs." She sucked in a lungful of nicotine and blew it out again. "One thing we did find out rather quickly was just how difficult it is to uncover which of these activities were officially sanctioned by the leadership of the paramilitaries, and which were simply fringe benefits used to feather the nests of renegade individuals."

She paused to gather her thoughts.

"There was an added dimension to all this that muddied the waters even more. Many of the breakaway cells from the main terrorist groups were involved in little else but crime in those days." She took another drag on her cigarette.

"Exactly where is this history lesson taking us?" demanded Jack, hoping something of interest was to follow as his patience was being sorely tested.

Mairead picked up the thread in the nick of time. "There was a period when we sought help from the local community in an effort to end the racketeering. Basically it involved paying money to anyone who supplied us with information that led to an arrest and a successful prosecution. Now that's where your guy came on the scene, Jack. I knew I had seen him before and I wasn't wrong." She stopped to puff on her cigarette one more time, leaving the conversation hanging in the air yet again.

"For Christ's sake, Mairead, cough it out." Jack yelled at her.

"Okay -- okay -- keep your bloody knickers on," she snapped. "As I was about to say before you so rudely interrupted me. We uncovered some fairly reliable information about a large consignment of drugs that were supposedly coming into the country, and naturally enough we were ordered to intercept it.

Unfortunately the operation didn't go quite as planned. The vehicle that was supposed to be carrying the drugs never turned up on the day it was supposed to, and when we went back to our source, he informed us there had been a last minute hold up of some sort that meant the delivery would be arriving late. What happened after that proved to be a bit farcical really as we completely lost the target and drew a blank. It was a major disaster for all concerned as you can well imagine, especially after the effort we had put in setting the whole thing up only to come away with egg on our face."

She took another breather, then realized she still hadn't got to the nub of the issue.

"Oh - sorry, Jack," she said hastily, "that's where your guy comes in. We never did manage to catch anybody with the drugs, but we did at least manage to identify the courier. In the end we stuck a tail on him, for bloody months as it happens, but it was a complete waste of time." She took another pull on her cigarette before getting to the real point of her call. "What you need to know is that the guy we were tailing was the same guy in that photograph you showed me. It all happened quite a while back, which is why it took me so long to recall where I knew him from, but I'm absolutely certain of it now. The guy we identified as the drug courier was without doubt the guy you've been hired to find." Jack collapsed on to the settee beside Peter, his mouth gaping open in disbelief. He simply couldn't believe what he was hearing. There had to be some mistake, the guy she was talking about could not be the same guy who was married to Roisin Byrne. Not the same 'sainted' pillar of society, the same church going charity worker who everyone praised for his good character and high moral standing. The very idea was too absurd to take seriously and he completely lost the plot, lambasting

Mairead in no uncertain manner.

"Absolute bollocks, Mairead -- you have got to be mistaken. You can't possibly be talking about the same guy."

It felt a bit strange defending a man he had never even met, but Jack wasn't about to accept that his professional judgment could be so far off the mark, not on such a fundamentally important issue. But it was being called into question, there was no doubting that, even if he refused to accept it.

"Look, Jack, I may have had to chase my memory up a bit on this one, but please don't deny me what I know to be fact. I'm certain it's the same guy, Christ --I shadowed him for long enough. He may be a bit older than I remember him to be, but he hasn't changed that much."

She sounded so convincing that Jack was momentarily speechless. It took a while for him to react.

"Have we any way of checking this out so we can be absolutely certain?" He was finding it very difficult to give in to Mairead's argument. He had never met Tony Byrne, didn't know him from Adam, but from what he had learned about the guy from his friends and fellow workers, and from his wife and the parish priest, he had developed a sort of kinship towards him.

"How certain do you want it to be, Jack?" she asked. "If I tell you his name will that convince you?"

Jack held his breath.

"The guy's name was Byrne." Having been professionally trained by MI5 suggested that if Mairead said she was certain then Jack had no reason to argue the point. But this latest finding was a huge set back that almost knocked the stuffing out of him. "Christ, Mairead, I don't know what to say. It looks as if you're right – that's certainly my guy-- but why the hell did you not remember all this when you were over here and we discussed the case?" He was full of resentful disappointment, and the misery of it carried through to his voice.

"That was down to you, Jack. You flatly refused to discuss the case with me, remember. All you asked off me was to check out this guy Barratt. I didn't even know the name of your missing man, so how the hell was I supposed to make the connection? Anyway it's not my case, as both you and Judy made abundantly clear."

She was right of course, it wasn't her case and she had no reason to know anything about it, but Jack was wishing now that he had given her a fuller briefing when the opportunity had been there to do so.

"I'm sorry if all this upsets your thinking on the case, Jack," she went on, "but it's the same guy right enough, and if you ask me to I could still take you to his house. I spent many a cold and miserable night staking it out."

"Why the hell did you not arrest him then?" he asked.

"Well it was all a bit peculiar in that respect, we followed the bugger for ages but never even saw him go anywhere near a truck, never mind drive one. In the end we thought our source-- who had some serious underground connections by the way -- was just setting us up to waste our time. It happens, Jack -- shit happens, even to the best of us." She was beginning to sound much too flippant, and if Jack hadn't been listening closely enough and paying attention he might have missed something of vital importance, something that suddenly hit him like a bolt from the blue when it did register.

"What the hell do you mean you never saw him driving a truck?" he asked, "the guy earned his living driving a fucking truck -- it's what he does -- it's all he does. There has definitely been some sort of cock-up here, we can't be talking about the same guy, it just doesn't make any kind of sense."

The expression of relief in his voice didn't go unnoticed by Mairead and she regretted having to prove him wrong yet again. "Piss off Jack -- you're the one who's got it wrong. I know what I know. I sat outside the guy's house on the Grosvenor Road far too often to be wrong about it." She was working up a real head of steam, convinced in her own mind that she wasn't mistaken. As a result their conversation was gradually descending into an argument, almost a battle of wills. But like earlier, it took time for the detail of what she said to register with Jack, and having got to his feet when things became heated he dropped down beside Peter again, a satisfied smile on his face.

"Bollocks, Mairead, it was Alfie Byrne's brother you were tailing. Tony Byrne lives off the Falls Road, not the Grosvenor Road." He was overcome with a feeling of elation, without really knowing why, but it passed abruptly when the realization set in that they could both be wrong, albeit for very different reasons.

"Hang on though, you might have been shadowing the wrong brother but I'll bet it was Tony Byrne you were meant to be shadowing -- after all he's the one who is employed as a driver, and he's the one who was on that bloody aid convoy that brought the drugs back from Romania. Although it's my belief that he was unaware of it at the time." Another thought popped into his head that needed dealing with. "You said yourself that he looked older, and that fits the bill perfectly because he is older. They look very alike and could easily be mistaken for each other, especially at a distance, although Alfie has a more receding hairline. Does any of that make sense?"

There was a short lull in the proceedings while Mairead thought it over.

"I guess it's possible, but one thing I am certain of -- the guy we were tailing lived right up at the top of the Grosvenor Road, and that's a fact. What more can I say?"

"Not a lot, sweetheart, unless you can tell me the name of the guy who put you on to him?"

"Jeez, Jack, I can't remember something like that off the top of my head. Joe somebody or other I think it was. It will probably come back to me if I sleep on it."

Jack shook his head in disbelief. "Not Joe Devlin, Mairead -- tell me it wasn't Joe Devlin who tipped you off." The very idea that it might be Devlin was too much of a coincidence to take in, too incredible to even contemplate. Why would Devlin pull such a crazy stunt? There was neither sense nor reason to it. Byrne had been transporting the drugs into the UK for Devlin, so why the hell would he want to call time on his own courier?

Mairead cut across his confusion of thoughts. "Yeah -- that's the guy -- Joe Devlin – it's all coming back to me now." She sounded vague and somewhat distant, but her confirmation that it was Devlin only succeeded in adding further confusion.

Jack's thoughts were all over the place as he tried desperately to grapple with the problem and find an explanation, but it was too irrational for a quick fix. What on earth could Devlin possibly gain from grassing up his own courier? What was the motivation behind it? Such behaviour was hardly in keeping with a thuggish reputation that dictated that you look after your own. But if Mairead was right, and Jack no longer felt obliged to doubt her, then his whole reading of the situation was blown out of the water.

He needed time to think things through, time to run it past Peter and see if between them they could come up with a logical explanation.

"Look, sweetheart," he told her, "your recollection on this has opened up a whole new can of worms. There are issues here that need serious consideration, and that's going to take a little time I'm afraid. I'll call you back when this bloody shambles makes some sort of sense." Even as he was speaking a tiny embryo of understanding was forming in the back of his mind, but he needed time to grow the thought and see how it developed.

"Whatever you say, Jack. Speak to you soon." She disconnected without another word.

Peter had heard enough to let him follow the general thrust of the conversation, and what he had not heard he could pretty well work out for himself, but seeing the look of intense concentration on Jack's face he opted to let him to sort his thoughts out uninterrupted and just sat quietly in abeyance.

A muted interval followed that gave Jack an opportunity to digest everything that had happened and time to sort things out in his own mind.

After a short while he found his voice again. "By God he's one crafty bastard."

"Who is?" asked Peter, believing he meant Devlin, but not certain.

"Devlin of course," Jack said irritably, his face screwed up in concentration as he sorted out his thoughts. "That bastard deliberately grassed Tony Byrne to the police to provide an acceptable rationale for his disappearance. It all makes sense to me now -- thanks to Mairead."

He left his seat and went walkabouts, his hands clasped behind his neck.

"You will need to explain that to me, Jack, because I'm afraid I haven't caught your drift." Peter warned him.

Jack turned to face him and lowered his arms, then pursed his lips in a thoughtful manner; he was clearly struggling to get his thoughts in order. "First of all we have to accept that Tony Byrne somehow got wise to what Devlin was up to, and if that's right, then it must have posed Devlin a real problem, especially at a time when Mairead says the cops were clamping down on the rackets. He must have been worried in case Byrne spilled his guts, especially when there was plenty of money being splashed about to loosen people's tongues. So rather than take any risks he decides to get rid of Byrne -- and what's the easiest way to cover it up? Grass him to the cops as a drug runner of course. Then when he disappears off the scene the cops think he's done a runner to avoid arrest. It's all beginning to make some sort sense to me."

He slid into a chair facing Peter, a satisfied smile opening up his face for the first time since he'd entered into conversation with Mairead.

"Okay, Peter -- I think I've just about got my head round this." He rubbed his face vigorously with both hands before telling his new employee he was no longer needed. "You might as well take off now, I've got some serious thinking to do, and I'll do it better if I'm on my own, but I'd like you back here around lunchtime tomorrow, if that's okay? We still have lots to sort out to prepare your trip over to Scotland." As he watched his new employee walk away he felt uplifted by the knowledge that his theory about the drugs had been right on the money, and while Mairead might have muddied the waters a bit with her phone call, she had at least confirmed that much for him.

34

It was late evening before Barratt returned Jack's call, and when he did he sounded overcautious and hesitant, showing absolutely no enthusiasm for what lay ahead. Having convinced himself that Devlin was too clever and experienced to incriminate himself as easily as Jack hoped he might, the Scot kicked off by making his protest as strongly as he might.

"There's no way Devlin is going to fall for this -- I just know it. I can see me ending up in the shit as usual -- the story of my goddamned life. If you ask me we should forget the whole thing." Unfortunately for Barratt his lack of enthusiasm only served to rile Jack and he let rip down the phone.

"Stop fucking whinging, Barratt -- you're in this whether you like it or not, so let that be an end to it." He took a deep breath to calm himself before carrying on in a more rational voice. "If it's your own safety that's bothering you, you can forget it. I have someone with the right credentials lined up to keep an eye on you. He'll be with you all the way. In fact he'll be acting as your co-driver -- the idea is that the two of you meet up over at your end and you travel back together on the ferry. That way you can get to know each other and not look like total strangers in front of Devlin."

Barratt's mutterings didn't sound quite so negative, prompting Jack to feed him a bit more by way of reassurance.

"This guy knows his way around and he'll be sticking to you like a second skin. Certainly close enough to ensure Devlin keeps his mischievous little hands in his pockets."

"Well," said Barratt, stretching the word out long enough to think about his situation, "I'll have to take your word on that, and while I'm not at all happy about it I've already made a loose sort of arrangement to meet up with Devlin either tomorrow night or Monday night at the

Larne terminal. All I have to do is confirm which night suits me best."

He sounded more at ease now, probably due to the fact that he would have someone else in attendance to protect him from Devlin, and the news about the meeting was a welcome boost to Jack's plan, although it had to be treated with an element of caution. There was a lot of preparatory work to be done before Peter could be dispatched to Scotland. For a start he needed to be put through his paces with the bugging equipment, and there were important security arrangements that had to be sorted out that forced Jack to kill off any hope of the earlier meeting.

"Tomorrow won't do," he told the Scotsman, "it will have to be Monday."

Barratt was clearly in a hurry to end the call, but Jack wasn't finished with him yet. "Tell me how Devlin reacted to the news that you'd been interviewed by the police?"

The Scotsman gave a fearful grunt. "He went buck fucking mad – that's what he did -- wanted to know why they had suddenly taken an interest in me after all this time. In fact he got himself really worked up about it --- gave me a right bucket load of shit."

The terror in Barratt's voice warned Jack not to dwell too long on the subject.

"How did you explain that one away?" Jack asked.

"I told him the cops had started a new line of enquiry, and they'd questioned me about my association with the aid convoy, and with him. I convinced him it wasn't safe to go into too much detail on the phone and suggested we meet up to discuss it. That's what you wanted me to do -- wasn't it?" He was less than brimming with confidence, but there was nothing Jack could do about that, he just had to keep him on side.

"Good man, Barratt -- you did just fine, but you had better remember that it's crucial you press Devlin really hard about what happened to Tony Byrne. Use every opportunity you get to raise that topic, because we won't get a second chance at this."

He was half expecting some form of acknowledgement from Barratt and when it didn't come he pushed him a little to get one. "I hope you appreciate that this is the best option you have -- the only way to get yourself out of this mess. You do accept that now -- don't you?"

"Yeah, yeah -- so you keep telling me -- but it's not your ass on the line -- is it? I just hope you've got all the angles covered pal because it's my ass that's gonna be in the hot seat -- not yours."

His remark sailed past Jack unheeded.

"I'll get my guy sorted out and let you know what the arrangements are for getting him over to your end. It's important that the two of you have some time together before you travel over." He was thinking specifically about setting up the bugging device in Barratt's cab, although rather than complicate things with the Scotsman, he kept that piece of information to himself, knowing he could rely on Peter to sort it out.

"Okay -- so that's it then -- I've nothing else to do until you come back to me -- right?" Barratt asked.

After sending him on his way Jack closed his eyes and ran the conversation he'd just had through in his mind. He was convinced he had put enough pressure on the Scotsman to make him stay in line, which meant he could start putting the rest of his plan in place, and as long as Devlin didn't get too jittery then he believed he could rely on Peter to keep a lid on things.

Having said that, his plan was no less fraught with danger and he knew it, even though he could at least take comfort from the knowledge that he was dealing with nothing more than a bunch of thugs, and not an organized group of paramilitaries. The threat however was still very real and not to be taken lightly; a distracting thought that remained on his mind for the remainder of the evening, though he did eventually go off to bed with the feeling that things were at last moving in the right direction and an end game might not be too far away.

The only weak link in his plan was Barratt, and whether or not he would stand up to the pressure, but that was for Peter to handle, and he wasn't about to lose any sleep over it as he rolled over and closed his eyes.

35

Jack had just driven away from the house when his mobile rang and brought him to an unscheduled halt by the side of the road. The readout flagged up Dave Jackson's name, and as he wasn't expecting to hear from the guy he dithered a bit about answering it.

"If this is an invitation to breakfast you're too late I've already eaten." There was an easy going, light hearted tone to Jack's voice, but if he was hoping for some friendly banter in return he was to be disappointed.

"I don't know where you are, or what you're doing right now, Jack, but I need you to come and see me right away -- and I do mean right away." His abrupt manner implied that a refusal was out of the question.

"What has your knickers in a twist so early in the day, mate? I think you had better tell me what's up otherwise you can join the appointments queue like everyone else."

"I'm not discussing it with you like this, Jack -- not over the phone. Just take my advice and get your ass up here right away, I have some people here who want a word with you, and I'm sure you would rather we kept this informal."

He made no attempt to conceal the threatening tone of his voice, or his threatening choice of words.

"What the hell's going on?" Jack asked, his mind buzzing with all manner of possible scenarios, none of which were confirmed or otherwise by Jackson's negative response.

"You'll know soon enough, Jack. Just get your ass up here as quick as you can, it's important."

Having other plans in mind Jack was in no mood to be ordered about. "I would love to oblige you, Dave, but I'm up to my ass in alligators right now with a very busy schedule and you're simply not on the radar, I'm afraid it will have wait until tomorrow."

Jackson almost snapped his head off. "Read my fucking lips, Jack -- get your ass up here right now."

There was no further conversation as Jackson had already hung up, leaving Jack looking totally mystified and somewhat bemused. His initial reaction was to stare at the phone in his hand as he questioned what was going on, then he tossed it on the passenger's seat with such force that it ended up bouncing into the foot well.

"What the hell is he on about?" he asked himself, trying to second guess from Jackson's attitude what the cause of the crisis might be. His only thought was that neither of them appeared to have any control over it – whatever it was.

Pulling away from the side of the road he headed off in the direction of the city centre, worried sick about Jackson's attitude and the possible consequences of ignoring his demands, which he fully intended to do.

The dignified silence of his deserted office was just what Jack needed to calm his strained nerves. It gave him an opportunity to gather his thoughts without interruption as Judy was still at home playing the domestic goddess. She wasn't expected to put in an appearance much before mid-day, and although he had plenty to be getting on with, his good intentions couldn't compete with the concern he felt over Jackson's mysterious phone call. He did his best to ignore it, but it kept bludgeoning its way to the forefront of his mind between each bout of activity, and every time his thoughts veered off in that direction his whole body tensed up noticeably.

He pressed on as best he could for about an hour or so without making any real headway, until eventually the peace and quiet he was enjoying so much was interrupted by the shrill ring-tone of the office phone. He tried to ignore that as well, but it went on and on until he eventually gave in, accepting that his caller wasn't going to give up.

He had a good idea who it was anyway, or at least he thought he did, so it was with a great deal of reluctance that he reached out and picked it up, his suspicions proving to be correct.

Jackson sounded so worked up about things that Jack had to take a deep breath and refrain from slamming the phone down and cutting him off.

"Listen to me, Jack -- whatever you do, do not hang up on me, I'm giving you some sound advice so please take heed of it. Get yourself up to my office without delay -- and please don't fuck about any more, the people who want a word with you are serious enough to lift you off the street if they have to."

Jack slammed the phone down without answering, turned on his heel, locked up the office and headed out to his car.

It took less than fifteen minutes to get to the police station, cursing and swearing every inch of the way as he vented his frustration on any other road users who happened to get in his way. After checking in at reception he was shepherded through to Jackson's office, his mind set on receiving a less than a friendly welcome. In fact the situation proved to be even worse than he had imagined, judging by the sorrowful look on the four faces lying in wait to greet him.

Two of the four he recognized immediately, having hosted them at his office earlier in the week, and of course he knew Dave, but the fourth man, who was much smaller than the others in stature, was a complete stranger.

Jackson locked eyes with him at the first opportunity, his head swivelling slowly from side to side in a manner that said he was not about to be very welcoming.

"Christ, Jack, you never do anything the easy way -- do you?" He looked anything but pleased, but then neither did Jack.

"What the hell is this all about?" he demanded, directing his question to no one in particular.

Inspector Campbell was wearing the same suit he'd worn the last time they'd met. In fact very little about him had changed in that short time -- except perhaps his attitude. Certainly his tone of voice was less abrasive than it had been on their last encounter.

"It's about time we had a serious little tête-à-tête, Mr. Brennan, if for no other reason than the fact that you are continually walking in our shadow. Dave here has explained to us all about our shared interest in this guy Devlin, but right now all you're doing is getting in our way and muddying the waters."

Realizing that Jackson had betrayed his confidence Jack rounded on him with a look that was nothing short of an accusation, but before he could put his thoughts into words the Inspector read his intention and intervened. "It's no good blaming this on Sergeant Jackson; he had no option but to tell us what he knows of your operation, and anyway, what do you expect -- he's a bloody policeman --- he has a duty to fulfil."

He pointed to a chair that was close at hand, but in all fairness everything was close at hand within the confines of the small office.

"Why don't you sit down, Jack -- may I call you Jack?" he added hurriedly.

Jack treated his request with silent contempt, although he did accept the offer to sit down.

"It's obvious that we both know what Devlin is mixed up in, and when I visited you the other day it was in the hope of persuading you to back off and leave Devlin to us." He folded his arms and cocked his head to one side as he prepared to explain himself. "You're making waves where we don't want them, Jack. We have maintained an interest in Devlin for some years now. We know he controls an extensive racketeering operation that stretches well beyond these borders."

He unfolded his arms.

"Okay -- it's true to say that initially we believed he was just a fringe IRA activist who was dipping his finger in the pie, but recent intelligence has revealed his true status. The guy is a serious racketeer, and may actually be responsible for two, or possibly even three murders."

Campbell looked for a reaction, but Jack presented him with a blank look, and his lack of reaction seemed to drain some of Campbell's resolve as he glanced round at the others in the room before going on. Although in fairness he didn't actually speak again until the well-dressed little man in the corner, a new face to Jack, nodded his head in silent agreement to some secret plan they undoubtedly shared.

It was only the slightest movement of the head but Campbell took it as a signal to go ahead and air their little secret aloud.

"We have someone inside their operation, Jack, but unfortunately he's not too well established just yet. He has been tasked to unravel the details of their structure and the extent of their criminal involvement, both locally and internationally. There have been a number of bank robberies that we believe track-back to this particular gang; its easy cash that helps finance their drugs operation." He only paused long enough to give Jack an unwelcome smile. "I'm sure you're wondering where all this is leading." He looked round the room at the others before continuing.

"Well," he said, dwelling on the word, "it's leading us to you, Jack." He stopped again and turned to face Dave Jackson, as if bringing him into the conversation was some sort of prior arrangement.

Jackson got out of chair with his hands clasped in front of his him and turned to face Jack, his thumbs rolling in a tumbling motion, his sheepish attitude a clear admission of guilt at having breeched their confidence. Although in the circumstances that hardly mattered anymore because Jack fully understood the young guy's situation, and conceded, to himself at least, that he would probably have done the same thing in similar circumstances.

"I had no option but to tell our people what I knew of your plans when they approached me the in the way they did. I hope you can see that, Jack?"

Jack shrugged his shoulders without commenting. He was still trying to figure out what they wanted with him, or from him, and until he did that he was saying nothing.

"We have a very specific problem right now, in so much as we can't afford to have Devlin frightened off and scampering across the border out of our jurisdiction. Not this late in the game, Jack -- not when we have invested so much time and effort and are so close to having the evidence we need to pull the whole bloody gang in."

Oddly enough Jack was enjoying a sense of relief at what he was hearing, relief that none of it had anything to do with their earlier threat over the assault charge; an issue that had been a sickening source of worry to him all day.

With that threat apparently lifted he was beginning to wonder what it was they needed from him that was important enough to drag him in the way they had. For now though he intended to wait for however long it took to see what crept out of the woodwork, since it seemed pretty obvious that nobody was in any great hurry to tell him.

At least that was what he thought -- quite wrongly as it happened, because Campbell heaved himself away from the wall and took up a position behind Dave Jackson who had returned to his chair. "Dave here is of the opinion that you're unlikely to give up on your investigation just to be helpful. So if that's the way of it then I believe it is in both our interests to at least co-ordinate our efforts and not go tripping over one another. Otherwise we might all end up with nothing more than a rear view of Devlin and his cronies heading south over the border."

Every eye in the room was suddenly on Jack, who although conscious of the fact, was dealing with the realization that he appeared to be the one controlling the situation, or at least could be if he so desired. In fact he saw it as a prime opportunity to negotiate something useful in return for his co-operation, and with that thought in mind he turned to Campbell and asked him quite bluntly. "What's in it for me and my client?"

The others immediately turned to each other with serious frowns on their faces, obviously caught off-guard by the directness of Jack's approach.

The small, well dressed stranger in the corner suddenly brought himself into play and entered the conversation, confirming Jack's initial belief that this quiet, unobtrusive little man was the real controller of events.

"What exactly have you got in mind, Jack?" he asked, in a pleasant, upper crust voice; his manner both calm and respectfully polite.

Jack rubbed his face and thought for a moment. The whole situation had been sprung on him without warning, and he was in no hurry to be badgered into something he might later regret. At least not until he had a clear idea of what could be gained from it, although he already had an inkling of that.

"Contrary to what everyone around here seems to think, I am not out to get Devlin, not as such anyway. To me he's simply a means to an end."

He was directing his attention to the anonymous little man in the corner, because whoever he was, his inquisitive expression made it abundantly clear that he was hanging on Jack's every word. Jack gave him a long, hard look in return, but the little guy didn't flinch or look away, he just stared back with the making of a glint in his eye that Jack accepted as an invitation to continue to engage with him.

"My job is to recover whatever there is left of Tony Byrne so that his wife can have somewhere to go on a Sunday morning. It would be a welcome bonus to discover who was actually responsible for his disappearance, and an even bigger bonus if that person was brought to book. I'm not actually interested in what Devlin's organization is up to, as that was never a part of my remit." He stopped talking and let his eyes travel round the faces of the other three, lingering momentarily on each in turn.

"You guys have your own agenda, and it's just bad luck that I'm getting in your way, but there's not a lot I can do about that." His eyes flitted from one to the other again, before settling on the face in the corner. "I don't imagine you dragged me in here just to pass the time of day, so if you have some sort of offer in mind then you had better get it off your chest in a hurry, because I have places to go, and things to do that won't wait."

The little guy came out from the corner and took up a position centre stage. He might well have been upstaged by the other much taller men in the room, but he had a certain presence about him, an authoritative manner that outgrew his lack of physical stature and set him apart, convincing Jack that he was the one he had to deal with.

"A few years ago we almost had Devlin in the bag," he explained, stroking his chin thoughtfully. "In all truth we really should have done -- but through one of those unforeseen human errors that can beset even the most disciplined organisations, we let him slip through our fingers. To be perfectly honest, Jack, we're still not sure exactly what went wrong, but that single mistake, or human error, call it what you want, resulted in a very large consignment of high-grade cocaine ending up on the streets of Dublin. You don't need me to tell you that we simply cannot afford to have anything go amiss this time." He twisted his neck to look round at Campbell, as if holding him responsible.

Jack maintained an air of marginal interest, even though his mind was buzzing with activity. This particular tale of woe had a very familiar ring to it, because unless he was very much mistaken, Mairead had related the same sorry tale to him just recently, and in much more detail.

He was convinced they were referring to the same operation she'd been involved with that had brought her into contact with Tony Byrne. More importantly, at least as far as he was concerned, from what she had told him he was probably the only one in the room who knew exactly why their operation had failed. It was for him to decide whether or not to divulge what he knew, or keep it up his sleeve in case things didn't pan out and he needed a bit more ammunition to bargain with.

Before he could make his mind up the little guy gave him something else to think about.

"The word is that another big delivery of cocaine is due in very soon. We are not sure exactly when just yet but our source tells us that it is fairly imminent." He cocked an eyebrow as a sort of warning of what was to follow.

"So you see, Jack, the last thing we need right now is someone rocking the boat. Even you must see that, and if you're not willing to be reasonable about it then I will have to make sure you are kept off our patch until this operation is concluded." He didn't look entirely comfortable issuing the threat, and glanced round at the others to gauge their reaction. Unfortunately the pained expression on Campbell's face made his feelings all too obvious, although in fairness to him he did his best to lighten the threat and keep Jack sweet.

"I don't think we need to take things that far -- do we, Jack?" he asked, his voice laden with mock charm that did little to raise his standing in Jack's eyes. At least the little guy -- whoever the hell he was, and Jack believed him to be MI5 or something similar, had the bottle to lay it on the line warts and all. Which was something he appreciated more than Campbell's smarmy approach, in any case he was about to put Campbell firmly back in his box.

"Why not, Inspector?" he asked stubbornly, causing everyone in the cramped little office to look at each other in despair.

The lingering silence that grew out of Jack's blunt retaliation was almost tangible, and would have lasted much longer if Dave Jackson hadn't intervened. Fortunately he and Jack still had a reasonable working relationship, at least he assumed they did, even allowing for today's little escapade.

"Come on, Jack," he coaxed, "you've had your pound of flesh, so how about joining the rest of us in the real world. We all want the same thing here so why not tell us what you're planning for Devlin and let's see how we can move things along. All this pussy-footing about is getting us nowhere."

Jackson's timely intervention was precisely what Jack had been holding out for, as it created an opportunity to show the young detective up in a good light. It offered a chance to have him credited with being the successful mediator, and that was more attractive to Jack than some unknown face who had just stepped out from a back office at MI5, or some other dark place.

He felt he owed something to Jackson for his generally helpful attitude, while he didn't owe the rest of them a spit in hell.

"Monday Night," he said unexpectedly, his announcement leaving them all hanging in mid-air and defusing their over-eager anticipation, while at the same time endeavouring to keep control of the conversation for as long as possible.

It was his belief, rightly or wrongly, that once he revealed his plan control would immediately shift out of his hands and revert to this not insignificant little pin stripe suit in the corner. Vacating his chair he got to his feet and surveyed the others.

"Monday night," he repeated, "that's when it happens. Devlin will be confronted at the Larne terminal by someone who has a close connection with him, someone who will be rigged so I can hear and record everything that goes on between them. Hopefully we will get some sort of admission about what happened to Tony Byrne, at least that's the plan as it stands at the moment. I don't know how that can help you lot, but I'm not about to change my plans for anybody"

The little guy came out of the shadows again to motion Campbell to one side and whispered quietly in his ear, too quietly to be overheard. Campbell nodded his head in mutual agreement and glanced in Jack's direction with an expression that revealed exactly what he was thinking, and what he was about to suggest. Jack had already read the signs and saved him the trouble.

"I take it you want me out of the way for a while." He was already reaching for the door handle as he spoke.

The little guy in the smart suit smiled knowingly. "That's very perceptive of you, Jack -- we only need a few minutes, if you would be so kind. Sergeant Baxter here will take you for some quiet refreshments."

Turning to Baxter he said. "Use any office you want to – leave your phone on and I'll call you when we need you."

Jack was already through the door and waiting for Baxter to join him.

It was a full twenty minutes before the call came through, and there was no doubting that the atmosphere was less tense and much more agreeable when Jack finally got back to Jackson's office. In fact the others appeared to be in a quite lively, almost animated mood. They were clearly very pleased about something.

"Ah -- Jack -- do come in." It was Campbell who welcomed him back. "We believe we have put together a plan that will suit both parties."

He looked far too smug and self-confident for Jack's liking, twirling both ends of his bushy moustache in a simultaneous waxing motion, like some outdated Colonel Blimp. Jack had a growing dislike for the man, but he didn't want to take on an attitude about it, he knew it was safer not to let his feelings show until a deal was struck.

"Really," he replied, without expression.

"We're all convinced about your willingness to be helpful, and we're agreed that you might have a genuine opportunity to gather some evidence -- or as you put it -- an admission that might implicate Devlin in the disappearance of this guy Byrne. We do have some concern that Devlin might get wind of what you're up to and go to ground, leaving us up the creek with an expensive three-pronged investigation that has hit the skids."

He took his hands away from his face and made a collective motion embracing the rest of his group. "You do see our concern?" he paused for effect before continuing. "On the other hand, if you were to succeed in tying Devlin to this Byrne murder it would present us with a very useful lever to help loosen his tongue. Particularly as we think it unlikely he would have pulled the trigger himself -- so to speak. So maybe -- just maybe he would feel like being more co-operative rather than face up to a murder charge. Believe me, Devlin knows everything there is to know about the goings on in the shady world he belongs to. He could open up a whole Pandora's box for us if we had the right leverage to help exert some pressure."

He stopped to take stock, but before he could get back in the swing of things the little guy in the corner, who Jack still had not been introduced to, decided to take over.

"Allow me to continue if I may, Inspector," he said, looking down at his feet for a moment, deep in thought before taking the few steps necessary to bring him alongside Jack. Reaching out he placed a hand on Jack's shoulder to draw him away from the others. Not that it was possible to achieve any real degree of privacy in such an enclosed space, but it helped create an atmosphere of confidentiality between them that he clearly felt useful.

"I'm about to give you your chance, Jack, but I need you to assure me that if your plan backfires, or fails in any way, you will pull out immediately and leave Devlin to us." His voice was little more than a whisper, soft and low, but his eyes carried the real message. They said he was unwilling to mess about any longer, which to some degree suited Jack, as he had long since accepted that he would eventually be forced to concede to the greater good. In any case it seemed inevitable that if he failed to prove a link between Devlin and Byrne's disappearance then his case would have nowhere to go and simply grind to a halt anyway. But in terms of his client's finances, well, he knew exactly what they amounted to because she had made a point of telling him, and the one thing he was determined not to do, if there was any way to avoid it, was to use up every last penny of the poor woman's savings. For that reason he was determined to squeeze every last concession out of the opposition to support her cause before agreeing to any compromise.

"What's in it for my client if I manage to pin a murder rap on Devlin?" he asked, mimicking the same hushed tone the other man had used.

"I suppose you get two things really." His arm drew Jack further into the corner, and further away from the others, but he hardly needed to because they were murmuring quietly among themselves so as not to be seen to be eavesdropping. The little guy stroked his chin thoughtfully. "Firstly, if the matter hasn't already been resolved by your own good administrations, we will make every effort possible to determine the whereabouts of Tony Byrne's remains for you, that's a guaranteed first priority as soon as we get the chance to interrogate Devlin." He gave Jack a pointed look and checked that none of the others were paying them too much attention. "Secondly," he went on, "there would be a sizable reward for any information that led to a successful arrest and prosecution of someone involved in serious criminality."

He reached up to sneak his arm further round Jack's shoulders with an intimacy that was decidedly unwelcome.

Jack shrugged his arm away none too aggressively. "How big a reward?" he whispered.

"Substantial, Jack, quite substantial." He made it sound very attractive. Jack angled his head and stared into the grey, blue eyes that were only inches from his own. He was intrigued by this apparently important little man and whatever office he held, but more important than that, he needed to decide very quickly if this diminutive little bureaucrat could be trusted.

The little guy refused to break the eye contact that locked them together, and in that brief moment of common connection Jack made his mind up.

"Okay," he said, "we have a deal -- now can I get the hell out of here and get on with some real work?" Escaping the stuffy atmosphere of the cramped little office had become a necessity as he was badly in need of some fresh air. But as he reached out for the door handle the nameless little man in the pin stripe suit got there before him, stopped, and turned back to look at him before leaving. "One last thing before I go, make sure you inform us of any change in your plans regarding Devlin. Sergeant Jackson will be your point of contact, you can brief him on the detail. He might even have something useful to tell you in return." With a motion of his arm to ensure his two companions followed he wheeled away and was gone, maintaining the same anonymity with which he had arrived.

They were no sooner on their own than Jack sought an explanation from Dave Jackson. "How did all this come about?" he asked, feeling a bit disgruntled as he was no longer sure of his feeling towards the guy, although deep down he very much wanted to trust him.

It was as plain as day from his expression that Jackson had no idea where to begin. It was even more obvious in his demeanour that there was something else bothering him as he stretched the silence longer than was comfortable for either of them. He suddenly got up from his chair perched his backside on the corner of his desk. "There was something else Inspector Campbell should have told you, Jack." He stretched his neck into his collar to ease the tension he was feeling. "He has good reason to believe there is a hit out on you." He paused to let it sink in. "You were actually mentioned by name, so don't go thinking we're just trying to put the frighteners on you. I only got word of this last night from Campbell, and when I reminded him of our duty to inform you, that was when the decision was made to haul you in for a chat." He pulled a sombre face. "This is a serious issue, Jack, we have every reason to believe you are in real danger. When I got wind of it I had no choice but tell them everything you confided to me, and I don't regret doing so because there was no other option." For once in his life Jack was at a loss for words, he hadn't expected anything like this and it took a while for the enormity of it to sink in, when it did his confusion quickly turned to anger. "And just exactly when were you lot going to inform me that I'm in danger?" he snapped, "After I'd been fucking shot?"

Jackson looked uncomfortable and hapless. "I'm telling you now, Jack, and this is the first fucking chance I've had for Christ's sake, and if you had been less bloody minded this morning you would have found out much earlier."

He pulled his jacket off and tossed it aside, paying no attention to where it landed.

"Get more than two people at a time in this damned place and it's like a goddamned sauna," he snarled, tearing his shirt collar open.

He would get no argument from Jack, the guy's office didn't even have a window and the atmosphere was laden with a mixture of sweaty body odours and stale nicotine.

"You need to be very careful, my friend. I don't need to tell someone like you how to look after yourself -- but you should bear in mind what happened to Tony Byrne."

Jackson looked thoroughly miserable and genuinely concerned for Jack's safety, so much so that it made Jack reconsider his earlier condemnations. But right then his only desire was to get away and be on his own to do some serious thinking, and after a brief word about keeping in touch he beat a hasty retreat from the building.

36

It was early Saturday morning, and although Jack didn't normally work at weekends, he did occasionally nip into the office to check the mail. On this occasion however Judy had booked him an appointment for nine thirty to see a potential new client. Unfortunately she had failed to advise him about it until late the previous evening, which meant he had to go in earlier than would normally be the case on his day off.

Judy was quite upbeat at the possibility of securing what sounded like a lucrative new deal with a debt collection agency. Had she left it to Jack the appointment would never have been made, not on his day off, and not when he had so much else to cope with, but of course she wasn't aware of everything that was going on and wasn't in a position to know any better.

But now, as he made his way through the slow moving traffic he was beset with a feeling of impending gloom, and hard as he tried he couldn't clear his mind of the gathering doubts about the forthcoming meeting between Barratt and Devlin. Not that he could do anything about it, except keep his fingers crossed; it was too late for anything else. It was up to Barratt to follow through with the arrangements they'd set in place, but for some reason Monday seemed a fearfully long way off.

When he finally got to the office building he found his normal parking space claimed by a scruffy looking little hatchback with a disabled sticker on the windscreen. And with no other vacant spaces in sight he was forced to go round to the loading bay at the rear of the building.

Returning to the main entrance on foot he pressed the buzzer to alert the security man and peered through his own reflection in the heavy glass doors for any sign of life. As a general rule the building wasn't open to the public at weekends, except by special arrangement, and Tom, who had the dual role of caretaker come doorman, might be anywhere inside the building attending to odd jobs or cleaning up. With nothing better to do he checked his own reflection in the makeshift mirror while waiting for the guy to put in an appearance. He wasn't to know it, but his plans for the day were about to be seriously disrupted.

The high velocity bullet that missed his head by the merest fraction of an inch left a whispered sound trail as it punched a furrow through the atmosphere millimetres from his left ear.

Quite often the displacement of air generated by a high velocity bullet can he detected by the human ear if it is close enough to the bullet's flight path -- Jack's ear was definitely close enough -- much too close in fact, but he heard nothing of it because it was masked by the sound of a passing car.

What he did not miss however was the sound that followed a split second later; a hollow thud of the steel tipped round impacting on the wooden structure beside his left temple. It was an unmistakable and all too familiar sound that he recognized instantly. With the doors in front of him locked and barring any forward escape, his instinctive reaction was to hit the ground rolling and scurry out of the line of fire. In fact he ended up crawling on his belly behind the little hatchback that was parked with its off-side wheels up on the pavement.

His evasive action proved to be a real life saver, as it took him out of the line of fire and the other three rounds that followed in rapid succession. They left tight little triangle in the splintered wooden structure where his head should had been. Unarmed, and only vaguely aware of the general direction of the attack he could do nothing to retaliate. His only option was to stay put behind the protective cover of the car, and after a heart thumping couple of minutes, when he thought it safe to do so, he got up on his knees and peered through the car window in search of any further danger, but there was nothing obviously threatening to be seen.

He was certain the shots had come from a high velocity rifle and not a hand gun, which meant it was most likely to have been a long range shot. Yet as he scoured the buildings and roof tops in the middle distance that might offer a direct line of fire on his position he was unable to identify anything that looked remotely suspicious. Whoever the shooter was, it was obvious he would not hang around in case he was spotted by a roving cop car or an impromptu army patrol. Most likely he had already taken to his toes and made good his escape, professional shooters don't hang around after taking their shot, and as this had all the hallmarks of a professional hit Jack stayed put behind the van until he was absolutely certain it was safe to break cover.

Glancing over his shoulder he spotted a couple of females observing his bizarre behaviour with childish amusement, and although they were unaware of his predicament, or the danger involved, they nevertheless concluded it was best to give him a wide berth. In fact they turned their heads away in the pretence that they hadn't seen him and continued their journey down the middle of the road. Jack's was about to wave them out of the way when his attention was claimed by a raised voice behind him.

"Mr. Brennan – quick – get yourself in here."

Spinning round he saw the doorman standing with his foot jammed against the open door waving like a mad thing for him to hurry inside. Being something an old soldier, and having witnessed what had taken place, Tom had put two and two together and made an accurate assumption. Jack dived through the narrow gap and into the safety of the unlit building.

"Christ, Mr. Brennan -- are you okay?" he gasped, looking terribly flustered and distressed. The elderly doorman might be getting on in years but he was still bright enough to deduce from Jack's weird behaviour that he had been shot at.

"I'll go ring the cops," he gasped, panting slightly as he made off towards the phone on the nearby reception desk.

"Leave it, Tom," Jack snapped, stopping him dead in his tracks. "Just leave it," he repeated. "I'll sort this out myself, no need for you to concern yourself, but thanks for getting me in off the street."

The old boy wasn't best pleased and gave him a very questioning look.

"Are you sure about that, Mr. Brennan? It doesn't seem right to me not to report it. I think you should call the police right away, they might still catch whoever it was who fired at you."

Jack gave him a wry smile.

"I very much doubt it, Tom, they'll be well gone by now if they've any sense, and it would only be an exercise in futility."

He looped an arm round the old guy's shoulder and guided him further into the building. "Thanks for your concern, Tom, but I'll be fine now, honestly."

The old boy shrugged indifferently. "You know best I suppose," he conceded, somewhat grudgingly, "in which case I might as well get on with the rest of my chores."

He took a few shuffling steps, then turned back at the foot of the stairs. "Let me know when you're leaving – won't you, Mr. Brennan."

"I'll not forget to do that." Jack promised, as he headed across the foyer to the lift.

Feeling much safer within the confines of his own office his first course of action was to get himself a stiff drink. The shooting incident had unnerved him sufficiently to make him dwell on his decision not to inform the police, indeed it took a lot of serious thought before he finally decided against it. The only good thing to come out of the incident was that it made him realize just how dangerous things had become. It also made him realize that this particular case was becoming something of a nightmare.

"You murderous bastard Devlin," he snarled, literally spitting the words into his glass, before tipping its contents down his throat. There was no doubt in his mind about who was responsible for the attack, and the more he thought about it the greater was his desire to go out and reap revenge.

It was only by sheer strength of will that he held himself in check. That, and the knowledge that if his plan ever came to fruition it would be no time at all before he had Devlin exactly where he wanted him. Bringing the case to a quick conclusion was even more important now, because he was fast discovering that the longer the investigation went on the more hazardous it became. This latest incident was another aspect of the case that he wouldn't be telling Judy about, and that concerned him greatly because he needed to protect her as well. "How many more bloody secrets do I have to keep from her?" he asked himself, his words filled with bitter regret.

"Damn this bloody case," he moaned, his frustration simmering marginally below critical as he topped his glass up and knocked it straight back. Then slamming the empty glass down on his desk he glanced at his watch a little anxiously, conscious of how quickly the time had gone-by since his arrival. If things had gone to plan he would be away from the office and clear of the city centre by now, but nine-thirty had been and gone without any sign of an appearance from his prospective client, consequently the seeds of doubts over the authenticity of the appointment were growing stronger and stronger. Indeed it was no time at all before he concluded that the whole thing had been nothing but an elaborate set-up. A clever ruse to ensure Devlin's thugs knew exactly when and where to find him.

"Thanks a million, Judy," he muttered, looking seriously pissed off with life. His angry outburst no more than a reaction to being shot at, but nevertheless totally unfair as the events of the morning had nothing to do with Judy. The problem was of his own making, he was the one who had slipped up, and seriously at that, he had been well and truly warned of a potential threat and had failed to take the proper precautions, more importantly, he hadn't even carried his personal weapon with him! The whole sorry episode had been a rude awakening and had given him other, much more important, issues to deal with. He was supposed to be meeting Peter later as well, but there was no way he was coming back to the office for that after what had just gone down. A hurried phone call changed the venue, and after a thorough check round the office, he locked up, left the office by the back door and headed home, keeping a close watch on the rear view mirror every yard of the way.

37

Jack's inexplicable reluctance to report the botched attempt on his life to the police met with fierce opposition from Peter Dunseith, and while his new boss sat somewhat belligerently nursing a mug of coffee he was letting off steam as he paced restlessly up and down the kitchen floor.

"There's no sense being bloody minded about things, Jack, your personal security is under threat, and whether you like it or not you're in need of protection. You've just had a blatant and very public attempt on your life and you need to do something about it." With Jack continuing to ignore his remarks he tried another tack. "Why don't you at least discuss it with Dave Jackson, privately even; it's absolute madness to leave things as they are now -- surely you can see that?"

He shook his head in despair.

"You can't let a thuggish bastard like Devlin go around shooting at people and do nothing about it. If you let him away with this there is no knowing what he might do next."

Having said his piece he turned his attention to the contents of his mug, swirling the remaining dregs round in little circles as he tried to figure out if Jack was taking the seriousness of his situation on board. In the circumstances it was wise to assume that he had taken his eye off the big picture, temporarily at least as he focused his energies on his more recent and more immediate problems.

If that was the case, then he was about to be reminded that it was ill-advised to do so.

"What if Devlin decides to go for an easier target next time?" Peter asked, meaning Judy of course, but shying away from actually using her name.

Jack cupped his chin in his hands and stared straight past his colleague, then closed his eyes in panic to block out the fearful image his warning had induced. The possibility of Judy being at risk sent an eerie shiver down his spine. He had always known she was a soft target, but he had never expected Devlin to make a direct attempt on his life in the way he had, and with that one solitary violation Devlin had created a wholly different set of constraints to be dealt with. The fact that he had unleashed his hit man into a crowded city centre, on a busy shopping day, convinced him that Judy might easily become a target. And terrifying as that thought was, it still fell short of convincing him to go to the police for help. Indeed if he was to choose that route then the cops would have no option but to pull Devlin in and investigate him for attempted murder, and that would scupper every plan he had.

Peter could argue himself blue in the face but it was to no avail, Jack had already calculated the risk as acceptable, especially if it brought him any closer to achieving his goal. Not that his decision in any way lessened his fears about Judy's safety, indeed, as he stood brooding over his mug of coffee, all sorts of potential hazards raced through his mind. He was so preoccupied thinking about Judy that he failed to notice he was the subject of close scrutiny himself. Peter studied his determined expression from no more than a few feet away, and it became obvious, even to him, that any further argument on the subject would be a waste of his time.

He'd met too many guys of Jack's ilk in the past not to recognize the trait. Guys like him were a breed apart, a dying breed perhaps, but the sort who never accepted second best, once they set their sights on a target they didn't know how to deviate, they just forged ahead no matter what the cost. It suddenly occurred to him that Dave Jackson hadn't been far off the mark when he had described him as ruthless, although when Peter took time to think about it, even ruthless fell some way short of the mark.

Sensing he was under scrutiny Jack looked up.

"We still have to determine exactly how Barratt should handle Devlin. There's so much riding on the outcome of this meeting that he has to make it work for us -- we won't get a second chance if he fucks it up."

Peter nodded his agreement and shifted his thinking to something more positive. "I couldn't agree more, but we can only point him in the right direction and give him a bit of protective cover, after that it's up to him. If he doesn't know by now what we're after then he never will. One thing he must not do though is push Devlin too hard, that could be fatal; he just needs to keep the conversation reasonably focused on Byrne's disappearance. It will improve our chance of success no end if we keep the plan simple and uncomplicated, because judging by your assessment of Barratt, I don't see him doing anything that needs a lot of brainpower."

Jack gave a wry smile. "You may be right, but once you and I commit to a plan I'll be leaving it up to you to brief Barratt, and between you and me we had better get a move on because I don't relish the idea of being here all night."

His prediction may have been made in jest, but the evening was growing a considerable beard before he was satisfied that they had covered all the angles. However, as soon as that moment arrived he wasted no time in wrapping things up.

"When you meet up with Barratt tomorrow make bloody sure he listens to everything you say. If you have any problems, anything at all that you don't like, or anything that smells fishy, I want to know right away. And regardless of anything else that's going on be sure to give me a call before you board the ferry -- I need an update on how you feel about things before you start heading across the pond." He cocked a warning eyebrow at his colleague. "That will be our last chance to call it off if there are any doubts, once you're on board the ferry -- we go through with it whatever happens. We simply don't have any other choice" Dunseith was visibly weary from the repetitive nature of the evening's work and Jack decided it was time to wrap things up. "You get on your way now, Peter, and good luck with Barratt."

It wasn't until Peter had gone that Jack began thinking negatively. He was placing a lot of responsibility on two people he knew very little about, both of them an unknown quantity, and while he trusted his instincts that Peter's experience would see him up to the task, he wished he could put the same faith in the Scotsman.

His concerns about Barratt were soon set aside when the forlorn image of Roisin Byrne encroached on his thoughts, and along with it the uncertainties that he imagined must tax her everyday existence. It was almost impossible to contemplate the legal wrangling she'd had to endure; the difficulties she faced over something as relatively simple as cashing in her husband's insurance policy. Such normal, everyday events become seriously complicated when there is no death certificate to support a claim -- but how do you get a death certificate when you don't have a body?

The poor woman was stuck in a time warp without even a grave to tend, she certainly couldn't erect a headstone when there had never been a funeral.

These were the unpleasant but simple things that normal people took for granted when a loved one passed on, but not so for Roisin Byrne. She lived her life in limbo, married to a husband who ceased to exist, clinging to a memory that chained her, both legally and morally, to a non-existent marriage. And all because of an event, as yet unexplained, that rooted her emotionally and legally to a day three years earlier when the man she loved, unwittingly, and hopefully unintentionally, put her whole life on hold.

Jack conjured up an image of his client standing beside her husband's grave as his remains were finally put to rest. That would be the day, when regardless of all the pain and the sorrow that Roisin Byrne would start to re-live her life, it would also be the day when he would hope to have justified her faith in him.

For now though it was all he could do to shake off the feeling of hopelessness that crowded in on him, making him regret having opened his mind to such misery; regret allowing his emotions to come into play.

But who else was there to share the burden of guilt over his lack of progress?

"Go to bed Brennan," he told himself, fearful that his present mood might all too easily tempt him back to the whiskey bottle. In any case, tomorrow was another day.

38

Barratt's mud splattered forty-footer rolled slowly down the unloading ramp bringing the reluctant Scot ever closer to his dreaded encounter with Devlin. Once clear of the unloading bay he almost turned it back on itself as he traversed a wide arc across the tarmac towards the open expanse of the terminal car park. Dunseith sat across the cab from the Scotsman, one foot resting casually on the dashboard, looking for all that mattered like someone who had occupied that same position most of his working life.

He was holding a newspaper at arm's length, open at the sports section, apparently unconcerned with anything else that was going on around them; while in reality he was acutely aware of everything that was happening that might affect their plan. Dressed in a navy roll-neck sweater, blue jeans, and a pair of steel capped industrial boots, he was satisfied that the story they had concocted to cover his presence was plausible enough to withstand scrutiny.

Barratt drove on in search of an isolated parking bay that was well away from the main entrance, ensuring he would have ample warning of Devlin's arrival. The down side to this meant that the terminal building itself, and the facilities it provided, were some way off.

Neither man had any idea when Devlin would turn up, so once in place all they could do was sit and wait. And as the first five minutes ran to ten, and then fifteen, Dunseith climbed out to stretch his legs with a short trip to the terminal building for a cold drink.

He was actually on his way back when he spotted the brown Mazda swing through the gates and cut across the tarmac in Barratt's direction. What he'd failed to see however were the two heavies who had leapt from the car just before it turned into the car park, a few yards short of the foot passenger's entrance. In fact it was more luck than judgment that got him back to the truck before the Mazda, but it was a close run thing.

Climbing back into the cab he found Barratt in a highly agitated state, the guy looked sick with worry and about ready to crap himself. Mind you, his fears increased tenfold when he too spotted the Mazda heading towards them and the realization sank in that his defining moment had all but arrived. To be fair he did at least regain some of his composure once Dunseith was settled beside him. His timely arrival a much needed morale booster that coincided perfectly with the Mazda coming to a halt just few feet from Barratt's cab door.

Devlin looked like something out of a horror story as he glared up through the open window. Indeed he looked even more brutish than Barratt remembered, and allowing for the fact that most of his face was masked behind a surgical splint --- that took some doing. The ugly looking contraption, that was designed to reshape his shattered nose, was held in place by a couple of broad strips of plaster that looked more like straps than strips. An angry gash that re-sculptured his right eyebrow was knit together by seven or eight spidery looking stitches. While the puffed up swelling round his mouth simply drew attention to the absence of any front teeth and created an altogether sorry looking image. One might even be forgiven for thinking that his injuries alone were justification for Peter's keen interest in him, but it was not so. He was more concerned as to why the battle scarred thug chose to stay seated behind the wheel of the Mazda looking sullen and wary, his eyes boring into Barratt in a way that said there was no love lost between them.

"Who's that bastard in there with you?" he snapped, pointing an accusing finger in Peter's direction.

Barratt shrugged and gave him a blank look. "Just a guy learning the ropes, he comes from these parts originally but he lives near me now and does me a bit of casual now and again, covers for me when I'm on holidays and things like that." He sounded plausible enough, off-hand almost.

"You might be glad of him one day when I'm not around and you're looking for something moved in a hurry."

Devlin stretched his neck through his open car window to get a better look at Peter, but gave it up as a bad job.

"Get him outta there -- we need to talk." he snarled, his words slurred and lisping due to the absence of any front teeth.

Turning to Peter, Barratt mimed the words 'stay close', before doing as he was told. "Go take a leak or something," he told him, in a voice loud enough for Devlin to hear, "I'll call you when we're ready to go."

Peter climbed out and ambled round to the back of the truck where he leaned against the tailgate looking thoroughly pissed off. Although he looked altogether more interested when the tiny ear-piece in his left ear suddenly bleeped a signal at him, confirming that Barratt had remembered to switch their device on.

"What's all this crap about you talking to the cops?" Devlin growled, as he hauled himself up into the cab beside the nervy Scotsman.

There was a scary moment when Peter couldn't quite make out what Devlin was saying, and his hand dived hurriedly into his jacket pocket to check the earpiece connection and adjust the volume. In fact he needn't have been concerned because as soon as Devlin got settled in the cab his voice came booming through loud and clear. Certainly loud enough for Barratt, because he went straight into attack mode.

"Maybe I should shut that big gob of yours permanently and have done with it."

The colour drained from Barratt's face and he edged to the corner of the cab away from Devlin's prying eyes.

"This thing with the cops has got damn all to do with me, Joe." Barratt pleaded, "Some guy by the name of Brennan put them on to me, according to them he's some sort of private investigator or something. Anyway, the cops said it was him that put me in the frame over that guy Byrne's disappearance -- the bastard even conned me into delivering a parcel to him so he could have a go at grilling me." Barratt knew it was wiser to come clean about his meeting with Jack, for fear Devlin already knew about it, or found out about it later. A slip up like that could be catastrophic, as none of them knew how trustworthy the transport manager at Zipline was, especially if the pound notes were waved in front of him. Either way, he wasn't about to take the risk, as Devlin might know more than he was letting on. Although what he came out with next indicated that it was unlikely he did.

"What the hell have you been saying to that snooping bastard?"

Barratt backed off again, at least as far as the cab door would allow. "How the hell could I tell him anything?" he argued, "I don't know anything. Not about Byrne -- or what happened to him. The guy just took to his toes and disappeared from what I hear, and that's got bugger all to do with me."

As the heated debate continued inside the cab, Peter was listening for any indication that things might get physical, but it seemed, for the moment anyway, that Barratt was holding his nerve pretty well and doing a good job. Strangely enough his main worry was that the Scotsman might get over confident and press too hard for information about Byrne.

Devlin might well have been reading Peter's thoughts because at that very moment he reached out and grabbed Barratt by the shirt front, dragging him across the cab until their faces were only inches apart.

"What did that bastard Brennan say about me?" He spat the words into Barratt's face with such force that he covered him in saliva.

Barratt wiped his face and tried to fight him off, but he was too powerful and had him in a vice like grip. "He reckons you're running drugs." His voice wavered as Devlin's sourness breathed into his face. "And he reckons you've been using my truck to transport them in for the IRA." It was much easier to sound convincing when he relied on the truth. "He reckons it was you who got rid of Byrne because he found out what you were up to -- he even said you moved Byrne's body down to Dublin in the back of my fuckin' truck."

Devlin's eyes opened wide in astonishment.

"What?" he screamed, hauling the beleaguered Scotsman across the cab, his shirt front ripping apart like tissue paper?

To Barratt's relief he released him almost as quickly, as if he'd been side-tracked by something more important, but the intense look on his battered face warned Barratt that he had very definitely said the wrong thing. "Don't go taking it out on me," he pleaded. "You asked me what he said, and I'm telling you." He pawed his shirt front back into shape. "Do you want me to tell you what happened or not?"

Leaning against the tailgate Peter recognized the fear in Barratt's voice, but he was in no position to be of any help, unless of course things turned really nasty, by which time it would no longer matter if he declared his hand. As things stood he was quietly pleased with the way they were going -- Barratt's feigned act of innocence was an Oscar winning performance, even if it was bolstered by the mistaken belief that he had ample reinforcements at hand.

"Yeah, I hear you, now just shut the fuck up and let me think." Devlin dismissed Barratt like some cheap flunky, allowing him a few moments respite.

"I'm gonna have to do something about this guy Brennan." His voice was low and menacing, making it sound more like a mumbled thought, and it suddenly dawned on Barratt that he wasn't talking to him at all but simply airing his thoughts aloud, convincing himself of what needed to be done.

Recalling Peter's instruction about keeping the conversation focused on Byrne he eased back towards the cab door again, ready to make his getaway if Devlin reacted badly to his next prompt.

"You mean knock him off like you did Byrne?" It took every ounce of his flagging willpower to get the accusation out, but he managed it, much to his own surprise. What surprised him even more was Devlin's reaction. The guy went absolutely ballistic.

"I didn't kill that little shit," he hollered, with so much anger in his voice that Barratt feared he was about to get clobbered and actually ducked out of the way.

If it did nothing else Devlin's angry denial made it abundantly clear that it was no feigned act of innocence on his part, the guy looked genuinely outraged at the suggestion he had killed Byrne.

Peter was of a similar mind, he was as certain as Barratt was that Devlin's response was an automatic reaction and in no way contrived, he had absolutely no doubt about that. It had been far too spontaneous to be anything else. The guy hadn't even taken time to think about it, but more importantly, if this was the truth he was hearing -- and he firmly believed that to be the case -- it made a total nonsense of Jack's theory.

Barratt's Glaswegian accent grabbed Peter's attention again. "Look, Joe, I want to help as much as I can, but I need to know more about all this Byrne shit so I don't cock things up with Brennan when he has another go at me."

This was Barratt's biggest challenge; the dreaded moment when he really pushed for information on Byrne's disappearance. If he cocked this up all his hard work could be undone in a flash.

"You help?" Devlin yelled at him. "How the fuck can you help?" He looked restless and troubled, nursing a simmering anger that had him on the very edge of his seat. And he remained perched like that for what felt like an eternity to Barratt, wringing his huge, hammer-like hands together and cracking his knuckles in brutish absentmindedness.

The Scotsman was taking no joy from the enforced silence; it was too unnerving and altogether too threatening.

"If there's any way I can ….." he got no further because Devlin was totally disinterested in anything he had to say. "Shut the fuck up," he snapped. "Can't you see I'm thinking?"

He cracked his knuckles more aggressively than before and squirmed back from the edge of his seat before turning to face Barratt.

"Did I hear you right just now? Did you say you were seeing that bastard Brennan again?" He sounded overly inquisitive, suggesting to the ailing Scotsman that something sinister was brewing behind his battered features. No doubt something that would have him involved, and something that he would have no wish to be part of. He began to question what he was doing in such a situation, why he was putting himself at such risk. Caught between a rock and a hard place he was nothing more than tool of convenience to be exploited by two totally unscrupulous adversaries. Neither of whom gave a tinker's damn what might befall him in their bloody-minded determination to outwit each other. All he felt now was remorse, a feeling of deep regret that he had ever allowed himself to become involved in the whole sorry episode.

"Answer the fucking question." Devlin's impatient snappiness shocked him back to reality.

"Sorry, Joe, I'm too knackered to even think straight. All this bloody driving -- I'm too tired to think properly." He might just as well have saved his breath for all the sympathy he got.

"What the hell do you take me for --some sort of fuckin' night nurse? I don't give a tinker's shit how tired you are -- I haven't got all night to sit here chewing the cud with you. Now give me a fucking answer -- are you or are you not seeing Brennan again?"

Barratt's head went up and down like a yo-yo. "Yes -- yes I am -- I told you I am," he stammered. "Brennan said he wants to see me again after

I've had a few days to think about Byrne's disappearance; like somehow my memory might suddenly improve and I remember something I knew nothing about in the first place."

Devlin tried to smile at Barratt's predicament, but it was nothing more than a grotesque apology in its ugliness.

"I think Brennan might be right you know, your memory might just take a turn for the better -- in fact I know it will, cause I'm gonna make sure it does." He sniggered contentedly to himself as if savouring some deep feeling of satisfaction. "With a little creative tuition from me I'm sure you can remember something quite useful." He rubbed his hands together quite briskly, demonstrating his enjoyment at whatever evil thought was going being concocted inside his twisted mind.

Leaning casually against the rear tailgate Peter allowed himself a wry smile, he'd just heard Devlin confirm that he was still willing to put his trust in Barratt, and that was an absolute necessity if their plan was to work. Although he was quietly cursing the Scotsman for letting him off the hook over Byrne's whereabouts, he should have followed up straight away after Devlin's rebuttal. As things stood a golden opportunity had gone begging, more worryingly, he doubted if such an opportunity would present itself again. Frustrated over their missed opportunity his concerns took on less importance as Devlin began mouthing off again.

"You go ahead and have your meeting with Brennan, but make sure you have it here in this very car park. Just let me know when it's going to take place and I'll arrange a cosy little reception for our friend." He locked eyes with Barratt. "You can do that -- can't you?" It was a blatant threat rather than a question -- a do it or else ultimatum.

Barratt hesitated momentarily, quite intentionally, not wanting to appear too eager and give the game away. As it turned out Devlin mistook his hesitation for defiance.

"I hope you're not thinking of crossing me -- because if you are, my boys are just a stone's throw away and eager for some entertainment."

A nauseous sensation engulfed Barratt, he was finding the atmosphere inside the cab almost unbearable. Devlin stank to high heaven of stale beer and iodine, or some such concoction, and the unpleasant stench within the confines of the cab was overpowering, and that, plus the undisguised threat he had just made was enough to make the Scotsman's stomach churn.

He wound the window down and sucked in a mouthful of the cool night air before defending himself.

"I don't want to get on the wrong side of anybody, Joe, least of all your friends, but I'm not up for murder -- that's not my scene. I can't have any part in that." His voice trembled with anxiety, making his plea sound all the more realistic.

"Who the hell said anything about murder?" Devlin spluttered, looking genuinely alarmed. "He'll just end up with a fuzzy head like that fuckin' idiot Byrne."

Thankfully Barratt was still facing the cab window and Devlin missed the surprised look of disbelief on his face, nor did he appreciate the impact his obscure revelation had on his listeners, who were both convinced Tony Byrne had been murdered. The seriousness of this latest revelation impacted on Peter Dunseith the harder of the two, if only because he was much more conversant with Jack's theory on the case, a theory that was now destined to become obsolete if Devlin's admission was to be believed. On top of that there were a number of interpretations that might explain what Devlin meant by a 'fuzzy head'? That was a bit of a mystery, and one that only Barratt was in a position to unravel, and to be fair to him, once he got his wits about him again he did his best to do just that.

"What the hell does that mean -- what's the hell's a fuzzy head for Christ's sake?"

Peter Dunseith had come away from the tail gate and was pacing up and down, mentally urging Barratt to keep going.

Devlin threw his head back and guffawed, a loud guttural laugh that was full of genuine enjoyment.

"You haven't a bloody clue -- have you?" he mocked; his smug attitude and arrogant belief in his own superiority affording him a temporary feeling of wellbeing. The same arrogant smugness that Jack had predicted would lead to his eventual downfall.

"Don't you bloody Jock's know anything?" he asked. "Haven't you ever heard of the happy sauce?" he chided.

The blank look on Barratt's face must have been a source of enjoyment to him because he burst out laughing again, really deep belly laughter that sounded obliquely threatening.

"The happy sauce," he repeated, "the white dreamer --angel dust -- memory buster --- call it what you want -- don't you know anything about anything for fuck sake?" He was gloating at the Scotsman's feigned naivety and obviously deriving a great deal of pleasure from it. But having been under severe pressure since Devlin's arrival Barratt welcomed the change in his attitude; he seemed to have lightened up and appeared to be enjoying himself; enjoying some pleasurable secret that brought purpose to his life.

39

Jack Brennan would have had something to say if he had been afforded the opportunity of listening in on Devlin's conversation. But he was well outside the effective range of any bugging device, an issue he had been aware of before he took up his covert position earlier in the evening.

Now, as he watched the sun creep out of sight below the horizon, and dusk begin its frustratingly slow transformation into night he lowered his binoculars and placed them carefully on the window ledge in front of him. It wasn't dark enough yet to make use of his night vision glasses, and he was quietly wishing the time away until it was. He was fed up trying to keep a tab on things from a distance and would have been much happier had he been able to eavesdrop the going's on inside Barratt's cab.

He was worried about the Scotsman's ability to cope, and he felt helpless at having to rely on Peter to intervene if things went belly up. On top of that he had Dave Jackson literally perched on top of his shoulder as part of the deal he had agreed with Inspector Campbell. Who had also arranged for them to have access to a conveniently sited room inside the terminal building, allowing them an overview of the situation from a relatively safe position. He had also insisted on a police minder being present to help swing the deal, which in effect meant that they had a mobile response unit within spitting distance just in case they gathered enough information to warrant an arrest.

Unfortunately any information gathered had to be conclusive, and had to be in the form of a disclosure regarding the murder of Tony Byrne.

To make things less easy than they might have been, any decision to enforce an arrest could only be instigated by Peter Dunseith, as he was the only person, other than Barratt himself, who was privy to what was being said within the cab. On the plus side, Jack's location within the terminal building did offer a perfect view of the terminal car park, and in particular the parking bay that Barratt was using, although that had come about more from luck than judgment.

A more restrictive part of their arrangement meant that if no positive evidence on Tony Byrne's disappearance came to light then Devlin was to be allowed to go on his merry way. After which he would become the responsibility of the RUC's Criminal Intelligence Branch and Jack would have to back off and cause no further interference.

"I wish to hell I knew what was going on in that bloody cab," he muttered, a noticeable hint of anxiety in his voice. From their elevated position he could see Dunseith idling against the back of the truck and was sorely tempted to call him on his mobile to find out what was happening, but as Alec had warned him that a mobile phone might interfere with the sensitive transmitter in the bugging device he decided, with some reluctance, not to risk it.

In any event things seemed peaceful enough, and although he had no idea what the topic of conversation was between Devlin and Barratt, at least things did appear to be under control. But as Jack knew from experience, such events can sometimes take on a life of their own, and if he had kept his eye on Peter for just a few seconds longer he would have seen him fiddling frantically with his earpiece as he struggled to hear what Devlin was saying.

Coinciding with this, a bunch of nerdy types in a beat up old Volkswagen Camper had just arrived on the scene and parked up less than twenty yards away, spewing out heavy metal music at an ear punishing volume.

Peter tore a small corner from the newspaper that was tucked under his left arm and chewed on it until it was moist enough to use as an ear plug, then jammed it in his free ear to block out the ear splitting racket. It was a simple enough remedy that did the trick, and he was soon back in touch listening to Barratt following up on Devlin's mysterious remark.

"What the hell are you on about, Joe? I can't keep up with you. I don't understand anything you're telling me." He was playing his part well, pretending to be dumber than he was and allowing Devlin's ego do the work for him.

Devlin threw his head back and laughed; another endorsement of his contempt for Barratt, who continued to amuse him with his lack of understanding of the things they were discussing, things that were an everyday part of life on the dark side .

"You really believe we killed that idiot Byrne -- don't you?" he said, with excessive smugness. It was obvious that he was toying with the Scotsman and enjoying the feeling of superiority he derived from it. "If you weren't so bloody thick you'd know there are less incriminating ways of getting rid of unwanted garbage. Mind you, I suppose we were a bit clever in the way we handled things," he admitted, gloating over his every word. "You see we made a sacrificial lamb out of our friend Byrne." He allowed himself another bout of laughter, really deep throated, unnerving laughter, clearly finding something humorous in whatever plot they had dreamt up to get rid of Tony Byrne.

"How the hell did you manage that?" asked Barratt, almost too eagerly, his eyes widening like some innocent underling seeking enlightenment from his more knowledgeable master.

"It's easy, when you know how," bragged Devlin, falling hook line and sinker for Barratt's feigned innocence. The smug look remained fixed on his battered features as he relaxed into the co-driver's seat and considered whether or not to reveal more.

Sensing his hesitation Barratt egged him on.

"You know you can trust me, Joe, and if I know what the hell is going on maybe I can feed a suitable story to the police and get them off our backs."

The smug expression deserted Devlin's face and his eyes suddenly lit up at Barratt's suggestion, clearly he'd been contemplating some devious new plan, and Barratt's suggestion appeared to have spurred him on.

A thoughtful silence ensued as his face took on a more serious, pensive expression, his damaged eyes, looking for all the world like those of a Panda, stared unseeingly at the cab floor between his feet. Barratt was quiet as well, just observing from the other side of the cab, happy to be given a breather to gather his thoughts. As a result it was rather unexpected when Devlin rounded on him and announced. "You might have hit the nail on the head, Jock."

Judging by the look on his face he was still putting his thoughts together, and to help him concentrate his hands went up to his mouth in a more studious pose, a pose that was totally out of context. But he sat like that for a while deep in thought.

"You weren't to know it, but the last shipment Byrne brought back for us was rumbled by Special Branch, but it only happened because the powers that be decided on a purge. They decided to pay huge sums of money to anyone willing to snitch on our activities, but that's by the by. The important thing is that we found out in time that they knew about our shipment, although we never did find out how they got to know, but that God lovin' little bastard Byrne was a prime suspect." He closed his eyes and shook his head despairingly as he recalled the upheaval involved.

"Anyway," he went on, "we decided to offer them a scapegoat and get them off our backs, so we put Byrne's name in the frame. That caused us a lot of grief at the time, because it forced us to re-route our shipment on the way back and our delivery was late getting here because of it. It earned us a loss of credibility with some of our major players, but by putting Byrne's name up to the fuzz we were offering them someone who was actually involved in the operation and would therefore be more convincing."

He winked knowingly at Barratt to reinforce how clever he had been, then his face took on an angrier look.

"But the last thing I wanted was that wee shite pointing the finger at me -- no way Jose -- so we gave them his name but his brother's address just to confuse the issue."

He cracked his knuckles aggressively.

"It was bloody clever really, because while they were following Byrne's brother around like headless chickens we got our shipment in and managed to get rid of Byrne at the same time."

A grotesque grimace that mimicked a smile spread over his ugly features as he relived his moment of glory.

"Of course when the cops realized what had happened I presume they took it as read there had been a cock up over the two brothers. Then when Byrne disappeared from their radar they naturally assumed he had somehow got wind of things and done a runner."

He stopped talking and his eyes glazed over as he drifted off in a temporary bout of sadistic delight. The ugly grimace he had given way to earlier remained firmly in place as a reminder of his utter contempt for his fellow man. Barratt felt contempt too, but he had to keep his feelings under wraps and well away from Devlin's prying eyes. Exhausted after his long day on the road, and with his nerves shot to pieces from all the hassle he was getting, he was suffering from an overpowering desire to get as much distance as possible between himself and his tormentor, preferably a couple of continents. He couldn't divest himself of the growing fear that if he got to learn too much about Devlin's business, then the chances were he would suffer the same treatment they had dished out to Byrne -- whatever the hell that was? But while Devlin allowed Barratt time to ponder his future, or lack of it, Peter was getting quite a buzz from the way things were developing, and was praying they would continue along a similar path. His gut feeling had him convinced they were moving ever closer to a disclosure from Devlin about Byrne.

Things were panning out almost exactly as Jack had predicted; the guy was falling foul of his own inflated ego, and was revelling unashamedly in the opportunity to brag about his criminal prowess. It made it easy to feel sympathy for Barratt, as Peter rightly did, the poor guy was on his own in the cab with a thoughtless brute of a man who would swat him like a fly if the mood were to take him, and if Peter was honest about it there was little he could do to stop it.

Barratt's Scottish brogue dragged him back to the conversation inside the cab. He was actually bracing himself to have one last go at Devlin, but his mind was made up that if he failed to get what he wanted this time, then he would use any excuse he could to get the away from Devlin and never come back. He wanted as much distance as possible between the two of them, and quickly too.

"So what did happen to Byrne then -- how the hell did you manage to get rid of him if you didn't knock him off?" he asked adding an element of false idolatry to his words. "You have me totally confused with all this bloody mumbo jumbo."

If he was intending to appear in awe of Devlin's superior intellect then he came very close to succeeding, certainly close enough to allow Devlin the opportunity to brag some more, and the brute was really up for that as he sniggered fiendishly and rubbed his palms together like a happy little schoolboy.

"Oh he's dead alright -- but not so as you'd notice." Once again he was seized by a fit of uncontrollable, manic laughter; it seemed to go on forever until eventually it petered out with him clasping his hands to his sides in agony.

Barratt had to raise his voice to be heard above the uproar.

"I wish you wouldn't talk in fucking riddles, Joe. I don't know what you've got me mixed up in but the cops are not going to let go of it, and if they ever find Byrne's body I'm gonna be in the shit, because I seem to be the only link they have to Byrne."

Devlin's laughter cut off abruptly as he rounded in his seat to face the Scotsman. He was about to grab him by the shirt front again until he saw the confused and frightened look on his face and went off on another laughing spree instead.

The manic intensity of his laughter frightened Barratt far beyond anything Devlin might have put into words, or any physical threat he might have made. In fact it raised genuine doubts in the Scotsman's mind about his sanity. After a while the outbursts grew shorter and shorter until in the end they petered out altogether. Devlin was posed with his arms wrapped tightly round his rib cage to ease the pain of his exertions, and when he opened his mouth his voice was cold and dispassionate, all humour having deserted him as readily as it had materialized.

"You dumb moron. They won't find a body -- not a corpse anyway, just one that can't tell them anything." There was a distinct calmness about him now as he asserted control, his moment of madness consigned to the back burner until the next time it was offered an escape route.

It suddenly became eerily quiet inside the cab but the tetchy silence did nothing to alleviate Barratt's frayed nerves.

Jack had maintained a steady vigil at the window since Barratt's truck had entered the car park, but with nothing happening by way of movement outside the truck he set his night glasses to one side and turned to face Dave Jackson.

"This is getting bloody tedious, the lack of activity down there is driving me nuts -- I wish to hell I knew what was going on." He shook his head despairingly. "This whole charade is in danger of turning into a bloody marathon. We would probably learn more if I went down and roughed him up a little."

It was easy to see why he was so frustrated, the business end of things was taking place less than a hundred yards away yet he could do absolutely nothing to influence it; an issue that was doing nothing to relieve his frustration.

Jackson on the other hand, who had much more experience with this particular kind of operation, was resting quite calmly in an armchair, his legs stretched in front of him leafing through a motoring magazine. He didn't stay that way for long with Jack's endless griping disrupting his concentration, and in the end he got up and brushed past him to get to the window.

"You know as well as I do that Devlin isn't the sort to give in to physical persuasion, especially not to us. No, Jack --- we have to play the long game here and see your plan all the way through. If we are to learn anything from Devlin, then I believe your idea to use Barratt as the bait is by far our best option." He shrugged aimlessly at Jack. "We don't know what the hell is going on down there, so let's just wait and see how things pan out." He stopped, talking and gave Jack a very pointed look. "I should remind you that this is your last chance with Devlin, if you don't get what you're after from our little exercise here then Devlin is off-limits. At least as far as any cooperation from the RUC is concerned."

He gave Jack a reassuring pat on the back and returned to his seat. "Take my advice, Jack, there's nothing to be gained by staring out of that window; you might as well be watching a silent movie."

Jack wasn't paying him too much attention as he had other things on his mind right then. "I hope you're keeping an eye on those two thugs who sneaked into the terminal building before Barratt arrived." Their presence was a real concern to him, especially as Barratt had told him that Devlin had turned up empty handed on all their previous meetings.

"Don't get yourself in a panic, Jack, we have people on their case." Jackson assured him. "We do know what we're doing."

Jack gave him a sideways glance. "I'll just have to take your word on that," he sniped; a hint of rivalry in his voice that exposed his lack of trust in the police to stick to their side of the bargain. Picking up his discarded night glasses he killed the conversation by turning his back on the young detective and returning to his vigil by the window.

Unaware of the protection that was in place to safeguard him, Barratt's desperation to get away was exasperated by Devlin's unaccountable and seemingly endless silence. He found this inactivity even more threatening than the verbal abuse he had been suffering only minutes earlier, and having waited in fearful expectation for longer than his nerves could tolerate he felt forced to say something.

"For God's sake, Joe, I can't get my head round any of this crap you're telling me. Why can't you just explain to me in words of one syllable what happened to Byrne without all this cryptic shite? If I've been party to the guy's murder I need to know so I can get offside, disappear somewhere over on the continent where nobody can find me."

Barratt's nerves were at breaking point, he was sick of being used like a football by everyone involved, and was even considering that it might be safer taking his chances with the cops, after all they could only charge him with drug smuggling.

Devlin stuck his face into Barratt's.

"Don't you tell me what you're going to do," he snarled, "you'll do exactly what I tell you to do, and believe me I'll have plenty more work for you before you reach retirement age." He stabbed a finger into Barratt's chest to reinforce his point. The Scotsman gave an involuntary shudder, and by way of a distraction reached out and switched on the cab light. A decision he immediately regretted, because in its muted yellow glow Devlin's face was a truly ugly and menacing sight. In fact Barratt believed it to be the most frightening thing he had ever set eyes on, and it was made even more menacing because of the grotesque injuries it had suffered.

Devlin stretched his legs as far as the foot well would allow, stretching out like he hadn't a care in the world, then without any warning his big hand shot out and wrapped itself round Barratt's thigh in a vice like grip as he leaned closer to him.

"You don't have anything to worry about, Jock," he whispered, a welcome calmness returning to his voice as he sought to dispel Barratt's concerns. "The Good Lord himself is taking care of our friend Byrne, or at least his maidservants are."

There was an evil twinkle in his eye as he said it. "Our wee man couldn't be in safer hands than that now, could he?"

His attempted smile slipped away like it had never been and he became strangely detached, as if something more pressing was occupying his thoughts.

"I have to go now, but I need to know that you're not going to do anything stupid behind my back. I need to know that I still have you on board -- otherwise ----" he left the rest unspoken, but there was no mistaking the menace in his words.

Barratt was so relieved that his ordeal was coming to an end that he actually felt weak at the knees, yet he still found enough resolve from somewhere to press Devlin one last time for an explanation that made sense.

"If you tell me Byrne isn't dead then I have to believe it, Joe, and you know I'll always be your man -- I don't seem to have a lot of choice anyway, do I? I have no intention of having a run in with the IRA. Christ knows I've got enough problems as it is."

Devlin released his grip on Barratt's thigh and gave him a friendly punch on the arm. "That's the way, Jock -- you keep the faith with old Joe here and nothing nasty will happen to you." His hand shot to Barratt's thigh and made a dive for the soft inner flesh, gripping it like a vice. The pain was excruciating, if short lived, but it knocked the message home to Barratt in no uncertain manner.

"When can I expect to hear from you?" Barratt asked, his voice no more than a whimper

"What are you on about, hearing from me. It's me who'll be hearing from you once you've set up your next meeting with that bastard Brennan. And you bear in mind what I told you, that meeting has to take place right here in this car park, after that you can leave the rest to me." He swung round in his seat and climbed out of the cab, his business with Barratt concluded.

The only sound inside the cab after Devlin's departure was a huge sigh of relief from the Scotsman as he watched him disappear round the front of his truck. He'd been living in fear for his life from the moment the Belfast thug had climbed into his cab, but having come through that dreaded encounter in one piece he could have jumped for joy. It mattered little to him right then that he hadn't achieved what he was meant to achieve.

Dunseith on the other hand wasn't experiencing the same level of joyful bliss. In fact he was disappointed at how little they had gained from their evenings work. Having listened to the conversation between the two men he was still trying to make sense of it. The only positive to come out of the whole charade was Devlin's oblique admission to his involvement in Byrne's disappearance, but there had been absolutely no admission to his murder. Quite the contrary in fact as Devlin had made an outright denial to that, and he had been clever enough to talk in riddles most of the time, which caused his listeners more confusion than enlightenment. It was an unwelcome outcome that left Dunseith worrying about what to do next.

Devlin sorted that out for him, because instead of getting into his car as expected, he carried on round to the rear of the truck in search of Peter, forcing the ex-cop to turn away hurriedly to hide the tiny receiver in his ear.

Devlin pointed an accusing finger at him. "I hope you weren't fucking eavesdropping," he snarled, "because if you were, you had better forget all about it, and quickly at that." He was noticeably less cocky with the ex-cop, but then he matched him pound for pound, and had a couple of inches of height in hand as well.

Peter gave him an indifferent look and brushed past him.

"I've got better things to do with my time, mate," he muttered, as he walked away and climbed into the cab.

Devlin tailed along behind him, and just as he was about to pull the door shut he grabbed it and held it open.

"Best you keep it that way and you'll be alright. I might even have a bit of work for you if you play your cards right, and keep your nose clean of course." He gave a fiendish grin and ambled off to get into his car, leaving both men watching him traverse across the car park in the direction of the Terminal building. Where it came to a standstill as Devlin's two heavies sprinted from the building and climbed into the back, then it took off again and disappeared through the exit gate.

Turning to the Scotsman Peter laid a hand on his shoulder.

"You should count your blessings, mate -- because believe me, there is only one reason why that pair of rock apes were in attendance." Barratt didn't need telling, his face had turned the colour of sun bleached parchment.

"I don't give a shit what Brennan says, or anybody else for that matter, I'm going nowhere near that mad bastard again." Peter gave him a wry smile before pulling out his mobile and dialling Jack's number, continuing to console Barratt as he waited for his boss to pick up. "All this can't have been easy for you, but I thought you handled things pretty well, in fact I'm quite impressed. I just hope to God it was worth the risk and we managed to get it all recorded. That bastard Devlin was talking such a load of drivel from what I could ----" he got connected with Jack before he could finish. "It's Peter here, Jack," he said hurriedly. "I imagine you saw our friend drive off, but I suggest it might be prudent to wait a while before you show yourself down in case he has someone keeping tabs on us, I'm about to rewind the tape to see what we managed to get, so keep your fingers crossed."

Jack was in no hurry to go anywhere. "I'm not intending to go anywhere just yet, Peter, but tell Barratt I'll give him a bell later this evening, and get him on his way as quickly as you can, he already knows where he has to go. We can meet up in the main lounge here as soon as you have yourself sorted out."

He began stuffing his night glasses and bits and pieces into a canvas bag ready to leave.

"It's time we were out of here," he told Jackson. "Peter doesn't sound terribly excited so I don't think they got very much out of Devlin. Whatever they got, it clearly wasn't what we were hoping for otherwise Peter wouldn't have let him drive off like that." Feeling frustrated, and disappointed that their efforts had been in vain he had no inclination to discuss it.

"It's all so fucking disappointing." That said, he snatched up the last of his bits and tossed them carelessly into his bag looking seriously pissed-off.

Jackson could see from his body language that he was more frustrated than angry and gave him a few moments to calm down before saying anything. "It's a bit premature to be taking that attitude," he argued, "We don't even know what we have on tape, or what Peter managed to find out. There will be time enough for making judgments when we know more."

If he was trying to put a positive spin on things then he was wasting his time, because all he got in return was a sullen silence from Jack as he hoisted the bag on his shoulder and bolted down the stairs.

A mad dash across the tarmac got Peter to the lounge a minute or two ahead of the others, and a few seconds ahead of the downpour that opened up as he raced for cover. Claiming an empty table just inside the door he set about rewinding the remainder of the tape.

He still had the recorder on rewind when the others came charging through the door, looking like a couple of drowned rats with their hair all over the place and drenched to the skin. They were in such an all fired hurry that they didn't even shake the water from their jackets before making a beeline for Peter's table.

"Well?" asked Jack, "what have we got?"

Peter shrugged his shoulders and inclined his head somewhat negatively. "I think we got it all down, but in all honesty Devlin didn't say anything that tied him into any murder. In fact when Barratt challenged him directly about it, he made a really robust denial that there had even been a murder, and to my reckoning his denial sounded genuine." He shrugged again. "Having said that, some of his conversation was bloody cryptic to say the least, it certainly had me confused." He shook his head despairingly. "I know this is probably the last thing you want to hear right now, Jack, but there's nothing more I can add."

Jack closed his eyes to block out any more disappointment, his face a study of abject misery. Nothing was panning out the way he had planned, and while he was deeply frustrated, the realization still filtered through to him that that neither Peter, nor Barratt, were in any way to blame for his lack of success. "It's not your fault, Peter," he told him, "you did what was asked of you and I can't expect any more than that." It took a real effort to muster up the enthusiasm to ask how Barrett had fared, and he only did so in the vain hope that it might help shrug off his own misery. "What about our friendly Scotsman -- how did he cope with Devlin?"

"Remarkably well for someone who was shitting bricks most of the time?" Peter explained, cocking a warning eyebrow. "You mustn't be too hard on him you know. What he went through tonight would have been extremely intimidating for anyone. That bastard Devlin really is a serious piece of shit." He stopped himself from going on too much. It wasn't part of his remit to analyse the evening's events, or to make any kind of judgment, at least not as he saw it. Nor did he see any justification for Jack's pessimistic attitude either, and he didn't hold back from saying so. "You know there was a lot that went on in that cab this evening, some of it very confusing, mostly due to that idiot Devlin talking in bloody riddles most of the time. I'd advise you not to make any harsh judgments. You're closer to the case than I am, and it could be that some of what's on that tape might make more sense to you than it did to me or Barratt."

Jack shook his head and grimaced, alerted to the realization that he was getting a little ahead of himself, after all he hadn't even listened to the tape yet.

"Point taken, Peter," he agreed, "but we need to get away from here before I listen to it. Let's go back to my place where we can have some peace and quiet and see what we've got."

He spun away and headed for the exit, leaving the others to follow at their leisure.

40

"Is that as loud as it will go?" Jackson asked, as they sat hunched over the table in Jack's lounge, staring at what was really a very small recording device.

"Don't panic just yet," Peter told him, "It just took a while to adjust the volume, that's all, it should settle down in a second or two. I had to do the adjustment by blind touch and it took a bit of getting used to as they're quite fiddly." Jack gritted his teeth as he strained to hear what was being said, but true to Peter's prediction the volume suddenly shot up and became much more intelligible. Although that didn't lessen their concentration to any degree and they remained huddled together in muted silence, absorbing every word, frowning occasionally as they queried some of the more puzzling remarks Devlin came out with.

Judy came into the room virtually unobserved, such was the level of their concentration, but sensing the taut atmosphere, she set the tray she was carrying on the end of the table and eased quietly into a spare seat. Her timing was very fortuitous as it coincided perfectly with Jack stabbing a finger at the pause button on the recorder.

"What the hell do you make of that?" he asked, referring to Devlin's threat to give Barratt a fuzzy head the same as Byrne. A threat that left him a little puzzled, while the blank expression on Jackson's face told a similar story. "It's hard to say," he admitted, "at least until we hear what comes next?"

Jack shook his head in frustration and hit the play button again.

***

Sometime later, when the tape had been played all the way through, Jack leaned back with his eyes closed in an effort to make sense of what he had been listening to. He stayed like that for a while before wriggling upright again, a look of sorrowful indifference on his craggy face. Running his fingers through his hair he gave a weary sigh as he looked to the others. "Does anybody know what the hell that lunatic was talking about? All that goddamned nonsense about being dead but no body -- what the hell does that mean?"

When nobody spoke up he carried on airing his own thoughts.

"I think that particular remark needs close attention, because when you tie it in with what he said about the Lord's maidservants taking care of Byrne, it has a certain synergy to it. At least it does for me."

The others avoided the issue by reaching for their mugs, leaving Jack to demonstrate his frustration by raising his fist and slamming it down on the arm of the settee. Ignoring Judy, who was sat next to him, he looked first at Peter, then at Dave Jackson. "If I had to lay a bet right now on whether Tony Byrne was alive or dead I'd stake my mortgage that he's still out there somewhere, alive and kicking." His remark failed to draw any comment from the others who hardly moved a muscle as he heaved himself up and addressed Dave Jackson.

"I agreed to back off and give your people a free run on Devlin if I didn't find any proof that he had murdered Tony Byrne. But I'm getting a different slant on this thing now." He paused for thought. "Maybe I'm barking up the wrong tree, but I'm beginning to question the assumption everyone has made that Tony Byrne is dead."

He rubbed the back of his neck to relieve the stress he was feeling.

"There's something I need to follow up on while the mood takes me, you guys can see yourselves out -- I have a call to make, and I need to make it right now while I'm in the right frame of mind."

Caught off guard by his sudden change of plan, his colleagues could only look to one another with a sense of dismay. Jackson was the first to get over the shock of being dispensed with in such summary fashion.

"Hold on now, Jack," he argued, "we need to work out what Devlin means by all this nonsense he's spouting, and three heads have got to be better than one if we're to think it through. For God's sake man, we haven't even started analysing the contents of that tape yet."

Jack gave him an apologetic look. "I'm sorry, Dave, but the thinking is done for now. At least mine is. I have someone to see, and I don't think he would appreciate a PC Plod walking through his door. But there's nothing for you to panic about, I'll stay in touch and keep you up to date with everything that's going on, that's a promise."

Sidestepping Jackson he placed a hand on Peter's shoulder.

"That was a good day's work, Peter, now you head off home and I'll see you in the morning bright and early. If you're still up for it that is?"

He turned away and picked up his phone, letting the others make their own way out as he got on with making his call.

41

It wasn't in Father Joseph's nature to go looking round corners in search of trouble, if anything, he preferred to shroud himself in a cloak of obscurity that he rarely cast off until absolutely forced to. Minded as he was to meander gently through life on the well-oiled wheels of procedural routine he was blissfully content to see only what was placed in front of him, while reserving his energies, little that he had, for that rare and genuine good cause that touched his soul.

Heading straight for his study after a late night service simply confirmed his unwavering devotion to routine. The first of his three routine drinks for the evening hardly touched the sides, while the second was normally carried through to the kitchen in search of whatever goodies his diligent, and somewhat frosty housekeeper had laid out for supper.

By normal standards it had been a busy enough day. Two funerals and a christening, all close together and well attended had left him feeling talked out and longing for some peace and quiet. Indeed he would freely admit, if anyone bothered to ask, that he found socializing at such events both tiresome and laborious, not to mention emotionally draining. So with his duties over for the day, and feeling once more content with the world, he slipped into his favourite chair with a well prepared tray of food on his lap, happy to settle down for an evening's viewing in front of his rather outdated but treasured television. And he almost got away with it, but of course almost is never enough, indeed were he not such a pious individual he might well have cursed his luck when the phone interrupted his coveted little soiree.

"Father Joseph," he announced calmly, successfully concealing his annoyance at such a late interruption. He was too astute to do otherwise, as his Bishop had recently acquired the annoying habit of phoning him late at night.

"How are you, Father? It's Jack Brennan here." Jack had the fingers firmly crossed down by his left trouser leg in expectation of a frosty reception.

The exhausted cleric bit his lower lip as he considered how best to get rid of his unwanted caller.

"I have had a very long and tiresome day, Mr. Brennan, and I'm about to partake of a well-deserved bite of supper, so you will understand that it does nothing for my well-being to have you call me at this late hour. In fact to be perfectly honest it does nothing for my well-being to have you call me at all. I was under the impression we had concluded any business we might have had together."

Jack failed to get a word in before he added.

"Or perhaps I should have said your business."

Jack winced and gritted his teeth. "I know it's late, Father, and I'm very sorry for that, but you must know that I would never contact you at such a late hour if it wasn't very important."

Holding the phone to his ear with one hand Father Joseph tipped the remains of the whiskey decanter into his glass with the other.

"I have to tell you, Mr. Brennan, that at this time of night the only things I consider to be important are matters of life or death."

"I'm pleased to hear that, Father, because that's exactly what I want to discuss -- a matter of life or death -- Tony Byrne's life to be blunt about it."

Father Joseph expelled a weary sigh. "You truly mystify me, Mr. Brennan – you really do -- perhaps it's due to the long day I have had -- or perhaps I'm hallucinating, but I seem to recall you telling me you were looking for Tony Byrne's remains. Am I now to believe there has been a resurrection that the church has yet to acknowledge?" There was precious little humour in his reply, nor was there meant to be, but Jack enjoyed a silent chuckle anyway. "Very funny, Father, but I'm trying to be serious. I'm in dire need of some advice and perhaps a little help right now, and unfortunate as that might be for you I can think of no one more qualified to provide both, otherwise I would not be disturbing you."

What sounded very much like a disinterested sigh greeted his plea, then, much to his surprise, Father Joseph capitulated without any further discussion. "Not like this, Mr. Brennan -- not over the phone -- you see I still believe in the old adage that matters of importance are best dealt with face to face. Anyway, with the church restoration fund the way it is my advice no longer comes free, and I'm afraid this telephone call is not going to deposit anything in the collection box. So whatever it is you have in mind, it will have to wait until tomorrow. Shall we say around noon?"

Jack was almost euphoric; he had expected much more resistance. "I can't tell you how grateful I am, Father," he said humbly, a little too humbly in the circumstance as the priest hadn't done anything yet to deserve it.

"Of course it goes without saying that you won't just be helping me, Father, but Roisin Byrne as well, and I must stress that I am fairly certain that you are in a unique position to advise me on a particular problem I have at the moment."

Father Joseph, having taken a mouthful of food grunted something unintelligible down the line before bringing their conversation to an end. "That such might be the case is the only redeeming factor for disturbing me. Goodnight, Mr. Brennan."

42

A troubled and restless night ended with Jack looking bleary eyed and jaded, but a generous helping of scrambled egg, washed down with a mug of strong coffee, lifted his spirits enough to prompt him into nipping out for the morning papers. When he got back he immediately refilled his mug with coffee and flopped back into his chair at the kitchen table, eager to see what the rest of the world was up to.

Having cast his eyes rather hurriedly over the headlines, the newspapers were soon dispensed with, mostly because he was unable to settle down to read them. He had almost convinced himself that the faint glimmer of hope he had been nurturing all night might grow into something concrete and really move his case forward. Unable to sleep, his mind had been running like an express train, endlessly regurgitating the taped conversation he had listened to between Devlin and Barratt.

The last thing he wanted to do was go off in a tangent before properly assessing the clues he had identified from the tape recording. Yet regardless of his doubts, he still remained convinced that his suspicions had sufficient credibility to justify what he now planned to do. Although with his expectations flying high, it would have suited him better had Father Joseph agreed to an earlier meeting, especially as he perceived the priest's involvement to be essential to any chance of success. He wasn't to know it, but the hapless cleric might well have agreed to an earlier meeting had Jack been a little more circumspect and made a genuine effort to convince him that he was on to something new and viable. Instead, he was contemplating the frightening possibility that any time wasted might increase the threat to Tony Byrne's life instead of doing something to save it.

That particular thought was at the forefront of his mind when he heard Judy's faint tread on the stairs. Her approach made him shake off his gloomy mind set and present her with a more upbeat greeting.

"You look decidedly perkier this morning," she mumbled sleepily, stifling a yawn. "What has you all hyped up?" It wasn't customary for her to be so alert and conversational first thing in the morning, but she had sensed an unusual intensity in her man's behaviour the previous evening, and had come out of her sleep with the same thought very much on her mind and with no one in bed beside her. She knew Jack well enough to detect when he was 'running hot' and her intuition told her that he was on the verge of some sort of a breakthrough, a breakthrough that he was keeping very much to himself.

"Can I ask why you are seeing Father Joseph again quite so soon?" This time the need to salve her curiosity was compelling enough to overcome her desire for a much needed mug of coffee. Jack lowered the paper he was pretending to read and peered at her over the top of his glasses.

"Nothing to bother yourself with, sweetheart, I'll explain later -- it's only an idea I'm playing with and it may not lead to anything. If it does you'll be the first to know."

For once in his life he wasn't being deliberately obtuse, nor was he teasing her like he usually did, although she would hardly see it that way. In fact it was a simple matter of trying to protect his pride, just in case he was heading down a cul-de-sac and ended up making a total fool of himself.

Judy soon got the message that her early morning rise and pleasant demeanour had failed to loosen his tongue, and she knew from previous experience that any further prying would only make him more defensive. Accepting the matter as a lost cause she resorted to her normal behaviour and gave him a right royal mouthful.

"Stuff you, Brennan, if that's your attitude I'm going back to bed."

Wheeling away she stormed out of the kitchen leaving Jack watching in total disbelief as she ignored the tempting aroma of freshly ground coffee, a tantalizing temptation that would haunt her all the way up the stairs. Truth be told Jack enjoyed their feisty little encounters and knew the running battles between them would continue unabated. In the same way that he knew she would waste no time in planning her revenge, and to his credit, he would gladly and lovingly let her do so.

The rain had become much more persistent as he made his way across town, and by the time he cleared the city centre it had turned into a serious tropical storm. Gale force winds had appeared out of nowhere, forcing unprepared pedestrians to scatter in all directions, causing havoc with the city centre traffic as they scattered this way and that in search of shelter.

The downpour reached its peak just as he turned into the grounds of the priest's residence, and as he approached the old Victorian house he was relieved to see Father Joseph rush out with an umbrella, although it was instantly threatened with destruction as the heavy wind took hold of it. They raced for the door in tandem beneath its limited cover, but still got soaked from the waist down before seeking cover inside the porch.

"The good Lord must be upset with someone to have us endure such an onslaught," Father Joseph commented, "I do hope it isn't something we have done, Mr. Brennan." It was a harmless, almost frivolous comment that suggested he was in a light hearted mood. Something Jack found a little disarming as he had prepared himself for a much frostier reception.

"Sorry to bring you out in such a downpour, you really should have stayed indoors." His remark went unanswered as he was led inside.

"Don't sit down yet, Mr. Brennan," he invited, "I have the heating on so we should dry out fairly quickly if we stand close enough to a radiator -- by the way have you eaten yet? I'm about to have a sandwich if you would you care to join me? You would be most welcome." Rather than wait for an answer he wandered over and tugged firmly on a corded bell-pull by the door, and as if previously rehearsed it swung open and a steely faced, middle aged woman wearing an immaculately ironed pinafore appeared as if by magic. Taking two tiny steps into the room she stopped and looked enquiringly at her employer.

"One extra mouth for lunch, Mrs. Connolly, can you manage that?" The request definitely sounded a mite timorous, and one look at his blue-rinsed housekeeper told Jack why that might be.

Mrs. Connolly angled her body awkwardly in order to get a good look at their visitor, a heavy scowl indicating her annoyance at the extra burden being placed upon her. Then raising her nose in the air, she sniffed noisily, perhaps even a little indignantly, turned on her heel and went out the way she had come in without so much as an acknowledgement.

Father Joseph shook his head despairingly.

"God knows, Mr. Brennan, that woman frightens the pants off me. She has the uncanny knack of making me feel that it is I who is in her employ." His rather solemn face offered a somewhat impish, boyish grin, indicating that he derived some secret pleasure from the thought.

"Mind you, when I think about it I suppose that is the case really, after all I am the parish priest, so I suppose that makes me a servant of the people." He gave Jack a sort of wistful look. "Do you know something, Mr. Brennan -- I had never thought about it like that before, so your visit today has made me recall something that is all too easily forgotten -- humility."

His face donned a more pious expression as he became momentarily immersed in some form of private penance. Although it vanished quicker than it had arrived when he leaned closer to Jack and dropped his voice to a whisper. "Let us both leave the purpose of your visit aside until the dear Mrs. Connolly has been and gone – I am led to believe she has very receptive hearing and an extremely active tongue."

Smiling contentedly he inched closer to the nearest radiator and pressed himself tight against it to dry out, making light conversation about the weather to while away the minutes until the said Mrs. Connolly returned.

Of the two, Jack was the least comfortable, he fell some way short of being adept at making small talk with people he was unfamiliar with, and it was no time at all before their exchange of pleasantries hit the buffers and became a little strained. Happily, his discomfort was short lived, when quicker than he thought she might, the iron lady came strutting back into the room with a large tray bearing two plates of sandwiches and a pot of tea.

Relieving herself of her burden she placed them, with annoying precision, on top of an over-polished side table before pouring the tea and stepping back a pace to survey her masterpiece.

"Thank you, Mrs. Connolly," said Father Joseph, "that will be all, you may leave us now." She was about to do just that when he added an afterthought. "In fact I have no need of your services until later this evening to prepare my supper, so you might just as well go home now and I'll see you then." There was a mild politeness in the way he addressed her, although it appeared not to be received as such by his overbearing housekeeper, whose only reaction was to raise a well preened eyebrow and repeat her earlier display of indignant superiority. At least that was how Jack read it, either way, the conversation remained on hold until they heard the outer door closing.

"Help yourself, Mr. Brennan," Father Joseph invited, "Then perhaps you can explain your mysterious behaviour of yesterday evening." He eased the tray of sandwiches in Jack's direction, only to find that Jack had other things on his mind.

"I need you to understand that I'm not here to waste your time, Father. Certain events have taken place since we last met that lead me to believe Tony Byrne might still be alive. It's not for you to know how I arrived at this conclusion, not for the moment anyway, but please accept that it is not something I just pulled out of a hat but is based on sound evidence that I have very recently acquired. If you can accept that possibility, and I hope you will, then it places a duty on both of us to try and find out where Tony Byrne is and return him safely to his wife.

Father Joseph was nibbling at a ham and chutney triangle without too much enthusiasm, giving the distinct impression that he was more interested in working out what was contained between the layers of bread than paying attention to anything his visitor had to offer. In reality he was reflecting upon their previous meeting, and while that event rested a little uneasily with his conscience he truly believed that he had identified something of a kindred spirit in his visitor. Not in any spiritual sense of course, but in so much as Jack's interest in Roisin Byrne's welfare appeared both genuine and sincere, and that was a common cause they both shared. Unfortunately that shared goal caused him something of a dilemma, because to disregard a plea for help in such circumstances was alien to every Christian belief and value he held dear. Nevertheless, such sensibilities did not balance out against the fact that he had no understanding of what he might have to offer by way of help, since he knew absolutely nothing about Tony Byrne's disappearance and had already made that abundantly clear to his visitor. As a consequence he found Jack's request for help quite puzzling.

"How on earth do you imagine I can help you find Tony Byrne?" he asked.

Jack reached for a sandwich and nibbled at it for a moment before answering.

"It's nothing very difficult, Father, I just want you to make a few phone calls for me." He raised his hands in the air to stop his host interrupting. "But before we go into that I want to draw on your knowledge of the Catholic Church, specifically here in Ireland. I'm trying to identify a secluded convent, or place of asylum perhaps that is run by the Sisters of Mercy, or something along those lines. I'm sorry I can't be more specific but I'm afraid I'm not terribly au fait with the organizational structure of your church." He pinched his lips between finger and thumb as he thought how best to explain himself. "I'm really looking for some kind of institution where a person might be hidden away from the rest of the world, or where a troubled soul might go to seek refuge."

His request came as something of a surprise to the priest, who studied his face much more intently as he attempted to second guess what Jack was up to, and what the consequences might be if he allowed himself to become involved.

"Is that what we are now to believe, Mr. Brennan? That Tony Byrne has been spirited away and is languishing somewhere within the confines of the Church these past three years, without so much as a thought for his dear wife's welfare or wellbeing."

He shook his head repeatedly, condemning the idea outright. "Why on earth would he do such a thing? If you knew the man as I do you would never entertain such a ridiculous idea? The very thought of it beggars belief -- it truly does."

He raised both hands to his lips, prayer like, and blew into them before continuing. "I'm afraid you have misplaced your sense of reason somewhere along the line," he declared.

Jack set his sandwich aside.

"If you knew as much about this sorry affair as I do you might see things differently. But you're right of course, I don't believe Tony Byrne is deliberately hiding away from his wife, or indeed his friends, and I'm not implying that he is. But if my theory is correct then he may not even be aware of where he is or what is happening to him. Because it's my belief that his memory, and perhaps even his sanity, might have been destroyed by someone forcefully overdosing his system with narcotics. I also believe it was a member of your own parish, an acquaintance and close neighbour of his who was responsible for arranging this to happen."

Father Joseph's mouth dropped open like he'd been poleaxed, either from shock or disbelief; it was hard to tell which, then his eyes glazed over and he stared vacantly at the wall as he tried to make sense of what he'd been told. Being a gentle creature by nature, and not given to understanding the vulgarity of violence, such a proposition was a totally alien concept to him and beyond his comprehension. He was undoubtedly shaken and even looked fragile enough for Jack to get a little anxious as he watched the contents of his mug tip perilously close to spilling down his trouser leg. He reached out prised it from his fingers.

"Are you okay, Father?" he asked, genuinely concerned. His host gave a strange little gasp that didn't sound unlike the last breath of a dying man, then his chest swelled up as he drew in a much deeper breath and straightened up in his chair.

"I'm sorry but you must forgive me, Mr. Brennan, I was totally unprepared for the horror of what you have just suggested. It rather shook me up I'm afraid, but I promise you I'll be fine in just a moment or two. Perhaps you would be kind enough to pour me a brandy while I gather myself together."

He waved an arm in the direction of the sideboard.

Jack poured him a brandy and watched the warming spirit gradually take effect as he sipped it nonstop until he had emptied the glass

"I must apologize for my delicate disposition, but I find your theory quite shocking, and very disconcerting, particularly as I believe it to be Joe Devlin that you speak of." He shook his head in despair. "Such a thought is altogether too shocking to even contemplate."

Jack was in no mood to argue the rights or wrongs of his theory; he needed a decision from the priest, and he needed it in a hurry.

"This is no time for meaningless discussion, Father. I have to know if you're willing to help me or not, and I need to know right now because it really is that important."

Father Joseph took on an anguished look, as if something he had no wish to surrender was being taken from him against his will. "What am I to do, Mr. Brennan? I believe you to be an honest and honourable man, and I know you believe in your own judgment on this, which I must then accept in good faith. It seems to me I would be failing, both as a priest and as a concerned human being if I did not do everything in my power to help end such barbarism, if indeed it actually exists as you say it does. And as I do not believe you have it in you to fabricate such a story I feel I am bound by pastoral duty to offer my assistance -- so yes, Mr. Brennan -- if you believe I can be of help then I feel obliged to do so. With the proviso that any action we take remains within the law." He made to get out of his chair, adding as he did so. "Please help yourself to a drink – I shall be back in just a few moments."

He looked a little unsteady on his feet as he left the room.

On his return Father Joseph looked much more purposeful than when he had left, his stride was bolder and he wasn't quite so tense and hunched up looking. He was clutching a large, hard back ring binder to his chest as he made his way past Jack on route to a nearby telephone table.

"This is our complete telephone listing," he explained, "It contains the telephone numbers for every Catholic establishment on this precious little island of ours." Inching his chair closer to the table, he asked. "Now tell me if you will, exactly what is it you want me to do?"

Jack pulled a chair up beside him and dropped into it.

"If my theory is correct then there's a good chance that Tony Byrne is being held, or cared for, by people who may not even know anything about him. I've been studying some very cryptic evidence that has become available, and if my interpretation of that evidence is correct Tony Byrne's mental condition may have been seriously damaged by an overdose of narcotics or some other lethal toxin. There is a strong likelihood that he may have no recollection or any memory of his former life -- in other words he might have been turned into a mindless junkie, in fact if I'm reading matters correctly he may even be beyond medical help."

He paused briefly before getting back to the question he had been asked.

"It would save an awful lot of time and trouble if you would phone around and see if someone fitting Tony's description and possible mental state is residing, or being treated, at any of your establishments."

"Right," said Father Joseph, "I think I'm beginning to get the gist of things." He rubbed his palms together enthusiastically. "I guess we had better get on with it then."

Flicking the cover of the file open he ran a finger down the page, searching for somewhere fitting to begin their search.

"Here we go then," he said, as he made the first of what was to be many repetitious calls before the day was through.

43

Working his way diligently down the listings Father Joseph was guided by his own local knowledge, a knowledge that enabled him to prioritize his calls in a structured way. Even then it was a seriously tedious ordeal having to repeatedly introduce himself to so many people, many of them strangers. Although, as one would expect, there was the odd occasion when he came across someone who knew him from the past, and those calls became much more protracted and even offered a bit of light relief. And while it was immensely boring he stuck to the task relentlessly. Jack on the other hand had very little to do except admire his seemingly boundless stamina and keep his caffeine levels topped up.

"Just a couple more calls, Father, then I suggest you take a break." The priest nodded gratefully and smiled tamely as he punched in another number. "I think it's about time we both had a stiffer drink – don't you?" suggested Jack, as another call got connected and Father Joseph delved into his well-practiced routine, giving a silent thumbs up to the offer of a drink as he prattled on. Jack left his side and headed for the drinks cabinet, but he hardly managed more than a couple of strides before something the priest said stopped him in his tracks.

"Can you tell me how long has he has been with you?" he asked, wriggling upright in his chair and taking a much keener interest. "Really," he went on, "and you have not been able to identify him in all that time?"

Jack couldn't take his eyes off the priest, he was hanging on his every word, waiting for what would next.

"I see, and how would you describe his medical condition at this time." There was a quite lengthy pause as he took in a fairly detailed recital of physical and mental ailments affecting the individual in question.

"I see -- right -- does he now? Yes I can well understand that, but I take it you would have no objections to me coming to visit with him?"

Jack could hardly contain himself as the conversation wound down with the usual farewell pleasantries, and no sooner had the priest replaced the phone before he was in his face, eager to know what he had turned up.

"Come on, Father," he urged, hardly giving the man time to catch his breath, "tell me what you've got."

Father Joseph yawned and stretched his arms above his head with a grunt.

"Well, as you must have heard, there is one poor soul being held in what is commonly referred to as a protective residence, and while that may give us some hope I have to say he sounds a bit older than Tony Byrne would now be, and from what I've been told, a lot slimmer and going bald." He shrugged offhandedly. "Having said that people do get thinner with age and hair does fall out." His eyes lit up as he went on. "Of more interest is the fact that he was taken into care suffering from a very heavy drug dependency, that, plus a whole host of more serous mental problems apparently led to him being sectioned under the Mental Health Act. Which I admit falls into line with your most recent theory about Tony." He crossed himself very deliberately twice over and muttered a few quick Hail Mary's before continuing.

"Whoever this poor soul turns out to be, Mr. Brennan, I sincerely hope it is not Roisin's husband, for her sake at least as he appears to have completely lost touch with reality and has no knowledge of his own past. A truly awful state of affairs I'm afraid." He reached for the drink Jack was holding out to him and raised it to his lips.

In spite of the priest's low key attitude Jack was bursting with enthusiasm. "It sounds to me like there's every possibility this could be our man, so where exactly is he being held?"

"A long way from here I'm afraid, and we could never manage a return trip today – it's some way south of Mallow."

Jack was finding it hard to contain himself and was far too eager get to going to consider any delay.

"Would they let me see him if I went there on my own?" he asked, toying with the idea that he could probably complete the round trip in a day if he didn't have the priest in tow.

Father Joseph had other ideas and was quite vehement in his opposition. "That's not to be advised I'm afraid – no -- indeed not, I very much doubt they would let you through the door as you have no connection to the man." He looked to the heavens as if seeking guidance. "No -- I shall somehow have to free up some time to accompany you, but I'm afraid you will have to be patient."

His offer to continue to help was a little unexpected and although it was very welcome Jack was unsure what to make of it, or how useful it might turn out to be. He was mad keen to get started and raring to go, especially now that he sensed they had a live trail to follow. But on reflection he wasn't in such an all-fired hurry as to ignore the benefits of having Father Joseph on board. The priest could open doors that he could only lean against, and more importantly, his presence would add a certain spiritual and moral legitimacy to their endeavours, especially where the Church was concerned, and unless he was missing something, they were very much involved.

Watching from a few feet away Father Joseph was having serious doubts about Jack's level of expectation, he was being far too optimistic, his own previous experience dictated the necessity to be much more circumspect when dealing with such delicate matters.

"I strongly advise you against building your hopes up unnecessarily, Mr. Brennan. There is nothing conclusive, or anything to guarantee that this individual is the person we are looking for." His hands were nestling prayer-like under his chin, although on this occasion he was not actually praying, he was simply imploring Jack to show some restraint.

"I know what you mean, believe me, Father, but please allow me to enjoy what I'm feeling right now. After all there is every chance we might find who we're looking for and bring this whole sorry episode to an end."

A rather meek, uncertain smile flickered across the priest's face. "As you wish, but please refrain from sharing your optimism with anyone else too readily -- I would not wish Roisin Byrne to suffer any further anguish because of it." He gave Jack a stern look. "Do I have your word on that?" His pale grey eyes, no longer mocking as they had so often been in the past, were now soft and pleading, seeking an assurance that Jack would keep his enthusiasm under control.

"I'm not a complete fool, Father," he replied stubbornly.

"That's good to know, so let us leave it at that. Since there isn't much more to be done for the moment, I will expedite things at this end and let you know when we can be on our way." He took a couple of strides towards the door, indicating to Jack that his time was up.

"One last thing before I go, Father. In a former life I had the unfortunate experience of delivering death and seeing death delivered -- time costs lives -- seconds are heartbeats and seconds can save lives. We don't know if Tony Byrne has many heartbeats left, so please remember the importance of expediency -- I'm relying on you for that." Having made his point he walked out through the door leaving Father Joseph feeling slightly disappointed that he'd felt it necessary to remind him.

Jack was feeling in a much more cheerful mood now that he had something positive to get his teeth into. His gut feeling told him they were onto something important, and it was a real boost to know that it was his intuitive insight into Devlin's manic mutterings that had put them on the trail. When he got back to the office Judy spotted it straight away and demanded to know the cause of his euphoria. He had been so uptight recently that she could hardly fail to notice the change in him, and of course when he explained the latest developments his enthusiasm rubbed off on her as well. Even more noticeably in fact, since she appeared, as Jack had done earlier, to be quite concerned at the priest's apparent lack of urgency.

"Why doesn't the bloody man just get off his ass and get on the road? You should be on your way to check this guy out for God's sake -- not standing here twiddling your thumbs."

"To be fair, Judy, we don't know what Father Joseph has in the pipeline for the next few days, maybe he has some funerals, weddings, or christenings lined up – who are we to know?"

Judy spun her chair round to face him.

"Okay – okay – I take your point, but do you really think it might be Roisin's husband?" More than anything in the world, she wanted it to be so, and that small embryo of hope carried through in her voice.

Having reflected on Father Joseph's advice Jack was reluctant to sound too optimistic and have everyone think they had already solved the case. He knew it was the safer option to be slightly more reticent in his expectations, publicly at least. "We'll know soon enough, but let's not mention it to anyone else for the moment. We haven't got anything positive enough to go building up people's hopes." His advice, though sensible enough in the circumstances, did not truthfully reflect how he felt inside, and he predicted that waiting for Father Joseph to get back in touch was going to be a trying time for both of them.

44

Standing in for Judy on the front desk Jack reached for the phone the third time it rang, and as it was less than twenty four hours since he and Father Joseph had parted ways he wasn't expecting to hear from him again for at least a couple of days, so it was a bit of a surprise to hear his voice at the other end.

"I have some good news for you, Mr. Brennan," he began, getting straight down to business and dispensing with the normal niceties. "I have made the necessary arrangements for my duties to be covered, and am now free to get under way. Might I suggest we make tracks and have lunch along the way; that would leave us enough time to make the return journey tonight if we decide to do so?" This sudden and unexpected burst of logistical forethought was greeted with a similar level of enthusiasm by Jack "

That's fantastic, Father, I'll pick you up just as soon as I can get there, and I have to say that I'm perhaps more grateful for your support than you might think -- more than I can say if the truth be known."

"There is absolutely no reason to thank me, Mr. Brennan. I just hope that our journey proves to be a fruitless one on this ocassion. I'll see you shortly." With no need for an answer he hung up, leaving Jack champing at the bit for Judy to get back and release him.

When she finally put in an appearance it was to find him pacing about the office like a cat on a hot tin roof, and no sooner had she discarded her coat before he rushed over, kissed her on the forehead and headed for the door without so much as an explanation.

"Can't stop, sweetheart, I'm off with Father Joseph – we might be staying overnight but I can't be sure about that." The words gushed out in his hurry to get away. "I haven't time to pick up an overnight bag so I'll make do as I am for a couple of days if necessary. I'll give you a bell when we stop for lunch,"

He took off, clattering down the stairs at a rate of knots before Judy had time to argue.

45

The first leg of their journey was as enjoyable as any journey might be between two relative strangers, and after negotiating a somewhat hazardous route through the heavy Dublin traffic they stopped for lunch at a little pub just off the south ring road that Father Joseph recommended. It turned out to be a good choice as the food, while fairly basic, was well prepared and the service excellent, which allowed them to be back on their way again much sooner than either of them had thought possible.

The second part of their journey however was much less enjoyable, especially for Jack, as having exercised his tongue over lunch his companion became less and less talkative, and as the miles clicked by any conversation between them soon dried up altogether. Turning to his bible for companionship Father Joseph only conversed spasmodically when quoting the odd passage that he considered relevant to their situation. Jack had never been a religious person, not in any real sense of the word, and although he had no strong feelings against it he found this continuous bombardment irksome and turned the radio on by way of a distraction. Sadly his attempted diversion had little effect and the quotations continued unabated, seemingly, at least in Jack's mind, to be directed at him personally. It was only when the priest fell asleep that he gained some welcome relief; even then it was only for a few minutes as he soon came across a road sign directing him to their final destination.

"Not far now, Father," he said, loudly enough to rouse his passenger and have him sit up and scan the countryside for any familiar landmarks.

"Ah yes, I know where we are," he said confidently, in a voice thick with sleep. "You need to take the next turning on the left; it's only about five hundred yards or so after that." Jack heaved a sigh of relief, grateful their journey was nearing its end as he was bored rigid and was making no effort to hide it.

Their destination proved to be a rather imposing, medieval, almost Gothic looking building that matched the description Father Joseph had related to him prior to starting their journey. Jack saw it as rather cold and austere, although it did maintain a definite air of grandeur from its previously illustrious past.

The main, central building was surrounded on three sides by a perimeter guard of smaller, less imposing buildings of a more recent age, which, combined with their immaculately maintained grounds and aura of peaceful solitude, made the whole scene quite inspirational.

As they drew nearer a sign directed them to a parking area close to the main entrance. Once there Jack allowed Father Joseph to take the lead as he appeared to be fairly familiar with their surroundings. He led them straight into the main building. Firstly through a massive stone archway, then through a set of intricately carved oak doors that led them into a circular, domed concourse that echoed loudly to the sound of their footsteps.

There was a table just inside the door with a fairly hefty looking brass bell resting on it. Father Joseph picked it and gave it a good shake. The sound reverberating noisily off the walls, and after what could only have been a matter of seconds a young novice nun appeared from a concealed doorway.

She shared a few whispered words with Father Joseph before indicating that they should follow her, then led them through the same door she had appeared from and along a narrow arched corridor, eventually stopping in front of another intricately carved wooden door where she knocked and waited. When invited to enter she slipped inside closing the door quietly behind her, leaving her visitors outside.

Jack chose to remain silent, in fact he wouldn't have spoken even if he'd had a mind to as the aura of peaceful reverence exuded by his surroundings seemed to forbid it. Thankfully they didn't have long to wait before their guide reappeared and invited them inside before taking her leave.

The room was unlike anything Jack had been expecting. The walls were covered with beautifully polished wooden panels, a priceless luxury that proved to be its only tie with its illustrious past, as all the other furnishings were quite modern and well-appointed, creating a pleasant, almost business like atmosphere. Seated behind a large desk at the far end of the room was a very grand looking Mother Superior, who quickly rose to her feet and greeted them with a welcoming smile.

"Father Joseph, how nice to meet you, I do hope you had a pleasant journey." She turned and smiled warmly at Jack while waiting for an introduction.

"I'm afraid I must confess that my companion is not yet converted to our persuasion yet, Holy Mother," he advised, his humorous remark meant as a warning that his companion might not be conversant with Church etiquette. The grand lady acknowledged with a curt nod, but retained the warmth of her smile. "We are what we are," she replied, her gentle Irish brogue very comforting and easy on the ear.

"Well now, gentlemen, I'm led to believe that you have an interest in one of our unfortunate guests. It will indeed be God's own blessing if you can throw some light on the mystery regarding his identity." She wrung her hands together as if she was applying hand cream. "This poor creature has been in our care for so long he is now completely institutionalized I'm afraid. We give him the best care we can of course, but it would be such a joy to discover where he truly belongs. We can do no more for him here I'm afraid."

Father Joseph was about to say something, but their host wasn't quite finished.

"We have named him Paul -- after Our Holy Father of course, he needed an identity of some sort and it seemed fitting at the time -- indeed we even suspect that he's beginning to respond to it." The last little aside was deliberately added to ensure they both fully understood the condition of his wellbeing.

Jack was mad keen to see the guy -- desperate to find out if he was who they hoped he was, but he somehow managed to hold his enthusiasm in check. He was in unfamiliar territory and had already decided to stay in the background and take his lead from Father Joseph, who, as if reading his mind, decided to finish what he had tried to say earlier. "Could someone take us to see him, Holy Mother?"

Without a moment's hesitation she rounded the desk, arms outstretched in a welcoming gesture. "I will be only too pleased to take you there myself."

Their short journey took them into another high roofed corridor, where the echo of their brisk footsteps on the tiled floor bounced erratically ahead of them off the panelled walls. As they neared the end of the corridor the Mother Superior turned sharply to her right and led them down a flight of stairs into a huge cellar that was lined on either side by a vast array of little rooms, or more accurately, little cells, for in essence that was really what they were.

The atmosphere was quite different down here, cold and austere, the monotonous glare from its whitewashed walls only relieved every ten or twelve feet by a regiment of solid wooden doors, all painted green, each with an opening no more than twelve inches square that was protected by three vertical metal bars. The temperature had to be at least two or three degrees below the more comforting atmosphere of the building above, and the eerie silence was only occasionally broken by a pitiful wail or an agonizing moan from one of its demented inmates. It was like nothing Jack had ever experienced before, and he could boast some dreadful experiences. He glanced quickly at Father Joseph to gauge his reaction, but his features were firmly set in an expression of firm resolve, with his eyes fixed straight ahead.

About halfway along the spotlessly scrubbed corridor the Mother Superior stopped at one of the cell doors and slid the bolt back. Turning to her visitor's, she was about to offer them a word of warning when she recognized the strained look on Jack's face and changed her mind, whispering in his ear instead as he drew closer.

"Lost souls need the security of a safe environment if they are to make peace with themselves." Her explanation was nothing more than that, and certainly not an apology for their medieval surroundings, but she was not yet finished, and in a more authoritative voice she issued a last stern warning to them both. "Please bear in mind that the sight of strangers, like your good selves, may well be a frightening experience for Paul. It would be helpful if you try to remain calm and don't allow any difficult emotions you might experience to show openly -- whatever the outcome of your visit."

It was sound advice, whether they realized it or not at the time, and she reinforced it by continuing to block their entrance until she was satisfied that her warning had sunk in, then she pushed the door open and stood aside to let them enter.

When the door opened a pungent and nauseating stench of human defecation invaded their nostrils, it was completely unexpected and overpowering enough to stop Jack in his tracks. The whitewashed walls inside the tiny cell were unadorned and slightly grubby, unlike the sterile, scrubbed floors of the outside corridor. Against one wall stood a very robust looking metal bed, securely bolted to a stone floor, with nothing but a solitary coir mat as the only other visible furnishing.

Tony Byrne sat zombie-like on the bare wooden boards, a brown blanket draped around his wasted frame. Dressed in a dull, grey smock that was heavily stained at the front. He appeared totally unaware of their presence, his lifeless blue eyes staring unblinkingly into his own lost little world. He looked emaciated and fragile, but he was Tony Byrne, of that there was no doubt.

Jack was speechless; his emotions were all over the place, but whatever he was feeling, it was not the feeling of elation he had hoped for. It pained him too much to look at the poor, pathetic creature they had found. Throughout their long journey from Belfast he had nurtured an image inside his head of rushing out and throwing his arms round Roisin Byrne's husband, if and when they found him, but he now genuinely wished that Devlin had killed the man, for what he had inflicted on the poor creature in front of them was nothing more than a torturous living death. Turning away from the others he went back outside, unable to stand the smell and the horror of what he was meant to bring home to his client. But if he thought he could rid himself of the smell quite so easily he was mistaken, it clung to his clothes and his nostrils and would remain with him for many days to come.

From inside the cell he heard Father Joseph try to converse with the poor wretch. "Do you remember me, Tony -- it's Father Joseph -- can you speak to me?"

The Mother Superior answered his question for him. "I'm afraid nothing registers, Father, I'm sorry to say you are really wasting your time." She paused, then to Jack's relief made a more sensible suggestion. "I think now that you have identified him we should go back to my office. I can see you are both struggling to come to terms with this."

She re-emerged with Father Joseph by her side and secured the door before leading them back through the maze of stone corridors that had become Tony Byrne's barren universe.

Jack's brain refused to function properly, he was unsure what he wanted to do, or what he should do, except for a compelling need to get in touch with Judy. Not to tell her the wonderful news she might be expecting, that he had found their missing man, but to express his regret for having done so.

Their journey back to the Mother Superior's office embraced a shocked and stony silence, each of them bedevilled by a confusion of thoughts about what to do next. It was the Mother Superior who broke the silence.

"I'm sorry if you found that depressing, gentlemen, but the sad truth is that we can only tend to our guest's spiritual and physical welfare, there is nothing that can be done to improve his mental condition." She sidled behind her desk and eased back into her chair. "What will your plans be now that you have confirmed his identity?"

Father Joseph made his decision unilaterally. "Return him to his wife of course, what else?" He glanced sideways at Jack to see if there was any opposition, then carried on. "We will need to prepare her for such an ordeal beforehand of course, and arrange some sort of medical assessment. I'm sure you understand that it might take a few days for that to be arranged."

Without uttering a word, or offering any excuse, Jack turned away and made a beeline for the door, preferring not to hear any more. Feeling stifled and claustrophobic he was desperately in need of some fresh air. Hurrying outside he went back to his car and sat on the front seat with the door open, his feet firmly planted on the ground outside. A whole host of emotions welling up inside him, none of them pleasant, and most of them aimed at the people responsible for what had happened to his client's husband.

It was some time before Father Joseph prised himself away from the Mother Superior and re-joined him, but of course a loose arrangement of some sort needed to be put in place, and Jack was grateful for the time alone to gather his thoughts and think things through. He was really struggling to quell the ferocious anger that had taken hold of him, and found himself overcome with a feeling of utter despair. Despair at being unable to prove who was responsible for what had happened, even though he had little doubt in his own mind that it was Devlin who had administered the cocktail of poisonous narcotics that had taken such a hideous toll on the man. It was almost certainly Devlin who had given the order to make it happen, shattering not one but two lives along the way. It was he who had given his client a much more punishing and costly burden to carry into the future than even the death of her husband might have put upon her, had that blessing only but happened.

Sat by himself he envisaged the years of torment that lay ahead for his client, chained to an empty shell of a husband who she undoubtedly loved without reservation, while having to endure the absence of any spiritual presence and companionship that she might justifiably have expected to enjoy into her old age.

They would be long, gruelling, and tormenting years; years without retribution. Years that would eat into her soul and turn her into God knows what. It was too dreadful a thought to even contemplate, worse still, at that moment in time Jack hated himself for having found Tony Byrne, even more than he hated Devlin.

46

Two months, two weeks, and four days had elapsed since Jack had accompanied Roisin Byrne to the south London hospital and reunited her with her husband. Father Joseph had been good enough to travel with them to offer spiritual support, and his presence had undoubtedly made a difficult task an awful lot easier for all concerned. Having said that, nothing anyone could have said or done at the time would have made things any easier for his client, who had been close to tears after just a few minutes in the presence of her husband.

The months of waiting while his chances of recovery were assessed by a series of consultants had made her woefully indifferent to her own physical and mental wellbeing. And when the news finally came through that her husband's time was limited she all but cracked up. The dreadful news, although not entirely unexpected, killed off every last shred of hope she had clung to that her husband might confound the doctors and recover sufficiently to recognize her presence at his bedside. The whole episode had been an extremely difficult time for everyone, especially Jack, who felt forever indebted to Father Joseph for his continuing support and advice. But the lengthy, drawn out saga had taken a heavy toll on him as well, and he was unable to shake off the oppressive burden of guilt that he had taken upon himself. He was drinking more than usual and generally hounding himself into a dark abyss of despair, while his neglected partner could only watch in silent protest, fearful of the effect it was having on his personality. All too frequently she found him withdrawn and snappy, failing to communicate for long periods, his behaviour so persistently out of character that she had simply given up trying to do anything about it.

Even now, sitting no more than a few feet apart either side of the fire, there was a stubborn wall of silence keeping them miles apart. The shrill sound of the telephone rescued her from her muted suffering and she pounced on it much too eagerly, silently praying that it might be a friend, or at least someone who could help get her lover involved in conversation. Anything at all to shake him out of his depressingly lethargic mood. Sadly there was to be no escape, and she was unable to hide her disappointment when she discovered it was none other than Roisin Byrne. Cursing her luck she placed her hand over the mouthpiece; the last thing she wanted was the Byrne case being dragged up again with Jack in his current state of mind, but she couldn't do anything about it, business was business after all.

"It's Roisin, Jack, she would like to speak with you."

He grimaced awkwardly, and Judy could tell from his body language, and the way he hesitated, that he did not want to come to the phone, but she knew him well enough to know he would do no less, so she held it out to him.

"Hello, Roisin -- how are you?" he asked, showing a distinct lack of sensitivity with his choice of greeting; he was well aware of her distressed state and didn't need reminding.

"I have been better, Mr. Brennan, I can't deny that, but we all have to get on with our lives as there are things that need doing," she told him. "I hope I'm not dragging you away from something important but I have a personal favour to ask of you." She sounded more purposeful than Jack thought she should, which lifted some of his own gloom.

"Anything I can do, Roisin, anything at all, you only have to ask." He could hear lots of noise in the background and wondered where on earth she was phoning from?

"I'm returning to Belfast and I wonder if you could pick me up at the airport and escort me home. I need to collect a few things and make some arrangements for the future. I know it's asking a lot but I would be very grateful if you could manage it." She sounded so restrained and reticent in the way she explained herself that he simply didn't have it in him to refuse.

"Of course I will, Roisin. Just tell me where and when and I'll be there." The prospect of doing something useful helped ease his own guilty conscience -- a kind of personal penance really.

"It's tonight at the City Airport if you can manage it. I get in at eight o'clock if my flight is on time."

The immediacy of her arrival took Jack by surprise, but rather than question the need for such suddenness he marked it down as some maternal instinct to get back to her roots, after all she had been commuting back and forth quite a lot, so maybe she was tiring from it all. Whatever the rationale behind it, he would quite happily do whatever was needed to keep her happy.

"I look forward to seeing you then, Roisin," he said, glancing at his watch, "but that only gives you a couple of hours, are you sure you can make your flight okay?" He knew how long the journey to Heathrow would take from Mairead's place and feared she might have underestimated the journey time. It entered his head to ring Mairead and check it out.

"I'm already at the airport, Mairead has kindly dropped me off." She sounded a little preoccupied, as if there were other things preying on her mind.

"Is she still with you?" Jack asked.

"Yes of course, it's her phone I'm using. I'll put her on and let you speak to her."

Mairead came on almost instantly.

"Hello, Jack, I didn't expect to be speaking to you again quite so soon." There was a detectable note of anxiety in her voice that Jack was quick to spot.

"What's going on," he asked, "can you talk freely?"

Her reply was a bit shielded and secretive. "Just about, Jack, I'm some distance away from her now. It's been bloody difficult over here since she left my place and moved herself into a hostel. It's been hard to maintain contact with her, although in fairness the hostel she chose is a lot closer to the hospital than my place, so I don't necessarily disagree with her reasoning. But it just makes it so much harder to be on hand for her if you get my drift."

Not happy with what he was hearing Jack pressed for more information.

"Where did this sudden urge to return home come from? What's that all about?" he asked.

"I guess she must have made her mind up yesterday. She spent the whole day with her husband and never left his side. The nursing staff said she talked to him relentlessly; they had to tell her to go home in the end, but when she rang me she sounded so much brighter than she had been that I just presumed she had made some sort of breakthrough with her husband. You know -- made some sort of contact because she was so much more purposeful than she has been. I think that's a good sign -- isn't it?" There was an element of uncertainty in her voice.

"I guess so," he replied, "at least she's doing something to keep herself occupied. Anyway, I'll meet her when she gets here and let you know how she gets on." After a few more meaningless niceties their call ended.

47

It was as black as your boots when they drove out of the short stay car park at the airport, which was a relief to Jack as it meant his passenger couldn't see too much of his face and the concern that was etched into it. He was pretty exhausted from a night of sleep denying, self-accusing guilt, and not fit for conversation. In any case he wanted his passenger to choose the topic for discussion.

"I suppose you're wondering why I should choose to come back to an empty house," she said, fulfilling his wish.

"No, not at all, it is your home after all. You must be keen to have familiar things around you again, and your property can't just lie there and grow cobwebs. You need to do something with it in the short term. Rent it out or something if you don't intend on coming back to it on a permanent basis for a while."

Jack had no knowledge of her future plans, but he was worried that he might say the wrong thing and upset her; and having no wish to face her tears if they put in another appearance, he was in entirely the wrong mood for such delicacy.

"Quite right, Mr Brennan, that's exactly how I feel about it too. I'm achieving nothing by sitting day after day beside a husband who knows nothing of my presence. I should be getting on with more important things, regardless of how Tony would feel about it. There are things in life that just have to be attended to."

There was a calculating edge in her voice; a coldness that Jack found slightly disconcerting, and it was sufficiently out of character to stop him from responding right away. Although when he thought about it he accepted that she was simply being practical and trying to get on with her life, a thought that actually cheered him up somewhat.

"I know we didn't discuss it when you phoned earlier, but I took it for granted you would stay the night with Judy and me." He held his breath while waiting for her to agree.

"That would be lovely, Mr. Brennan, as long as you don't mind taking me to my house early tomorrow morning – say around eight o'clock?"

Jack could feel her eyes on him, but he managed to mask his surprise at the needless urgency in her demand.

"I don't have a problem with that, Roisin," he agreed with a timid smile, although behind the forced smile was a niggling concern over her need for such an early start. She had all the time in the world at her disposal, so why go rushing around and putting herself under pressure? Her apparently pre-planned timetable made him wonder what she was up to, but he kept his thoughts to himself as the conversation dwindled to a mutual accepted silence for the rest of their journey. A useful break that gave Jack time to think about what to do if they bumped into Devlin while he was taking her home?

48

Roisin Byrne was clearly agitated and impatient to be on her way, and having declined Judy's offer of a cooked breakfast she settled instead for a single cup of tea with which to face the day. Jack was making short work of his own breakfast, aware of their guest's need to expedite her departure with what he considered to be unnecessary haste.

"Can we be on our way now, Mr. Brennan?" she pleaded. "I'd like to get this over with." Before he could answer she had donned her outdoor coat and was waiting for him by the door, her hands clasped protectively over a large handbag that was held tightly to her bosom. Jack pushed his unfinished breakfast aside, took a last gulp of coffee and stood up.

"Right then -- that's me -- we're on our way." His remark was aimed at Judy as he slipped into his jacket and kissed her goodbye.

"If you're ready, Roisin?" he invited, quite unnecessarily as she was already making her way through the door without even saying goodbye to Judy, whose eyes followed her from the room with a rather enquiring look.

Jack had allowed a little over twenty minutes to get to the Byrne household, and as they were on the road pretty early he knew they would miss the commuter traffic and any serious hold ups.

There was a distinct lack of conversation in the early part of their journey, which was nothing new to Jack, he was used to the silent treatment from Judy most mornings. But it was a quiet spell he was thankful for as he never quite knew what to say to his client these days; there was little by way of sympathy that he hadn't already expressed many times over.

"I'm very grateful for everything you and Judy have done for me, Mr. Brennan, I'm sure you already know that, but could I please ask just one more favour of you?" This was another request that was unexpected, and with his thoughts focused on something else entirely, like the possibility of bumping into Devlin, Jack found himself agreeing to it without knowing what might be asked of him.

"You really don't need to ask, Roisin, if it's in my power to help then I will. You should know that by now."

She hesitated quite noticeably before explaining what she had in mind. "You might not feel quite so eager when you hear what it is." Jack glanced anxiously in her direction, invited to do so by a sinister undertone in her voice that set his alarm bells ringing.

"I want to go and see Joe Devlin."

Jack slammed his foot on the brake pedal and whipped the car in to the side of the road, then turned in his seat to face her.

"Have you taken leave of your fuckin' senses?" he snapped, struggling to control himself. The very idea that she would contemplate such an insane notion was too ludicrous for words. "I'm sorry for swearing at you, Roisin, but how in God's name did you ever come up with such an insane idea?" He immediately regretted using the word insane, because of her husband's situation, but it was out now and past retrieving. Thankfully it seemed to go past her unnoticed.

"If I'm ever to have any peace of mind then I have to face the monster who you tell me is responsible for what happened to my husband. I believe he at least needs to know what I think of him." She clutched the bag nestling on her lap more tightly. "I feel like I'm being eaten up inside by this awful thing that happened to my lovely soul mate. It's driving me crazy that up to now I haven't had the courage to face Devlin and ask him why he did it. I feel so guilty about it each and every time I face my husband."

She was crying bitterly, making it all the more difficult for Jack to maintain his hard-nosed opposition, but he had a real understanding of what she meant by 'guilt'. That was a universal infliction, one that clung like a blood sucking parasite to anyone willing enough to indulge it.

"This is not a very clever thing to do, Roisin. You have no idea how that evil bastard will react if you just turn up on his doorstep out of the blue." It was far too late for niceties now that her determination for such an early start began to make sense. It was obviously her way of ensuring that Devlin would be at home, which left Jack with the uncomfortable feeling that she had planned the whole thing very carefully, and well in advance.

"This is something I have to do, Mr. Brennan. I have to confront that man and hear what he has to say for himself, for my own peace of mind if nothing else. I think it would be better if you were with me, but I will go it alone if I have to." Jack could see no way out. The stubborn look on her face told him she meant every spoken word, and he could hardly hold her prisoner against her will, or let her face a thug like Devlin on her own.

"Christ, Roisin, this is absolute bloody madness. The RUC are still actively working to make the connection with Devlin, you should walk away from this and leave it to them. I didn't expect anything like this when I agreed to help -- I'm not properly prepared for what you're asking of me."

Turning away from him she gazed through the side window at the passing traffic, momentarily at least, then turned round in her seat to face him again.

"I can well understand how you're feeling, but you mustn't fret yourself over it, I'll just go and see this awful man by myself." She paused to look at him. "It was unfair to ask it of you, but I need you to understand that this is something I absolutely have to do." She was unfaltering in her determination and Jack could hardly stand aside and let her face a brute like Devlin all by herself. God knows what the outcome would be if he allowed something like that to happen?

"If I can't make you change your mind then of course I'll go with you, but you're forcing me to do something that I believe is entirely wrong." He clinched his hands together and gave an involuntary shudder. "When do you propose to make this visit?"

She looked him straight in the eye. "There's no time like the present, it's always best to get these little difficulties over with and out of the way, then perhaps the day might improve as it gets older."

Jack sighed, resignedly. "Alright," he conceded with a sigh, "let's do it, but be warned, nothing good will come of this. Guys like Devlin are not swayed by what normal people like you or I think of them. They live in a different world to the rest of us." He centred himself in the driving seat, stuck the car back into gear and pulled out into the passing traffic.

49

It took a couple of knocks before the door opened and Devlin's ugly bulk filled its frame, his broken nose, and the deep scar above his eye providing Jack with a pleasant reminder of their last encounter.

"What the hell?" he gasped, startled to see who was at his door, added to which he was almost naked, apart from a pair of tartan boxer shorts that made him look vulnerable and defenceless, regardless of his massive bulk. It took him a few moments to get a hold of himself and gather his thoughts.

"What the hell do you two want?" he demanded, going straight on the offensive.

Roisin Byrne's calm response seemed somehow unreal in the circumstances. "I had to come and see you, Joe. I have to know why you did those awful things to my poor husband. It was a wretched thing to do to such a wonderfully caring man like Tony." Her hand dived into her pocket and Devlin flinched defensively. Even Jack, fearing the worst, made a grab for her arm, but he was too slow, not that it mattered because when she raised it up it held nothing more than a photograph that she shoved into Devlin's face. "That's what you did to him, that's what my poor husband looks like now," she said, her own sadness masked by the force of her accusation. "I want you to look closely at it, Joe. I want you to see what you have left me to live my life with." She pushed it into his face.

"Take it," she demanded angrily, "or haven't you the stomach for it?" She shoved it into his unwilling hand, forcing him to look at it as

Jack watched on intently, worried that things were getting out of hand.

Perhaps if he had been watching Devlin less intently he would have spotted Roisin Byrne's hand creep furtively into her bulky shoulder bag. But he failed to do so, as did Devlin, and when they realized what was happening it was too late to do anything about it. She unscrewed the rubber top from a large bottle she was holding and tossed its watery contents into Devlin's face, then shoved the neck of the bottle deep into his gaping mouth as far as she could get it, and in the blink of an eye his face began to smoulder as Jack looked on helplessly.

An acrid stench filled the air as the undiluted acid vaporized his skin and burned its way through the soft tissue of his flesh. Caught off guard Jack was slow to react as Devlin's frantic contortions, and the thought of the pain he was suffering, held him immobile. Time seemed to stand still as his inhuman screams rang in Jack's ears; a sound that quickly turned to a stomach retching gurgle as the burning acid melted his tongue and began eating through the soft tissue of his throat. Devlin was choking to death right in front of him.

In a panic he reached for the bottle in Roisin's hand, but he wasn't quick enough as she had already backed away out of reach. He spun back to help Devlin who was writhing on the ground but he knew there was nothing he could do, there was no hope of saving him -- he was beyond help. All he could do was watch the other man's contorted features as his body jerked in violent spasm and he struggled for a last breath that wasn't there.

Roisin Byrne's voice came to him from just inside the garden gate that she had closed behind her to keep him at bay. "Goodbye, Mr. Brennan -- I don't expect you to understand any of this, nobody will. I'm truly sorry that I made you witness it, but some things just have to be done."

They were the last words she would ever speak, as she lifted the bottle to her own lips and poured the remainder of its contents down her throat, bringing her own sad life to the same hideous and torturous end as the man she had once thought of as a neighbour. Both bodies lay squirming on the ground in the final throws of death, and for the first time in his adult life Jack Brennan felt a tear run down his cheek as he pulled out his phone and hit the pre-set code that would connect him to the emergency services.

50

Standing by the graveside as Roisin Byrne's remains were lowered into the moist, freshly dug earth Jack was overcome with a disturbing mixture of guilt and grief. Logic should have told him that none of this was his doing, but he was suffering from an overload of mental anguish and pain at his client's tragic death, and particularly over the manner in which she had chosen to end her life. An act of utter desperation that had clearly come from no spur of the moment decision on her part, since she had planned it well enough in advance to have ensured that her executors made good on her debt to Brennan Associates without delay.

It was this glaringly obvious element of pre-planning that hurt him most of all, as it condemned him for lacking the foresight to pre-empt what she intended to do on that fateful morning. That, and the sad awareness that he, and only he, had been in a position to divert such a tragedy. But how, in such gruesome circumstances as those that had taken place, could logic ever prevail?

As expected, it was Father Joseph who administered the service, which proved to be a muted, edgy affair, with many of the local parishioners collectively sharing in Jack's remorse. The horror of two close neighbours suffering such a violent death had roused feelings that had touched the very heart of the community, giving rise to a feeling of communal responsibility. And as Father Joseph delivered his graveside eulogy, many of the mourners fidgeted nervously as they mentally debated whether or not they had subscribed, in kind or part, to Roisin Byrne's demise.

Jack was stood on one side of his client's brother in law with Judy on the other. All three looking pale and red eyed as the service came to an end. He had stayed close to Alfie Byrne throughout the ordeal, offering what little support he could muster out of respect for their client. Of course the one person who had been central to the whole affair, Roisin's husband, was not in attendance. He only had weeks to live and would not have understood anything of what was going on. It would have been undignified to say the least to have made him a part of the arrangements, and in any case his dementia and frail state of health was such as to ensure he did not leave his hospital bed.

Once Father Joseph had concluded his business, and the customary handshakes and platitudes were dispensed with, the foursome of Alfie Byrne, Father Joseph, Jack, and Judy all departed the scene as a group. It had been decided well in advance to forego the traditional tea and sticky bun gathering, thinking it might have been socially awkward for some of Roisin's neighbour's, especially those who had been less than supportive in her time of need. So her brother-in-law had planned for only those who were now accompanying him to go back to his local pub for a bowl of soup and a few drinks. Jack thought it a sensible decision that he happily concurred with, although he would like to have seen the same invitation extended to Dessie Graham and his wife as well, but that wasn't to be. Judy had also declined the invitation to join them, believing it prudent to leave the men to their own company. She would make her own way back to the office and allow them to travel the short distance to the pub in Jack's car, a journey that afforded little conversation, apart from giving Jack directions on how to get there.

"I'll get these in," Jack insisted, as the waitress approached their table. He didn't know Alfie Byrne at all well and was more than happy to be otherwise occupied and leave it to Father Joseph to keep him entertained. In any event, he was unsure what to say to the dead woman's relative that hadn't already been said.

"A most terrible tragedy, Mr. Byrne," declared Father Joseph, clinging doggedly to the same solemn tone he had used throughout the service. More noticeable than his tone of voice was the formal way in which he addressed Alfie Byrne, a trait that caused Jack to wonder if he had known Tony the better of the two brothers, even though they were both members of his parish. The thought stuck with him for a while, but he made his mind up to keep it to himself and not quiz the priest about it at such an inappropriate time. Nevertheless, it did make him wonder.

"Terrible indeed, Father," Alfie Byrne agreed. "It's been a terrible time altogether and no mistake. I suppose in a way it's rather fortunate that Roisin didn't have any other close family. It would have been much more of an ordeal for her had her parents still been alive." Father Joseph just nodded in agreement; he was already talked out, leaving Jack to wonder if he suffered from some sort of social disability? The secret humour in his thought brought the makings of a smile to his face as he had a developed a soft spot for the priest.

"Sadly I didn't know Roisin for very long," Jack admitted, to no one in particular, "but she impressed me in a lot of ways. She certainly didn't deserve any of what happened to her, and no matter how you look at it, she was the real victim in this whole sorry mess." There was more he wanted to say now that he'd got going, but fearing it might be misconstrued he chose not to.

"I would never have considered her capable of doing what she did," Father Joseph confessed. "She was always such a gentle, caring soul. She must have been terribly disturbed to take her own life in such a tragic and disturbing manner. It goes against everything that I know she believed in, especially her faith, which I know was such an essential part of her life."

Alfie Byrne declined to comment, as did Jack. He sensed the other two were struggling with the conversation as much as he was. In fact it dried up completely soon after, as they each focused their attention on their drinks as an excuse to let someone else carry the burden. If it did nothing else the prevailing silence gave Jack an opportunity to study the man sitting beside him.

He was intrigued to know why Alfie Byrne looked so inexplicably jittery; he kept fiddling with his face, and his right knee, which was in light contact with Jack's left leg, was constantly in motion, jerking up and down in a nervous, quivering motion, as if he was impatient to be doing something else. Jack wondered if it was his presence beside him, or perhaps that of Father Joseph, that was the cause of his agitation. On the face of it, there was no other reason for his noticeably strange behaviour, except perhaps what he came out with next.

"I need to visit the little boy's room," he announced, as if guessing what the others were thinking. He got up and squeezed past Jack and was on his way before his admission had registered with either of his guests. Such a hurried exit seemed unnecessarily abrupt to Jack, who was finding the whole situation a bit bizarre to say the least. Father Joseph appeared to be of a similar mind, judging by the quizzical look on his face.

"What do you make of that?" enquired Jack, unable to hide his concern. "Do you think he's okay?"

Father Joseph didn't look at all concerned as he raised a hand to placate Jack.

"Don't alarm yourself, Mr. Brennan, it's likely nothing more than the stress of today's events taking their toll. It happens that way sometimes. Believe me, I have enough experience of such matters not to get too worked up about it." His explanation seemed reasonable enough, even if it lacked sincerity.

"I think I should go and keep an eye on him anyway, just in case he's in some sort of difficulty." The priest raised a hand in protest but Jack was already on his way, and although he wasted no time in getting to the toilet he was amazed to find that Alfie Byrne was nowhere to be seen. A problem that immediately lessened his concern, especially as the toilet was sited very close to a rear entrance and right next to a stairway leading to the floor above. At a loss to know which of these he had taken Jack decided to return to their table rather than leave Father Joseph on his own.

As it turned out he was the one left on his own, because Father Joseph had vacated their table and was stood at the bar having a good old chin wag with some old lady he obviously knew. Feeling a tiny bit neglected he went back to his seat and quietly nursed his beer, while waiting patiently for his company to return.

The whole sorry saga leading up to today was proving to be a bit of a nightmare, and while he tried to concentrate on Alfie Byrne's sudden disappearance, and what had prompted it, his mind unwillingly returned to the awful events that had been blighting his happiness over the last few months. It was obvious now that he should have taken Judy's advice and given the Byrne case a by-ball, but it was too late for recriminations, what with everything that had happened, and he drew little pleasure from knowing that his investigation had actually been successful, in part at least. After all, he had found Tony Byrne, and that was what he had been paid to do. Admittedly he had failed to prove, in any legal meaning of the word, who it was that had actually spirited him away, and with Devlin now out of the picture he had little hope of ever doing so.

But that was all water under the bridge as he was no longer serving a client, and no good would come from punishing himself over things he couldn't control, even if they didn't rest easily with his conscience. As he was sat at the table inflicting more misery on himself, Father Joseph finished his little chat and came hurrying back to join him. Timing his return to coincide with Alfie Byrne rushing back through a door that should have taken him to the toilet, his hair windswept and untidy looking. One thing in his demeanour was instantly noticeable to Jack; the guy had the appearance of someone who had been rushing around outside and not someone who had simply been to the toilet to relieve himself.

"Sorry to leave you on your own like that, Mr. Brennan, but I spotted someone at the bar that I haven't seen for a while, and it would have been inconsiderate of me to have ignored her. Please do forgive me." Father Joseph's apology rested easily with Jack, who was much more interested in how Alfie Byrne would explain his rather mystifying behaviour.

"Are you feeling okay?" he enquired of Byrne, as he joined them and seated himself beside the priest.

"Yeah, I'm fine thanks, just a bit of a tummy upset, sorry to have been so long at the toilet but you know how it is."

If Jack hadn't followed him to the toilet he would never have had any reason to disbelieve what he was being told, but having done so, he knew the guy was lying, although for the life of him couldn't understand the reason behind it.

Father Joseph on the other hand was completely unaware of Jack's discovery and gave Byrne a sympathetic grimace. More interestingly, for Jack at least, Alfie Byrne appeared oblivious to the fact that he had gone in search of him, he was also unaware to the fact that he was displaying a noticeable change in his attitude. There was no doubt that he much more relaxed and at ease with himself, and the nervous leg quiver that had been so distracting before he'd left the table appeared to be under control.

On closer inspection Jack noted an alarming and more damning difference -- the pupils of Byrne's eyes were noticeably dilated. A condemning piece of evidence to those who knew what it meant, as Jack did -- Alfie Byrne had just had a fix!

Keeping his finding to himself he decided that if the priest couldn't work out what was going on, then he wasn't about to enlighten him. It was almost tea time before Jack decided to call time on what had been a positively horrendous day, in fact he had felt more like a prisoner of conscience than a welcome contributor to the day's proceedings. So it came as music to his ears when Father Joseph declined his offer of a lift home and opted instead to make the journey by taxi.

While for his part Alfie Byrne showed little sign of going anywhere while he still had a drink in front of him. A situation, that for reasons known only himself, Jack chose to exploit by buying him one last pint before leaving.

CLOSURE

Patience was a virtue Jack rarely subscribed to, which made sitting in his car with nothing but the radio for company a decidedly tiresome occupation that he had no wish to repeat. But having held his patience in check for the best part of three hours, he was fully intent on maintaining his vigil no matter how long it took. He wasn't going anywhere until Alfie Byrne came out of the pub, even if it meant staying where he was until they threw the guy out at closing time. His strange behaviour in the pub was one thing, which in the context of the day's events might easily be ignored, but his obvious character weakness added a more serious complication that aroused Jack's suspicions.

Right now his solitary vigil, if providing nothing else, at least gave him time to consider the possible implications of what he had uncovered. There was no doubt in his mind that Alfie Byrne was a drug addict, or at least a user to some degree, and that posed a serious question that needed investigating. If he was a druggie -- what else might he be?

That tantalizing thought was enough to make him recall Peter's advice that he should look more closely at Tony Byrne's brother, advice that he had chosen to ignore, and over which he now had some fairly serious regrets. His consideration of the problem might have lasted longer had the pathetic figure of Alfie Byrne not come staggering out of the pub and pushed it from his mind.

Jack didn't follow him straight away, choosing to let him get some distance up the road before getting out of his car and tailing along at a respectable distance. Although in his present state of inebriation Jack could have been walking alongside him and Byrne would hardly have noticed. An issue that brought into question the validity of what he was actually doing, and whether anything was to be gained from following a drunk man home. Indeed had they not been closer to Alfie Byrne's home than they were to his car when the thought struck him, he might well have called time on the whole idea.

"To hell with it," he conceded under his breath, "in for a penny -- in for a pound. I can at least make sure the guy gets home safely." A task that wasn't made any easier by Byrne's erratic meandering, indeed Jack had to hold back at regular intervals in order to keep his distance.

He was doing just that by taking refuge in a shop doorway when a car came tearing up the road and skidded to a halt beside his quarry. A couple of heavy duty thugs leapt out and bundled Byrne into the back seat like a sack of rubbish, leaving Jack a frustrated onlooker as they sped off up the road. He was about to head back to his own car when the Mazda turned off the main road into the street where Byrne lived. Having recognized the other car Jack had a very good idea who it was had lifted Byrne off the street, even if he didn't know what they were up to. And he sure as hell knew where they were going once they'd turned into the street where Byrne lived.

It only took a couple of minutes to reach the same turning, and as he rounded the corner he saw the Mazda parked directly in front of Byrne's house just as he expected. Although it looked more like it was abandoned than parked, with both off-side wheels up on the pavement, almost blocking the gate to Byrne's house.

The narrow, dimly lit street was totally deserted, and although the lights were on in Byrne's front room the curtains were so tightly drawn that it was impossible to see what was going on inside. However that was only a secondary issue as far as Jack was concerned; at least for the moment anyway, the main issue was the appearance of the Mazda in the first place. It was without doubt the same car that had tried to follow him home a couple of months back, which gave his belated suspicions about Tony Byrne's brother a little more impetus, since it linked him, willingly or unwillingly to Devlin's gang of thugs. By itself that was enough to persuade Jack to find out a little more about this 'clean cut' young man of whom everyone spoke so highly.

From his vantage point on the opposite side of the street Jack could see absolutely no movement, or any indication that someone might be lurking in the shadows outside the house, but that didn't deter him from pulling the weapon from his waistband and loading a round into the chamber. He knew enough about the people inside Byrne's house to know they were extremely dangerous, so he wasn't about to take any unnecessary risks, even though he considered that all risks were calculable. It was a situation where he couldn't help himself, as he still retained a sense of loyalty to his dead client, and he could hardly shirk from unravelling the mystery of her brother-in-law's connection to Devlin's henchmen.

Demonstrating a deceiving lightness of foot he sprinted round to the back of the house and climbed over the fence into Byrne's back yard. There were no lights on in any of the back rooms, but the curtains on the sliding patio doors were partially open and spilling light from inside the house. Once he was close enough, he found an unobstructed line of vision into the dining room and on through to the lounge beyond. It was impossible to see the whole of the lounge because of a curtain divider that separated the two rooms, but there was a big enough gap to at least see into it. It was certainly enough to see Alfie Byrne sprawled out on a settee directly facing him, with a couple of heavies standing over him. Knowing there had been three people in the car when they picked Byrne up meant there had to be another lurking somewhere else out of sight.

It was impossible to hear anything of what was being said, but the two guys in front of Byrne appeared to be quite animated. They were having a heated debate about something, and if Jack was to find out what it was he knew he needed to get inside the house. A quick inspection identified a bathroom window on the next level that was slightly ajar and looked to have possibilities. Right next to him was a wooden shed that had been built against the rear wall of the house, and when he climbed on top of it he was able to scramble up a metal drainpipe until he was level with the open window. With less difficulty than he imagined, he secured a foothold on the concrete sill and swung across, gaining a solid grip on the narrow opening. Reaching inside he released the main window catch and within a matter of seconds he was inside and groping his way in the semi darkness.

Stopping at the bathroom door he listened for a few seconds to ensure the all-clear before venturing out onto the landing. There was enough light filtering up from the lower level to help him get his bearings.

He could hear intermittent bursts of laughter emanating from down below and used this as a cover to ease his way down the stairs, while at the same time retrieving his mobile phone and switching it to record.

"Look at the state of that would you -- pissed as a fucking newt." The voice from inside the lounge was loud and mocking. And although Jack was still some way off at the other end of the hall from the lounge door, he knew the owner of the Armagh accent had to be talking about Byrne. The door leading into the lounge was wide open, and as he was now only a matter of four or five steps away from it, he was in a very vulnerable position should someone choose to step outside. Fearful that this might happen he pulled out his gun again, and holding it in one hand with his phone in the other he pressed himself as tightly as he could against the wall.

"Get some bloody coffee into that waste of space and sober him up, he has some questions to answer." The owner of the Armagh accent appeared to be the one giving the orders.

"That won't do any good I'm telling you -- the bastard's been shooting up, he's away in a little world of his own for Christ's sake. All the coffee in the world won't straighten him out, not for a while anyway." It was a much younger voice that was putting up the argument, albeit with a similar accent.

"Why did your stupid cousin have to complicate things for us?" he went on, "We could have been rid of this idiot's brother without bringing all this crap down on ourselves. What the hell made Joe think he could control this useless piece of crap by getting him hooked on drugs? That was a big mistake – sheer fuckin' madness if you ask me. What did we get back for all the drugs we plied into him? Sweet bugger all. Even Devlin's pushing up the daisies. Some fuckin' plan that turned out to be."

The conversation died for a while, making Jack fearful of moving a muscle in case the floorboards creaked and gave him away. As it turned out, a third voice, one that Jack hadn't heard before, decided to make itself known and ease some of his worries. While at the same time confirming that all four men he knew to be in the house were grouped together in the same room.

"So -- our wee junky friend here is a grass just like his brother. Well if he's been talking to the cops why don't we just shoot the bastard and get the hell out of here. Why are we wasting time making coffee for a crap head like him? What are we? A bunch of fuckin housemaids?" There was a bit more movement inside the room before anyone spoke again.

"Oh yeah, that's your answer to everything, isn't it? Shoot now and ask questions later. We need to look for a way out of this situation – not create an even worse mess to clean up."

Whoever was arguing against the idea of shooting Byrne seemed to be moving closer to the door causing Jack to hug the wall much tighter in case he came out into the hallway.

"Did it ever occur to you that we might be able to use this situation to our advantage? We all know this little crap head has been grassing us to the cops, but let's not forget that he was the one who handed his brother to us on a plate. Okay, so maybe he didn't know what the consequences of that would be, but he's still culpable, if only as an accomplice, and that gives us enough leverage to keep him in line. Anyway -- useless pieces of shit like him will do anything for a fix, so we'll always have him by the balls no matter what happens."

Jack could hardly believe his luck; he hadn't expected to uncover anything as revealing as this when he'd decided to follow Byrne home, especially as he had only made his decision to do so on a seemingly groundless whim; more out of curiosity than anything else. But what he was hearing now slotted the last pieces of the puzzle into place for him, proving, beyond any doubt who had been responsible for what happened to Tony Byrne.

Knowing this should have had him jumping for joy, but he took no comfort from it; quite the opposite in fact, for although the deaths of Roisin Byrne and Joe Devlin had brought his case to a grinding halt, and had him believing he would never solve it, he now had all the information he needed to put the whole worthless gang behind bars for a very long time.

He should have been feeling on top of the world, regardless of the dubious situation he found himself in, but the only emotion he could muster up was one of deep sadness. Sadness in the knowledge that Alfie Byrne had been complicit in what happened to his brother.

He wasn't given time to dwell on the matter as the conversation inside the room took off and claimed his attention once more.

"How the hell do you figure that out, Pat?" The younger speaker challenged, "All he did was lie about dropping his brother off at work and that's hardly the crime of the century --- I don't think he gives a tinkers damn about the cops finding out. I bet he's been sharing a bed with those bastards for a lot longer than we knew anything about. Our latest intelligence tells us he's after some of the money they're throwing around, and you have to ask yourself why the cops would give a monkey's toss what else he's been up to, just as long as he keeps feeding them information."

Jack was convinced the 'Pat' referred to was none other than Pat Towey -- Joe Devlin's cousin. A nasty piece of work who would stop at nothing to protect his criminal interests, including murder. A thought that warned him to shift his ass before he found out just how ruthless the thugs inside that room could be. Time was running out and he knew it, the longer he stood listening to their conversation the greater his risk of being caught, it was time to either put up or shut up.

What needed to be done was hardly rocket science, he already knew that at least one of the men in the room had a gun, so it was essential that he ascertain exactly where everybody was positioned before charging in like a bull in a china shop. Even he, with all his military training, couldn't be looking in three directions at the same time if he moved in on them. He needed the whole group to be in front of him if he was to eliminate the risk of being taken from behind, but he didn't know the situation inside the room, and he couldn't exactly see round corners. However when he gave it a little thought he realized that was exactly what he should do because hanging on the opposite wall was a large wall mirror that would allow him do to do exactly that. In fact it was sited directly facing the open door to the lounge, and only needed a slight re-positioning to let him see what was going on.

Reaching across he angled it sufficiently to allow him a good view of what was happening inside of the lounge.

Apart from Alfie Byrne, who was sprawled out in a drug-induced coma on the settee, the others were grouped fairly close together in the middle of the room with their backs to the door. It was the perfect scenario for him, having them grouped so closely together afforded him a massive advantage, making it very much a case of now or never. Without a second thought he took the few strides necessary and entered the room.

"Good evening, gentlemen -- what a pity we didn't have a priest on hand to hear that interesting little confession, but never mind, at least you've told me everything I need to know. And just so you know, I've recorded every word of your little conversation." His voice was confident and forceful, belying how he was feeling inside. Having been in similar situations in the past, he was conscious of just how easily and unexpectedly things can go array in situations like this, even when you think you have all the angles covered.

All the three men rounded on him in unison, their mouths gaping open in shock at his sudden and unexpected appearance. Two of them looked to be in their mid-forties, and beefy with it, the third was much smaller, and probably no more than twenty two or twenty three years of age.

Towey stood out from the others because of his uncanny resemblance to his dead cousin. Jack recognized the same brutish expression on his face that he had seen on his deceased relative the day they'd had their little 'get together' in the pub. But this was no time for sight-seeing, or reminiscing, he needed to assert his authority before anyone had time to react.

"Get your sorry asses over to that wall and lean on it with your weight on your fingertips, keep your feet away from the wall and spread your legs. I'm sure you all know the drill by now." He waved the gun menacingly. "And in case any of you have any doubts-- this thing is loaded and I'm fit to use it. In fact nothing would give me more pleasure, so let's not have any heroics."

Nobody moved an inch, well not right away, but rather sooner than Jack expected Towey took a menacing step towards him.

"You're that fucking private dick who did a job on Joe Devlin," he said threateningly. "I knew we should have gone back and finished you off when we missed the first time round, that's what happens when you use a fuckin' rifle that hasn't been zeroed in properly."

Jack had no idea who had taken the shot at him on that Saturday morning, but since Towey had been stupid enough to volunteer the information he wouldn't need much of an excuse to take his revenge. Lowering his weapon he aimed it directly at Towey's groin.

"That's about close enough -- you take one more step in my direction and I'll spray your wedding tackle all over this fuckin' carpet."

Towey hesitated, for a fraction of a second, but it was pretty obvious from his aggressive stance that he wasn't put off by Jack's threat. An issue that proved to be the case. Again rather quicker than Jack expected as he took another bold step forward, bringing him to within an arm's reach of his quarry. He would have done better to have heeded Jack's warning as he was primed for just such an eventuality, and without a second's thought he adjusted his aim and released a single shot that reverberated round the room as the bullet shattered Towey's left ankle.

The big man collapsed in a heap on the floor, writhing in agony and screaming like a banshee. One of the others, the bigger of the two, made a threatening move in the same direction, although it was really more of an automatic reaction than a planned attack, and as soon as Jack aimed the gun between his eyes he stopped dead in his tracks.

"Now then, gentlemen," he warned, "up against that wall like you were told before someone else ends up in a wheelchair – I'm not convinced our Health Service can afford it."

Having seen their boss so ruthlessly taken out both of Towey's accomplices felt less inclined to argue.

Jack held his station, towering over Towey's prone figure, his legs straddling the wounded man, and now that he felt in control of the situation he gave the thugs damaged ankle a little extra attention by tapping the toe of his shoe against it several times.

"Now you be a good little boy and don't try anything stupid. Just lie still and behave yourself." Bending to the task he used his free hand to frisk the injured thug for a weapon; a sinking feeling running through him when he didn't find one, especially as he had it mind that there was at least one weapon in play, and he had fully expected Towey to be the one carrying it.

With his sense of awareness bordering on panic, he rushed across the room to the others and kicked their legs so far apart that they almost fell flat on their face. The older of the two got his attention first since as he looked to be the bigger threat, and after a hurried search that uncovered a .22 Star pistol he turned his attention to the younger man, relieving him of a .38 Smith and Weston from the back waistband of his trousers.

Satisfied that he had all the weapons secured, he made both men take off their belts and kneel down facing the wall. Once he had their hands firmly secured behind them he backed off and sat down on the settee next to the comatose figure of Alfie Byrne. Now in complete control of the situation he took out his phone and switched it to record; ten bent over and held it close to Towey's face, once again placing his foot on the injured man's shattered ankle, applying a little pressure in the process.

"Now my friend, before I give you an opportunity to find out how much I weigh, maybe you'd like to tell me which one of you bastards took a pot-shot at me on my day off?"

Towey face contorted in agony, but he gritted his teeth stubbornly and refused to answer, leaving Jack with little option but to get to his feet and apply a bit more pressure to the shattered ankle. An agonizing scream filled the room as Towey squirmed on the floor like an epileptic eel in a vain attempt to escape his tormentor, inadvertently causing himself more pain in the process. He would have done better not to have crossed Jack right then, as he simply applied a lot more pressure to the wound, and would continue to do so until he got the response he was looking for.

"Okay – okay," screamed Towey, conceding defeat, "it was me you twisted bastard and it's a fuckin' pity I missed – now piss off and leave me be."

Jack had a look about him that said he'd already guessed who was responsible, and smiling contentedly to himself, he straightened up to his full height and applied his whole body weight to Towey's ankle, forcing him into a bout of uncontrollable convulsions, his agonizing screams bouncing off the walls as his pain tolerance shot off the Richter scale and he lapsed into unconsciousness.

Having secured the confession he was after Jack had no further interest in Towey, and left him to come round again in his own good time.

Turning away he seated himself beside the prone figure of Alfie Byrne yet again, and with his phone still in his hand he switched it to call and punched in Dave Jackson's mobile number, having to wait longer than he felt comfortable with before being connected. Without going into too much detail he gave the detective a hurried update on the evening's traumatic events, leaving all mention of Towey's injury to the very end in the expectation that it would get him a right royal earful in return.

As it turned out he was to be pleasantly surprised.

"Couldn't you have aimed just a little bit higher, Jack – say between his pearly blue eyes?"

"I can't say I wasn't tempted, Dave, but I'm trying to follow your well-intended advice and be nice to people for a change." Any intended humour in the remark was completely lost on the young detective, who cut him off without ceremony in his eagerness to get a mobile response unit under way. His concern for Jack's safety an overriding priority as he had no wish to leave him in his current situation any longer than necessary, not with three hardened criminals keeping him company.

To his credit though he did ring back and confirm that both he, and a mobile response unit were under way, and would be at the scene within a matter of minutes.

Having set the wheels in motion Jack felt a little less apprehensive, especially now that he knew help was on its way and he would soon be handing his captives over to the proper authorities. Clearly there would be some explaining to do about Towey's injury, he fully accepted that, but it wasn't exactly weighing on his mind, in fact he had already convinced himself that the action he had taken in defending himself against a trio of armed thugs was perfectly reasonable. Certainly Dave Jackson's light hearted reaction to the matter during their phone conversation had given his spirits a real boost, mainly because he had sounded almost euphoric at the possibility of getting Towey under lock and key. And more importantly, as he had explained to Jack, with Joe Devlin's participation no longer an issue, it eradicated any likelihood of paramilitary involvement and left the whole scenario much less complicated. It was really just a matter of locking up a bunch of murdering scum and throwing away the key.

Taking everything into account he should have at least felt vindicated, if not elated, that his investigation had come to such a positive and unlikely conclusion.

There was no hiding the fact that the painful events he'd been involved in since Roisin Byrne had first entered his life continued to weigh heavily on his conscience. And by way of adding to his on-going guilt complex over the experience his eyes latched on to a photograph that was staring down at him from the opposite wall. A photograph that portrayed his dead client sandwiched between her husband and his thankless brother, each with an arm round her shoulder, looking for all the world like a happy and contented family group. Jack allowed it to hold his attention far too long, forcing all kinds of recriminations over his handling of the case to resurface. Recriminations that dragged his eyes, and his thoughts, away from the photograph to the motionless figure sprawled out on the settee beside him.

A seething anger at the innocent expression on the man's face took hold of him, goading him into exacting some form of personal revenge. It mattered little that Byrne knew nothing of what was going on around him, immersed as he was in a drink and drug induced coma. The only thing that quenched Jack's overwhelming desire for revenge was the thought that it would be a lot more than a hangover his client's brother-in-law would be waking up to. That thought alone afforded him a temporary feeling of gratification and held his rage in check, but it was only temporary. His thoughts quickly returned to his dead client, and how painful it would have been for her to have known that it was her own beloved brother-in-law who had determined her husband's fate. It wasn't a thought he had any desire to hold on to, not while he still had a gun in his hand, and the thugs responsible for all that had happened right here in front of him. It took every bit of will power he could muster, and then some, to just sit and wait for the sound of the police siren without pulling the trigger.

Although now that he thought about it, and he had some time to do that, he realized it wasn't only his own willpower that held him in check. It was something more important than that, something intangible and entirely alien to him; something to do with the haunting image of a remarkably dignified little lady who had turned to him for help, an image that was haunting enough to stop him from exacting his own form of justice. An image of that diminutive little lady, who regardless of anything else that happened in the rest of his life, would remain forever embedded in his memory banks as a reminder of what genuine dignity and loyalty to ones loved one truly meant.

Taking his phone out one more time he dialled Father Joseph's number; a call he was looking forward to as much as anything else, since the priest had played such a pivotal role in helping him find Tony Byrne. It was also a call that surprisingly ended with him making an unexpected admission before saying goodbye.

"Perhaps there is a place for religion in my life after all, Father."

Lightning Source UK Ltd.
Milton Keynes UK
UKOW04f0632100316

269948UK00003B/65/P